"Everyth

Waylon.

Christina

The knot of ~~n~~
was sure ever

"My sister ma
of them. Heck
poor decisions
her fingers over
was one mistake. . .
an *error in judgment* that. . . well. . . We all. . .
We. . ."

"We are just as much at fault as Alli," his mother said, her voice high with nerves. "We should have told you sooner. Years ago, but—"

"Wait," he said, with a raise of the hand. "*What* exactly should you have told me years ago?"

"It's about Winnie. . ." Christina began.

His heart stopped at the sound of the little girl's name.

Christina looked up at him and her eyes were filled with a look of apologetic fear. "Winnie is yours, Waylon. She's your daughter."

MR SERIOUS

BY
DANICA WINTERS

MILLS & BOON

First Published in Great Britain 2017
By Mills & Boon, an imprint of HarperCollins*Publishers*
1 London Bridge Street, London, SE1 9GF

© 2017 Danica Winters

ISBN: 978-0-263-92924-9

46-1017

Our policy is to use papers that are natural, renewable and recyclable products and made from wood grown in sustainable forests. The logging and manufacturing processes conform to the legal environmental regulations of the country of origin.

Printed and bound in Spain
by CPI, Barcelona

Danica Winters is a multiple award-winning, bestselling author who writes books that grip readers with their ability to drive emotion through suspense and occasionally a touch of magic. When she's not working, she can be found in the wilds of Montana, testing her patience while she tries to hone her skills at various crafts—quilting, pottery and painting are not her areas of expertise. She believes the cup is neither half-full nor half-empty, but it better be filled with wine. Visit her website at www.danicawinters.net.

To Mac.
You're the mac to my cheese and the butter to my bread. Thanks for making life such an amazing adventure.

Chapter One

It was Waylon Fitzgerald's firm belief that most people were the same when it came to their wants. People were driven to desire four major things: good-enough sex, at least a comfortable amount of money, to be happy most of the time and to find someone to love them. Lucky for him, he'd never been like most people. His dreams were so much bigger—he wanted it all, and more. He wanted to travel the world, to help those in need, to live the dream and have a life driven by passion—not by *good enough*.

The helicopter's headset crackled to life. "Where do you want me to put her down?" The pilot motioned out the window of the Black Hawk as they passed over the stock pond in the pasture where his mother normally put the horses out this time of year.

His family wasn't going to like that he was bringing the helicopter to the ranch, but thanks to the disappearance of his ex-wife, Waylon had had to catch the next available flight. As luck would have it, his friend was relocating bases from Fort Bragg to Fort Lewis and he got to come along for the ride.

He'd always loved the feel of the chopper, its blades cutting through the air and the thump they made, just like the thump of a heart. Maybe that was what the chopper and the army were—his heart. He glanced down at Dunrovin Ranch and the guesthouses speckled throughout its expanse.

As much as he had loved the place where he spent most of his childhood, the lifestyle it symbolized was exactly what he feared the most—boredom. A life spent in habitual motion. Feed the horses, take care of the guests, take care of the ranch's maintenance, take care of the animals and go to bed, ready to repeat it every day until one morning he just didn't wake up. It wasn't that he judged his adoptive mother and father, Eloise and Merle Fitzgerald, for their need for complete stability. It was because of their stability and values he had even made it out of childhood alive. He owed them everything.

"Waylon?" the pilot asked again. "You got a place?"

"Put her down just there." He motioned toward the gravel parking lot that stood empty in the midmorning sun.

That was strange. This time of year, Dunrovin was normally hopping with life—winter-themed weddings, riding classes and parties to celebrate the coming of Christmas.

As the pilot lowered the bird toward the ground, people started spilling out of the main house. His adoptive mother waved at the helicopter, and even from a distance, he could see the smile on her face. In just the few years since he'd left the ranch, she'd grown gray and her back had started to take on the slight curve that came with age and osteoporosis. His father, the quiet and stoic man who was always working, stood beside her, holding her hand.

Next to them was a blonde. She was tall and lean, the body of a rider, but he didn't recognize her. She turned slightly, and he could make out the perfect round curve of her ass in her tight blue jeans. Perhaps she was one of their trainers. Either way, he'd have to watch out for her. She looked like the kind of woman who would end up in one of two positions with him— either toe to toe in a shouting match, or between the sheets. As it was, he just needed to get in and out of the ranch and back to work. The last thing he needed was any more drama than necessary.

The blonde shaded her eyes as she frowned up at him, but after a moment her gaze moved to the apple tree in the corner of the lot. Standing high in its branches was a little girl who looked to be about three years old. Her brunette curls blowing in the rotor wash as she gawked at him.

What in the hell was a girl that little doing standing in a tree?

The blonde jogged toward her as if she'd had the same thought.

"Be careful," Waylon said to the pilot, pointing to the toddler.

The pilot pulled back on the stick, and the powerful draft at such a low altitude kicked up a thick cloud of dust.

The little girl in the tree started to sway, and Waylon called out a warning into the deafening roar of the chopper's wash.

The girl trembled as she struggled to keep hold of the bark. She looked up at him as a gust of wind set her off balance, and her left shoe slid from the branch. The girl's blue dress moved against her like an unwieldy sail and propelled her out of the tree. She careened toward the ground.

From where he sat, it looked as though she landed face-first at the bottom of the tree.

"Bring this bird down, dammit!" he shouted.

Hopefully the little girl was still alive.

Chapter Two

What kind of man thought it was okay to fly into a quiet ranch like he was some kind of freaking hero? Who did Waylon Fitzgerald think he was? All that man ever did was leave destruction in his wake, and as far as Christina Bell was concerned, this was just another example of how little he cared when it came to how his actions affected others.

She rushed to her niece as the girl tumbled out of the apple tree and landed on the ground. The girl let out a shrill cry, but it was nearly drowned out by the chopping of the blades of the bull-in-a-china-shop helicopter.

"Winnie, are you okay?" Christina called above the sound.

Tears streamed down Winnie's dusty face, cutting through the dirt and exposing her unmarred skin below. "It hurts."

"It's okay, Win. You'll be okay." Christina ran her hand over the girl's head, smoothing her curls and trying to comfort her. "Where does it hurt, sweetie?"

Winnie cried, and her sobs stole her voice, but she motioned to her right arm and wrist. Of course it would be the girl's arm. She'd probably put her hand down during her fall in an attempt to catch herself.

As soon as the helicopter touched down, Waylon ran over, dropping his bag on the ground at Winnie's feet. "Are you okay, kid?"

Christina turned toward him, and she could feel a snarl take over her face. "You leave her alone."

He took two steps back, like he was afraid a bite would follow the growl. It might have been the smartest thing he'd done so far. All she wanted to do was come at him. He was the reason Winnie was hurt—in many ways, he was responsible for the bad things in her life.

She stared at him as the helicopter lifted off the ground and set to the sky. Alli had told her that he was a military police officer for the army, and she had seen pictures of him in the main house, but none of that did him justice. The man, all two hundred-ish pounds of him, was lean, and from what she could see, his chest was just as muscular as his legs. Even his forearms were thick, so much so that the muscles stressed the cloth of his rolled-up plaid sleeves.

He gave her a small smile, like he hoped that it would be his get-out-of-jail-free card, and she forced herself to look away from his almond-shaped eyes, buzzed black hair and copper-toned skin. He was a far cry from the scraggly teenager whose pictures adorned Eloise Fitzgerald's walls. Christina didn't like him, but she couldn't deny he might have been one of the sexiest men she'd ever seen in real life. She could certainly understand how her sister had fallen for the man. And regardless of Alli's latest drama, she had been right in divorcing the man if his entrance was any indication of his character.

Just because a man was ridiculously handsome and knew how to make an entrance, it didn't make him a man worth calling a husband—or a father.

Yep, she definitely hated him. Maybe it was just her hatred of every man who'd left his wife in the lurch, or it could have been all the things Alli had told her about the guy, but there was nothing redeemable about him. Not even that stupid grin he tried to ply her with.

"Is the kid okay?" he asked, his rough voice suddenly taking on a silky edge.

It wouldn't work with her. No way. No how. Especially when he referred to his daughter as "the kid," but then again, he didn't know who she was to him.

Winnie looked up at the man and wiped the tears from her cheeks with her good hand. "My arm," she said, lifting her limp right arm for him to see. "It hurts."

He squatted down next to Christina, far too close. He smelled like motor oil and spicy men's cologne— if she had to explain it, she would have said it was the scent of a real man. On the other hand, it was the scent of Waylon Fitzgerald—notorious father at large.

He didn't reach for the girl; instead, he leaned back on his heels as though being that close to a hurt child made him deeply uncomfortable.

"Does your back hurt, sweetie?" Christina asked.

Winnie shook her head and stood up, being careful not to put any weight on her arm. The area around her wrist was red and had already started to take on a faint bruise. It had to be broken, yet amazingly the little girl had stopped crying.

"What's your name, kid?" Waylon asked.

"Winnie. I gonna be three."

"You're such a big girl." He looked over at Christina. "Is she yours?"

She snorted at how ridiculous his question was. "I'm her guardian."

Waylon frowned as though he was trying to connect the dots. "So you are…"

She ignored his question. As far as she was concerned, he didn't need to know her. He'd missed his chance to know her and her family when he'd chosen to elope with Alli. He'd never cared before—and he didn't need to start now.

Eloise and Merle Fitzgerald made their way over to them as the helicopter disappeared into the distance. Eloise looked torn between worry and excitement. "Waylon!" she called, waving. "Hey, kiddo!"

Christina stood and wrapped Winnie in her arms, holding her against her legs as she chuckled at Eloise's welcome—calling Waylon a kiddo was about as fitting as calling a wolf a Chihuahua.

Waylon didn't look back at them as he made his way over to his mother and gave her a solid hug and a quick peck to the cheek. He turned to his father and shook the man's hand. Apparently, Waylon was the serious kind, a guy who was all business. His father deserved a hug—even if Waylon thought he was too much of a man for that kind of thing.

She sighed as she thought of all the reasons she had to keep the secret about Winnie from him. He definitely wouldn't be as good a parent as she was—and Winnie deserved the best care she could get.

Eloise glanced over at her and, almost as though she could read Christina's mind, gave her a slight raise of the brow before she knelt down to talk to Winnie.

"You gonna be okay, pumpkin? That was a pretty big fall, but you were so brave."

"Nana, I tough." Winnie smiled, the action tight from pain, but thankfully Eloise's compliments were taking her mind off her arm.

"Nana?" Waylon interrupted.

"Oh, yeah." Eloise waved him off, but from the way she didn't answer her son's question, Christina could tell that she was also questioning exactly if, how and when they should give him the news. Eloise turned back to Winnie. "Let's go see Dr. Richards. I bet he would like to hear about how brave you were. Okay, pumpkin?"

"I want Wy-ant." Winnie said, giving Eloise her special brand of puppy-dog eyes—the ones that worked on everyone who lived at the ranch and especially Christina.

For a brief second, Christina felt guilty for not telling Waylon then and there about Winnie being his. It wasn't really her secret to tell, and even if it were, the revelation would change everything—he would likely want to step into his role as a father and take Winnie away from Dunrovin. Even the thought of more change broke her heart.

She glanced over at him, hoping he would crack a smile—anything that would make him seem like a man who deserved to be Winnie's guardian. He just looked back at her, a solemn look on his face. So much for that.

Perhaps all she could hope for was that he wouldn't want to take the girl away. Maybe he would want his daughter to stay at the ranch while he continued to roam the world, but it wasn't a risk she was willing to take. She loved the girl entirely too much to risk her future on Mr. Serious and a life that he most likely didn't want.

"I'll call Wyatt," Christina offered, but in truth it was just an excuse to get away from the infuriatingly handsome army man.

Sometimes, when things were this confusing, the only thing to do was run.

ALL WAYLON WANTED to do was get out of this place. He hated hospitals. Thanks to his time in Iraq, there was no place he dreaded more. If a guy was in the hospital there, bad things had gone down.

Truth be told, in Iraq, the name of the game was bad things.

Every second there was another enemy, another battle to fight, another person to protect. And here, back in the civilian world, no one seemed to understand how ugly the real world was. Waylon's brother Wyatt tapped his foot as he sat next to him in the waiting room, agitated that they hadn't been invited to the examination room with Winnie, where they were going over the results of the X-rays.

"She'll be okay, man," Waylon said. "Kids are resilient. And, honestly, except for the bruise, she seemed fine. Who knows, maybe her wrist ain't broken."

Wyatt nodded. "That kid's tougher than you think. If she cried, there had to be something majorly wrong. I've seen her get stepped on by a horse and barely bat an eyelash."

He'd nearly forgotten how tough even the youngest members of the family were expected to be. There was no time for weakness when they were out checking on cattle during calving season or when they were breaking a new horse. If there was weakness, animals would sense it, and undoubtedly use it to their advantage. The ability to disguise pain was a vital part of existence out here in the wilds of Montana, where it often came down to survival of the fittest. Since he'd left three years ago after his divorce, he'd barely thought about the ranch—and he had completely forgotten how much Mystery, Montana, felt like a throwback to a bygone era. It really was a different culture, a tiny microcosm of society where the values revolved around family and community.

It was a different world than the one he'd been in overseas.

It surprised him, but for a moment, a feeling of sadness and nostalgia overtook him. He hadn't realized how much he'd missed home. Well, he'd missed *some* things about home. He glanced over toward the door that led to the examination rooms, where the blonde and his mother were with Winnie. The blonde seemed to hate his guts. When he took off again, he'd miss a lot of things, but her hate wasn't one of them.

Hopefully he had time to make her change her mind about him—he'd overcome worse odds with women before. Heck, Alli had really hated him when they'd first met. She had been waiting tables at the little diner in Mystery, the Combine, making money before moving along to the next town. The first time she'd seen him, he could have cut glass with her sharp glare. He'd loved that about Alli, the way she was so strong and always ready to stand up for herself. So many women just let men walk all over them, but not Alli. Then again, it was that same strength that had pushed him away and led her into the arms of another man, and then another, and another.

"Have you heard anything new about Alli?" Waylon asked, trying not to notice the way his gut clenched when he thought about all the hard times he'd gone through with the woman.

Wyatt shifted in his standard-issue plastic hospital chair. "They have her car at the impound lot. We're holding it until we get the full forensics report. But thanks to Lyle, it may take a while."

"Lyle is still working for you guys? Can't you find anyone better?" he teased his brother, but he knew exactly how it worked with small-town politics—where the good ole boy system was still alive and well.

"Lyle isn't all bad," Wyatt said with a laugh. "Though he probably could use a refresher course or two. He did find the photos that pointed us toward Alli in the case of Bianca's murder."

"Even a blind squirrel finds a nut once in a while."

"You got that right." Wyatt's laughter echoed through the nearly empty waiting room. "If you want, when we're done here, we can run up to her car. Maybe you can spot something we've missed. Though, I gotta say, there ain't a whole lot there."

"Maybe you just needed your little brother to come home and show you how to do *real* investigative work. Like we do in the military," Waylon said with a booming laugh.

"Is that what they're calling the Girl Scouts these days?" Wyatt smirked.

It was moments like these, when his belly hurt from

laughter, that made him realize being home wasn't just about a change of location. It was more about family—and family was something he could never replace.

Danica Winters

Chapter Three

Waylon was certain he shouldn't feel guilty for the state
of Winnie, yet he couldn't help the tug at his heart each
time he looked at her clunky, Ace bandage–wrapped
arm as they all made their way into the main house.
Dr. Richards had said it was only a sprain, but just to
be sure he hadn't missed a microscopic crack, Eloise
and the girl's guardian had gone along with his plan to
keep it wrapped for at least the next week.

Waylon followed the blonde woman toward the
kitchen as Winnie pushed past. The woman had barely
spoken to him since they had left the hospital. *Pissed*
didn't even seem like a strong enough word to express
the vibe she was sending his way. It was going to be a
long week at the ranch. He'd thought war zones were
bad, but at least there he wasn't the sole focus of a
woman's wrath.

His mother stepped up beside him, and as she noticed him watching the woman, she chuckled. "Don't
worry about Christina—she'll come around. She's just
a bit protective of Winnie, that's all."

"Christina?" He let out a long breath. "As in Alli's
sister, Christina?"

"The one and only. She's been a real asset to the ranch. Didn't you recognize her?"

He'd only ever seen pictures of Alli's sister. Alli had made sure to keep him at arm's length from her family—when he had suggested having them at their wedding, it was in that moment Alli unilaterally decided they should elope. He should have seen it as a warning that she had some issues, but no, love had made him blind. So blind he hadn't noticed when she had started to keep him isolated; after a couple of years he never saw his friends or even his brothers.

If he'd been smarter, he would have seen what she was really doing—using him to take care of her while she pursued another man. As much as he had the right to, he didn't hate her. Emotions were crazy, and love was even more illogical. Not that he still loved her. No. That feeling had died the moment he'd left the ranch and run away to the military. The day he signed his papers was the day he had let his past go—that was, until now.

Christina turned around, standing in the doorway of the kitchen, and glared at him. "For some reason, Winnie is asking about you. You may want to go see her."

He could almost hear the hiss in her words. Yep, she hated him. *Sweet.*

He sighed, and his mother gave his arm a little squeeze. "Don't worry, kiddo. I'm telling you, her bark's worse than her bite."

He had a feeling he would get the chance to see if his mother was right, but if Christina's attitude toward him was any indication of her bite, he was sure he'd come away with at least a mark or two.

Winnie sat at the table while Wyatt set about grabbing supplies for a peanut butter and jelly sandwich. As he walked to the table, Wyatt turned to Waylon. "Want one?" He lifted the jelly. "This is what you eat for lunch in the Girl Scouts, right?" His brother laughed.

Stepping behind Winnie so she couldn't see, he flipped his brother the bird. "It's still better than a solid diet of doughnuts, Deputy." He rubbed his stomach. "In fact, I think you're growing a bit around the middle."

Wyatt laughed. "You need to move back to the ranch."

"You looking for someone to help you with your *Dumb and Dumber* act?" Waylon teased.

The girl wiggled in her chair. "Yeah, Way-lawn." She said his name like she had to think about each syllable on its own, and it made it sound like a children's rhyme. "You come back. And you know what? We have party."

Waylon chuckled. "Is that right?"

"Uh-huh," she said with an overly exaggerated nod. "Way-lawn, you and me, we dress up. You help me?"

He'd had bullets whiz by his head in active combat zones, and he'd stepped in front of high-value dignitaries, ready to give his life for the greater good, yet, as Winnie looked up at him, he couldn't help the fear that rose within him. He had no idea what to do with a kid—especially a kid who wanted to do a craft project. Maybe he'd have more of a clue if she wanted to strip down an assault rifle, but costumes—he was totally out of his league.

Christina gave a wry laugh from behind him. "Waylon doesn't do that kind of thing, sweetheart. If you want, though, I can help you later."

He noted the jab she was taking at him, and he couldn't help rising to the fight. "Nah, Ms. Winnie.

Don't you worry, I got you. You want a costume? I'm your man." His stomach clenched as he thought about how ill equipped he was for the promise he'd just made.

"Don't you have a *job* to do? You know, trying to find my missing, fugitive sister? Or are you going to just let her get away with murdering the vet and William Poe's wife?" Christina rebuked.

She stared at him, and some of the anger that had filled her features seemed to melt away, replaced by shame. "Look, I'm sorry," she said, not waiting for him to talk. "I didn't mean it like that. I'm just…just…"

"Hurting," he said, finishing her thought.

She sighed, not admitting he was right, but he could see from the way her posture softened that he'd hit the truth. Of course she would be hurting and scared, and probably overwhelmed. Her sister was her only family, since their mother had passed away a few years back.

"I want to find her. Alli needs to come home," she said, her gaze moving to Winnie and the bandage on her arm.

What was he missing? There was something happening that they weren't telling him—he could feel it in the air.

"What's going on?" he asked, tired of skirting the issue.

"Huh?" Christina looked up at him, a look of shock flashing over her features. "What do you mean?"

"You guys are hiding something." He turned to Wyatt, who all of a sudden seemed wholly consumed by the process of making another sandwich. "What is it that you don't want me to know?"

His mother walked into the kitchen, almost as if the question had beckoned her to the room. She glanced around at Christina and Wyatt, as if giving them some signal. "Everything's fine, kiddo. We're all just worried about Alli."

"Did she do something you aren't telling me? I mean, besides murdering Bianca and that other woman and then going on the run?"

His mother smiled. "It's not what she did but what she didn't do that is the problem."

"What's that supposed to mean?"

His mother touched his shoulder. "Just work on finding Alli. Then we can deal with everything else."

Some of the fondness he was feeling toward being home drifted away. He'd forgotten how the family always turned inward first—and because of his time away, he now stood outside the circle.

"Look, why don't we run over to the impound lot?" Wyatt said, waving the peanut butter–laden knife around in the air.

"You're not leaving me here alone to wonder what's going on," Christina pressed, but she glanced over at his mother with a question in her eyes.

"Don't worry, I'll watch Winnie," Eloise offered.

Whatever was going on revolved around that little girl. Waylon glanced at Winnie. How was she involved with all of this? Was it possible she was Alli's daughter? Was that why there was such a rush to find the woman—and why they had been adamant that he come home to help them in the search? He pushed the thoughts from his mind. Alli had always told him she was unable to get pregnant. The child couldn't be hers.

THE IMPOUND LOT was attached to the prerelease center on the outskirts of town. It wasn't much of a place.

Wyatt punched in his key code, and the gate of the chain link–enclosed lot opened with a grinding sound. There was a collection of beat-up old cars and one late-model Mustang. Most of the jalopies had flat tires or shattered windshields, and more than a few had both. The lot even had a few campers that looked like they'd escaped the show *Breaking Bad*, complete with what Waylon was sure were meth labs inside.

He chuckled, but his humor was short-lived as they drove around the corner and came into view of the convicts' exercise yard. One of the prisoners looked over, and as he caught sight of Wyatt's patrol unit, he spat on the ground and flipped them the bird. As the other prisoners noticed, the middle finger came in almost a concert-style wave, rippling through the yard.

"Nothing quite like the royal welcome, right?" Wyatt said, ignoring his fan club.

"I'm acquainted with the lifestyle," Waylon said with a cynical laugh.

Christina tapped her fingers on the car door. "That's what you guys get all the time? No wonder you both have chips on your shoulders."

He and his brother looked at each other and shared a smug grin. A few middle fingers were nothing compared to facing down a drunk man with a gun who wanted to kill him for some past injustice he felt he had suffered at the hands of the police. It was a strange feeling to know that most of the time, wherever he went, people despised him.

Sure, it was true most of the population weren't criminals, but the people they worked with every day weren't the general public—in his case, the criminals he worked with were even worse than Wyatt's. For

Waylon, when he was working on a base between de-
ployments to war zones, the people he arrested were
well trained in weapons and self-defense—his job
was to handle trained killers. Wyatt just had to handle drunken idiots.

Wyatt parked his car next to a black Hyundai Gene-
sis. "It was pretty beat-up by the time we got the report
that it had been abandoned. You know how that goes,"
his brother said, motioning toward the wreckage.

The car had a flat tire on the passenger's side, and
its windshield was shattered. For a moment, Waylon imagined Alli's car on the side of the road, people smashing it just because they could. People had a
strange, innate need to destroy things that stood alone
or abandoned. It was almost as though anonymity was
enough justification for them to give license to their
destructive nature.

"I went over this car with Lyle, top to bottom,"
Wyatt said, getting out and walking toward Alli's car.

"What all did you find?"

Wyatt shrugged. "We ran fingerprints, but nothing came of them. And all we found inside was the
normal crap—wadded straw wrappers and a few fries
under the seats."

"But nothing that you think would help us figure out
where she could have gone?" Christina asked.

Wyatt looked over at her. "You and I both know
she's in Canada somewhere. She's probably watching
a hockey game, drinking Molson and laughing at how
stupid she thinks we are."

"She's not like that. She knows you aren't stupid.
She just got herself into a bad spot, and it escalated. I
don't condone what she did, but there has to be more

to it than we know. She had her problems, but I never thought she was capable of…you know," Christina said. She looked down at the ground with what Waylon assumed was shame.

He wanted to tell her he was just as confused and upset a woman he had once loved had made such a stupid series of decisions, but there was no making any of what Alli did better. There was only bringing her back so she could pay for her crimes—and so he could ask her all the questions he was dying to ask. He just couldn't understand how she had fallen into such a pit of self-destruction. Sure, she had never been exactly healthy, but he'd never thought she was capable of taking a life.

Then again, if he'd learned anything on the battlefield and as an MP, it was that all people were capable of pulling a trigger if the conditions were right.

"I'm sure when we find her we can get to the bottom of this," Waylon said in his best attempt to make Christina feel better. From the tired look on her face, he had failed.

"So," Wyatt said, opening the car's door, "we did find a receipt on the floor on the passenger's side. We tracked it down—it was to a gas station just outside Mystery. Alli filled up with gas, but beyond that there wasn't anything usable."

Waylon stepped beside his brother and leaned over the passenger's seat. The car was filled with the dirty, stale scent of the long neglected. He pulled the odor deep into his lungs. Over the years he had been around more than his fair share of abandoned vehicles that had been left behind by people on the run. The one scent the car didn't carry was the putrid odor of death. Its absence was really the only thing they had going for them—at least, for now.

He opened up the glove box. It was empty.

"We took all her documents out. They are in evidence, but there really wasn't anything unusual, just her insurance card and registration."

He closed it. "Huh." He stared at the headliner for a second.

Almost as if it were a sign, a wayward fly crawled out from behind the black felt. He reached up and ran his fingers along the edge of the liner. It gaped where the bug had exited. His fingers brushed against something rough—paper.

He pulled the paper out and held it in his hands as he stared at the thing in disbelief. "You went through the whole car, huh?" He lifted the paper high for his brother to see.

"What's that?" Wyatt asked, his mouth open slightly with shock. "I swear, we went over this thing from top to bottom."

It was total dumb luck Waylon had found the paper. It was almost like the proverbial needle in the haystack, but he wouldn't admit that to his big brother. "Hold up your hand," Waylon said with a mischievous grin.

Wyatt frowned, but he played along, lifting his hand and extending his fingers.

"Oh, yep," Waylon said. "It's those stubby fingers that are the problem. You just couldn't reach it."

Wyatt balled his fingers into a tight fist, but he laughed. "Real funny, jackass. You just got lucky and you know it. In fact, it probably got loosened up when they towed the car."

"Wait," Christina said, "if you guys are done picking at each other, what is on it? Is it from Alli?"

Waylon opened the folded page. Inside was a note in Alli's jagged, hurried scrawl. All it said was "I'm sorry. But, William, I don't understand. Why?"

It was almost as if while she had been writing the note, she had been interrupted and she had stuffed it half written in the headliner. What in the hell was it supposed to mean? And why would she leave such an obscure note behind? Had she meant for them to find it, or was it meant for someone else?

He thought he didn't hate Alli, but in this moment, the feeling threatened to overwhelm him.

Christina glanced over her shoulder and he could hear her breath catch.

"That doesn't make any sense," Christina said, mimicking his thoughts. "What did she mean by 'I don't understand'? She's the one who started all of this mess. She set the rules to this game."

He handed the note over to Wyatt. His brother shook his head and slipped it into his pocket. "I'll get this into evidence, but I have a feeling it's going to be just about as helpful as the straw wrappers. Do you remember William Poe?"

Waylon had met the county tax appraiser a time or two in passing, but aside from Poe's relationship with Alli and a brief mention of him in the newspapers thanks to the murder of his wife, Monica, Waylon didn't know much about the man.

Waylon shook his head.

"Poe is like a greased pig," Wyatt said. "Just when I think I can pin him down for something, he slips out of my grasp. I thought for sure he was involved with

Bianca's and Monica's murders, but the guy always has an alibi. Always."

"And from what I hear, it usually involves politics or a woman's thighs," Christina added.

Wyatt laughed. "And sometimes a combination of the two."

"Did you check his alibi?" Waylon asked.

Wyatt looked at him with a raise of the brow. "Really? Dude, I'm not completely incompetent at my job."

He instantly regretted asking his brother such a stupid question. Of course Wyatt knew what he was doing—Waylon hadn't meant to step on his toes, but he was just so used to working alone, or rather, being in command, that coming here and being second in line in the investigation was out of his comfort zone.

"Boys, boys, you are both good at your jobs. Wyatt, I don't think that's what your brother meant," Christina said, trying to smooth the ground between them. "Right, Waylon?" She put her hand on his shoulder and gave it a light squeeze.

"Of course. Sorry, man."

Waylon stood up, and Christina's fingers slipped from him. He looked back at her, and he couldn't help but notice the way the midday sun made her normally icy blue eyes sparkle with warmth.

He forced himself to look away and walked toward the back of the car, stopping by the rear tire on the passenger's side. As he looked down, something odd caught his eye. "Wyatt," he said, squatting down and pressing his finger against a deformation in the rim's surface, "look at this."

Wyatt came over. "It's just a rock chip." But he knelt down beside him.

"No." Waylon pressed. "Look closer. That, Wyatt… is a bullet hole."

Chapter Four

Wyatt dropped them off at the ranch so Christina could get her truck and they could set to work. She sent a quick glance over at Waylon. His copper-toned skin glistened in the midday sun, and she couldn't help the little wiggle of attraction that rose up from her core.

Seeing him in his element, working over the car and finding what the rest had missed, had made some of the anger she had been carrying for the man fall to the wayside. He was good at his job, and he looked even better doing it.

This would have been so much easier if she could just stay firmly planted in her dislike. It made it easier to compartmentalize and keep him as an enemy. Yet every time he joked around, she was tempted to think of him almost as a friend.

He turned to her as Wyatt drove off. "You sure you don't mind driving me around? I could just borrow one of the ranch's trucks. You don't have to keep me company."

She appreciated the out, but her whole body pushed her to stay with him. "I'm doing this for Alli. I can't stop looking just because you're here."

"Have you been looking for her nonstop since she

went missing last week?" he asked. A frown crossed over his face, like he was surprised she had not given up.

"Of course. She's my sister. I don't have to agree with what she does, or the choices she makes, but I love her and I want to make sure that she's safe."

"If she called or you found her, do you think you'd be able to turn her in to the authorities—or Wyatt?"

She chewed on her lip. She'd already thought about that question, but she had pushed it to the back of her mind. "I need to know she's safe first, then I'll make that choice."

"Does that mean you would let her stay on the run?"

Alli deserved to pay for her crimes. She had murdered, but Christina had to think about Winnie, too. The girl was already bearing the weight of her mother's choices. If Alli went to prison, Winnie would have to visit that terrible place, but if Alli stayed on the run, things could be kept from Winnie until she was old enough to understand a bit better.

"Like I said, I'll make that choice when I'm faced with it," she said. "All I want now is to know that she's alive and well."

Waylon glanced down at his hands. "You know what? I get it," he said, looking at his tanned and calloused fingers. "Your sister has a good heart. I don't know why she acted like she did, but that doesn't mean I don't care about her and what happens to her. I want her to be safe—just like you do."

The way he spoke about Alli was endearing and completely unexpected. Alli had never spoken of him with anything close to the same warmth. In fact, if Christina had to guess, regardless of what Alli had told her, it was not a breakup he had instigated. If anything, it seemed like he might still have had feelings for her sister when they had split and maybe even now.

Which made the feelings Christina was starting to have for him all that much more wrong. How could she possibly be attracted to her sister's ex-husband? There was something so daytime gossip show about the whole thing.

She chuckled at the thought.

"What's so funny?" Waylon asked.

"I wasn't laughing at you," she said, trying to backpedal from her bad timing. "It's just that…" She couldn't tell him she was laughing about the way she was starting to feel about him.

"What?" he asked, spurring her on.

"It's just that I think we're one step away from being asked to be on the *Maury* show." She covered her mouth as she laughed and, as she did, the look of pain on Waylon's face disappeared and he smiled. It was filled with a jovial warmth, and there was even a look of something else in his eyes…something that resembled attraction.

Nope. She had to have it all wrong. There was no way he could be attracted to her.

"I…er…" she said. There was a faint warmth in her cheeks, and she tried to keep it in check. She walked toward her truck with him at her side. "I don't mean your family. Your mom and dad are great. It's just with the murders and everything…you know."

He motioned that it was okay for her to stop her rambling. "It's okay. I get it. And though my parents' lives are in order, you and I both know the same can't be said for the rest of us. That's without even mentioning this thing with Alli." He paused. "I can't even begin to imagine what she told you about me over the years." He glanced over at her, as if trying to gauge her reaction.

She bit the inside of her cheek. Alli had made a personal habit of ripping her ex-husband to shreds. Alli hadn't done it in front of Winnie as she had wanted to keep Winnie's father's identity a secret from her, but that didn't change the fact that over the years, some of the things she had told Christina had begun to wear her down and made her dislike him on principle.

"Yeah, I thought so," he said, as though he could read her mind. "Listen, Alli and I had a *tough* relationship." He said the word like it tasted of spoiled shellfish. "We never should have gotten married. I just thought that what we had was what love was supposed to be. I supported her—emotionally, mentally, even physically sometimes. It only made sense that we took the leap and made things official. But as soon as we got married, it was like a switch flipped. She went from bad to worse."

Christina should have been offended that he was saying her sister was bad, but she really didn't have a platform to argue anything different. Alli made poor choices on a regular basis.

"I thought I could handle her mood swings, but in the end—when she started sleeping with other men—I just couldn't have her in my life anymore. We weren't good together. We never were. It was just time that I left. She's the reason I went back to active duty. And you know what? I'm glad that I left. It was far better than letting your sister rip my soul apart."

His candor came as a surprise, so much so that Christina didn't quite know how to react. She should have stood up for her sister, yet at the same time, she could feel for Waylon. Her sister had a way of tearing down the people she loved. It was just a part of her personality, as if by pushing away the people she loved the most, she could protect herself from being vulnerable or at the mercy of others' feelings. It was almost as though she wanted to hurt them before they had the chance to hurt her.

It undoubtedly came from their childhood. Their parents had been emotional train wrecks—a world of constant cheating and berating. It was the reason Christina had sworn off men for the last few years. She had come too close to following in her parents' footsteps. Not loving was just so much easier than living a life like that of her childhood.

"Alli had her fair share of problems, and maybe a few extra, too," she said, giving him a knowing smile.

"I have mine, too," he said, making the desire she was feeling for him even more intense.

Waylon wasn't a perfect man, but Alli had been wrong when she'd told her that he didn't have a heart. Even now, when he had the chance to make Alli the fall guy, he took his lumps.

She threw him her truck keys. "Remember how to get around?"

His face pinched. "This old town ain't that big. I think I can remember where the Poe place is." He got into the driver's seat and revved the old truck to life.

Christina laughed as she slid onto the truck's bench seat—far too close to the man who was starting to make her heart do strange things. "You got that right." Sometimes, just like this truck, the town was entirely too small for comfort.

"Why did you come here?" he asked as he steered the truck onto the road. "I mean, no offense or anything, but there's so many amazing places in the world—places where anything you want is at your fingertips. Why would you, a woman in her late-twenties who could have anything—and anyone she wanted—come to a place like this and stay?"

Did he really think she could have anyone she wanted? She almost laughed at the thought.

The only men who had ever seemed to be attracted to her were emotional nitwits. They were just too much like her father—wanting her when it was convenient for them, and then forgetting about her when it wasn't.

She refused to chase another man. She wasn't the kind of woman who pursued men and made things fit when they truly didn't. She wanted the elusive unicorn—the kind of guy who actually made the effort, the kind who wanted her for her and not what she had between her legs, and the kind who fit into her life naturally instead of feeling like a fish out of water.

She glanced over at Waylon as he drove. He would fit right in. It was his family's ranch. He knew everyone. It was neutral ground and a commonality that she would have with only a few, but his passions didn't seem to lie within the boundary lines of the guest ranch. Rather, they seemed to be following his heart all around the world—living for adventure. He seemed like the kind of guy who was far more at home jumping out of an airplane than sweeping a floor.

He lived for his dreams.

She closed her eyes and leaned her head against the window. If only she had the same freedoms.

There had been a brief period of time, right after she had moved out of her mother's house after her parents' divorce, when she could have escaped. She could have gone anywhere in the world. At the time, she'd barely had two dimes to her name, but if she had truly wanted to get out, she could have. There was nothing holding her back—except her own fears and feelings of inadequacy. She hadn't wanted to travel the world alone. Adventures alone were nothing compared to adventures with someone you loved—and that feeling had led her straight to her sister, and the gates of Dunrovin.

Until now, she hadn't looked back. Yet, sitting next to Waylon—a man who was living his dreams—Christina couldn't help but feel like she had missed a chance of a lifetime. Now she couldn't go—she had to think of Winnie. She had to think of her life at the ranch. Family, and the ability to support them, came first.

The truck slowed down, and they bumped up the driveway leading to the Poes'—or rather William Poe's—house. She still hadn't gotten over her friend's death. Every time she thought of Monica, she had to remind herself that she was gone. It was surreal. So many times over the last few days, she had lifted her phone to text her friend, only to remember that she was gone.

Though everything had changed in her world, the Poes' house hadn't. The siding was the same gray it had been a few months ago, and the garage stood apart from the house, filled with William's collection of cars, its walls adorned with *Sports Illustrated* posters of scantily clad women.

She'd never liked stepping foot in the garage, and she had liked William even less—especially after Monica had told her about his private habits, which mostly centered on getting himself between the legs of as many women as humanly possible. How Monica had put up with it was still a mystery to her, but she'd always supported her friend. It wasn't her place to judge her, but only to stand by her side.

Monica's car was parked outside, like now that she was dead, there wasn't a place in William's home for any of his wife's leftovers.

"You okay?" Waylon asked as she noticed him glancing over at her.

"Yeah, I'm fine. I've just made it a habit over the years not to hang out here. Monica was good about it—she normally let me meet her somewhere else."

"You were friends with Monica? The lady your sister…" He stopped, like he was afraid that the words *your sister killed* would break her once again.

She couldn't deny the fact he might have been right in his assumption. Even the thought of what her sister had done to her friend, and her reasons behind it, made a feeling of sickness rise up from her belly.

"Yeah. Monica is a cool—I mean, *was* a cool chick. She loved to ride horses. We'd spend hours riding the trails around the ranch. Honestly, looking back, I think it was just an excuse for her not to be around her husband."

Waylon chuckled. "It's funny how hindsight is always twenty-twenty."

"Is that how you feel when you look back at your marriage with my sister?"

His face pinched slightly at the question, like he wished she hadn't gone there. Lucky for him, as they pulled to a stop in front of William's house, the man in question came out the door. William grimaced as he caught sight of them, and Christina would have sworn she could see him mouth a long line of curse words.

Instead of answering her question, Waylon jumped out of the truck like he would rather face the cussing county tax appraiser than talk any more about his failed marriage.

She couldn't blame him. Relationships, and what came of them, were a tricky thing—especially in their case. Even as she thought about their confusing circumstances, she couldn't help but watch as Waylon strode toward William.

His jeans had to have been made especially for him. There was no way something that fit that well around the curves of his ass could have simply come off a rack.

She giggled as she thought about the many web articles she had read about men who didn't wash their jeans so they could get them to fit that way. Was Waylon among the no-wash crew? It was a random thought, but in a way it made her like him even more. It was almost as if the thought of him standing over his jeans at night and deciding whether or not they should be cleaned made him more human and less the imposing MP who had literally landed on her doorstep. More than anything, it made him real. Human. Attainable. But was he someone she really wanted to be with?

Waylon turned around and waved for her to come out of the truck.

She'd much rather have stayed—she had nothing to say to William Poe that she hadn't already said. They'd had their moment together at Monica's funeral. He had barely spoken to her or looked at her as they had stood at the cemetery, watching as people threw handfuls of dirt onto his wife's casket. Yet, afterward, when everyone was saying their goodbyes, he'd made his position clear when he'd leaned in and said a few simple but inflammatory words: "This is all your fault."

At the time, she hadn't understood his thought process. How could he have possibly thought she had anything to do with his wife's death? Sure, she had ties to all involved, but that didn't mean she had taken a role in anything. On the other hand, she wasn't completely innocent—there had been the night in the office when she had been talking about William and his actions with Monica. Alli had been just outside the door, listening to their conversation. No doubt that night she had drawn her sister's crosshairs onto Monica's back, but William couldn't have known.

He was just angry, and she had been his easiest and closest target. Maybe because he couldn't go after her sister, he had simply decided to come after her. Regardless, she hated him and how his choices had been an atomic bomb in all of their lives. If he had just kept himself in his pants, lives could have been saved and Alli would have never disappeared. He was like this town's Helen of Troy, but instead of his face launching a thousand ships, his manhood had launched a thousand hours of tragedy.

She clomped out of the truck and made her way over to the two men. William gave her the same look of disgust he had given her at Monica's funeral, like he had bitten into a wormy apple. The only worm here was him.

"I believe I answered all the questions when your brother brought me in, Waylon." As William spoke, a small dark-haired woman walked out of the house. William, noticing the woman, turned and pointed toward the door. "Get back inside, Lisa."

"Why are *they* here?" The woman pointed toward her with a shaking finger. "Did they find Alli?"

"Shut up and listen to me, Lisa. Go inside."

Lisa looked taken aback, but she hurried inside.

"Who was that?" Christina asked.

William waved her off. "*She* is none of your business."

Was the woman just another in his long line of conquests?

"You people have no right to be stepping on my property, and you have no right to be asking me any questions," William continued.

"You're right. You're under no real obligation. Nothing you tell me would be admissible in court," Waylon said, in an almost jovial tone, as if he could win the slimeball's favor by acting like a friend. "However, I would think you would want to bring your wife's murderer to justice."

"You don't want justice," William said with a snort. "You just want to find Alli. You think if you can get to her first, maybe you can get her a lighter sentence when the crap rains down. But here's the deal…" William pointed at Waylon, the move aggressive and escalating. It was the move of a politician. "*Even if* you find her, she's going to pay for what she did. She'll get the full weight of justice upon her. I will make sure of it."

"*Even if?* What, do you think there's a chance we aren't going to find my sister?" Christina asked, enraged by the man's tone. "What did you do to her?"

"Better yet," Waylon interrupted, "what didn't you tell my brother about what you know?"

William waved them off. "You and your screwed-up family aren't my problem. You people are trash." He looked into her eyes. "*You* are trash. And if you think I'm going to play your effing games, you're wrong."

"*Our* games?" Waylon looked genuinely confused by the man's accusation. "What games are you talking about, Will?"

"My name's William, not Will, Bill or Billy. Unlike you, Waylon, I wasn't named after a dead country singer. My family wasn't a bunch of rednecks."

Up until that point, Christina had thought she had the corner on hating William Poe. Yet, based on the flaming-red color of Waylon's face, she might have just lost the lead position.

"Listen here, bastard," Waylon seethed. "I would've liked to go about this whole thing amicably. You could have made this all easy."

"Who the hell do you think you are?" William interrupted him, making a thin sheet of sweat rise to Waylon's forehead as his hands balled into tight fists. "You came here. You're accusing me of who knows what. You have no right to be here—and the only bastard here is you."

Waylon lunged forward, but Christina stopped him by grabbing his hand. "Come on, Waylon." She pulled him toward the truck. "If nothing else, now you know the type of guy that would lead a woman to kill."

Chapter Five

Eloise had been cooking constantly since Waylon had stepped foot back onto the ranch, and the rich odors of roasting meat and butter wafted throughout the house. After their run-in with William, Christina was more than happy to settle back into the warmth and comfort of the kitchen as she helped Eloise put the finishing touches on the meal.

Waylon and Colter walked in, but they were so wrapped up in whatever they had been talking about that neither of them seemed to notice her sitting at the bar.

Colter looked a lot like his older, biological brother. They both had the same copper-tinted skin, dark brown eyes and jet-black hair, but beyond their looks, the two were nothing alike. Waylon carried himself as though he were ready to take on the world, while Colter…well, it could be said that he was constantly at ease. It was almost as if Waylon carried a chip on his shoulder big enough for the both of them, so big that Colter had never felt its weight.

"Heya, Colt," Christina said, giving him a small wave.

He smiled brightly, the simple action lighting up his

face with his characteristic warmth. "How's it going, lady? Long time no see." He walked over and gave her a hug so big that her feet came off the floor.

She laughed, but she couldn't help but notice the frown that flickered over Waylon's features at his brother's display of affection. Or was it that his brother had suddenly displayed a bit of affection toward her? Either way, she pried herself out of Colt's arms.

Winnie came running into the kitchen. There was dirt streaked over her face, and her Ace bandage was covered in sticky greenish-brown mud.

"Winnie, were you out in the barn again?" Christina asked, giving the girl an admonishing look.

"Lewis and Clark gotta have cookies," Winnie said, like giving horses their treats was a vital part of any growing girl's day. "They so hungry."

Christina fell victim to the girl's big brown eyes—eyes that looked entirely too much like her father's. She instinctively glanced toward Waylon. He was smiling at the girl, and the warmth made her heart shift in her chest. He wasn't supposed to like children—especially Winnie. If he fell for the girl's charms and the time came when he was given a choice of having her, Christina would undoubtedly lose out to him and the girl would be taken away.

She wrapped her arms around Winnie, claiming her even though Waylon had no idea she was up for grabs. "Why don't we go get you cleaned up before supper. Your—" She stopped before she let the word *nana* fall from her lips. She didn't want him to ask about the moniker again. The less he knew, the easier it would be.

"What?" Winnie looked up at her.

"Nothing. Let's just get you cleaned up. You don't want to be a mess when it comes time to eat."

Winnie pulled out of her arms. "You're gonna play dress up." She pointed toward Waylon. "Yeah, Way-lawn?"

His handsome and confusing smile disappeared. He might have liked Winnie, but he probably wasn't any closer to wanting a kid than at the moment he'd landed.

"Ah, yeah," he said, pulling the word into a long collection of syllables. "You still want to do that, eh?" He looked over toward Christina, sending her a questioning glance.

She shrugged. He could stay in the hot seat for a little while longer. Sometimes all it took for a man to go running was an hour with a mercurial toddler—especially his type, the kind who didn't know the difference between a sippy and a bottle.

Winnie ran over, took him by the hand and started to drag the begrudging Waylon toward her room at the far end of the ranch-style house. She and Alli had shared a room, but now she was on her own.

"Come on, Way-lawn. It's gonna be fun!" Glee filled Winnie's words, so much so that Christina was tempted to let him off the hook and take his place.

She didn't mind living in the land of Pinterest costumes and childish dreams. She embraced country living—a world of quilting parties and Sunday dinners. She found great comfort in the fact that they had their own lifestyle and their own brand of perfection.

Even though Waylon had grown up in this world, the tight look on his face made it clear he didn't have the same sentimental attachment. He looked like he would be far more comfortable in the throes of war than the throes of pink felt and glitter.

Eloise walked out of the kitchen carrying a bag of frozen corn as Waylon made his way into the girl's room. "Is he really going to go with her?" she asked, her eyes wide with surprise.

"You know Winnie. She has a way of convincing even the stillest of hearts to start beating again."

Eloise gave her a soft, knowing smile. "I don't think it's just Winnie who has that gift."

She wasn't sure exactly what the woman was implying, but the thought made Christina shift her weight uncomfortably. She wasn't having any effect on Waylon, and whether or not Waylon was making her feel unexpected and somewhat unwelcome things…well, there was no way the woman could have known.

Before Eloise could make her think of anything else, she escaped down the hall after the keeper of hearts. She stood outside the bedroom door, listening to Winnie telling Waylon about her stuffed animals. Apparently, according to the story she was telling him, her favorite was her orange-and-white plush cat she had dubbed Mr. Puffy Face. Yesterday the cat had been dubbed Hank; regardless, their interaction made Christina laugh. Winnie hadn't been herself since her mother's disappearance, and it was nice to see some happiness return to the girl.

She leaned against the doorjamb, the door open just far enough to see in but not far enough to interrupt the two from their play. Winnie had put on her pink Sleeping Beauty dress, and Waylon had a purple bejeweled tiara perched at an awkward angle on his head.

Christina chuckled as she turned back to the kitchen.

Eloise pulled out the roast from the oven as Colter stirred the vegetables. From the formal dining room, she could hear the titters of laughter as Wyatt and his fiancée, Gwen, set the table. As she stood watching, a comforting feeling of home filled her.

It felt so good to be a part of all of this—and the family. If she had been on her own with Alli's disappearance, she didn't know how she would have been able to make it this far—just taking care of Winnie was a full-time event, and that was to say nothing of her job at Dunrovin, taking care of the animals and helping to train the horses, and the daily needs of living. It felt so good, standing here and letting life go on around her.

It made her wish this moment could last forever—but bad or good, all things in life were dictated by the fickle hands of time. Even intangible things like love fell victim to it—love ebbed and waned, or at least it always had when it had come to the men in her life.

The only time that wasn't true was when it came to her love for Winnie. To love a child was an incredible experience. They could drive her to the edges of madness, they could treat her worse than a stranger, and yet at the end of the day, all their trespasses could be forgiven with the whisper of *I love you*, or their scent on her skin. Christina hugged her arms around herself as she thought about how close those days could be to coming to an end.

"Is Waylon going to make it out of that bedroom alive?" Wyatt asked, pulling her from the pits of her thoughts.

"I—" she started but was cut off as Waylon appeared in the kitchen's doorway, sadly without his sparkling tiara.

"Is there any tinfoil?" he asked, a childlike smile on his face.

Eloise opened up a drawer, pulled out a blue box and handed it over to Waylon. "You're not going to make her dress up like leftovers, are you? Winnie isn't going to go for the idea," she said with a chuckle.

He raised the box like a wand. "No worries, I have this under control."

"Is that army-speak for you are letting a two-and-a-half-year-old run you?" Wyatt asked with a raise of his brow and a thin smirk.

Waylon laughed, and his whole face lit up. His copper skin made the crow's feet nearly invisible at the corners of his eyes, but if she looked closely, she could just make them out, almost as if they were a secret about him that was there only for her. She tried to control the drive she felt to move nearer to him, but as she stared, her desire intensified.

"Hey, now, I've let worse women control me. At least this one's cute, she likes me and she enjoys having me around—it's a lot more than I can say about some others," Waylon joked, but as he looked at Christina, he shut his mouth like he wished he could have reeled the words back in. "I… I just mean…" he stammered. "Not that I meant Alli or anything."

"I'm not going to say anything," she said, cutting him a little slack. "I have no room to judge anyone when it comes to relationships."

She could have sworn she saw Eloise and Gwen share a look. They were wrong if they thought something was happening between her and Waylon. There weren't any feelings between them—at least not any that came from Waylon—and her feelings were probably nothing more than her trying to come to terms with his new bond with Winnie. Regardless of whatever those two women were thinking, the only thing she and Waylon would share was the love they each felt toward one curly-haired two-year-old.

She turned away as Waylon brushed against her, making his way back to the girl. Where he had touched her burned with an unexpected and unwelcome heat, and she rubbed her arm as though she could make the feeling disappear by wiping it away.

The door to Winnie's room clicked shut, and Wyatt peeked around the corner before turning back to everyone in the kitchen. "Have you told him yet?"

She glanced down at the floor, afraid that if she looked at Wyatt he would be able to read each confusing thought and feeling that ran through her.

"Don't you think he has a right to know?" Wyatt pressed.

Eloise waved him off. "He has every right to know, but it's already been nearly three years. What's another few days?"

"He's going to be furious when you tell him. He's never going to understand. I know I wouldn't," Wyatt continued.

Gwen walked over to him and wrapped her arm around his. "This isn't our choice, Wyatt."

"That doesn't mean that we aren't going to be accountable when he learns the truth." Wyatt put his hand on his fiancée's and made small circles on the back of her skin.

The simple action made Christina want to hug herself tighter. Gwen was so lucky to have found love with one of the Fitz brothers. They all had their issues, but they were all good people, even Waylon—or rather, especially Waylon. She could only imagine how good it would feel to have him making small circles on her skin, especially after him merely brushing against her had almost brought her to her knees.

She forced herself to look away from the cute couple, reminding herself that as picturesque as they were, a relationship wasn't what she wanted. Sure, it started out with flowers, sweet words and tender touches, but nothing that good lasted forever.

"If we tell him," Eloise said, pulling her from her thoughts, "there will be no going back. Once the truth is out there, he's going to have to make some major choices in his life. He's innocent in all this. He has always done his best, and I'm sure if we tell him the truth, he will try to make the best choices he can. But who knows what those choices will be."

Wyatt shook his head. "We can't stand in his way."

"I know," Eloise said. "Right now, with all the uncertainty with Alli and what she may or may not do… Well, he's already burdened enough. Don't you think?"

"Give him more credit. He's strong. He can handle the truth. And he needs to be able to make his own decisions." Wyatt motioned toward the bedroom.

"No one is arguing that, Wyatt," Christina said, trying to come to Eloise's aid. "It's just that we need to make sure he's ready."

"Come on," Wyatt said, shaking his head. "No one's ever really ready to be a parent. Even if you think you are ready, it's not until you're thrown into the situation that you really know what you're in for."

Eloise smiled as she raised her brow. "Is there something you two need to tell us?" She rubbed a small circle on her lower belly.

Gwen's mouth dropped open. "No... I... Not yet..." she stammered.

Wyatt chuckled. "Mom, come on. Don't tease her."

Eloise laughed. "There's nothing wrong with me hoping for a few more grandchildren. It's never too soon to start trying." She gave them all a little wiggle of the finger. "Little Miss Winnie needs a partner in crime."

Gwen's face was bright red, and Wyatt had started to take on a sweaty sheen. Christina felt for them and the pressure the matron of the family was putting on them. At least she wasn't in their shoes. She might be asked about her relationship status all the time—it was the curse of being over twenty-three and not married—but those questions were far easier to field when compared to talk about babies.

Thankfully, before any more uncomfortable questions, the door to Winnie's room opened. They all went silent.

Waylon walked into the kitchen. He frowned. "What's going on? Why are you guys so quiet?"

Eloise smiled. "What, kiddo? We aren't being quiet. We were just waiting on you two rascals to be done playing around before we sit down to eat." She motioned to the roast, once again taking control of the situation like a master.

Christina smiled. She could learn a few things from Eloise.

"Okay." From the way Waylon stood there looking at his mother for a moment, it was easy to see he didn't believe her, but he didn't press them further. He shook his head and turned away from them toward the hall. "If you are all ready, I'm proud to present Princess Leonia of Leo Land and her cat, Mr. Puffy Face." He gave an over-the-top whirl of the hand and a deep, exaggerated bow.

He stood up and started to hum the theme song for the Miss America pageant. Christina couldn't help the laugh that escaped her. It was surreal to be watching the oh-so-handsome MP doing tongue trills for the entrance of a two-year-old.

Winnie marched into the kitchen. Her walk was more like the cowgirl she was instead of the princess she was pretending to be. She had on the pink Sleeping Beauty gown, her bandaged arm was wrapped with tinfoil to make it look like a clunky sword and she wore a foil crown. The crumpled and uneven crown had two large spikes Christina was sure were supposed to be purely decorative but looked conspicuously like devil horns.

Winnie had on bright pink lipstick that was smeared over her teeth as she smiled, and it was heavy on the left side of her mouth, like Waylon had pressed too hard while applying. Winnie smiled brightly, the motion filling her eyes with joy.

Oh, what it would have been to be a child once again, to find true, unadulterated joy in things most stodgy adults thought ridiculous. It would have been so nice to go back to those moments in life, where a thing like playing dress-up was all it took to forget one's troubles. There were no concerns of what was to come, bills that needed to be paid or the things that were required to make another person happy. There was just one pink dress and one ill-fitting tinfoil crown.

Wyatt leaned in close so only Christina could hear him. "He isn't perfect, neither is his life, but maybe he wouldn't be such a bad dad after all."

He hadn't needed to tell her what she was already thinking. Some things—like the look of pride that Waylon was giving Winnie—spoke volumes about what it meant to truly love. And love was the only thing that really mattered.

Waylon had never been one for sleep much, but last
night had been long and filled with dark shadows.
It was almost as if Dunrovin had started to move in
around him, threatening to trap him with its candy
canes and pink princesses. He had managed to escape
once before, but it had been when things had been

Chapter Six

Waylon had never been one for sleep much, but last
night had been long and filled with dark shadows.
It was almost as if Dunrovin had started to move in
around him, threatening to trap him with its candy
canes and pink princesses. He had managed to escape
once before, but it had been when things had been
ending with Alli. Now that he was back at the ranch,
it was hard to remember any of the other reasons he'd
left besides his disastrous marriage.

Rolling out of bed and making his way to the
kitchen, he was surprised to find Christina already
standing in front of the coffeepot as it percolated and
bubbled with life. The scent of hot coffee filled the
kitchen, but beneath it was the heady aroma of the
woman standing with her back to him. The strange
mixture made him suck in a long breath, pulling the
scent of her deep into his lungs. She smelled like sham-
poo, hay and something earthy. It reminded him of
something he couldn't quite put his finger on.

Christina swayed her hips as though she were dancing to a song only she could hear, but as she moved,
she hummed a few bars. A piece of hair fell from the
butterfly clip that held up her blond locks. She was so

dang beautiful. If he wasn't here about her sister, if he was just living his everyday and somewhat mundane life back at Fort Bragg, he would have made his move. As it was, he simply stood there, taking her in.

Last night there had been a moment when he'd been dancing with Winnie in her princess dress and he had caught Christina smiling. That look had almost made it seem possible she liked him, but he wasn't sure he was qualified to get a good read on that woman. She was so confusing. Mad one minute, and the next she was giving him a look that in most circles meant they would be exchanging more than phone numbers.

He chuckled.

Christina turned around with a jump. "How long have you been standing there?" She pulled at her Van Halen nightshirt. There was a hole over her left hip, and her hand found the spot like she hated the thought of him seeing any part of her naked flesh.

He smiled as he stared at her fingers and thought about the word *naked*. Just the thought made his body quiver to life. Yes, he could handle seeing her lying on his bed, waiting, wanting.

"Waylon, how long have you been there?" She gave him a look as though she was wondering if he had lost his mind.

"Huh? Not long." He forced himself to look at the clock on the stove while he tried to get his body back under control, but mornings and him…well, it was just another battle that he rarely seemed to win. He shifted his weight to hide anything that might have slipped into view. "Actually, I was just going to grab a cup of joe before heading up to where they found Alli's car."

"I thought you might have something in mind. I'm glad I caught you. I want to go."

"Haven't you already gone up there?" A minute ticked by on the clock.

She turned back to the cupboard and took out two travel mugs. "Yep, but after I saw you work the investigation on the car yesterday…well, I would love to think that you might be able to pull something from the scene, just like you pulled that note out of the headliner."

That was pure dumb luck, but he wasn't sure he wanted to admit it to her. He liked the thought of her thinking he had some special gift when it came to an investigation. He would take being her hero any day.

"I doubt there's anything left up there for us to find. They went over that scene pretty good, according to Wyatt's notes. And it's been nearly a full week. By now, between the weather and normal wear and tear— well, we'd be lucky to even find the exact spot."

"I've been up there. I can show you where they found the car." Christina sloshed the coffee into the cups. Her hands were shaking slightly.

"Are you okay?" he asked, motioning toward her unsteady hands.

She set the coffeepot back in the maker and balled her fists, like she was mad at them for giving her weakness away. "I'm fine. Just fine." As she looked up at him, there was a faint redness to her cheeks.

He didn't push it. It would make all their lives easier if they could get along for the few days he was here, and he had a feeling that if he questioned her, things had the chance of slipping back into a place where she barely seemed to tolerate him.

"Here." She handed him one of the travel mugs. "You take it black, right? Every cop I know always takes their coffee black. I always thought it was some statement about being so tough that you all don't need cream and sugar, but when I asked Wyatt about it, he said it was that you all were just too lazy to put extra work into something that was good just plain." She was rambling, and as she spoke, the redness in her cheeks grew more pronounced and she was forced to put her hands around her own cup to keep them from shaking.

"Yep, I'm one who takes it black. But I got a buddy back at Bragg who loves so much cream that I always say it's just cream with a splash of coffee," he joked, trying to make her feel better. He took a sip of the steaming liquid.

The woman knew how to make a good cup of joe, and it made him wonder what else she was good at.

"Are you sure you're not going along just so you can spend more time with me?"

She gave him a cute smirk and a raise of her eyebrow. "It's about my sister. Not you and me."

"You and me?" he teased. "Don't you think you could just call that *us*?"

She took a long drink of her coffee. It was so long, in fact, he couldn't help but wonder how she wasn't burning her tongue.

"It's really all just semantics," he continued. "I'm not saying there is an us. Just that…"

She lowered her coffee, and there was a smile on her lips. "You can stop. We both know where each other stands—and it certainly isn't something that needs to be discussed." She refilled her cup. "By the way, when are you thinking you're going to head back to your base?"

"I have a week's leave. The only reason I got it at all is that my CO owed me a couple of favors. They don't like giving leave when a person only has a few months left before reenlisting."

She frowned at him. "So you're going to go for another four years?"

He shrugged. "I only have about six months left this round. I love my job and my buddies in my unit. We are like family."

"*Like* family," she said, repeating his words as though she was trying them on for size. "Is your job pretty dangerous?" She looked up at him, and there was something in her eyes that made him glance away out of fear that she would be able to see into his memories.

There was always danger in his job. Each day was something different. The last major incident had been when he had stepped in the way of a sniper's bullet in Fallujah for his CO. Luckily, the bullet had mostly impacted Waylon's Kevlar, but a small fragment had managed to break loose and hit him in the elbow. From time to time, his left arm still pinged, reminding him of how close he could have been to losing his life for the greater good. Yet, from the look on Christina's face, the last thing he needed to do was admit that he was always toeing a thin line between life and death.

"Let's go," he said. "And no more questions."

Her frown deepened. "Look, if you don't want me to go…"

"You'd stay here?" he asked with a playful smile. "We both know you aren't the type who is going to sit by and idly twiddle her thumbs. No matter what you think of me, you won't miss this chance."

"Let me go get dressed," she said, setting down her coffee. "Don't go anywhere." She gave him a threatening look.

Waylon raised his hands in surrender. "Cross my heart."

She rushed out of the room and he could hear her run down the hallway. A couple of minutes later she returned, cowgirled out—complete with a pair of ostrich-skin boots, a tight-fitting pair of jeans, and a purple plaid shirt. She had her coat draped over her arm.

"You ready to go?"

"Always."

He walked to the car, holding the door as she followed.

Each time she drew close to him, he couldn't help his need to pull her scent deep into his lungs. Dang, she smelled so good.

They drove in silence, passing through the gates of the mountains that led to the Montana/Alberta border. He hadn't made this drive in a long time, and as they passed by the crystal-blue lakes and clear rivers, he just took it all in. This place was so beautiful. It really was the Last Best Place, just as its slogan said. There was something about Montana that beckoned to days gone by, of the untamed nature of life and the ones who dared live it.

"I'm sorry about yesterday. When you flew in. It was just…with Winnie and all… I guess… Just know that I don't hate you or anything. Sometimes I can just be a little prickly," Christina said, breaking the silence between them.

She sounded sincere enough, but he wasn't sure he entirely bought what she was trying to sell. "Honestly, I get it—I mean, if you hate me or whatever. Divorce leads to division among friends and even more among families. You have your sister's back, and I admire that kind of loyalty—even if it's to my disadvantage."

She stared at him for a moment, like she was surprised by his candor, but she didn't say anything.

"My family had their fair share of dislike when it came to your sister. It would only be right that you would have the same feelings toward me. But I want you to know that, regardless of what Alli told you, there was a lot more to the situation. I doubt she told you everything that led up to our divorce." He gripped his hands tight on the steering wheel of her truck. "I mean, I wasn't without guilt. I certainly made my fair share of mistakes, but I wasn't the only one who made some bad choices."

She glanced down at her hands. "I know I only got one side of the story. I've come to realize that, thanks to you being here. I can see the way you are with your family and how you're trying with Winnie. You don't need to worry about my opinion. Besides, I heard something the other day that kind of put things into perspective for me, and I know it's as true for me as it probably is for you."

"What did you hear?"

She looked up at him and sent him a soft smile that made his stomach flip.

"They said that everyone's life is a book, and in each book there is one chapter no one is willing to read aloud."

He chuckled. "Just one chapter?"

Her smile widened. "Hey, it's just what they said." She shrugged.

For a moment, he considered reaching over and taking her hand, but he couldn't bring himself to do it. They had finally started to move together. He would hate to screw it up by taking things in a direction that she had no intention of going. For now, he would have to be happy with just seeing her smile and ignore the way his body seemed to want to pull him closer to her.

"The spot was right up there," Christina said, pointing to a nondescript little pullout on the side of the nearly deserted highway.

There were tall dead grasses on the side of the road, and down the embankment was a pond and a meadow that brushed against the toes of the mountains that stood like sentinels around the valley. Snow had started to accumulate on the peaks of the range, a visible reminder that icy storms lurked just over the horizon.

He parked the truck, and they got out as a big rig barreled down the road past them. It made the air shudder as the driver changed speeds, the sound almost deafening.

"Where do you think he's coming from?" Waylon asked, motioning toward the truck as it rumbled north.

"Truckers use this highway when the weather is good. It's a bit longer in mileage than the main highway, but they make up for it in speed. It can cut up to an hour off their transit to the border. The people who live along here hate it. Two years ago, a big rig carrying crude oil overturned. Ruined their groundwater. The EPA had to come in and do all kinds of studies. They finally cleared the area for general use again, but if you ask anyone who actually lives around here, there is still oil that seeps through the ground and into their water."

He would have asked how the oil company had gotten away with dodging responsibility, but he knew all too well how the feds liked to work. He'd been living in their world for too long to be oblivious to the fact that they often were willing to accept a little bit of collateral damage when millions of dollars were at stake.

"There are a few locals who like the truckers, though," Christina continued.

"Who's that?"

She motioned down the road. "There is a small town about fifteen miles from here that pretty much only exists thanks to the long-haul trade. It's the last stop for gas and grub before the truckers head over the border."

His mind went to the receipt Wyatt said he'd found in Alli's car. He'd said it was of no use, but maybe it was from the town Christina was talking about. It could have been more of a clue than his brother had realized, but what did it really matter if Alli had stopped for gas in the little town before heading over the border, or had she come back sometime later in the day? It would be a normal thing to do. Wyatt had said he'd looked into the lead. If it had been anything, his brother would have figured it out. He was a good cop and an even better brother.

Waylon walked to the edge of the pullout. No matter how badly he wanted to find something definitive that could point them in Alli's direction, there was nothing besides gravel on the side of the road. He stood there for a moment, taking in the mountains and the aroma of winter. The cold air bit at his nose, sharp and clean—a far cry from the dry and dusty air of Iraq.

"You okay?" Christina asked, stepping beside him. "You're being quiet."

"Just thinking," he said, looking over at her. His gaze moved down to her hands. Her fingers looked so inviting. He could almost feel them slipping between his, and the sensation made his hand twitch.

"About?" she pressed.

He couldn't tell her that he was really thinking about how badly he wanted to touch her, and how she reminded him of how lonely his life had been ever since he'd left Montana and Alli. Maybe that was all his desire to touch her was—a need to stave off the loneliness. No, that probably wasn't it. He'd had plenty of chances to be with other women, and none of them had made him give even a passing thought to anything resembling a relationship. Yet something about Christina and the way she pushed him made him wonder if he'd made a mistake in leaving Mystery. But if he'd stayed, there was no way they would have ended up together, either.

Oh, Alli. When they found her, she would never let him and Christina be together. She would do and say everything she could to stop her sister from being with him.

Everything about him and Christina and the attraction he felt wasn't going to work—a relationship with her wasn't just unlikely, it was almost forbidden.

As much as he wished the thought would push him away from her, it only made him want her that much more.

If he was going to have a chance with Christina, he had to make things happen before Alli came back into their lives and had the chance to screw everything up.

He reached over and took Christina's hand. Alli had already messed up enough in his life—he wouldn't let her stand in the way of him following his heart. Christina jerked as their skin touched, but she didn't pull away. Rather, she moved her fingers between his and drew him closer.

His heart leaped into his throat. Maybe he wasn't alone in his desire.

There was the rumble of another big rig, but this time the roar seemed deeper and the rig slowed down, pulling to a stop behind their truck. He frowned in the trucker's direction. He'd finally made his move with Christina and the dude was ruining it.

She pulled her fingers from his and moved a few steps away from him, almost as if she regretted her decision to let him touch her.

"Heya," the trucker said as he stepped down from the cab. His hair was long and unkempt, and as he looked at them, he ran his fingers through the greasy mess. "You guys need help?" he asked, his voice flecked with a Canadian accent even though his rig had Montana plates.

Waylon had forgotten about Montana and its unspoken pay-it-forward code. If someone was broken down on the side of a road like this, there was always someone willing to help. The system came from the days of the pioneers. Not much had changed from those days, because in the dead of winter, in a place like this, it might be hours—if not days—before a person ran into someone else. In such a barren world, a single act of kindness could sometimes be the difference between life and death.

"We're good," Waylon said, trying his best to make himself smile at the well-intentioned interloper.

The trucker didn't stop; instead, he turned to Christina. "Are you okay, miss?"

Christina's eyes widened with surprise at the man's implied assumption that she might be here against her will. "I'm… I'm fine. Thanks for asking."

The guy dropped his hand. Until now Waylon hadn't noticed he was hiding a bat behind his leg.

Did this guy really think he was the kind of guy who would bring a girl out here to the middle of nowhere against her will? Or had the guy been around the world enough to jump to that kind of conclusion?

In a strange way, he was glad there were still guys out there like this trucker, men who were willing to come to the aid of a woman they didn't know. It gave him a little bit of hope for mankind.

"Army?" the trucker asked, motioning toward him.

"Huh?" Waylon glanced down at his clothes, half expecting to see his ACUs, but he was wearing jeans and a red plaid shirt. "Hoo-ah."

"I could tell from the look of ya. I can't believe they let you out of the desert playground."

"Ha," Waylon answered with a dry laugh. "Let me guess, you're a jarhead?"

"Some of us were born to be real men." The guy laughed, the sound high and tight.

Christina glanced over at him, like she was trying

to figure out what she was supposed to be doing while they chided each other.

"Sorry," Waylon said, motioning toward her. "This is my…" Dang, what did he call her? His former sister-in-law, his friend or his girlfriend? "This is my *friend* Christina. And, buddy, you are?"

The guy shook her hand. "I'm Daryl, Daryl Bucket," the man said, his voice flecked with a Canadian accent.

"Nice to meet you, Daryl," Christina said. "Thanks for stopping. That was noble of you. Let's chalk one up for the marines." She gave Waylon a teasing glance.

"Hey, now, you can't really give him a point. I traveled all the way across the country for this." He laughed.

She smiled, giving him a soft look that made it clear she was just joking around.

He turned to Daryl. "But really, that was something, man. It's been a long time since I've been home. I forgot how selfless people around here can be."

"It ain't no thing." Daryl waved them off. "About a week ago I ran across a girl around here who was down on her luck. This is a hell of a spot for bad things to happen."

"You found a girl here a week ago?" All of Waylon's MP senses kicked into high gear. "What did she look like?"

The guy shrugged. "Average height, kind of skinny, dark haired. Nice enough lady."

"Did you catch her name?"

Daryl frowned as though he were trying to pull the name from somewhere deep in his thoughts. "Can't say that I did. I don't recall her giving it, though I think I asked."

The woman's description vaguely matched Alli's. Was it possible this guy had some connection to her?

"She was pulled over right here," Daryl continued, motioning toward the small pullout.

"Do you remember what kind of car she was driving?"

Daryl nodded. "Oh, yeah, it was a black Hyundai. Couple of years old. My ex-wife bought one just like it right before she and I split."

Waylon tried to play it cool, but his mind was buzzing.

"Did the lady tell you why she was pulled over?"

Daryl scratched his head. "She said she had a flat tire. I offered to change it for her, but she said she didn't have a spare and told me not to bother. Instead, she asked if I would give her a ride."

"To Canada?" Christina asked.

Daryl shook his head. "Nah, she wanted to go to some little town a ways south."

"Remember the town?"

"Of course I do, I live there. Moved to the place just after my divorce," Daryl said with a nod. "Lucky for her I was headed back home."

"Where do you call home?" Waylon pressed.

"It's a place called Mystery. You know it?"

Waylon looked over at Christina, and she gave him the nod that said she was thinking the same thing he was—they had just found the break they needed. They were one step closer to finding Alli, one step closer to going back to a life where the last thing they could have would be each other.

He stared at her blue eyes, taking them in like it was the last time he would really be able to look at her. She'd never be his, no matter how much he hoped for things to be different.

Chapter Seven

At least there was some kind of good news. Finally. Her sister was alive. Or at least Alli had been alive when Daryl had found her. Only the fates knew if she was still alive and kicking, or what was going on in her mind, but for the first time in a week, the sick feeling in Christina's stomach lessened.

Though when the trucker had told them he'd taken Alli back to Mystery, she wasn't sure if she was furious or relieved. How could her sister have run away only to come back the same day? She must have been running purely for show, but why? Why had she come back to town? Moreover, had she been watching them at the ranch?

There had been so many whispers about her sister still being a danger to the residents of the ranch and the town, but until now Christina had brushed them aside. Alli had wanted to kill Bianca and Monica because they had stood in the way of her relationship with William, but that didn't make her a threat to the rest of the population.

But maybe she had her sister all wrong. Maybe Alli was far more dangerous than she had assumed. Maybe Alli really had lost her mind like some people thought.

Maybe she really did want to go on some kind of murderous rampage—or perhaps she had some kind of hit list. It was impossible to know until they found her.

Even though it was her sister, the thought of Alli lurking in the shadows as she waited to take her next victim made Christina's skin crawl. Alli had been having so many issues, most circulating around her tumultuous relationships with men, and most recently William Poe. Maybe that was why she had come back—to watch William. Or was it possible she had something else in mind for the man, something more sinister?

Alli had always been the kind to hold a grudge.

Even though Christina hated the guy, she wasn't sure she could resist the urge to tell William that his life might be in danger. He had a right to know. She tried to tell herself it was unlikely, but with how strangely Alli had been acting before her disappearance, it was hard to tell what exactly her sister was thinking.

Christina sighed, watching the road as she and Waylon drove back toward the ranch.

"It'll all be okay." Waylon rested his hand palm up on the bench seat, waiting for her to slip her hand into his.

She stared at his fingers. With everything going on with Daryl, she had nearly forgotten about their moment, yet as she recalled the feeling of her hand in his, a warmth rose up from her core. There had been something so right about the feel of their entwined fingers.

In the still of the Montana roadside, she had even been able to feel his heartbeat, fast and erratic, as though he had been as anxious as she was. He was a beautiful specimen of a man. She had never thought of herself as ugly or unworthy, but there was no reason he should be nervous around her, a woman with no game and even less sexual acumen.

"I hope everything will be okay. I hope we can find her," she said, almost unaware of her words as she moved her trembling hand ever so slowly toward his waiting fingers.

It was funny how when she didn't have time to think about their actions, she had taken his hand and just lived in the moment. It had been unquestionably right to stand there, holding him. Yet, now that there was a chance to think of all the things that stood in their way, and all the reasons that they shouldn't be together, she wasn't sure that letting the wants of her body overrule the needs of her life was the right choice.

If they became anything more than acquaintances, she could only imagine what the rumor mill of Mystery would have to say. She wasn't a person who was overly consumed by what others thought or her image, but even a simple act like going to the grocery store would be met with whispers and poorly masked jabs at their choice to be together, as he had once been her sister's husband.

She could just have him for a few days. No one would have to know what went on between them— that was, as long as she could keep her head and her heart separate. She could enjoy his sexy body without the weight of worrying about the future. She'd never done the whole one-night-stand thing, but at her age it didn't seem like such a taboo. Perhaps she could even be empowered by living in a world where she could have sex just to have sex.

Throughout her life, her heart had only gotten in the way. This time she could just ignore it.

She smiled as she moved the last few inches and slipped her fingers between his.

It already felt good to do a little living.

Waylon squeezed her fingers. The action was small, but it ran through her entire being.

"I…" She wasn't sure of what to say, or if she should tell him that she wanted this to be a no-strings type of thing.

"Alli is going to be all right. Now that we know she's alive, I'm sure we will find her," he said, going down an entirely different line of thinking.

She considered moving the conversation back to what she needed to say, but she stopped herself. It was better just to leave some things unspoken. Maybe that was what Waylon was thinking, too. He had to understand anything that came to be between them had a limited shelf life.

"Wait." She paused, letting what he'd said sink in. "You thought she was dead?"

Waylon's fingers tightened for a moment. "Well, she hasn't been seen in a week and no one has heard from her. You would have thought, with all the police and law enforcement involvement, if she was out there somewhere, someone would have at least reported seeing her by now. The only tips Wyatt has gotten so far are from a few folks who also reported seeing Elvis at the grocery store."

Alli couldn't be dead. Oh, the thought had crossed her mind. She just hadn't given it any room to grow. It just wasn't possible. Sure, some people would call her refusal to think about the possibility denial, but

Alli being dead didn't even make logical sense—who would have wanted to kill her? Bianca's family hadn't taken the news of her death and Alli's involvement well, especially her mother, Carla, but not even she seemed like the type who would try to murder out of revenge or anger.

No. Alli had to be alive.

"She just dropped her car," Christina argued. "She didn't want anyone to find her. Really, it was smart."

"Sure," Waylon said with a slight nod. "It was smart. She could travel with truckers, get lost in a sea of faces as she moved around the states. But there are a couple of things wrong with the idea. First, if she was going to drop her car and come back to Mystery, why would she have stopped at the little gas station and purchased enough gas to keep going for hours? And I'm still not sure how and if the note and the bullet we found are related."

He was right. It didn't make sense. "Maybe she wrote the note before everything fell apart and someone shot out the tire after she left the car. Who knows?" Christina said, trying to quell the fears that were rising within her about Alli's well-being.

"You're right, I don't understand your sister. And I really don't understand why she would have run away only to come back to Mystery."

"Maybe she just couldn't leave—" She stopped before she said Winnie's name aloud. "I think we need to get back to Mystery, fast." Her thoughts raced to Winnie and the possible implications Alli's return to the town could have on the child's safety.

"Why?" he asked, pressing down hard on the accelerator without waiting for her answer. "What are you thinking?"

She shook her head. She had to tell him. If she did, maybe he wouldn't question things too much. And even if he did, she didn't have to answer him.

"Winnie... Winnie is Alli's daughter. I think she may be coming back to get her."

"Wait. She's *Alli's* daughter?" He jerked his foot off the gas pedal and stared over at her. "What? She couldn't get pregnant."

The way he said *pregnant* made it sound like some kind of expletive.

"She could and she did. And if Alli's come back, it's probably for Winnie."

He turned away from her and stared out toward the road as he stepped back on the gas. He sat in silence for a moment, just as she had feared he would. "So, how old is Winnie?"

Christina considered lying for a brief moment, but nothing good would come from it. "She's two."

His fingers moved on the wheel as though he were counting backward on them. He shook his head and gave a sigh of relief that made the knot that she didn't know was in her stomach loosen.

"She's two...so who's the father?"

Several of her own brand of expletives rolled through Christina's mind.

"I... She... You know Alli," she said, her voice as weak as her resolve. She should tell him. Now. He had asked her point-blank.

"She'd been seeing Poe, right?" Waylon asked. "You think he could be the girl's father?"

"No. She had Winnie before she started sleeping with him."

She hated being in this position. She hated this, but it wasn't just her choice to make to tell him. She and Eloise had agreed it would be better to break the news when everyone was there. If she let it slip now, Waylon would be so angry, and his mother wouldn't be there to defend herself. She had to protect Eloise by keeping the secret a little bit longer—Eloise was the closest person she had to a mother. It was only because of her that she wasn't living in some dank apartment on the wrong side of the tracks. She owed her everything—and that included her loyalty.

Yet that didn't mean she felt good about omitting the truth.

There was no right answer. There was only here and now, and what needed to happen.

"If Alli gets her hands on her daughter, we'll never see her again. We need to keep Winnie safe. She needs to be protected."

"If Alli was going to take her, why would she have waited this long?"

He made a good point. "We really haven't left her alone. Someone is always with her."

"Even at night?" he asked with a raise of the brow.

Christina looked down at her hands. "Winnie has been sleeping with me ever since her mother disappeared. She's been having some abandonment issues and hasn't let us out of her sight."

"Oh, I see," he said as though he was suddenly reminded that Winnie was just a child, with childish needs. As Mystery came into view, he took in a long breath. "Do you really think Winnie's in danger? If she is, maybe it's best if I take care of her."

"You?" She didn't mean it to come out like it did, with an air of shock and revulsion, but there was no taking it back.

From the look on Waylon's face, he was surprised and far more annoyed than she had intended for him to be.

"I just mean you have a lot on your plate already. The last thing you need while you're here is to have to take care of a child. The best thing you can do to keep Winnie out of Alli's hands is to make sure that you find her before she gets a chance to do something unspeakable." She paused. "Besides, Winnie is safe at the ranch."

He glanced over at her. "First, that's the first place Alli's going to come looking for the girl when and if she comes to get her. So we can't leave her there. Second, Alli may not even know I'm here. That gives us a little bit of an advantage when it comes to keeping the girl safe. She won't look for her with me. And third, I don't know who you think I am, but I swear I'm not some monster with kids. I like kids. Just because I don't have any doesn't mean I'm completely inexperienced. Remember, I was in foster care for a long time. And when I was growing up, my mom and dad regularly took in foster kids that I helped care for."

"Having your own kids, or the sole care of a child, is totally different. You aren't ready." Her voice cracked like a whip, and she wished for a second time that she had better control of her tone.

He sucked in his breath. "You're right," he said, giving her an assessing glance. "I know it's different.

And I know by what you are saying, and by the way you are saying it, it's probably coming from a place of deep hurt and pain—I know about your parents—but you can trust me."

"We can't fight about this. We just need to find Winnie. She can go with Wyatt and Gwen," Christina said, not giving an inch.

She could trust a lot of things—the sun dawned in the east, the wind blew and time would always pass—yet she hadn't ever trusted a man. Not really. She wasn't about to start now, not when her niece's life could possibly be hanging in the balance.

Chapter Eight

She wasn't telling him something. Waylon could see it in the way she wouldn't look him in the eyes. He didn't know what she was holding back, but one thing he did know was that she was in full panic about Winnie. There was something about that little girl and Christina's concern for her safety that he couldn't ignore—or question.

She would tell him the truth if and when she was ready. He would just have to be patient.

His thoughts drifted to Winnie. The girl was two. He had divorced Alli three and a half years ago. That put Winnie well outside the range of the possibility of him being the father. At least, probably.

He tried to recall the last time he'd had relations with Alli, but all he could remember were times while they had still been married. He hated to think about that time in his life too much. Thoughts of what had transpired with Alli only brought heartache.

Wyatt and Gwen were in the barn with Winnie when they got back to Dunrovin.

Everything about the ranch was the same—the same weathered red barn and green stock fence around the corrals, the same red and green Christmas lights strung up around the barn, and the same American flag on the flagpole in the middle of the main house's front yard. It waved reverently, for a minute reminding him of what and whom he'd pledged his life to and why.

He followed Christina into the barn, watching her hips move and the Wranglers she was wearing stretch over the round curves of her ass. Her long blond hair fell down her back like a lion's mane, perfectly matching her proclivity for roaring. He didn't know a lot about astrological signs, but if he had to guess, she was probably a Leo.

As much as she drove him crazy, it was those same qualities—the tendency to push him away, to keep him guessing and to make the whole room turn with her smile—that made him want her more. She challenged him like no other woman ever had, and it was that mystery, that need to learn more, that made him wonder what it would be like to move back to the ranch—make a go of it here for a while.

He had planned on reenlisting, but now he wasn't so sure.

"Hey, guys!" Gwen said, looking up from the horse she and Winnie were brushing. "How's it going?"

Winnie ran up to Christina and threw herself around her aunt's legs. As he watched, he recalled how Christina had told him she was merely the girl's guardian. Why had she been so evasive? She had said the father wasn't William and it wasn't him, so who could it be? And why wouldn't she just tell him?

Winnie let go of Christina and wrapped herself around his legs, then squirmed her way up, using her bandaged arm like a lever to move herself higher until she was snuggled into his arms. "Wy-ant said I can't

wear my crown," she said in her slightly garbled toddler tongue. She pointed to her head.

"Why not?" Waylon said, pulling her higher into
his arms so she could perch on his hip like a little bird.

She shrugged and popped her dirty thumb in her
mouth.

"Weren't you just brushing the horses, kid?" he
asked.

She smiled, not letting her thumb out of the cage
of her teeth. "Yep. It was so funny. Lewis was being
naughty." She nodded toward the bay gelding as he
shifted his weight from one side to the other.

"I can't believe you wouldn't let her wear the crown
we made. You're such a killjoy, man," he said to Wyatt
with a laugh.

"Hey, now, little Miss Winnie, you know Lewis
doesn't like shiny things. It spooks him. We don't want
to scare him with your devil horns, do we?"

"Devil horns?" Winnie said with an overly exaggerated frown.

"Oh, I mean your *beautiful* crown." Wyatt laughed
and pointed at his brother. "He may be good at a lot
of things, but your buddy Waylon shouldn't be put in
charge of costumes."

Winnie's frown deepened. "I looked bee-u-tiful."

"Of course you did, sweetheart," Gwen said, walking over and pulling the girl out of Waylon's arms.
"Why don't you and I go have a little chocolate milk.
Sound good?" She gave Wyatt a knowing look as she
set Winnie down, and the girl took off toward the house
without answering.

"Thanks, Gwen," Wyatt said, giving his fiancée a
quick smack on the rear end.

"You need to put Lewis away, okay?" she said.

Wyatt nodded with a smile. The way he looked at Gwen made something shift in Waylon's chest. He couldn't recall ever looking at Alli the way Wyatt looked at Gwen.

He glanced over at Christina. Maybe there would be a chance he could love someone the same way Wyatt and Gwen loved each other—like it was from the deepest part of their souls.

Wyatt unclipped Lewis's rope from the wall and led the horse back to his stall. The horse nickered as Wyatt closed the door. Wyatt walked over to the bucket, took out a few pellets and fed them to the gelding.

"So…" Wyatt said, "how'd it go up north? Did you guys find anything?"

Christina gave Waylon an uncomfortable glance and then her gaze fell to the floor.

"Actually, we ran into a trucker," Waylon said, telling him about Daryl Bucket and the ride to Mystery that he'd given Alli.

Wyatt's face tightened with anger as Waylon spoke.

"Why the hell would she come back here?" Wyatt asked, but as he looked over at Christina, he shut his mouth tight, like he'd suddenly answered his own question. "Winnie?"

"He knows she's Alli's daughter," Christina said, but her face was tight. "I think she's going to try to kidnap her."

"She wouldn't come back here for Winnie. That can't be it," Wyatt said, shaking his head in disbelief.

"There's no other reason, at least no good one, for her to be here," Waylon said. "We were thinking it would be best if we kept Winnie out of sight for a little while, at least until we have Alli in custody."

"I'll let Gwen know, and I'll stay with Winnie non-stop until we have Alli behind bars," Wyatt said. "Alli can't get an opportunity to get her hands on Winnie. If she does, I hate to think that Winnie's life would be in danger, but the truth is, I just don't know. All I know for sure is that if you give people the right motivations, they are capable of just about anything."

Waylon couldn't agree with his brother more. They couldn't trust his ex. The only people they could trust right now were family. No one could protect the little girl better than the people who loved her the most.

"I don't think Alli would hurt Winnie," Christina said, coming to her sister's defense.

"Are you really willing to put Winnie's life at risk just because you don't *think* your sister would do something sinister?" Wyatt asked.

"You were the one who suggested Winnie stay with Wyatt," Waylon said, arguing his brother's point.

Christina's eyes filled with tears. "It's just… I never thought Alli would do something like this."

"Don't worry, Christina. Gwen and I will take good care of our girl. In fact, I'll go grab them and we'll get out of here." Wyatt turned to Waylon. "Make sure to let Mom know we have Winnie when she gets back from the store, or she'll freak out."

"No problem," Waylon said as Wyatt rushed out of the barn.

Christina looked over at him, and he could sense her contempt. "My sister isn't as evil as you are both making her out to be."

He could understand why she was upset. If one of

his brothers had done something like this, he would love them just as she loved Alli, and just like her, he would be stuck in a place between love of a person and hatred for their actions. Not for the first time since he'd met Christina, he wished he could pull her into his arms and heal her with his kiss.

NOTHING MADE SENSE. Her sister was out of control and acting in a way she never had before, and Christina had no idea what to think or do. She wished her sister would just turn herself in. Everything would be so much easier, and at least they would know she was out of harm's way.

Lately it seemed like wherever Alli was, trouble followed—and she was the source.

Christina sighed. Alli was trouble. There was no doubt about it, and as much as she loved her sister, she hated her equally.

She could feel Waylon looking at her. She glanced over at him and caught his eye. There was something in the way he looked at her that made her body come to life.

He smiled, and the sensation she was trying so hard to ignore boiled within her. No. It was nothing more than lust that she felt...tense, hungry, desperate lust. If she fell for that feeling, it would be far more dangerous than her sister. It would tear her world to pieces.

Then again, on the edges of lust was love. But falling in love with the man who promised nothing except his imminent departure was madness.

Danger and madness. It was the recipe for a disaster.

"Is there anywhere you think your sister would go?" Waylon asked, rescuing her from her thoughts.

She shook her head. "All she had was this ranch."

"Do you think it's possible that she went back to Poe? Would he shelter her from the police?"

"After what she did to Monica? No. Never. He hates her for what she did. He hates this entire ranch and everybody who works here and isn't afraid to tell everyone about it," Christina said. "Besides, Poe's already moved on to greener pastures."

"You're right. But if she's here in Mystery, she has to be staying somewhere. Somewhere that no one would have noticed her."

The thought of someone hiding in the small town of Mystery was nearly laughable if it wasn't for the fact that, so far, Alli had been able to pull it off. There was no way she could go anywhere without someone knowing her, especially after the news of her role in Bianca's and Monica's deaths had hit the papers. She was unwelcome number one.

Even Christina had found herself getting the cold shoulder from some people within the community, especially those closest to Bianca. It was almost as if they blamed her for being the sister of a murderer— like in some way she could have stopped her sister from going mad.

Not for the first time, she wondered if she could have.

If she had just known more about her sister or if she had taken a more active role in her life, maybe she could have stopped things from ever going as far as they had.

She sighed. Whether or not the community eventually forgot or forgave her—and the scarlet letter she seemed to wear was removed—her mistake in not being able to stop Alli was something that would haunt her for the rest of her life.

"Why don't we get out of here. Take a break." Waylon reached over and took her hand. He gave her fingers a light squeeze. "Sometimes I find the answers I'm looking for in moments when I'm not concentrating on the problem."

She knew exactly what he meant. She did that all the time—for some reason, her best ideas always seemed to come to her when she was in the shower. Yet she wasn't about to say that to Waylon. They weren't quite ready for a shower or talk of one—at least not yet.

She blushed as she realized her thoughts had devolved into her and Waylon making sweet, sweet love. It wasn't like she was a teenager who couldn't control herself, or who let her hormones drive her. She was a grown woman; she should have had far more restraint on her feelings.

That was what she was feeling—just some animalistic draw to the sexy Waylon Fitzgerald. Some primal instinct for sex. Simple procreative needs. Nothing more.

A strange calm filled her as she found a tendril of logic in her swarm of illogical feelings.

She let him lead her out as she stared at their knotted hands. Logic had to be her guide, not the feeling of heat that rose up from their melded touch or the happiness that threatened to overtake her at the mere fact he was touching her—moreover, that he *wanted* to touch her.

He must have had so many women interested in him. The thought made an unwelcome flutter of jealousy move through her. She looked up at his brown eyes and the almost imperceptible fine lines at their corners. He ran his thumb over her hand.

"What?" he asked, his voice raspy with something she recognized but refused to acknowledge even to herself.

"We've gone through all the guesthouses on the ranch from top to bottom." She tried to talk about something as distanced from feelings as possible. "Now that the main tourist season is over, we're buttoning up a few of them for the winter. And the rest we are keeping up and running for the fall guests and winter skiers." She knew she was rambling a bit, but he seemed to have a habit of making her do that.

His smile grew almost impossibly larger, as if he realized he was making her nervous. "Did she know the schedule of guests and which cabins you guys would be closing down for the season?"

"Everyone who works here would have had access to that information."

"Then it may be a good idea if we start looking around those places. It would be the perfect place to hide. No one coming around. No prying eyes."

It didn't feel quite right, but she didn't argue. As long as they got out of this place, and she could start ignoring her feelings again, everything would be okay. As it was, she was growing far too close to him for her own comfort.

Chapter Nine

The whole thing felt like a wild-goose chase. Other than knowing his ex-wife was somewhere in town—or rather, *had been*—they had little to go on. Maybe Alli had left again. Maybe she'd just wanted to throw everyone off her scent by taking the car north, then she'd come back and taken off south. It was a good maneuver—the double back. He'd used it in hundreds of his military exercises. His favorite was doubling back and moving in behind the enemy, gaining the high ground. If it was successful, there was almost a guarantee they could overcome their enemy.

Was that what Alli was doing now? Going for the high ground?

She had surprised him by coming back. He couldn't let her surprise him again. They had to be prepared for anything. She wasn't stupid. She'd never been stupid. He couldn't underestimate her, not if it meant anyone—especially Winnie—could be put in danger.

The more Waylon thought about Winnie, the worse he felt for the girl. She was just another of Alli's victims—another heart that had been left shattered in the woman's wake.

He knew all too well how it felt to be left by a parent. He and Colter had been down that road, though Wyatt and Rainier had gone through their own versions of hell when it came to their own biological parents. Some wounds never went away, they simply fell further into the past. And just when a person thought they were gone, those old wounds had a way of rising to the present and even scarring the future.

He glanced over at Christina as they made their way up the steps to the Sacajawea guest cabin. The place hadn't changed much since he had last been there. There was a model of a papoose above the door of the cabin, and there was a picture of Sacajawea and her baby on the door. He'd always liked this place; it had an air of the Old West, complete with pictures of bison and framed projectile points on the walls.

"It doesn't look like she's been here, either," Christina said, pressing her face to the glass and looking inside. "Nothing is out of place, at least as far as I can tell. It looks just like the others."

They had been all over the ranch, but there hadn't been any evidence that anyone, let alone Alli, had been to the cabins in the last week. They were just running in circles, and he hated the feeling of impotence that filled him.

He sighed, and Christina turned to him. "It's going to be okay," she said. "At least we're checking everything we can off the list. And right now, we know that Winnie is taken care of. Gwen and Wyatt won't let her out of their sight."

He looked at her as she pushed a wayward hair out of her face. As she moved, she licked her lips, and the simple action made his body stir to life. Her lips were damp, and as he looked at them, he wondered exactly what it would be like to kiss them. She was so sexy. She was probably the kind of woman who took a kiss slow at first, taking in the moment their lips met like it was an expensive scotch—and everything could be found in the first burning sip. In that moment, a person could taste all the things that had come together to make the kiss what it was and what made it special. It was like that first kiss held the promises of what their relationship could be—both good and bad.

He couldn't deny that even just the thought of kissing her was better than any scotch in the world—and probably far more addictive.

His phone rang. It was his mother. "What's up?"

"You need to come home. Where are you?" There was a high and frantic edge to her voice that made all of his senses spark to life.

"We're not far. What's going on?"

"Is Winnie with you?" his mother asked, not answering his question.

"Oh," he said, his stomach sinking as he remembered Wyatt's request to tell his mother that they had taken her back to their place. "She's with Wyatt."

His mother let out a long sigh. "Thank God she's all right."

"Is everything okay?"

Christina passed him a questioning glance and moved closer so she could hear his exchange with his mother.

"I was just worried when I came home and saw the door open and found Winnie's room destroyed. Did you get whatever you guys were looking for in there?"

He looked over at Christina. "No one was in her room. Were they?"

"Gwen went in there to pack her a bag and grab a few things, but she wouldn't have made a mess, and I was the last one out of the house. I *know* I locked the doors when we left. I made sure of it."

The knot in his stomach returned. "We'll be right there. Is Dad with you?"

"Yeah, he's here."

"Good." He took Christina by the hand, led her back to the truck and started the engine. "Don't go outside the house. We found out that Alli may be in Mystery and…well, who knows what she's capable of. You both need to stay safe."

THE TRUCK BUMPED down the dirt road that led out of the back forty as Waylon tried to steer around the abundant ruts in the road. It was no wonder they'd closed these cabins down—once the snow started to fall, these roads would be nearly impassable. One bad decision, one ill-prepared couple trying to drive down it in more than a few inches of snow, and without a doubt the ranch would have another mess on their hands. People constantly underestimated Montana's wild power. She was a fickle beast. One minute it could be sunny and hot, and the next it could be snowing, with hypothermia a legitimate threat.

Alli had always hated living here, a place with such extremes, but maybe it was because she was already living with more than enough extremes within herself. She couldn't compete with another thing like her.

When they got back to the main house, every light was on, even the strands of Christmas lights that ran down the fences and around the barn's windows. If the circumstances had been different, he would have said the place looked beautiful with its array of greens and reds, but as things stood, the cast of the red lights on the bone-white fence posts only reminded him of spilled blood.

Eloise stood at the bay window, watching out for them. She was hugging herself, and as she spotted them, she turned and called out behind her. His father came to the window and gave them a small, relieved wave.

He hadn't seen his parents scared before, especially not his father. The man was the picture of steely resolve. He was the kind of man who'd spent many a night pulling calves, only to watch them pass in his arms. Even before his years on the ranch, he'd seen so much tragedy and death thanks to his years in Vietnam. He didn't talk about his time spent in the jungles. The one time Merle had even mentioned it had been after a night of heavy drinking, when he'd told a story of men in his unit stealing the gold teeth of the dead. It had made Waylon's skin crawl. Yet it was also the moment that he'd realized he needed to serve his country.

His father had been through hell and back. He was a hero. Even as a young man, Waylon had known that was what he wanted to be as well. He wanted to right the wrongs of the generations before him. He wanted to make the world a better place. And, thanks to his dark past and the demons that filled his soul, he found an insatiable need to protect those who didn't have the power or the strength to protect themselves.

He had wanted nothing more than to follow in his father's footsteps. And though he'd found himself deep behind enemy lines in Iraq, and coming under fire to protect those he'd been ordered to serve, he'd never really felt like a hero. It was strange, but most of the time he felt like nothing more than an impostor.

It was all thanks to Alli.

He had promised to stay by her side, to keep her safe in a world that promised a million forms of danger and pain, yet when push came to shove, he had left her in the middle of Montana.

He gave a cynical chuckle at the thought. He was no hero. Heroes didn't run away.

His father pulled his mother into his arms and smoothed her gray hair. It was perhaps the most touching thing he'd ever seen his father do, to put aside his strong exterior and put the needs of the one he loved the most before his own.

Perhaps true love wasn't found in strength, but rather in moments of weakness. Moments in which the soul lay bare, when fears and insecurities were open for the world to witness and judge. Those who truly loved each other didn't disappear behind their masks of strength. No. Instead, they moved into each other's arms and found all the support they needed there.

As they got out of the truck, his mother and father rushed outside to them. "What took you so long?" Eloise pressed.

Waylon glanced down at his watch. It had taken them only ten minutes of speeding down logging roads to get back, yet she was acting as though it was a lifetime.

"Did something else happen?" he asked.

His mother shook her head.

"Eloise," his father said, taking his mom by the hand, "don't be upset with him."

"How can I not be upset with him? He and his

brother didn't bother to tell me that they had taken Winnie. You know how I feel about our children going missing."

He had nearly forgotten about the time Rainier's biological mother had kidnapped his brother. Rainier had maybe been eight or nine. His mother had shown up in the night, pulled him from his bed, and no one had realized he was missing until the morning. They had all thought the precocious boy had simply found his way out into the expanses of the ranch, but after turning over every rock, they hadn't found him.

Eloise had been beyond distraught. He'd never been able to forget watching her fall to her knees on the floor of the living room and dissolve into sobs when she had realized what had happened.

It had taken nearly two weeks, and dozens of law enforcement officers searching, but they had eventually found his brother and brought him back to the ranch. Ever since, his mother had been adamant about knowing the comings and goings of all their four children and any foster kids that were in their care. He was sure her need for that type of control was out of her misplaced guilt from letting his brother fall into the wrong hands. If something had really happened to Winnie, he would have felt the same way—and just as culpable.

"I'm sorry. It slipped my mind," Waylon said, truly humbled by his error. He could only imagine the terror that must have filled her when she came home to the scene.

Eloise nodded, but the fear and anger on her face remained. "I swear, I almost had a heart attack. I don't ask much, but if you're going to be around here, you need to follow the rules."

He had no problem following the rules—his life was dictated by them—but all he could think of was that he wouldn't really be here long enough to worry about them. A deep sadness filled him as he realized he had only a few days of leave left, and then he would have to return to his world of ACUs and PT—a world of acronyms—and a far cry from the ranch.

He pushed the thought out of his mind. He couldn't have *feelings*. He didn't have a life that allowed for them.

"And make sure that you guys close the doors when you are coming and going."

"We did. I swear," Christina said. "I even locked them."

"Wait." Waylon stared. "Were the doors open when you came home?"

She shook her head.

"Did anyone come in the house? Any staff or guests that you know of?"

"We don't have any guests staying. Not since…" Eloise didn't bother finishing her sentence. "And there were only a couple of the hands around. However, when we got home, they had only just returned after taking a couple of the horses for a trail ride. When they got back, they said they saw an open door."

"And they didn't think to close it?" Christina asked.

Eloise shook her head. "You know the trainers. Some of them may have actually been born in a barn."

Christina and Merle laughed, but all Waylon could think about was the fact that someone, maybe even Alli, had been inside the house after they had left.

"Did you call the police and report a break-in?" he asked.

"No, I wanted to check in with you guys first."

"Why don't you go ahead and call Wyatt and he can get in touch with his crew. In the meantime, I'll take a look inside. Did you touch anything?"

His father shook his head. "We just went inside, realized someone had definitely been in there and then waited for you to get here. I already called Wyatt. He's on his way."

"Good," Waylon said. "I'll be right back. If Wyatt gets here, let him know I'm inside." He took a few steps toward the house.

"You aren't going in alone," Christina said, hurrying to catch up.

He smiled. He wasn't sure if she was coming with him because she didn't think he could do the job or if it was because she wanted to be with him, but regardless, he was happy to have her company.

Aside from the open front door, everything in the living room was in its place, and it looked as though nothing had been disturbed—at least that he could tell. As they made their way down the hallway and toward the bedrooms, it was a different story. Winnie's bedroom light was on, casting a finger of light into the hallway, where the toys spilled out of the room. A blue teddy bear that had been on Winnie's bed the night before looked unnervingly out of place in the hall, its beady black eyes peering down the hallway toward them like some terrified witness to an unspeakable crime.

"Wyatt still has Winnie, doesn't he?" Christina asked, almost as though she were as unsettled by the reality in front of them as he was.

"Yes, they have her. She's safe," he said, but as he

spoke, a new sense of urgency to find Alli and put her behind bars welled within him. They couldn't live like this—no one should live their life in fear for their or their loved ones' safety. If he didn't hurry, they would have to continue on in this terrifying reality.

Winnie's room was destroyed. Toys were scattered everywhere, pictures had been pulled off the walls and even her bedding had been pulled back and thrown to the floor. The sight of her discarded bedding made the hair rise on his arms. Maybe it was the fact that the bed was a place of safety for children—where even he had pulled the sheets over his head when he'd been afraid of monsters—but the sight was chilling.

"Thank God we had gotten her out of here," Christina said, her voice flecked with terror.

"Why would Alli turn over her daughter's room? What do you think she could have been looking for?"

Christina chewed on her bottom lip, and her gaze moved to the closet. She hurried to the small door and, pulling it open, lifted a black fireproof safe off the top shelf. Someone had left it unlocked. She set the safe on the floor and opened the lid. Inside was a collection of papers, most of which looked like deeds and a car title. She riffled through the papers, taking them out and gently stacking them on the floor.

"What are you looking for?" Waylon asked, squatting down beside her.

"Alli and I…there was only one thing our grandmother left us. We are the only ones who knew about it," she said, only half explaining her maniacal digging and stacking.

"What is it?"

She stopped for a brief second and looked up at him.

"My grandmother left me a three-carat diamond ring. It's flawless. Cushion cut. Inlaid sapphires around it. It's beautiful."

"You had a three-carat diamond ring in a lockbox in a two-year-old's bedroom?"

She frowned and gave him an are-you-kidding-me kind of a look. "Don't judge me. It was in a safe at the main house—I thought this would be the safest place."

He hadn't meant to make her defensive or to comment on anything that had to do with their child-care choices.

"That's not it," he said, trying to deescalate the situation as much as he could. "I'm just surprised you didn't keep it in your bedroom, is all."

The look on her face disappeared, and she seemed to relax slightly. "In truth, I haven't thought about the ring in a long time. My grandmother wanted me to have it as my engagement ring someday. It's beautiful, but I never thought I'd use it, so I just tucked it away in the lockbox in hopes that one day Winnie would get it."

"You thought you'd never use the ring?" The thought that Christina didn't think she would get married surprised him. She was beautiful and smart—any man would be lucky to have her in his life.

She went back to pulling out the last of the papers. In the corner was a small black velvet box, and Christina sighed with relief. "Whew. It's still here," she said, gingerly lifting the box out, as though a simple jarring could destroy the precious ring inside. "Maybe someday Winnie will have better luck than I have and she'll actually get to use this thing."

"You have to have been in a serious relationship before." He paused. "Wait, weren't you with some guy?

Steve or something? Weren't you seeing him when Alli and I were dating? I thought she mentioned something about you guys."

Christina scowled at the sound of the man's name. "Steve? I haven't thought about him in years." She spun the velvet box in her fingers. "He and I, we didn't fit. You know?"

He knew all too well about not really *fitting* with a person he loved. "Did you love him?" The moment the question left his lips, he felt strange for asking. It really wasn't any of his business, but he couldn't resist the urge to know more about her.

She looked up, staring at him in silence for a moment as though she were trying to understand exactly why he'd asked her and how she would respond. "I... It's not that easy," she started, then looked back down at the box.

"It's okay to have loved someone and lost them."

"That's not it." She shook her head. "I don't know how much my sister told you about our parents, but let's just say they weren't the best examples when it came to what a healthy relationship should be. They were constantly fighting. Then they'd cheat." She spun the box again like it was a talisman that could keep the dark thoughts at bay. "I just never wanted to have a relationship like theirs."

"So you push people away?"

She sent him the sexiest guilty smile he'd seen in all of his life. "So Alli told you a few things about me, did she?"

He laughed, the sound echoing off the empty bedroom walls. "Actually, she didn't. I picked up that little gem on my own."

She laughed, and the sound was so unexpected and beautiful that he held his breath, as though if he moved, her laughter would vanish just as quickly as it had appeared, like some skittish animal.

"I don't know how you got there, but there are some things I guess I can't deny. It's just," she said, smiling at him, "well, I don't want to waste my time falling in love with the wrong man."

Was she talking about him? Was she falling in love with him, or was she implying that she wouldn't fall in love with him because she didn't want to waste her time?

The thought made his head hurt. Women made everything so complicated. If she liked him—or didn't, for that matter—she could have just said it. She didn't have to dance around the attraction that seemed to simmer between them.

On the other hand, he wasn't about to fall on that sword by saying something. Clearly she wasn't interested in him. He stood up and started toward the door, unsure of exactly what to do other than to go.

"Wait." He turned around as a thought crossed his mind. He motioned to the ring box. "Look inside."

The box clicked as she pulled it open. She let out a long, raspy breath as though someone had punched her in the gut. "No. She didn't."

Christina turned the box so he could see. There was nothing inside. Once again, they were left with only questions.

Chapter Ten

Why would Alli ever steal the only possession that meant anything to her? Christina kept her tears in check, but they threatened to spill over her resolve at any second. It was all too much.

Christina clicked the box closed and dumped it back in the safe. The lockbox slid off her lap and onto the floor. It would have been more prudent to be more careful, as she sat in the middle of a crime scene. Yet, at the same time, she was so beyond caring. She had been through so much emotional upheaval lately, it was almost as if this all had beaten her to the point of numbness.

She looked at the black rectangular box. They wouldn't have been able to pull prints from the box, but maybe the police could pull some off the other items in the room. Then again, she doubted they would even try. The only people who knew about that ring were her and her sister. It wasn't much of a mystery who had taken it—the only question that remained was why her sister would have been so ruthless.

"Did Wyatt check out your sister's bank accounts?" Waylon asked, pulling her back to the wreckage that surrounded her.

She nodded. "He's been monitoring it, but nothing has been drawn since the day she disappeared."

"Did she empty them out before she left, or take out any large sums of money?"

"What large sums? Alli was living hand to mouth—basically everything she made went to Winnie."

"I had been paying her alimony. Didn't she save any of that money?" he asked, his face was pinched as though he was thinking about all the money he'd given to her since their divorce.

Christina shrugged. "I don't know what my sister did with her money. I didn't have anything to do with that part of her life. But having Winnie was hard on her, both emotionally and financially."

Waylon's mouth opened and closed as if he had an idea but wasn't sure he wanted to tell her exactly what he was thinking.

"What?" she asked.

"Huh?"

"Just tell me why you are standing there guppying. There's nothing you can possibly say that I probably haven't already thought about my sister—especially after everything that's happened lately."

"Do you think that any of this has something to do with her mental health? Or do you think maybe she wanted the ring for herself? Maybe she was jealous?"

"Are you implying that you think my sister is crazy?" She tried to sound mad, but the numbness she felt made her voice flat.

"Not that harsh, but you know. She was having affairs when we were together. Maybe she was depressed about this thing with William dissolving. It could have

sent her off the deep end and made her think everything and everybody is fair game."

"Are you implying that you think my sister would
hurt me out of a jealous rage or something? That's silly.
She wouldn't do something like that. Maybe she just
wanted the ring to sell. She may have just needed the
money—like you said."

She wasn't sure what to say, so she simply sat watching him as he shifted his weight from one foot to the
other with discomfort. Regardless of whatever he
thought or felt about her sister, Alli would never hurt
her—at least she hoped she wouldn't.

"You know, I gave her about forty thousand dollars
when we divided our assets during our divorce. She
should have at least been able to put a down payment
on a little place. I bet my mother would have helped her
get a place, too, if she'd wanted. So why didn't she? I
mean, where did the money go? She's been erratic and
dangerous. What if she had other problems?"

Christina stood up and brushed off a wayward Lego
that had embedded in her thigh when she had sat down.
"Do you mean you think my sister might have been
a drug addict?" she asked ever so slowly. If Waylon
was as smart as she assumed he was, he would hear
the warning in her tone.

"No!" he said, panic filling his voice. "No. God,
why do you always have to jump to the worst conclusion first? I just was wondering if she had gotten
herself into some kind of trouble. I guess, yeah, she
could have been into drugs." He glanced over at her.
"Is that what you think was happening? That she had
some kind of drug addiction—and that's what moved
her toward murder and theft?"

Christina believed this had all happened because Alli had fallen in love with William Poe. Sure, falling in love was sometimes just like being an addict—her sister had always been chasing the next hit. And toward the end, before she'd left, she hadn't let anyone or anything stand in the way of getting the man she had wanted—even when it meant killing Bianca and Monica. Yet drugs and love weren't the same—not at all. You could only do so many drugs before you overdosed.

Christina looked up into Waylon's brown eyes. He was still staring at her like he wanted some kind of sign that she agreed with his thinking. In truth, she agreed with him—Alli had more going on than anyone knew. Heck, every time they looked into her sister's activities before her disappearance they learned some new deeper, darker secret. And everything came back to men—either Waylon, William or any number of her other lovers.

Men and love were more trouble than they were worth.

Waylon took her by the hand. The sensation of his warm fingers against hers made her wonder if she was wrong. Was Waylon right, and her sister was involved in something far more sinister and dangerous than Christina had assumed? Everyone had simply presumed that Alli had done what she had out of jealousy, but what if there was something more at play? Something that could affect them all?

"You know how Alli is…or at least *was* when you were with her. She is impulsive. I guess it wouldn't surprise me if she got into something and got in way over her head," she admitted.

"There was this one time, when we were together…" He stopped, almost as though he hadn't realized that he was reminiscing until it was already out of his mouth. He looked at her as though talking about his relationship with Alli suddenly made him uncomfortable.

He gave her a sexy half grin, and it had an air of apology to it.

"You don't have to stop. We both loved her once," she said, secretly wondering if his feelings toward her had something to do with his reluctance to talk about her sister.

She hated to even think about what he felt toward her, fearing if she did it would somehow make things between them more real—and even more tense. She didn't want more of her body or her mind telling her that she needed to kiss him.

In fact, if he talked about her sister more, Christina was sure she could pull herself back to reality and out of the fantasy that seemed to fill her thoughts every time she let her mind drift. No matter how good the dream was of taking his lips, letting him lace them over her skin and down her neck, it wasn't healthy to give her daydreams any room to grow.

She drew in a long breath, and at its edges was his scent. He smelled of men's cologne and the sweet crisp scent of winter air.

"I guess right now it doesn't matter what pushed Alli to her breaking point," he said. "What does matter is the ring and Winnie's safety. After she sells that ring, it may be only a matter of hours before she comes to get her daughter. Maybe she just needed the money in order to run."

"There are all kinds of things that she could take

from this ranch and sell if she wanted to make money. This can't be about that," she said, trying to find some other reasonable answer behind her sister's illogical behavior. "She had to have done this just to send me a message."

"You're right." He nodded. "Maybe she could have stolen some other things from the ranch and that's how she's been getting by. But what if someone connected some of the things that she was selling to this ranch? Maybe she had to steal something that wasn't so obvious—maybe she was afraid that someone would come to the family with information…information they wouldn't have wanted to give to the police."

"Not everyone wants to protect this family, Waylon," she said, but the words came out much harsher than she had intended. "I mean, there's more than a few people out there, just like William Poe, who would go out of their way to make sure Dunrovin fails."

He stopped her with the wave of his hand. "I know we aren't the Kennedys, Christina, but we have a lot of love and support in this community. My mother and father give a lot to charity, they bankroll the high school extracurriculars when they can and, heck, you know how much they foster."

Waylon wasn't wrong. His family as a whole was nothing if not altruistic and kind. They were the picture of giving. Yet not everyone in the world appreciated that kind of people—and more often than not, they were the first ones to get taken advantage of. Heaven knew she had stopped more than one employee from taking advantage of Eloise. Just two months ago, they'd had a young woman apply for a job. She'd plied Mrs. Fitzgerald with a sob story about getting kicked out of her parents' home after they had caught her with a man they hadn't approved of.

Of course, Eloise had hired the girl, letting her work as a housekeeper. In only two weeks, the girl had robbed at least three guests that they knew of, to the tune of nearly two thousand dollars' worth of jewelry and cash. Eloise had covered the loss, but it had been up to Christina to fire the girl. If she hadn't, Eloise without a doubt would have kept her on.

Almost exactly the same thing had happened with Alli when she had arrived at the ranch, except instead of jewelry, she had stolen Waylon's heart.

Christina glanced over at him. He was staring at her, and there was a whisper of empathy on his face as their eyes locked.

"It's not a secret that Alli has stolen before."

"I know." She walked out of the bedroom. There was nothing more they could do here. Alli had sent her message—she wasn't coming back, and she didn't care about Christina.

"Wait," Waylon said, calling after her as she made her way down the hall. "Where are you going?"

She had no idea. She just couldn't be in the center of her sister's mess anymore. "Your brother and his team can handle this. I'm out. I'm so tired. I can't handle this…any of this."

She made her way through the living room toward her bedroom on the other side of the ranch-style house. Partway down the hall, she stopped. She didn't want to be in this house or anywhere near it for a while. Yet there was nowhere else to go. She didn't have anything but this place, and thanks to Wyatt and Gwen, she didn't even have her niece to keep her company.

All she had was Waylon and the feelings that flooded her whenever he was near.

She turned back to him and, taking him by the hand, pulled him toward the front door. "Let's get out of here."

"What?" he asked, but he didn't resist her leading him out of the house and to the truck. "Wyatt's on his way."

"Whatever," she said, motioning for him to get in as she made her way around to the driver's side. "He can handle this."

Mr. and Mrs. Fitzgerald were standing in the yard next to Wyatt, who was sitting in his squad car. He gave them a two-finger wave as they made their way out of the house.

She sighed, letting go of Waylon's hand as they changed direction toward his brother's car. They were never going to be able to get out of this place now. Why was it, when all she wanted to do was run away, there was always something that had to be done, or someone who needed something from her?

No wonder Waylon had taken the chance to escape when he could. And it was no wonder, now that he was back, all he wanted to do was leave. This place was like a giant pit of quicksand from a cheesy action movie. Put even a toe in, or give a little bit of your heart to the ranch, and pretty soon you were in over your head, and the more you struggled to pull your way out, the deeper you sank.

Waylon walked ahead of her as she trudged toward Wyatt. She could hear him telling his brother about the state of the bedroom and the missing ring.

Wyatt looked around his brother and waved her

over. "Do you have a picture of the ring we could give to the pawnshops in the area?"

So even he thought her sister was going to sell it. Perhaps it was time she saw her sister for the person she really was—everyone else seemed to get it. They all saw Alli for the terrible person she had become, and they weren't tethered to the past by their emotions. She had made choices that were unforgivable. She had cost people their lives and others their families. She had cost Winnie her mother, and she had cost Christina a sister.

Some things were unforgivable—and heartbreaking. It was time that she truly let go of the person she had always thought her sister was. Alli simply wasn't the girl Christina had known; rather, she had become some warped and heartless stranger.

Waylon put his hand on the small of her back. "Do you have a picture of the ring?" he asked, repeating Wyatt's question.

She shook her head. "I don't have one," she said, trying to ignore the pain in her chest. "But the ring is one of a kind. It's a three-carat cushion-cut diamond inlaid with blue sapphires." Her voice cracked as she talked. It was unlikely she would ever see the ring again, and it was the last tangible thing that connected to her grandmother.

"Don't worry," Eloise said, coming over and wrapping her in her arms. "The boys will find it and your sister. She couldn't have gone far. It'll turn up, and we'll get this all figured out. We'll find it."

The way Eloise repeated herself made it obvious that even she didn't believe what she was saying, but Christina appreciated the attempt at comforting her.

"And who knows," Eloise said, giving Waylon a

questioning look. "Maybe you will be getting a new ring soon."

What in the hell was the woman talking about?

Christina pulled herself out of the woman's grasp. There was no possible way Eloise could have known what Waylon felt for her, or what she felt for him. Heck, she barely knew what *she* felt toward the man. Sure, he was good-looking, and she kept imagining him between the sheets, but that was where things ended. She didn't have the time or emotional space to deal with a man like him.

She turned and started to walk away, unable to stand Eloise's teasing look or the surprise on Waylon's face. She couldn't do this anymore. She couldn't stand all the emotions that seemed to fill this place. Everyone had an agenda, and none of them were making her any less confused.

"Where are you going?" Eloise called after her.

She didn't turn around. Instead, she waved behind her.

"Wait," Waylon called. She heard the crunch of gravel as he jogged to catch up. "With your sister out there, I don't think it's a good idea for you to be going anywhere alone. What are you thinking, anyways?"

She got in the truck and waited for him as he jumped in next to her, but she didn't say anything.

"Are you going to tell me where you're going?" Waylon asked again, pressing her for answers that she wasn't ready to give.

Christina started the truck, letting it rumble for a moment as it warmed up, and tried to collect her thoughts. The clouds that collected on the mountains had started to thicken and take on the dangerous gray color of a looming storm. It was an eerie reminder of her life. Just when she thought she had figured herself out and was on a forward path, storm clouds threatened to overtake her and make her lose sight of who she thought she was and what she thought she wanted. Yet with storms came the refreshing promise of rain, as long as one could survive the winds and lightning.

She sighed at the thought.

"What?" Waylon asked, looking over at her.

"Nothing."

She looked up to the clouds one more time. She couldn't decide who, exactly, was the most destructive force in her life, between her sister—who left pain and chaos in her wake—and Waylon, who, equally sexy and frustrating, seemed to make promises with his touch and his gaze that she knew he couldn't keep. At least with her sister there was a hope that when they found her and she went to prison, maybe she could go back to the girl Christina had once known. If Christina allowed Waylon any deeper into her heart, she would be left with nothing but an identity in tatters.

If she fell for him, her whole life would have to change again. And she couldn't change what she wanted or who she was for him.

The gravel of the driveway slipped and spattered as she gunned the engine and they roared out of the ranch and into the vast expanses of the pastures. Regardless of the threatening storms that rested on the horizon, she needed to get out of the place and escape her reality, if only for a few moments. She needed to find a sense of peace.

Waylon reached over and put his hand on her thigh. The action was so unexpected and his hand was so warm that she jerked the wheel slightly, and the truck drifted off the road, catching a bit of the grass, which made a whipping sound against the metal.

"Whoa, cowgirl. You okay? Are you sure you're up for driving?" he asked, but he didn't move his hand from her thigh.

She shook her head and tried to ignore the way her heart thrashed in her chest as the heat of his touch intensified on her leg and radiated up to more forbidden places. She wasn't going to find peace with him touching her like that.

"I'm sorry about Winnie's room. I'm sure that Wyatt will pull something usable from it," Waylon said, having completely misread her emotions. "And at the very least, we got Winnie out in time."

Though he was thinking about something far different than her, she was glad he was talking about something that didn't involve his hand on her thigh, or the way she didn't really want him to move it, no matter how much he should. It felt so good to be touched by a man—and not any man, but Waylon Fitzgerald. The man she'd sworn to hate for a lifetime—but after having met him, she couldn't even manage the feat for a day.

Did he have that effect on all women?

He was so serious, but under the facade was something so lovable, so kind and unexpectedly gentle that it was hard not to fall. Not that she was falling. No. She was just dipping her toes in the cool waters of Waylon Fitzgerald.

After a few miles, they hit the deserted wilds of an old logging road. She'd been on it before, but only a few times, and when the road forked, she passed him a questioning glance. Without a word, he smiled and gestured to the left with his chin.

Apparently, he was more than willing to take a minute and get lost together.

She followed the dirt road deeper into the timber, until they were high on the mountain and the clouds seemed so close that if they reached out the window they could have touched them. She'd always loved this part of living in Montana, where it seemed like in just a few minutes all were within a finger space of heaven.

Bits of wet snow started to flutter down from the clouds, a tentative warning of what could come. Yet instead of turning around and getting off the hill that promised nothing but icy roads and danger if the storm cut loose, Christina pushed the truck deeper into the depths of nowhere.

She glanced over at Waylon to see if she was making him nervous.

For once, she could understand his desire to constantly be on the move. It was so much easier to live in the moment, to let the wind be her guide.

The wet snow collected on the windshield, finally forcing her to turn on the wipers. Before the first pass moved over the glass, one front tire hit a rut, sending them jumping in the bench seat. Waylon had been jostled closer, making her heart race.

She veered into a pullout next to the narrow road and threw the truck into Park. "Let's go," she said.

"What? Wait," Waylon said, grabbing her hand and stopping her from getting out of the truck. "Where are you going?"

Christina motioned feebly toward the small game trail beside them. "Let's hike."

He frowned. "We can't hike. It's starting to snow, and it's going to be dark soon. What's going on with you?" He took hold of their entwined fingers with his free hand. "What's the matter? Is there something you're not telling me about you and Alli? You know you can tell me anything. I'm not going to judge you."

She didn't know if she believed him, and she most certainly didn't dare admit the thing bothering her the most was her growing feelings for him.

Waylon reached up and pushed a stray hair behind her ear as she turned to him. She looked up into his face. The gray clouds were reflected in his dark brown irises, but in his eyes the storm didn't have the same ominous tone; instead, his eyes only seemed to promise that with one simple blink the storm would be gone and the sun would shine once again.

She leaned into his hand, letting him cup her face.

He moved closer, his breath hot against her lips, and he waited, almost as if he wasn't sure if she would move out of his touch. But she didn't move. All she wanted was him. His touch. His lips against hers. His hands on her skin.

She wanted all of him.

His lips grazed hers, making her need for him roar to life. She wrapped her arms around his neck and let his kiss overtake her. She had imagined this moment, but it was nothing like the reality. His tongue moved against hers, pressing and teasing and making her think of other things that she wanted him to do with his tongue.

Leaning back, she pressed her back against the truck's door. Reaching under her, he lifted her hips and pulled her down so she could lie flat on the truck's bench seat. He smiled as he looked down at her.

"Have I ever told you how beautiful I think you are?"

She giggled, covering her face with her hands. It had been so long since a man had talked to her like that, or since a man had given her *that* look. She felt silly as she gazed up at him from between her fingers. She should have been so much more confident and secure—she was old enough to know how to act around a man who wanted her.

His smile grew impossibly wider as she smiled up at him. Instead of reaching up to lower her hands, he leaned down and pulled her gingham shirt out from her jeans, exposing her stomach. He ran his rough, calloused hand over the soft skin of her belly, making her skin tingle to life as she grew wet with desire.

She groaned, the sound thick and guttural, at the sensations that threatened to overtake her. She couldn't remember the last time she had wanted a man as badly as she wanted Waylon, here and now.

"Waylon," she whispered, the sound as rough but tender as his hands.

He didn't answer. Instead, he leaned down and kissed around her navel. Her hips arched upward, her body responding on instinct. Yes. She wanted this. She needed this. It had been too long. She needed to feel alive again.

He sat up and slipped his fingers from under her shirt, unbuttoning each button as he slowly moved up her stomach and toward her breasts. Opening the last button, he let her shirt fall open on the seat next to her, exposing her black lace bra. He sat back and just looked at her for a minute.

Vulnerability wasn't even close to what she was feeling. No. It was something rawer and more frightening. She sucked in her stomach and pushed up her breasts in an attempt to make her body look as beautiful as possible, and to hide the effect of the years of hard work and ranch life.

"Stop," he said, his voice gentle and understanding. "You don't have to be something you're not with me. You're perfect just as you are."

She could have sworn her heart stopped for a brief moment as his words melted into her. Just when she thought she couldn't possibly be more attracted to him.

He ran his fingers up her abdomen and over the top of her bra, moving between her legs and leaning down. Pushing back the edges of her bra, he pulled her nipple into his mouth. He sucked it, before moving to the other side. She arched her back, letting him feel the heat that he was making erupt from her center.

"Waylon," she whispered. His name tasted like cotton candy on her tongue.

He felt so good between her thighs, the weight of him pressing against her. Rubbing as he rolled her nipple over his lips.

"I want you," she whispered, her voice hoarse with desire. "Please, Waylon."

He leaned back, letting go of her nipple and giving her a wolfish smile. "Are you sure?"

Her body screamed yes, but there was a nagging thought in the back of her mind, in the area where logic reigned, that screamed no—this was a bad idea. For her, when two bodies came together, the hearts were quick to follow. And, in this case, her heart was entirely too close to falling over the precipice into love as it was.

This was a bad idea. Letting her body win was a rookie mistake—a mistake made by those who hadn't become cynical about love, those who still believed the world was a fairy tale and when it came to following the heart, there was always hope. In other words, love was for people who weren't like her. She was too strong for love.

She put her hand on his chest and gently pressed him off her. "Wait," she said, the weak resolve she felt sounded even weaker when voiced. "I want you. This, Waylon."

"I want you, too," he said, the wolfish look in his eyes still feeding on his lust. "You know what?"

She was glad he was changing the subject, and that for at least a moment, she had time to think with her head and not her body. "What?"

He sat back as he ran his hands over her stomach. "You are so freaking sexy."

She giggled like a teenager even though her mind protested the adolescent sound. She had to fight the urge to go backward in time and continue to follow her lusty impulses.

"And?" she teased.

"And I'm glad that you are who you are. You are so strong and kind. And I love that you always tell me the truth. Whether or not I want to hear it. I appreciate it—your honesty."

His words struck a raw nerve, pulling Winnie and his family's omission to the forefront of her mind.

If he was attracted to her for her honesty and forthrightness, then he didn't know who she really was—in fact, she was exactly the opposite of the woman he assumed she was, the woman he wanted her to be.

Forget falling into each other's arms; if they were even going to be friends, he needed to know the truth—no matter the consequences.

Chapter Eleven

Waylon didn't have a clue where things had gone wrong. One minute he was feeling her quake beneath his touch, begging him to continue with the motions of her hips. She had looked and acted as though she had been enjoying herself just as much as he had, but in the next moment she had pushed him away.

He ached as he thought about how badly he had wanted her, and how sweet she had tasted. She carried the flavor of peppermint gum and sugar on her lips, and it was a heady mix. Every kiss he searched for the same flavor, pushing deeper and harder. Her touch was intoxicating—it was something he was never going to forget.

It was funny, but he'd never really thought about a kiss before; for him a kiss was a kiss was just a kiss. At least it had been with every woman before Christina. With her, it was entirely different. It was almost as if when their lips came together, they were the keys to unlocking another existence. A world where love was free to move unchecked by time, space or the needs of others.

Yet she mustn't have felt the same way. If she had,

they would be covered in sweat and making believe they were the only two people in the world.

What was wrong with him?

He ran his hands over his face and sighed as they bumped down the country road that led back to the ranch. It had been stupid to fall into her body. Now everything between them would be even more tense than it had been before. It was going to be a long few days until he would have to leave.

Was that why she had pushed him away? Because she was afraid he would leave her in the cold?

He wanted to reach over and touch her again, to feel her tense under his fingers, but he resisted the urge. Her body was so far from him that she pressed hard against the door, as though she couldn't get enough distance. His touch was probably the last thing she wanted right now.

He opened his mouth to tell her they could try to do the long-distance thing if she wanted, but he stopped. Nothing like that would ever work. Long-distance relationships were almost always doomed to fail. There was no way people could really get to know another just based on talking. So much of what happened between two people was in the body language. Just like when they had parked. Much of what she wanted to tell him was in her eyes, in the way she had looked up at him from behind her thick black eyelashes and the way her hips had pressed against him, showing him how she ached for him just as badly as he ached for her.

She had wanted him. Right up until the point they had started to talk. He shouldn't have opened his mouth—it always got him in trouble. Though it wasn't a bad thing they had taken a step back. If she wasn't feeling it, then she wasn't feeling it. He wasn't about to rush her, and thinking about it now that he had a clearer head, it was a relief it hadn't happened. He liked and wanted her, and they could have a thing while he was here, but there was no future in their relationship.

She didn't seem like the type who would want anything to do with his lifestyle. He was a military nomad, moving from one place to another based on his orders. It took a special woman to want to follow her spouse around, and that wasn't saying anything about what happened when he was deployed. And deployment in his life was never an if—it was always a when.

She deserved a man who could dote on her, who could give her the world and everything that she wanted from it. That couldn't be him. His life was already promised to the country, and her life was promised to the care of Winnie. Plus, she'd made it clear that the ranch was her life. Or had she?

"Do you ever think about leaving Dunrovin?" Waylon wasn't sure he wanted to know the truth, but he couldn't keep thinking in circles about Christina. He needed at least a soft yes or no when it came to the feelings growing within him.

She nibbled on her lip, making him think of their lips touching and her taste. His body quivered to life, but he tried to control himself.

"I've thought about moving away, but now that's not really an option." She sucked in a long breath and exhaled it slowly as she gave him a searching look. "Though that may change. I guess we just never know what the future will bring, do we?" Her expression was strange, and it reminded him of a person who was trying in vain to keep a secret.

He'd seen that kind of look before, normally when he was interrogating people. Just a few months before, he had been the lead investigator on an attempted murder at Bragg. According to the wife, her husband had come home late after a night of heavy drinking with his buddies. It wasn't an uncommon occurrence, and a fight had erupted about his behavior. Allegedly, the man had taken a small hatchet and come after the woman, threatening to kill her. She had been lucky, walking away with only a few scratches and bruises.

As Waylon had interrogated the husband, the man had been evasive, never really wanting to answer his questions. He had given Waylon the same look Christina was giving him now—a look that told of deep secrets. That look had made all the difference. Going back to the crime scene, he'd reconstructed the events and eventually found the man hadn't been the one wielding the hatchet—it had been the wife.

If that was what marriage was like behind closed doors, he could do without it. He cringed as he thought about how, from the outside, most marriages were the picture of the American dream, yet when you opened the door and delved into the reality, many were the stuff of nightmares. His relationship with Alli, while not murderous, had definitely been just as dark.

"The future…" He started but paused as he tried to collect his thoughts. "There's only a few things in life we can control. Hearts and futures aren't on the list of things we can conquer. You know what I mean?"

She turned the steering wheel, pulling into the ranch's parking lot. She threw the truck into Park and dropped her hands in her lap. For a moment, she just sat there silently staring, but she finally looked up at him. "Conquer? That's not something that applies to one's heart. You can change it, you can fill it and you can own it—at least for a time—but you can never keep what isn't yours."

What exactly did she mean? Was she trying to hint that he had part of her heart or that he didn't? Why did she have to talk in riddles all the time? Women were so complicated, especially Christina. She was a mystery to him, and as much as it should have gotten under his skin, it only made him want to get to know her that much more. It would be an incredible thing to have even a part of her heart.

He moved to touch her, but before he could, she stepped out of the truck and rushed toward the barn. As she opened the door, he could see his mother standing inside, grabbing a flake of hay and stepping toward one of the older mares' stalls. Eloise stopped and turned as Christina said something, and dropped the hay she was holding. Turning slowly, Eloise looked over her shoulder at Waylon. She looked surprised, but then as she noticed him watching, she gave him a weak, empathetic smile. She mouthed what looked like *okay* as she turned back to Christina.

Something was very, very wrong, and based on his mother's expression, whatever was going on wasn't something he was going to like.

He made his way toward the two women in the barn. He couldn't handle the looks or the strange tension that seemed to reverberate through the air.

"What's going on?" he asked, his gaze moving from one woman to the other, but neither seemed able to meet it.

"Are you absolutely sure this is the best time?" his mother asked, looking toward Christina.

"There's never going to be a right time, but if we wait any longer..." Christina finally looked to him, and there were tears welling in her eyes. "I'm so sorry, Waylon."

"Sorry for what?" He hated the way she was looking at him, with pity and hurt in her eyes. The last time anyone had given him that look had been the day he'd been taken from his biological family. The woman with child protective services had given him that exact same look...it was the look that told him nothing was ever going to be the same again.

Part of him wanted to turn around and run. It could have been his instinct taking over, or perhaps it was the pain of his past, but he couldn't just stand there and take a blow he could see coming.

He started to turn, but his mother grabbed him by the arm, stopping him. "I know you, Waylon. This isn't something you want to run away from. At least not yet." She let go of him and gave him a weak smile, which helped to quell some of the panic that was welling within him. "Just listen."

He balled his fists but then slowly relaxed his fingers. "Fine. What in the hell is going on?"

Christina took his hands in hers. His mother gave him an approving nod.

"Everything's going to be okay, Waylon. Nothing has to change," Christina started.

The knot of nerves in his belly tightened. Now he was sure everything was about to flip on its head.

"My sister made a lot of mistakes. You know most of them. Heck, you were the victim of most of her poor decisions," Christina said, running her fingers over the back of his hand. "But there was one mistake…well, not mistake, but rather an error in judgment that… well… We all… We…"

"We are just as much at fault as Alli," his mother said, her voice high with nerves. "We should have told you sooner. Years ago, but—"

"Wait," he said, raising his hand. "*What*, exactly, should you have told me years ago?"

"It's about Winnie…" Christina mumbled.

His heart stopped at the sound of the little girl's name.

Christina looked up at him, and her eyes were filled with apologetic fear. "Winnie is yours, Waylon. She's your daughter."

Chapter Twelve

The Dog House Bar was packed, and as Waylon walked in, he had to weave his way around the throngs in order to find the only open seat at the bar. He shouldn't have taken Christina's truck without asking her, but considering the bomb she had just dropped on him, he couldn't feel bad. In fact, all he felt was the sting of betrayal.

How the hell had his family come to the decision that it was okay to keep a secret—not just a secret, but an entire child's existence—from him?

His mother and Christina had made feeble attempts to apologize as he'd walked out of the barn. They had both sworn they had wanted to tell him before and they were just doing as Alli had begged them to do, but all their excuses had fallen on deaf ears. There was no reasonable explanation that could justify the fact they had kept his being a father a secret.

He was someone's *father*.

He was Winnie's *dad*.

He waved at the bartender. "Whiskey."

The bartender poured the shot and handed it over. "Anything else?"

He motioned toward the taps. "And I'll take a Coors."

The guy looked at him with a raise of the brow. "Rough night?"

"If I told you, you wouldn't believe me."

The guy laughed, poured Waylon's beer and slid it down the bar to him, not slopping a single drop. "That one's on the house, but I'll lay a bet to say your story probably wouldn't even compare to some of the things I've had people tell me."

He snorted—that, he could believe. Booze and secrets always seemed to spill together. It was one of the reasons he rarely drank. He hated to open up the doors to his heart any wider than necessary, but in his defense, it was a rare day when someone learned they had a two-year-old daughter. A daughter who had already made a place for herself in his heart…but he doubted he could make room for her in his life.

What in the hell was he going to do now?

He downed the first shot. The whiskey burned his throat, but he welcomed the feeling. He pulled air through his nose, letting the burn move through him completely. It had been a long time since his last drink, and as the sensation overtook him, he relished it.

He was a father. The thought felt as airy and burning as the alcohol on his breath. How could it have happened?

He smirked. The last time he and Alli had been together had been before he'd filed for the divorce. He stopped. No… Wait… There *had* been one more time…one time after the divorce had been finalized. It had been the night he'd told her he was leaving for the military. It had been their farewell to one another. One last time. One last night together.

Apparently, it had been one heck of a farewell.

He wasn't sure whether or not he should laugh or jump into action, but he wasn't going to feel sorry for himself—he couldn't—and he wasn't going to let his daughter go through a childhood like his. At least not as far as being abandoned or mistreated. She'd be fine at the ranch, just as he had been. It was a great place to grow up, a place surrounded by horses, water and the shielding strength of the Rocky Mountains. Yet he couldn't be there. He had a job. He had a life. He had people to protect—people needed him. That was to say nothing of his commitment to the military—it was his everything. The army was him.

He ran his hands over his face, stopping for a moment to scratch at the stubble on his cheeks. He needed to shave, but then again, he needed a lot of things—starting with a family he could trust to always tell him the truth.

Seriously, how could they have done this to him? And why? He just couldn't make sense of it. Maybe they were trying to protect him, but even then, from what? A child wasn't something that he should be protected from. Was it that they thought he wasn't ready for a kid? Did they think he would be like his biological parents and just abandon the kid? They were wrong if they thought he could put a kid through a life like his.

He sighed as he thought about his first run-in with Winnie, when she'd fallen out of the tree. Sure, he might not have had a clue about how to raise a kid, but that didn't mean he wasn't willing to learn. Or was he? He tented his fingers over his beer and stared into the foam. Two bubbles rose, almost staring back up at him, and he shook the glass. He didn't need anyone or anything else to judge him—or his ability to be a decent father.

He was more than able to be a father. He could handle the responsibility. He could be a dad—far worse men than him did it every day. He could do the whole thing far better than any one of them. He'd sign Winnie up for ballet and T-ball. She could even get into hockey like he had when she got older.

As he thought about all the things he wanted to do with Winnie, he realized the immense time commitment it would take to raise a two-year-old. She wasn't in school or day care. Even if he started her in some kind of program, he would still have to take her there and pick her up. At Bragg, he would be completely on his own with her—there would be no extra sets of hands to shuttle her around or make sure she got to where she needed on time.

And all that was without taking his schedule into consideration. In the last three years, he had been deployed nearly a third of the time. If he reenlisted, it would probably be the same. That meant Winnie would constantly be waiting for him to come home.

If only Alli had just told him. He stopped. She probably hadn't wanted to share the kid with him—or play pass-the-kid-around. Though they had spent one last night together, they really hadn't ended things on a good note; if they had added a kid to the mix, it would have undoubtedly made things between them worse. And when parents fought, it was always the kid who paid.

He didn't agree with the lie, but for a brief second

he could almost understand why they had done what they had. Winnie didn't deserve to be some pawn in a game of divorce. At least Winnie was being raised with the love and safety his family provided—Alli had given the girl that much of a leg up. It would have been all too easy for her to simply disappear with the baby and never look back. Yet she had decided to let the girl be a part of his family's life—if not his. Then again, maybe it was just her easiest option. His family had given her a free ride in exchange for the time they got with the secret child.

The thought of how much she must have hated him made his chest ache. She didn't trust him, and, well, he certainly didn't trust her. As it turned out, the mistrust he felt had been completely justified.

Now that she had disappeared, the burden of the child should have fallen on him, but she had chosen her sister—and to still keep the truth hidden. She could have simply called him, left a message and let him handle things. Yet she hadn't, and the thought made him ache even more.

It might have been her plan all along, to come back for her daughter the moment she thought the police were off her trail. If she kept Waylon out of it, kidnapping the girl would have been easier—at least she knew no one was threatening to take Winnie away from the ranch or from Christina. Alli probably was just waiting for the right moment to strike. First, she took the ring, got a little mad money, and then she and his daughter would be gone.

Alli was the epitome of selfishness. Everything she had ever done, every choice she had ever made—even in marrying him in the first place—had been to advance herself and her desires. She didn't have a self-less bone in her body—apparently not even when it came to her child.

Bottom line, she couldn't get her hands back on Winnie. It was impossible to know what she was capable of, and no matter what the future had in store for him, he couldn't let Winnie's safety be compromised—by anyone. Even if she wasn't his daughter, her safety would have been number one, yet now that he knew the truth, it made everything more real and more immediate.

*His daughter...*the words echoed in his mind. It felt so strange to hear them rattling around in his thoughts, to feel the weight of the words on his shoulders. Yet, strangely enough, he welcomed the weight. It was nice to think he wasn't alone in the world and just maybe he could keep the girl safe.

He moved to stand up, then stopped—he could save his daughter from many things, but her mother was not someone he could completely protect her from. The woman would always have a place in the girl's heart and she would figure out a way into her life. Even if that meant she would ransack her daughter's belongings for a ring that he assumed Alli wanted just for the money.

There had to be something else missing. Something else going on.

He normally loved this part of an investigation, where he searched for the key to the puzzle. Yet, with so much at stake, he hated this case. It was best that Wyatt was the one investigating this. There was no way he could remain objective now. Especially if Alli laid a finger on their daughter.

The word echoed again, and this time it didn't sound as foreign.

He took a long drink of his beer. There was no way he was ready to go back to the ranch and his waiting family. He wasn't ready to face their apologetic faces and downcast gazes. It would take a long time to get used to the word *daughter*, but it would take even longer to trust them again. Trust would have to be earned. Yet, if he looked into Christina's glacial-blue eyes, a color so clean and pure that it seemed bottomless, he wasn't sure he could continue being as resolute as he felt now. It was easy to be angry when he didn't have to face her, when he didn't have to hear her soft voice.

If his brothers had asked him to keep a secret, as Alli had done with Christina, he probably would have made the same choice she had. He had to respect her and his family's honor and loyalty—albeit to the wrong person.

Of course, this all could have come back to the fact that they didn't want to lose the baby, either. They really must have believed what they were doing was for the best.

There was no getting around it—he had to talk to them.

He moved to stand up but stopped as he turned to face the main bar area. Sitting two tables over from him was William Poe. There was a woman with him, with dark hair and heavy makeup; she looked like the woman he and Christina had seen at Poe's house the day before. Lisa.

He turned back to the bar and waved down the bartender. The man dried a pint glass as he made his way over. "Need another round?"

He waved him off. "Nah. But, hey, do you know that guy over there?" He pointed at William.

"Sure, that's William Poe. I think he does something for the county. He's in here a lot. Why?" The guy leaned in closer in an effort to keep their conversation a little more private.

"You know the woman he's with?"

"Yeah," the guy said with a nod. "Her name's Lisa. Lisa Chase, I think."

"Are they in here together often?"

The guy shrugged. "She just started hanging around with him in the last month or so. Poe's always got a new chippie on his arm. I'm sure she'll be replaced in another few weeks. Usually I don't even bother learning their names."

"Why this time? I mean, why do you know her name?"

"She's the one who's been paying the tab."

It made sense that the one thing the bartender would care about was the person paying the bill. Waylon would have felt the same way in the guy's position. Especially in a place like this.

"Does William normally buy the drinks for his dates?"

The bartender nodded. "The word on the street is that his wife's assets are in probate and he's been spending a lot of money trying to track down the woman who killed her—at least that's what I heard him say. You hear about the case?"

It was a relief the guy didn't know who Waylon was or what his connection was to the local events. There was a certain amount of freedom in anonymity.

"What about it?" he asked.

"Apparently, one of Poe's exes went batty. Killed his mistress, who was a local veterinarian, and his wife. Bloody business when it came to the wife." He made the motion of slicing a neck. "But hey, at least it was quick. When I go out, I'd choose that over cancer any day."

Waylon couldn't help but agree with the dude. He'd seen more than his fair share of death. The worst had been seeing bits of flesh stuck to a mud wall after a suicide bomber had detonated in Tikrit. If nothing else, though, that type of death was dehumanizing—if he didn't think about it, the bits of flesh didn't add up to a person. It was that thought alone that had allowed him to keep his sanity.

He thumbed the rim of his pint glass. He probably needed therapy. It was probably one of the reasons his family hadn't wanted him to know about Winnie. With a life like his, it would be challenging to have a normal relationship with a child. He would always be overly protective, wanting to make sure his daughter was cared for and out of harm's way. It was the reality of any parent who had seen the worst and come back to civilian life.

He couldn't blame them for wanting to protect the child—not from the world, but from him.

He took out a fifty and laid it on the bar. "Thanks for the drinks, and the information. If you hear anything else about William and his crazy ex, my name's Waylon. You can get ahold of me at Dunrovin."

The guy's eyes widened with surprise as he must have put two and two together. "Waylon? Waylon Fitzgerald?"

He gave a tight nod and turned away before the bartender asked him any more questions. As of late, the only thing he had in high supply were questions—what he didn't need was more being flung at him.

Thankfully, as he made his way through the bar, William and Lisa were too busy making out to notice him. The way they were completely lost in each other's faces made his stomach churn. William's wife had just died, yet here he was flaunting his newest fling in public.

He never wanted to be that kind of guy who moved from one woman to the next without a thought. No. He wanted one woman for the rest of time.

For a second he could think only of Christina, and how beautiful she had looked lying back on the truck's bench seat. And though he was annoyed at her for the secret she had kept, he couldn't help but imagine her porcelain skin and how it had felt to kiss the soft lines of her belly and the arc of her ribs. He'd screwed up his chance to be with her. In all ways it was as if he was the dark and she was the light—they were in perfect complement.

If he played his cards right, they could come to some kind of agreement when it came to the child, but finding himself in agreement with that woman was almost as unlikely as finding a unicorn. Perhaps it was the tension that always seemed to reverberate between them, but when it came to Winnie, he had a feeling the only common ground they would find would be the fact they each loved the child and wanted to keep her safe.

Chapter Thirteen

Christina stood by the window, watching and waiting for Waylon to come back. He had every right to be angry with her—and she wouldn't have been too surprised if she got a call that her truck had been abandoned in front of the airport. He probably hated them all right now, but most likely no one more than her.

She should have convinced Alli to tell him before, but her sister wasn't the kind who backpedaled once her mind was made up. Sure, Christina could have gone around her sister and told Waylon, but until now it would have done far more harm than good. Or at least she had thought it would. She wasn't so sure anymore.

The more she thought about the wrong they had done Waylon, and the more minutes that ticked by, the more she was convinced Waylon had run away. He had done it before. She couldn't blame him. Sometimes the only thing a person could do when they had been repeatedly broken was run. It was the only effective way she had ever learned to protect her heart—and he had probably learned the same lesson.

Her thoughts went to when she was in the truck with him, lying on the bench seat and looking up into his eyes. She had been right to stop things from going any further, but now she regretted her choice. Well, kind of regretted it. Sure, it made things easier now that he was apparently gone, yet she wished she had taken the chance to live a little. She couldn't help but imagine what it would have been like to have him further his advance, and to have him kiss places that even now begged for his touch.

She moved to the chair across the living room and sat down in the dark, still watching for him, though it was more out of desperation than an actual belief.

It felt good to sit alone in the dark. It was the first time in what felt like an eternity that she had a moment that wasn't filled with talk about what had happened and what they could do to fix things. There was always something that required her attention and action. She didn't mind when it was about Winnie, but she never had a moment to herself anymore.

She closed her eyes and drew in a long breath. This was what Waylon's life was probably like—quiet and serene. She could understand if he didn't want to take over the care of his daughter if this was what he was used to. It would be an extreme change to go from living alone in the routine of the military to caring for a two-year-old he barely knew.

He was probably scared out of his wits.

She had been scared, too, when she had read Alli's note designating her Winnie's appointed guardian. Even though she had been there for all of Winnie's life, the thought of just picking up where her sister had left off had been more than terrifying. Though she hadn't had the time to pay her own feelings too much attention. No, she had only one choice—take the girl and raise her, or give her up. She would never give up her niece. Never.

Yet if Winnie went with her father, it wouldn't be Christina's choice. It would be his, his decision whether or not he would whisk his daughter away. She had to accept it—there was no sense in going to court to fight over custody when in the end it would undoubtedly be given to the biological father. He was a good man, a good provider and Winnie's closest relative. She couldn't compete with him—she owned nothing but one beat-up old truck and she trained horses, which paid her bills but not much else.

She ran her hands over her face, looking out at the moon between her open fingers.

Her breath hitched in her throat, and she couldn't control the sobs that overtook her as she thought about Winnie sitting beside Waylon in a plane, flying to a state where she'd never been and where Christina was unlikely to see her. Sure, they might have the occasional week and maybe a holiday here and there, but it would be nothing in comparison to the time they'd had together over the last few years. Basically, she would lose the girl forever.

She dabbed at the tears that poured down her cheeks. She couldn't bear the thought of losing her niece, but she also couldn't risk her safety, and she couldn't make choices on Winnie's behalf.

If Waylon ran away, as a woman who longed to feel his touch and be held in his arms, she would be broken. Yet, as Winnie's guardian, she couldn't help the feeling of freedom and relief at the thought that he might have gone. She shook her head at the realization that she could be so selfish. Even if he left, she couldn't keep Winnie. Not as her own child. No, not now that the truth was out. From this day on, Waylon would be Winnie's father and she would only ever be merely Winnie's aunt. Nothing more.

The girl would need her father to help her learn how to tie her shoes and to ride a bike, and maybe someday she would need him to walk her down the aisle.

The thought only made Christina's tears come down that much harder, and she gasped for air as her emotions moved through her unchecked—so much that she didn't realize Waylon was standing next to her until he gave her shoulder a soft squeeze.

"Christina, are you okay? Did something happen?"

She stood and buried herself inside his arms. He smelled of liquor and the woody aroma of a bar, but she didn't care. He was here. He had come back to her. To them. He hadn't run away, even though it would have been all too easy to disappear into the night.

"I'm so sorry, Waylon. I'm so sorry," she said between sobs. Her tears wet his neck and made their skin slick, but she didn't move.

He sighed. The sound was heavy and slow, the sound of someone who might have been just as confused and upset as she was.

She leaned back, looking up into his face. He gave her a smirk, the one he seemed to reserve only for her, as it so rarely made an appearance except when they were alone. She loved that smile, the way his eyes met hers and how, in that moment, he could make all her fears disappear.

He cupped her face with both hands, wiping away her tears with his thumbs. The feeling of his rough fingers against her soft cheeks made the need she felt for him intensify. She wanted him. All of him. All the time. Yet she would have to be satisfied with only this moment. He would have to leave in a few days, taking her world and her heart with him.

But they had tonight.

She could take this one chance to make him hers and to become his.

"I'm sorry I didn't tell you. I couldn't—"

"I get it. Let's leave it at that," he interrupted. He kept running his thumbs over her cheeks. "You did what you had to do."

The way he said the words made her wonder if there was some hidden meaning, like he was going to do what *he* thought he had to do. But she had no idea what exactly that would entail.

She opened her mouth to ask him what his plans were, but she changed her mind and clamped her mouth shut. She didn't want to know. It would only ruin this moment. There would be plenty of moments to talk after she felt his touch, after she felt his kiss on her lips.

"I... Do you want..." she stammered. She was so bad at making the first move. Except for their brief time in the truck, it had been forever since she had seduced a man. No matter what anyone said, it wasn't like riding a bike. Just because she had done it a long time ago didn't mean that it would ever come naturally.

She looped her arms around Waylon's waist and laid her head on his chest. His heartbeat was hard and fast under her ear. It was a comfort, as in its rapid cadence she could almost confuse its sound with her own heartbeat.

"Did you call Wyatt to check on Winnie?" he asked, almost as though he wanted to talk about anything other than what their bodies were saying to one another.

She held her breath for a moment, wishing the question could disappear into the thin air between them, but his body tensed with each passing second. Reality pressed in on her, and she finally forced herself to move, looking up at Waylon as she stepped back. Instead of letting her go, as she had expected him to do, he reached down and took hold of her waist.

"How is Winnie?" He frowned. "Is she the reason you're crying? You don't have to be worried about her. She's safe. She'll always be safe."

He really was a good man.

Maybe he would be a good father, too.

A tear slipped down her cheek, but she quickly looked away in an effort to keep him from seeing her cry again. "I called your brother. Winnie is doing just fine. Gwen put her to bed a couple of hours ago. Winnie was a little upset tonight. Apparently, Gwen forgot her favorite doll."

"Do I need to run it over there so she can sleep?"

Christina's knees weakened. He was so sweet and caring.

She wiped away her tears with the back of her hand. "No. Winnie eventually went to bed. She'll be okay, but with everything that's been going on in her life, it's not a huge surprise that she has been regressing lately."

"Regressing?" He frowned.

She nodded. "She's been potty trained for some time, but lately she's been wetting the bed."

His eyes widened. "She's still in diapers?"

Some of the swoon factor receded. Maybe he wasn't the perfect man after all.

"Are you afraid of having a child in diapers?"

He laughed. "No. It's been a while, but I changed more than my fair share of diapers when my parents were working more with the foster care system. It's just that I guess I really hadn't thought about all Winnie must be going through." He nodded. "That kid is a real trouper."

She thought about not speaking her mind, but she'd never really been the kind to sit quietly and let a man take the reins—she was far too strong for that kind of thing. "And putting her through much more…it will only make Winnie's separation from her mother that much harder for her."

He nodded and gave her hips a light squeeze before letting her go. "I know."

No. She should have stayed quiet. The last thing she wanted to lose right now was the healing power of his touch.

"But you need to do what you think is right. She's your daughter." She reached down and took his hands in hers and interlaced their fingers. "Do you know what you want to do?"

"Honestly…" He paused and drew their intertwined hands up to his mouth and he kissed her fingers. "I have no idea. The only thing I know for sure is that, right now, all I want is you."

He led her down the hallway, and to his old bedroom. His parents hadn't changed it since he'd last lived at home as a kid. There were still posters of early 2000s football player Brett Favre, and a model of the Millennium Falcon hanging from his ceiling. She smiled at his bit of kitschy coolness. It wasn't every day that a man like him would willingly take a woman into a room filled with the memories of his past.

She'd walked by his room a thousand times, but she'd never really paid it any mind and, as he clicked the door shut, for the first time she noticed the *Star Wars* sheets on his bed—complete with Darth Vader on his pillowcase.

"When did you stay here last?" she asked, trying not to think about the lurid, silent promises their bodies were making to one another.

He smiled, and there was a faint redness in his cheeks as though he understood what the place must look like to her. "I have the same exact setup on base. Like it?" he joked. "Though, since I'm older, my action figures have only gotten better." He ran his hands over her curves with a devilish grin.

She giggled. "I had no idea you were this big of a nerd," she teased, relishing the way he gently squeezed her hips.

"Don't get me started on *Star Wars*," he said, but his tone made it clear it was the last thing on his mind.

"Is there something else you'd rather be doing?" As the words fell from her lips, a feeling of delightful naughtiness whispered through her and made heat rise in her cheeks.

He chuckled, the sound throaty and raw and just as wicked as her words. She loved the erotic sound of his laugh. He wrapped his arms around her waist and pulled her tight against him. So tight she could feel his body's answer to her question.

She reached up to his short, dark hair. It looked sharp but was soft as she ran her fingers through it. It was just like the man it belonged to—high and tight on the outside, but once she really got to know him, he was just a softie.

She had a feeling he let very few people see the man he really was. The thought made her feel even more special and honored to be in his arms and surrounded by his former life.

He lifted her up, and she wrapped her legs around his waist.

"I don't know how we got here. Or why. But I'm so glad we did," he whispered, his hot breath brushing against her lips as he spoke.

The sensation made her shudder.

He closed the gap between them, not waiting for her to answer, and took her lips with his. She ran her tongue over his lips, teasing him with her touch. His lips were strong and giving— So much could be assumed about a man just through his kiss, and from his all she could feel was a passionate future together.

He moved to the bed, but as he walked, his hands slid down to her curves. He cupped his hands over her ass and moaned. She swallowed the sound, relishing its delicious complexity. She rolled her hips slightly, forcing him to hold tighter to her as she pressed against him in all the right ways.

He leaned back slightly to look at her, his eyes heavy with the high of lust and the hunger for more. "What are you trying to do to me?"

"What do you think?" she asked with a playful quirk of the brow.

"Are you sure you want to—"

She pressed her lips against his, the action hard, forcing him to silence. He chuckled, his lips still pressed against hers, and she matched the sound.

He laid her back, their bodies barely parting as he set her down on the bed and moved atop her. Moving down, he laced his kiss over her neck, driving her crazy with desire. When she arched her back, he ran his hands down her front, slowly unbuttoning her shirt as he kissed down her neck and to her collarbone. He pushed back her collar, the dry air brushing against her skin a sharp contrast to the damp trail of his kiss.

She popped open the pearl buttons on his shirt in one swift motion. "Slow," he said with his sexy half grin, the words barely more than a moan. "I want to have you all night long."

Her thighs clenched at the thought. She wasn't sure exactly what her body could handle, but she was willing to test it out. Her mouth moved slowly as she searched for words. She could find only one that her tongue would agree to make. "Please."

She loved the sound of his deep chuckle and the way it reverberated through her, especially through those places where she most yearned for his touch.

He undid the last of her buttons and slipped her shirt off her shoulders. "One thing I've always been trained to do is take orders."

The heat at her core intensified as she realized he wanted her to instruct him on how to touch her. It was definitely outside her comfort zone, but it was what made his request even more desirable. She loved that he pressed her to go further, to trust him and to find pleasure in ways she never had before.

Yet she found it hard to speak her desires as he looked up at her while kissing the soft skin of her belly.

He must have sensed her tentativeness. "Do you like it when I kiss you here?" He pointed at a little freckle on her hip, just above the waist of her jeans. Leaning down, he gently sucked her skin and released it with a kiss.

She smiled. "Yes."

He ran his rough fingers over her lower belly, making the blood rush to the place he had touched. "Do you want me to move lower?"

She nodded, the action slow and deliberate.

He reached down and unbuttoned her pants. His lips moved over her stomach, and he traced the top of her panty line with his kiss. She squirmed under his touch, aching for more but enjoying each individual kiss as though any one of them could be the last.

If she had a choice, she would live in this place— relishing his kisses and falling deeper and deeper into the euphoria of his touch. She'd never felt anything or anyone better.

He slipped her pants down her legs, caressing each place where her jeans scraped against her flesh. It was a strange sensation, the mix of harsh cotton and the tenderness of his touch. If he wasn't careful, he wouldn't get his turn.

He dropped her pants to the floor, and she sat up, taking him by the flap over his zipper and pulling him closer. His eyes were wide with anticipation and excitement as she slid open his zipper, tooth by tooth. She lavished in the sound of his breath hitching in his throat as she grazed her hand over his responding body. He was hot with want. So hot that her hand was drawn to the heat like a moth to a flame, and just like the moth she couldn't deny there was a certain amount of danger in the choice she was about to make. Yet close on danger's heels was thrill.

But *thrill* didn't fully encompass the feeling she had as she reached inside his open zipper and ran her hand over his length. He groaned as she lowered his pants with her free hand. They fell to the floor with a thump, and he didn't even bother stepping out of them. Instead, he seemed fully consumed in what she was giving him.

She smiled up at him, and their eyes met. It was so sexy when men wore boxers. Especially the kind she could slip her hand into.

"Christina." He whispered her name and he arched his back slightly, almost in warning of what could happen if she continued.

She considered taking him into her mouth and bringing him to the point of release, yet she wanted more. This was her time to experience all of him, every perfect inch of him.

Slipping her hand out of his boxers, she tugged them down his hips, exposing the dark hair that made a line from his belly and filled in around his ample assets. A giggle escaped her lips as he pulled off his shirt and dropped it to the floor.

"What's so funny?" he asked.

"Nothing."

There was absolutely nothing funny about what was happening between them; rather, the giggle had been an ill-timed attempt to get rid of the nerves that pulsed through her. She wasn't twenty anymore. There were lumps and curves where her skin had once been smooth and inviting, and her breasts were definitely far from the perky peaks they once were.

He pulled back from her touch and stared down at her, almost as though he could sense what she was thinking.

"You know what I like best about you?"

She raised an eyebrow, almost in warning that he'd better get the answer right, as she lay back in bed and rested on her elbows—her breasts taking center stage and looking slightly perkier than they had moments before. In fact, they were almost back to their former glory if they were viewed in just the right light.

"What?"

"I love how confident you are. You're a solid ten anyway, but dang, when you move…"

She smiled. Clearly, he didn't live in her head and hear her thoughts, or he would have known what a self-deprecating and insecure mess she could be. Maybe she was better at faking her confidence than she thought. "What do I move like?" she asked, prompting him to continue his flattery.

"You move like no one else. I guess the best way I can explain it is that when I watch you walk, it's like you are walking only for me." He moved between her legs, pressed her down to the bed and pulled her nipple into his mouth, claiming it.

"Don't you think that's a little selfish?" she asked, trying to ignore the intense rush of feelings that moved through her as her nipple popped out of his mouth.

"Selfish?" He gave her a wicked glance. "I promise you, I'm the least selfish man you will ever know. In fact…" He lowered his hand between her legs and found her, making her gasp. "I think it's better if I just show you how giving I can be."

His fingers moved into her, filling her with his gentle but confident touch. "Do you like that?"

"Yes," she moaned, "but I want you…all of you…"

He kissed his way up to her lips as his body moved

over hers. He slipped inside her. He felt even better than she had dreamed he would. In fact, he fit so well, it made her wonder if their bodies had been made for one another.

As he moved within her, she felt the edge moving closer and closer. From the rhythm of his breath and the way his body was tensing, he was close, too. Before she could say anything, her body defied her and she gave herself completely.

Chapter Fourteen

Sometime in the night, snow had fallen, blanketing the ground and piling up on his window ledge.

Christina's head was on his chest and, as if she could sense him thinking about the chill that awaited them, she snuggled closer.

He'd had to make some hard choices in his life, divorce being right at the top of the list, but nothing was going to be harder than having to decide what he was going to do with this relationship. He had no idea what he was going to do—he'd fallen harder and deeper than he had intended.

Her hair was loose and splayed on his chest. He picked up a strand and wrapped it around his finger. Even her hair was soft, strands of blond silk that were just as strong as the woman they belonged to. Everything about her, even down to her pit bull–like stare when she had first met him, was perfect.

He gently ran his fingers through her hair, careful not to wake her up, but he just needed to touch her. They had only a few days until he had to get back on a jet and fly all the way across the country.

It struck him how everything had moved so fast. It was crazy to think they had been strangers only a matter of days before, and now he was thinking about changing his life for the woman in his arms. Even though it had been quick, he wasn't afraid—and that thought was what scared him the most.

He wasn't new to the world of falling in love. He should have been more controlled, more metered in his approach, but there was just something about Christina that made him throw caution to the wayside. Hopefully he wouldn't come to regret his reckless behavior—he wasn't sure that he could handle another Bell woman breaking his heart. He could only spend so many years in the military.

Waylon's body tightened when he heard the thump of footfalls in the hallway. After a brief knock on the door, the doorknob twisted. He moved quickly to cover their entangled bodies with a blanket, and if he'd been a little younger, he would have pulled it all the way over his head, but there was no hiding the facts.

Wyatt barged in, and though it was early, he must have already been at work, as he was decked out in his uniform. "Get your a—" Wyatt stopped midword as he stared at them. "Dude." His mouth opened and closed for a minute, then he turned away and stepped back into the hall, closing the door behind him.

Great. Waylon sighed. Now his morning would be filled with knowing glances and his brother's hounding.

There was a light tap on the door, as though Wyatt was going for strike two.

"What?" Waylon grumbled.

"Um," Wyatt started. "We need to talk. I got some news. Take your time."

Waylon snorted. Like he needed his brother's permission or direction to do anything, especially when it came to women. Admittedly, though, he couldn't deny the fact there were times, just like this one, when he wasn't exactly sure what his next move should be. Talking to his brother about his situation sounded just about as fun as going to the dentist. He and Wyatt could talk about a lot, but the topic of Christina somehow seemed off-limits. On the other hand, Wyatt knew her better than Waylon did.

He moved from the bed, pulling himself out from Christina's hold ever so slowly to keep from waking her. It was strange how cold the room felt now that he wasn't wrapped in her arms. He'd spent hundreds of training hours covered in mud and lying in stagnant swamp water, and in those moments he had thought he was cold, but it was nothing in comparison to the chill he felt without her against him.

He looked back at her as he slipped into his clothes.

She stirred slightly and moaned, as though she was protesting his absence in her sleep. Her moan made him think of the way she had sounded and looked under him last night. The thought made his body stir, and he forced himself to look away. There wasn't time to do the things he wanted to do to her now, but given another chance, he would ravage her and make her purr like the sexy lioness she was.

He chuckled at the thought. He would give just about anything to have enough time to make her go from a purr to a roar.

Wyatt, standing in the living room, turned toward him as he made his way down the hall. Waylon sighed as he imagined all the things his brother was probably going to say.

"Say whatever it is you're dying to say," Waylon said, motioning down the hallway toward his room.

"Hmm?" his brother asked, a mischievous grin on his face. "What do you want me to say?"

Waylon snorted. "Nothing. Nothing at all."

"I get one, then I'll leave it alone," Wyatt said. "Just don't hurt her. She's a good one. She may come off like she's as tough as nails, but she's not. She has been through a lot, especially with everything going on with her sister. Gwen and she are good friends, but even Gwen may not be able to save her if you decide to go on and break her heart."

"I have no intention of breaking her heart."

"Intention or no intention, if you've got her in your bed, you are only setting her up to fall."

He couldn't deny the fact his brother was right.

Wyatt gave him *that* look, the look that he'd given him every time he'd been in trouble as a kid. "There's no good way out of the hole you've started to dig with her."

There was a good way out, but not one he would dare whisper. The second he started to talk about something more, something like a future, was the moment everything had a way of going wrong.

"I wouldn't call what we are doing digging a hole."

"Then what exactly would you call it? You are going to love her and leave her. Just like you did with Alli, and we all know exactly how well that turned out." Wyatt motioned around them, like Alli was some kind of omnipresent being.

"Are you kidding me?" Waylon tried to control his anger. He couldn't be mad at his brother for warning him—he was just stepping up to the plate and making sure no one got hurt. In a way, his brother might be far wiser than him. Then again, Wyatt didn't have a right to try to lay the blame of everything that had happened with Alli on Waylon. "None of this is my fault. Alli is a big girl. What she does or doesn't do is on her."

"I know. You're right." Wyatt let out a long breath as he pinched the bridge of his nose. "It's just…"

"You don't want anyone to get hurt," Waylon said, finishing his sentence. "Believe me when I say I don't want her to get hurt, either."

"If that was true, you wouldn't have—"

"Stop," Waylon said, putting his hands up in surrender. "You said you only got *one*. One was enough. You're just going to have to trust me when I say I only want the best for Christina, and I care for her."

Wyatt nodded. "Good. Just as long as we know where we both stand. I don't want to be the one stuck here holding the emotional baggage you leave behind. Again."

"Enough," Waylon grumbled. "If you just woke me up to have a talk, I'm going back to bed, and to her."

"Wait," Wyatt said, stopping him as he started to walk out of the room. "I'm sorry. Seriously, man, I guess that—" he motioned down the hall "—just caught me by surprise. I'll be okay with it, I swear. You know, Gwen and I…you know how we've been over the years. I guess maybe I don't have any room to judge how you go about your love life."

At least his brother had stepped back into the land of the reasonable. "Thanks, man. You know how it can be. Sometimes things just happen."

"You mean like *love*?" Wyatt scanned him, looking

at Waylon like he was trying to find some twitch that would give his true feelings away.

Did he love Christina? There were definitely things he really liked about her—her personality, how smart and driven she was, how her hair fell down her back and caressed her skin. She was so dang sexy. Yet she could set his teeth on edge in a matter of seconds when she wanted—especially when they talked about Winnie.

If he made the decision to take Winnie with him back to Fort Bragg… Well, whatever fondness Christina felt for him would probably disappear more quickly than his independence. Yet if he left the girl with them at the ranch, she would undoubtedly come to resent him and his inability to be a father.

The old adage "Danged if you do, and danged if you don't" came to mind.

"Why did you wake me up?" Waylon asked, mostly out of a desire to avoid answering Wyatt's prying question.

Wyatt smirked. "I thought you'd like to know we got a hit on the ring that went missing from the lockbox. Apparently, someone pawned it to a place in Flintlock last night."

"There have to be at least four pawnshops between here and there," Waylon said, trying to recall the town just south of them that was little more than a speck on a map.

Wyatt nodded. "Maybe Alli thought she was far enough outside our range."

"It's still in Flathead County. She had to know you would get a call."

"Unless she thought she could get away with taking the ring without anyone noticing it was missing."

"Did you go through the documents in the box? Was there anything missing from those? Something that Christina might not have noticed?"

Wyatt shrugged. "Lyle and my team went through the room. It had been rifled through, but I wouldn't know if something else was taken. When I talked to Christina, not even she knew exactly what was in that box."

"Don't you think it would hold official documents? Maybe something like Winnie's birth certificate? Or her Social Security card. Did you find any of those kinds of things for Winnie?"

"There were only a few deeds and a car title."

Waylon motioned toward the room. "I bet you a hundred bucks if you go back in there and look in that box, that stuff is missing."

They made their way down the hall to Winnie's room. Someone had picked it up, as the little bed was made and all the toys were back in place. Wyatt walked to the closet and pulled the safe off the shelf. He opened it and shuffled through the papers. After a moment he looked up. "How did you know they wouldn't be in here?"

"I don't know. I guess ever since I found out about Winnie, I've just been thinking about all the things I would need for her. If Alli is going to take her, she's going to need those documents—especially if she wanted to take her over the border. Does Winnie have a passport?"

The color drained from Wyatt's face.

"Let me guess. It's missing, too?"

Wyatt nodded. "But Gwen would never let Alli get her hands on the girl. Don't worry."

"If she gets her hands on Winnie and makes it over the border, we'll never get her back. Under no circumstances is Gwen to leave Winnie alone. Got it?"

"She knows. Don't worry," Wyatt said. "If you think she wouldn't do everything in her power to keep Winnie safe, you're crazy. She loves that girl—maybe even more than you do. She's known Winnie since the day she was born."

His brother's words stung, but Waylon didn't have time to dwell on it. If anything, he would just have to get used to everyone judging him for a mistake he hadn't known he'd made. If that was the price of having his daughter in his life, then it was a price he was willing to pay.

There was a knock on the door. Christina stood there, looking in at them. She was dressed and her hair was pulled back into a messy bun, but the haze of sleep was still in her eyes. "What are you guys doing in here?" she asked, her voice sounding as groggy as she looked.

"I'll explain it on the drive," Waylon said, taking her by the hand and leading her to the truck.

"On the drive? Where are we going?" she asked.

At least she had finally come to trust him and the fact he wasn't out to hurt her or his family. Unfortunately, Wyatt was right. In a couple of days, that was exactly what he'd be doing—hurting the woman he cared about.

There was no doubt in his mind that they shouldn't have slept together, but when her fingers laced between his, his heart told him he had made the right choice last night. Spending the night holding her in his arms, her head on his chest, had been the best night he'd had in a long time. It had been something so beyond a one-night stand, even though he had the impression that neither of them intended to make it more than just that.

It was strange how things could change in just a few seconds when they chose to open up their hearts. There would be no going back to the way things had been between them. For the rest of time, regardless of what the future brought, they would have the special bond that only lovers were blessed to experience.

Wyatt walked over to his patrol unit. "I'll lead the way. Try to keep up."

Waylon answered with a nod as he helped Christina into her truck.

"If you're going to drag me around, I'm going to need a cup of coffee. Especially after last night," she said, an air of satisfaction in her tone.

"If we had time, I'd make you a cup, but we need to head out."

"Okay, then you'll at least have to tell me where we're going."

"We're heading to Flintlock," he said. "We got a hit on your grandmother's ring. Apparently, someone pawned it."

Her early-morning smile disappeared, and he instantly wished he hadn't told her, but there was no avoiding the reality that last night, and what had happened between them, was officially over—no matter how badly he wished he could scoop her up in his arms and carry her back to his bed, *Star Wars* sheets and all.

He laughed as he thought about how often in high school he'd dreamed of bringing a girl back to his room, and how it had never happened. Yet now that he hadn't been looking, it had come to fruition.

He slipped into the driver's seat and followed Wyatt out onto the highway that bridged the gap between the two towns.

Some of the ease they'd had with each other before had disappeared now that they were alone in the truck. It was like she also realized their time was coming to an end. She laid her hand between them on the bench seat, palm up. He almost reached for it, but as he started to move, she closed her fingers and pulled her hand back, balling it up in her lap.

"Did your brother have anything to say about finding us in bed together?" she asked, her words as tight as her fist.

"Yeah, he definitely had an opinion."

"One you care to share?" She glanced over at him.

He put his hand atop her fist in an attempt to stop her from closing off more and more to him. He couldn't handle being back on the outs with her. As long as he was here, he wanted things to be as they had been last night—open and filled with laughter. Yet he couldn't deny the fact that some desires couldn't survive in the glaring light of day—they were burned away by the harsh reality of their lives like shadows in the sun.

She didn't loosen her fist, so he drew his hand away. She didn't want him. Or at least, just like him, she was realizing all the reasons she had to close herself off and protect her core. That was what it was—a protective measure. He would be smart to follow her lead.

"You know Wyatt," he said, gripping the wheel hard with both hands. "He thinks just 'cause he's the oldest, he has all the right answers."

"What does he think the right answer is when it comes to you and me?"

He shrugged. "He's not always right."

"So he thinks it's a bad idea?"

Waylon wasn't sure what he wanted to talk about less—her grandmother's ring being pawned or the state of their relationship—or rather, the *lack of*, based on the state of things. Both topics seemed to make her tighten up. He would give anything just to make her easy smile return.

"Some of the greatest things in life have started out as bad ideas."

She laughed. The sound was warm, and he found it impossible not to laugh with her and mimic her intoxicating sound. What it would have been like to hear that sound every day.

"You and I, we've done too much living to believe in some idealistic notion that the heart always leads us in the right direction. The heart is a fickle and mercurial thing."

"Are you saying you regret what happened last night?" He felt almost at a loss at the fact that he wasn't the one controlling the conversation and that she was taking the lead in what would undoubtedly be her attempt to push him away.

She looked down at her fingers. "I know, as I'm sure that you do, too, that last night…it was great, but…"

"But you don't want anything more from me?" he said, trying to steel himself against the stinging truth of her words.

"That's not it…" She gazed over at him, and there was the faintest hint of tears in her eyes. "It's just… this…it can't be. Our lives are too different. You don't belong here anymore. You have the world at your fingertips. If I asked you to stay, or to come back to me, I'd be asking you to give up the world. I'd never ask that of you."

"Then why don't you come with me?" The words flew out of his mouth without him really thinking about what he was asking her to do.

"It's not as simple as that. With everything going on with Winnie and with the ranch…your mom needs me here. My life is here. Besides, if I went with you, what would there be for me to do?"

"We could be together. What's more important than that?" The pain that pierced him made its way into his voice, but he didn't have the power to keep it in check.

"Waylon, you don't know me well…"

"I know you better than you want to admit," he argued. "I know the face you make when you are truly happy, and the face you make when you think someone you love is in danger." A tiny smile lighted over his lips as he thought about her standing on the front porch of the main house as he'd landed in the Black Hawk. "And I know how much you try to control every situation in order to keep yourself from getting hurt."

She sucked in a breath as though he'd struck a chord. "You're right, Waylon. I don't want to get hurt. And I don't want to get hurt a year from now. Let's just tell it like it is. I mean, think about it. What would I do while you're off working every day? What would there be for me at Fort Bragg? And what about Winnie? You can't think that raising her on a military base would be better than raising her on the ranch."

"Plenty of kids grow up on the bases."

"Sure, they move from one place to another. They make friends, and then those friends leave."

"They grow up strong," he argued. "They grow up knowing that the only thing they can really rely on is themselves and their family."

"Don't you think that Winnie can grow up just as strong here? Here she would have stability—and that's something that has been desperately lacking in her life since her mother disappeared."

This time, she was the one who was right. Winnie deserved to have the best in life. And maybe Christina had a clearer view of exactly what that was.

Christina reached over to him, but he wouldn't let go of the steering wheel. No. He couldn't let her see his pain. He was too strong for that. He'd already opened himself up too much. He'd been an idiot, and it had been too long since he'd been down this road. He'd almost forgotten how much it hurt to have himself torn apart.

There was no possibility of a future. All he could ever have with her was a friendship and thoughts of what might have been if their lives had made their dreams possible.

He was relieved when they passed the log sign that said Welcome to Flintlock. At least he could get out of the car and away from the conversation that would only lead him farther down a path he didn't want to travel.

Flintlock was made up of a railroad track, a gas station, two bars, two churches, a pawnshop and a bank—it was little more than a place in which a road-worn traveler could make a pit stop before getting back on their way. Waylon followed Wyatt into the pawnshop's parking lot.

The pawnshop was a squat, square building with shake siding that had little chinks in it where pieces had rotted out and fallen to the ground. The place's windows were dark, but the Open sign was on, making Wyatt wonder if the windows had been tinted in an effort to mask whatever nefarious deeds normally happened inside.

He hated the place before he even stepped out of the truck, but he reminded himself that maybe it wasn't as bad as he assumed—at least they had called in a tip. The owner or an employee could have simply bought the ring or turned Alli away and never reported anything. It would have been easier for them not having to deal with the police.

At a place like this, probably the last thing they wanted was police to come sniffing around.

Waylon stepped out of the truck, thankful for an escape from their conversation. Christina shook her head as she got out and followed him over to Wyatt, who was waiting beside his car.

"A guy named Herb called in the tip. He should still be working. He's a nice guy, been in this game a long time, but you want to be careful. In fact, I'll just take the lead on this one. Cool?"

Waylon nodded, but the last thing he wanted to do was play second fiddle to his brother. Yet this wasn't his investigation—or his jurisdiction.

Most of the lights were off in the pawnshop, and it was barely bright enough for them to navigate through the racks of old guitars and outdated DVDs. The place beckoned of lost paths and sadness.

An old man sat behind a long glass counter in the back of the store. Inside the display case was a collection of handguns and expensive jewelry. It struck Waylon as funny that the guns didn't really seem out of place next to the pawned wedding bands—rings that had likely been sold by those who'd had their hearts destroyed.

Or maybe that was just his pain talking.

"How y'all doin'?" the guy behind the counter asked as he stood up from the bar stool. He had gray hair and a barrel chest, and though he was crooked from the ravages of age, he stood at least six and a half feet tall. Beneath him, the little wooden bar stool teetered as if it feared the man would sit down on it again.

"Doin' real well, Herb. We appreciate you giving us a call." Wyatt shook the man's hand and motioned toward them. "This is my brother and his girlfriend, Christina. Actually, it was Christina's ring that was reported stolen."

Waylon tried to pretend he didn't notice the look of surprise on Christina's face at Wyatt's introduction.

"Ah," the guy said, looking her up and down. "That ring is almost as pretty as its owner." He whistled through the gap in his front teeth.

Christina looked away, suddenly passive in the presence of the man.

"Did you purchase the ring, Herb?" Waylon asked, trying to help Christina escape what could become the man's full-court press.

Herb reached under the counter and pulled out a receipt book, the kind that most stores didn't seem to use anymore, but that were common in parts of the world where internet service and sometimes even cell phones were a luxury. "The guy was selling quite a few things.

A few pieces of artwork and two rings." He tapped the receipt as he spoke.

"The guy? The person who came in and sold you the ring was a guy?" Christina asked, shock filling her voice.

Waylon was just as surprised as Christina. There had been no talk of any man in Alli's life except William Poe. Was it possible that William had been the man here selling things? It seemed like a long shot. William would never stick his neck out, not now when so many people were watching him.

"What did the man look like? Was he a business type?" Wyatt asked. He must have been thinking about William as well.

Herb waved him off. "No. The guy was hefty, big belly, and long, greasy hair. Nice, liked to chat, but I have a feeling it's because he spends a lot of time on his own. If I remember correct, he mighta said he was a trucker."

"A trucker?" Waylon glanced over at his brother, who gave him a small, almost imperceptible nod. "By chance did you manage to catch the guy's name?"

Herb shook his head. "Can't remember the guy's name off the top of my head, but I got a little card with some information."

Waylon had to reach deep as he tried to recall the name of the trucker they'd met at the pullout where Alli's car was found. "Does the name Daryl sound familiar?"

Was it possible the man was more involved than he had let them believe? Had he been helping Alli ever since he found her along the side of the road? Or that he had known Alli even before he'd picked her up and they had been following all the wrong leads?

A thousand questions and even more possibilities came to mind—followed by a litany of mistakes Waylon had made. He had been so wrapped up in uncovering the secrets within his family and following his heart's wants that he had managed to miss a clue that had literally stared him in the face.

On the other hand, the guy hadn't given them much to work with, nor had he given them any indication he was more involved with Alli than he had told them. It was possible that the man who'd brought in the jewelry and art wasn't the same guy they had met on the side of the road. Or maybe Alli had set them up and she wanted them to chase their tails.

Herb reached under his counter and took out an old metal box. Opening it up, he frowned at its contents for a moment before turning the box around for them to see. Inside the box was a gold band with a large cushion-cut diamond flanked by sapphires. It was a beautiful ring; Christina's description had barely done it justice. Yet, as with so many things in life, being told something was a poor replacement for living it.

He glanced over at Christina. She had her hands clapped over her mouth. "How much?" she asked from between her fingers. "At least tell me how much you gave the guy for my grandmother's ring."

"I paid five hundred, but you guys don't owe me a dime. I barely gave him anything for the paintings." Herb pointed to two paintings leaning against the back wall behind the counter. They had dabs of paint here and there and looked like something Winnie could have made. "The guy who came in seemed to know a lot about the ring, but he barely knew anything about art. Those paintings are worth ten of those rings. They're originals. I think I'm gonna go ahead and send them off to Sotheby's for auction."

Waylon stared at the paintings. One had a red glob surrounded by sharp black lines, and he could tell exactly why the seller had thought the thing was worthless. When it came to art, he didn't understand why someone would be willing to pay hundreds of thousands of dollars for something they put on their wall and could just say they owned—not when they could spend that same money on living their lives and experiencing the world.

"Did he mention where he got the paintings?" Waylon asked.

"You know how it is," Herb said with a shrug. "Some people want to tell you their whole life story, but the ones you want to hear are the ones that you don't get. You're lucky I even managed to get his name and address. He wanted to dicker over that as well. I wouldn't be surprised if the information he gave me ends up being phony." Herb reached into the metal box and handed the ring and the card beneath it over to Waylon.

Waylon stared at the name: Jeb Bush. Herb was right; the guy had definitely given him a fake name.

"Wyatt, you ever heard of Running Deer Lane?" Waylon moved the card over so his brother could see it.

Wyatt took the card and threw it down on the counter. "Yeah. The guy was full of crap, there's no such address. Did you ask to see his driver's license?"

"No," Herb said, shaking his head. "But I did manage to get his license plate number before he drove off."

Finally, they had a tie to Alli—hopefully they could get to her before anyone got hurt.

Chapter Fifteen

Five hundred dollars. Not only had her sister murdered, but she had also stolen from her and pawned a symbol of what little was left of their family, and she had done it for five hundred dollars. A lump rose in Christina's throat, and though she shouldn't have let this hurt, she couldn't help but succumb to the lashes of her sister's actions.

Perhaps Alli *was* on drugs. It wasn't the first time the thought had crossed her mind, but she always tried to have a little bit more faith that her sister would make better decisions. Looking back, though, she felt like a fool. Maybe if she just started thinking the worst of her sister, then she would no longer be surprised or agonize when Alli did the things she did.

Christina twisted her grandmother's ring around her finger. It was a little tight for the ring finger on her right hand, but until she could put it back in its box and get it tucked away somewhere Alli would never find it, she could think of no better place than her own hand to keep it safe. It was funny. She could protect things by keeping them close to her—everything except her feelings.

Wyatt was across the parking lot, running the plates

in his squad car. Tiny, almost ash-like snowflakes fell from the sky and, as the wind picked up, scattered like secrets throughout the small town.

The thought of secrets and the power they wielded made Christina rub the ring finger on her left hand. Her sister's secrets had nearly cost them everything—even a chance at a future.

She glanced down at the ring as a snowflake drifted down and melted on the surface of the diamond. She thought about slipping the ring off and putting it on her other hand, feeling the weight of the engagement ring and what it had the potential to mean—loyalty, fidelity, love, trust and being loved forever by the man of her dreams.

She glanced up and caught Waylon looking at her.

"You all right?" Waylon asked, nodding toward her hand. "I'm sure she was just desperate. You know, selling the ring and all. And when people are desperate, they do desperate things."

"I know. It's just that…" As she looked over at him, her thoughts moved to him between her legs, looking down at her with something that was well beyond lust—and a lot like love.

"Just what?" Waylon moved closer but stopped short, almost as though he wasn't sure whether or not he should come any closer.

"I'm not a wild dog. I'm not going to bite," she said, but even as she spoke, she knew it had come off just like a snip. The look on his face confirmed her fears. "Sorry, I'm not upset with you. It's just…well, I wish Alli would just stop doing what she's doing. It's almost like everything she is doing and trying, she is doing to hurt me and her daughter. I just can't figure out what

I did to her that would make her want to hurt me like
this. All I ever did was try to help her. I came here for
her. I agreed to take her daughter. All I ever wanted to
do was be the best sister I could. We were all we had
for each other…" She tried to continue, but she couldn't
get any more words past the lump in her throat.

Waylon rushed over to her and pulled her into his
arms. His chin rested on her head as she let him hold
her. It was all too much. Being with him. Losing Alli.
Fighting for Winnie. Being strong…all the time. For
this moment, and just this moment, she let herself be
weak.

Sometimes the soul needed a moment of weakness so a person could really appreciate its moments
of strength.

Waylon rubbed her back as she laid her head against
his chest. It felt so good to be held by him. Being with
him was what she hadn't known she was missing, but
now that she realized it, she couldn't imagine him being
anywhere else but with her. She didn't have a clue what
she was going to do with herself once he was gone.
Things could never go back to the way they were—
and once again, her life would be in flux.

When would life just *be*? Why did everything have
to be a fight? Why couldn't she just have what she
wanted—a future with him?

She sucked in a long breath as she tried to take back
control over her feelings. Right now, she couldn't dwell
on them. There was too much to lose and too much at
risk to start wallowing in a land of what-ifs.

She pulled out of Waylon's arms just as Wyatt
stepped out of his car and made his way over to them.

"Everything all right, Christina?" Wyatt asked, his face filled with concern.

Of course he would be worried. As long as they had known each other, he had never seen her fall into the arms of a man in a moment of need, but if the events of late had taught her anything, it was that anything was possible—even the things she feared the most.

"I'm fine," she said, attempting to swallow back the lump in her throat. "What did you find out?"

"We ran the plate numbers and it looks like the truck does, in fact, belong to Daryl," Wyatt said. "You guys want to run over there and question him with me?"

"Let's go. If Daryl knows where we can find Alli, maybe we can have her in custody by this afternoon."

"And you can hit the road?" Even Christina heard the acidic tone as it burned away any softness from her voice.

Waylon reached toward her, but she stepped away from his touch. His eyes widened, and he looked shocked and confused by her refusal. Instead of falling victim to that look—the look that said he needed her—she forced herself to turn away.

Wyatt's phone rang, and he motioned for them to hold on for a second as he answered it. "What's up, babe?"

A fast and erratic woman's voice came through the speaker—Christina assumed it was Gwen, but she couldn't quite make out the words. Wyatt's face blanched as she spoke.

"No..." he said, almost on an exhale. "It's okay. It's going to be okay. I'm sure she's okay. How did she get her?"

Get who? She glanced over at Waylon, and his

mouth was pinched and a storm raged in his eyes. "He's not talking about Winnie, is he?" she asked, though she already knew the answer.

Wyatt leaned against the front of the pawnshop and ran his hand over his face.

"Don't worry. I'm on my way. We'll get her back. Come hell or high water, we will find Winnie." Wyatt looked up at Christina, and this time there were tears in his eyes—tears that made her entire body go numb.

WINNIE WAS GONE, stolen from Gwen's care. One minute she had been safe at home, and the next she had simply disappeared.

Waylon had promised Christina they would keep her safe, yet he had let Alli take her—and if anything happened to her, he wasn't sure he would be able to live with himself. He'd known he was a father for a day, and as already culpable in letting his little girl fall into the wrong hands.

Christina had been right in thinking him incapable of being someone's father. In fact, he shouldn't have even had the right to call Winnie his daughter. He didn't deserve something that good in his life.

Wyatt had gone straight over to his house to get Gwen, who had grown more and more hysterical over the phone. He could imagine how bad she was feeling right now, but no matter how badly he wanted to push the blame on her for what had happened, he couldn't blame anyone but himself. He shouldn't have let Winnie leave his side, yet instead of taking her under his wing, he had let others care for her.

He glanced over at Christina as he drove toward the address Wyatt had given them for the trucker. Christina's face was steely, and she was staring out of the truck with such intensity he wondered how the glass wasn't melting. She was being strong—and that was exactly what he needed to be as well.

This couldn't be about emotions. From now until Winnie was found, they could only focus on the things they could control. They should only have one objective—to get Winnie back. After that, he and Christina could focus on Alli and perhaps talk about a future, but as it was, there was no way he could think about the needs of his heart. Not when it was utterly broken at the thoughts of what his daughter was possibly facing.

"Alli would never do anything to hurt Winnie," he said, trying to not only make Christina feel better but to reassure himself as well.

Christina didn't even bat an eyelash. "Sure. Of course she wouldn't." Her voice was flat and emotionless.

He could handle her display of emotions so much better than her arctic front.

"I'm so sorry about this, Christina," he said, trying again to comfort her.

This time she glanced over at him, and the chill in her voice had overtaken her gaze as well. Some of the iciness penetrated his core and seeped into his heart.

"I told you this was going to happen. I told you Winnie wasn't safe. We should have brought her with us."

He didn't want to bring up the fact that they had been busy doing other things—things that would have never happened if they had a child with them—but he stopped himself. She hated him. Bringing up anything that had happened between them would be disastrous. In truth, he didn't blame her. He hated himself just as much for what he had allowed, albeit passively, to happen to Winnie.

"You're right," he said, submitting himself to her derision. He deserved whatever punishment she wished to deliver. "I never should have let her out of my sight. No matter how bad you are feeling right now, just know I'm feeling a thousand times worse. I know this is my fault. I was stupid to think Gwen could have kept her safe. Alli knows too much about the ranch and Gwen's movements. If I'd trusted my gut, none of this would have ever happened."

"Maybe everything…everything has been a huge mistake."

"That's not what I meant," he said. "You have to know that's not what I meant. What you and I shared last night—"

"Was stupid," she said, finishing his sentence. "If we just hadn't lost focus, none of this would have happened." She glared over at him, and her lip twitched with anger. "I told you almost the second you set foot on the ranch that Winnie was, and will always be, my primary concern. I am her guardian. You coming here put her at risk."

"My coming here has nothing to do with your sister coming back and kidnapping Winnie. And what happened between you and me wasn't stupid. You can't tell me you didn't enjoy it just as much as me. You are hurt and angry. I get that. But don't forget we're on the same side."

"We are not on the same side. We've never been on the same side."

She was pissed, and she had every right to be, but

she was wrong. Yet trying to argue with her would be futile.

He could only watch and listen as she attempted to shatter the bond they shared.

He'd always been one to be the hero, to save those who needed saving and help people through their darkest moments, but he hadn't had a clue that when he came back to Montana he would be facing his own personal version of hell.

All he could do was hope that he would be able to save Winnie. If she got hurt, or if Alli made some stupid decision, he would let his rage take over. He would no longer be a hero—he would be a man thirsty for vengeance.

"Winnie is going to be fine. They are going to start searching the ranch. For all we know she's still there. Safe and sound." He said it aloud, but the words sounded muted, like they were coming from the other side of the glass.

Christina said something under her breath he was glad he couldn't hear.

They barreled down a dirt road just on the edge of the county line. A trailer sat at the end of the drive, its roof was covered in bits of tarp and one of its front windows was held together with duct tape. Even by Montana standards, the place was a crap hole.

For a passing moment, he wondered if Alli had brought Winnie to this rat-infested place. He had to brush the thought aside. He needed to treat this case like it was just any other missing person—and not his daughter. If he let this be personal, he wouldn't have the control required to do the job that needed to be done.

He pulled in behind the big rig parked beside the

trailer. Now that they were close, he could see the place listed a bit to the left, almost as though it, too, was ashamed of the wreckage it had become.

He got out and came around to open Christina's door for her. It was a feeble gesture, but hopefully she would see it as the peace offering he intended.

"If you think you're going to tell me to sit here and wait, you've got another think coming," she said, pushing out of the truck. She didn't even look back as she made her way toward the front door of the house.

He rushed to catch up. "I'm not the kind of guy who would ever ask you to stand by and watch as a man does the work. Do you really think I'm a jerk?" He instantly wished he could reel the words back in. He wasn't sure he wanted her to answer.

She snorted slightly, but then as she turned to face him, she stopped. "You are not a jerk." She stared at him for a moment, and some of the iciness of her gaze melted away. "You just need to do everything in your power to save my niece." She turned back away and took the steps leading to the door two at a time. She knocked on the door; the sound was hollow and echoed through the house as though it was made of nothing more than cheap particleboard and spackle.

The cheap blinds rattled, as someone must have looked out at them from the living room.

"Daryl! Daryl Bucket?" she yelled. "We know you're inside. Answer the damned door!"

Waylon could hear heavy footfalls as the man made his way down the hall. Daryl opened the door just far enough that Waylon could see one of the man's eyes. His cheeks were covered with a day's worth of stubble, and from what Waylon could make out from the array of stains on the man's white shirt, he must have eaten a week's worth of Cheetos and used his T-shirt as a rag.

"What the hell do you want?" Daryl's voice was hoarse from lack of use and, from the tarry scent of the trailer, a hefty addiction to cigarettes.

"I'm not sure if you recognize us, but—" Waylon started.

"I know who you are. Why are you here?"

"We just wanted to ask you a few questions. No big deal, man, but we would appreciate your help," he said, trying to act as chummy as possible, though every cell of his being wanted to reach through the crack in the door, take the man by the throat and make him answer every one of his questions to his satisfaction.

"Hmm." Daryl ran his fingers through his greasy hair. "All right, army boy. You can come in, but I got stuff to do." He opened the door, and in his right hand once again was his trusty bat.

They followed him down the narrow hall. It was covered in old grainy photographs of green-clad marines posing with antiquated tanks and helicopters in what looked like the jungles of Vietnam. Daryl rubbed the bat on the wall, making an unsettling sound as he walked into the living room.

He flopped down in a threadbare recliner and set his bat across his lap as he looked up at them.

Waylon couldn't help but wonder what kind of life the old marine had lived that he thought he always needed a weapon. Though they were in different branches, he had a certain level of understanding of the world outside the United States.

When a person had experienced the brutal reality of combat, there was no going back to a life in which they could ever really feel at peace. Safety was merely an illusion—an illusion he had perpetuated by telling Christina that Winnie was safe. How could he have been so stupid? How could he have looked past the lessons that had been drilled into him—the lesson that the only person he could really trust was himself?

He stared at Daryl and his bat. The only real difference between him and that man was Waylon wasn't carrying a bat—they were both equally a mess by the hand life had dealt them. Daryl just had the luxury of trying to forget.

"What kind of *stuff* do you have to do?" Christina asked, nearly spitting the words.

"That ain't none of your business, eh," the guy said, his warm Canadian accent in juxtaposition to his harsh words.

"I know, man. We don't have any business coming here and buggin' you when you got places to be. I get it." Waylon tried his best to overcome the jagged edge of Christina's tone. "We just had reason to believe that you might know a thing or two that could come in handy in helping us."

"Helping you all with what?" Daryl asked.

"We heard a little rumor that you sold some things to a pawnshop last night. Is that correct?"

Daryl didn't say anything; he simply spun the bat around in his hands.

"There's nothing wrong with pawning a couple of things to make an extra buck here or there," Waylon said. "Heaven knows I've needed a couple extra bucks now and then."

"You're still active. You don't got a clue. You would have thought my going to fight for your country woulda proved my allegiance and set me up for retirement, but that ain't happening. Ya know?"

"What do you mean? Isn't the VA treating you right?"

Daryl twisted the bat again. "As a former Canadian, I was only ever eligible for jobs that didn't require security clearance. You know what I mean, eh? The only good thing to come of my enlistment was my citizenship, but now that I been in the States most of my life and saw what a mess your political system is, I may just have to turn around and go back up north." He laughed.

"I wouldn't blame you, man." Waylon stepped over to the window and turned slightly so the guy could be a little more comfortable. "So you sold the ring. No problem." He glanced over at Christina, who slipped her hands behind her back in an effort to hide the ring from view.

"Then what's the problem?" Daryl asked. "What brought you all the way up here to my door?"

"We were just wondering where exactly you got that ring. Do you remember?"

"Did she steal it?" Daryl asked, staring at the bat in his hands.

"She did," Waylon said. "Do you know where we can find her?"

Daryl shook his head. "Truth be told, I don't even know how she found me, but she musta searched my name or something. Anyways, she showed up on my doorstep in what I now gotta assume was a stolen car and asked me if I could help her out by taking a few things off her hands. In my defense, she didn't tell me they were stolen. I wouldn't have bought none of it if I'd known for sure they were hot."

"Yet you gave the pawnshop owner a fake name and address when you sold him the stuff?"

Daryl twitched. "Is someone on the way here to arrest me? I swear I didn't know for sure. I just had a feeling. And I needed the money. She gave everything to me for a real good price. It was a good investment. That was all," he rambled.

"You're not in trouble, and the cops don't have a reason to come on out here and bother you, if you give us the answers we need."

"Look, army boy, I really would love to help you all, but I don't know nothing." He glanced back down at the bat in his hands, but not before Waylon noticed the faint redness in his cheeks—a color that told him there was far more to the story than the man wanted to admit, especially in front of a woman.

Waylon turned to Christina. "You mind if I talk to him alone for a minute?" He felt bad for asking, especially since he had just told her he wasn't the kind of guy to push a woman to the side, but there was no getting around it with the retired marine.

Christina opened her mouth to say something but stopped as she looked at him. "Daryl, do you have anything to drink in the kitchen?"

He pointed farther down the hall. "There's some coffee from earlier this morning. And there might be a few beers left in the fridge. Help yourself."

Christina frowned but made her way out of the room and toward the kitchen.

Waylon turned back to Daryl. "So was she good? You know, the girl who you bought the ring from."

Daryl jerked as he looked up at him, and the way the

man's mouth opened and closed—like he was searching for air—told Waylon he'd hit the nail on the head.

"A man has needs. You're fine," Waylon said with a shrug. "Not to mention that Alli is a beautiful woman. I don't blame you for making a move on her." Actually, he hated the thought of the things Alli had done and continued to do, but that was hardly the man's fault.

"Alli? Who's Alli?" Daryl frowned. "She said her name was Sharon. At least I think that's what she said."

It didn't surprise him that Alli would have given the guy a fake name. There seemed to be a lot of that going around. In fact, it might even have been where Daryl had gotten the idea, but he didn't bother to ask.

"What did Sharon look like?"

"I told you before, dark haired, about five foot six, skinny—though she looked like she'd lost weight from the last time I'd saw her. It's another reason I wanted to help her out."

Daryl could try to make it sound like he was helping the woman out of the goodness of his heart, but he'd already admitted to letting her exchange sex for favors and profiting from a stolen item. He was no saint.

"Is there anything else you can tell me?"

Daryl shook his head.

"You saw her naked. Did she have any kind of birthmarks? Tattoos?"

The guy's face pinched as he thought. "There was… She had a strawberry birthmark on her inner thigh." He wiped the sweat from his brow as he looked over his shoulder toward the kitchen, checking to make sure that Christina wasn't within earshot.

Alli didn't have a birthmark.

"Is it possible that the birthmark was a bruise or

some other kind of mark?" Waylon asked, trying to make sense of exactly what the man was saying.

"No. It was a port-wine mark," Daryl said, making a circle with his fingers on his thigh. "It was about this big. Dark red. She said she had it as a child. She never liked to wear shorts."

Alli lived in shorts in the summertime, or at least she had. It was possible that she could have been lying to the man about the story, but there was little to no way to replicate a birthmark like that. Yet Alli did have a tattoo of a small lightning bolt on her ankle.

"Did Sharon," Waylon said, the name sounding as foreign as the woman Daryl was describing, "have any tattoos?"

The guy looked up toward the ceiling as though he was trying to find memories on the tiles. "No. Not that I can remember. To be honest, she didn't seem the type. She was a bit by the book—if you know what I mean." He gave him a look that told him Daryl wasn't talking about tattoos.

Alli had always been anything but by the book. There was no possible way that the woman Daryl was talking about could have been Waylon's ex-wife. But if it wasn't her, he had no idea who else would have had the ring and the paintings. Maybe it was possible that Alli had given this other woman the items to sell, but something about it all just didn't fit.

He was missing something. He had to be. But what was it that he wasn't seeing?

"And you said that the woman who came to your door was, without a doubt, the same woman you picked up on the side of the road and brought back to Mystery?"

Daryl nodded. "Yep."

"And where did you drop this woman off? Did you bring her back here the first time you met her?"

The sweat dripped on Daryl's brow, and he tried to wipe it away, but it returned just as quickly. "I didn't bring her back here then. She didn't seem like the type who wanted…you know…at least not with me."

"So where did you take her?"

Daryl looked away and tapped his fingers on the bat in his hands. Everything about his body language screamed that he was trying to come up with a convenient lie, and it made the hairs on the back of Waylon's neck rise. The man hadn't seemed like he really had anything major to hide, but the way he was acting now made him think otherwise.

"Don't bother lying to me," Waylon said, not waiting for the man to answer. "If you do, I will have the police here within minutes."

Daryl gripped the bat and looked back up at him. "I don't want her to get in trouble. I don't want anyone to get in trouble. She seemed like a nice-enough woman."

"She's not *nice enough*," Waylon spat, finally losing his patience with the man's game. "Trust me. We have a reason to believe she may be involved with the kidnapping of a little girl. It's why she needed the money. Why she came to you. So the faster you can give me answers, the faster we can get to that little girl. If you just tell me what you know, maybe we can even save the little girl's life."

"She made me drop her off on the frontage road— about a mile from anything on the north end of town. I don't think she wanted me to know where she was going. She was good at keeping her secrets, you know?" Daryl spoke fast, flustered. "The only thing I can think of is that she kept talking about this ranch. Dunrovin. You know it?"

His stomach sank. "What did she say about it?"

"Only that she was going to take the place down. One person at a time."

"And you thought this woman was innocent?" Christina asked as she walked down the hallway toward them. The glass of water in her hand was shaking. "Where is she, Daryl? Where can we find her? Where can we find my niece?"

"I don't know anything. I swear, I don't know nothing. All I know is she had some kind of vendetta. I don't know why." Daryl stared at Christina, an apologetic look on his face. "If this were my deal, I would start looking there. At that ranch. Flies are always drawn to things they think are rotten."

Chapter Sixteen

"It has to be Alli. If the woman wasn't Alli, who could it possibly be? Who would want to hurt Winnie? Us?" Christina asked as she tried to keep her rage in check.

None of this made any sense. Winnie was innocent in all this. Alli was the only person who could have wanted her—she was the only one with any motivation to do it. That was, unless Daryl had been right and the person behind Winnie's disappearance had been carrying a vendetta toward the ranch and everyone who lived there.

It felt like they were chasing a ghost—a ghost who knew their weakest points.

Everyone loved Winnie. If a person wanted to hurt everyone at the ranch, the girl was the best place to start. She was the heart of the place and everyone in it.

Waylon reached over and took Christina's hand, gripping it hard as he pressed down on the gas. Her body flew back in the seat as he raced the truck back toward the ranch. "I don't have a frigging clue why this person did what she did. But whoever this woman is, she's not going to get away with anything else. And if she touches a single hair on Winnie's head, I will make it my mission in life to make sure she never draws another breath."

His words carried the weight of truth to them.

"You don't really think this mystery woman would hurt a child, do you?"

"Don't underestimate people. Evil is evil. And truly evil people, they don't have a sense of right or wrong. They believe whatever they do is right. For all we know, this woman is psychotic, or a sociopath. She's capable of anything."

She leaned over to read the speedometer on the truck—the needle pointed at seventy. "Can't you drive any faster?"

He slammed his foot down on the gas pedal, and the truck bellowed. They squealed down the road, and the ranch quickly came into view. The parking lot was full of flashing red and blue lights, and people were milling around the barn. Even the horses were alarmed, and as they drove past the pasture, a mare raced down the fence line next to them—almost as if the horse knew who was missing and feared what could have happened to Winnie just as much as they did.

It was amazing how quickly the love for a child could bring even the most unlikely people together.

Christina squeezed Waylon's fingers. She needed him, and she had a feeling he needed her just as badly. It was inconvenient and unwieldy, but she loved him. Looking at him, the intensity in his gaze, the strength in his body and soul, she loved everything about him. No matter where in the world he went, or what the future would bring, she would love him. She hated it, but there was no fighting the truth deep in her heart.

Mrs. Fitzgerald ran up to the truck as they struggled

to find a parking spot in the melee of emergency vehicles. There was even an ambulance parked toward the edge of the parking lot. The EMTs were standing among the police officers, and everyone had a look of concern on their face.

Waylon let go of her hand and rolled down the window as his mother stopped beside them.

"We're organizing search parties. We're going to go over every square inch of this place. Wyatt is setting up a grid in and around Mystery, and the highway patrols are watching all roads. Everyone is helping. Everyone," Eloise said, her voice cracking with nerves.

Waylon jumped out of the truck and drew his mother into his embrace. Christina followed him. "Don't worry, Mom. We'll find her. They couldn't have gotten far. How's Gwen doing?"

Eloise pointed a shaking finger across the yard toward Gwen, who was sitting on the porch steps. She was moving back and forth, hugging herself. Wyatt was with her, rubbing her back, but he was talking to one of the officers.

"She's doing just about as well as you'd expect," Eloise said. "If something's happened…"

"Don't go there, Mom," Waylon said, his voice firm with resolve. "She's going to be okay."

Christina doubted what he said was true, but she nodded. They needed to be the backbone of the family; they needed to stay strong so everyone around them could as well.

"What did Gwen say? Did she see the woman who took Winnie or anything?" Christina asked.

"She's having a hard time processing everything. She said she didn't see anything—one minute Winnie was in her house at the edge of Dunrovin with her, playing with her toys, and the next minute she was gone. Wyatt said there weren't even any tire marks in the gravel or signs someone had driven up to their trailer. He's thinking that either the person responsible is still somewhere on the ranch or there may have been more than one person involved."

The thought made Christina stop. "How many are involved?"

Eloise shrugged. "At this point we don't know."

Christina looked over at Waylon. His lips were puckered and the lines of his frown seemed deeper than ever before. "What if Alli wasn't even the one driving her car? Think about it. She may have never even left this town."

"Or she could have gone south. She could have hitchhiked to Mexico by now."

"Or she could be…dead." Eloise covered her mouth. "I'm so sorry, Christina. I shouldn't have said it."

"No," Christina whispered, stunned. "Alli isn't dead. She can't be dead. She's probably with Winnie right now. Wyatt's probably right. Maybe Alli had someone working with her, someone she convinced to drive her car. And take Winnie." Even as she spoke, she knew how far-fetched the whole thing sounded.

Alli wasn't the kind who normally kept a throng of female friends. If she had one named Sharon, Christina would have thought she would have heard about the woman at least in passing from her sister before she had disappeared. Then again, maybe she wouldn't have. Her life was nothing if not a jumbled mess of dangerous secrets.

IT WASN'T HIS first search party, but it was the first one in which Waylon thought there was hope they'd find the victim alive. That hope might be misplaced, but he couldn't bring himself to believe anything else.

No matter how hard he tried to compartmentalize his feelings, there was no escaping the emotional reality that it was his daughter's life at stake.

As his team moved through the pasture, their motion made some of the dry, light snowflakes rise in the air. It was almost as if the snow was floating upward, disobeying the laws of nature and following only its own desire to get back to the safety of the sky. If only it was that simple to escape the constant beating life wrought.

One of the police officers Wyatt had sent with them flagged him down. "Mr. Fitzgerald, does this belong to your daughter?" The man lifted up a pink hooded sweatshirt with Dora the Explorer on the back. Its sleeve was stretched a bit, like it had been pulled over the girl's Ace bandage.

Waylon didn't want to admit that he didn't know his child well enough to know what kind of clothing she wore, or even if she liked Dora or not, so he looked to Christina. She gave him a small, almost imperceptible nod instead of calling him out in front of the group of rescuers.

"Yeah," Waylon said, rushing over to the deputy.

A sense of relief flooded him. Finally, they had a clue to Winnie's whereabouts—and proof that she might still be on the ranch. Now it was just a matter of finding her in the nearly thousand acres of the place.

The sweatshirt was partially frozen where it had been lying on the ground and covered by a thin layer of snow, and as the deputy turned it around, on the left breast, Waylon noticed a brown dot of dried blood. He looked over his shoulder to Christina. The pink in her cheeks disappeared, and her mouth fell open as her gaze moved over the shirt in the deputy's hands.

"It's probably not hers," Waylon said, stepping between Christina and the sweatshirt. "If she's anything like me, maybe she bit her attacker. My girl would fight."

Christina just stared at him like she could still see the sweatshirt through his body. "We have to find her, Waylon. We have to find her right now."

She started to move again, pacing around the area, searching the ground. It didn't make him feel any better that she was no longer looking up; instead, everyone was now looking for more blood on the ground.

He tried to ignore the sick feeling in his stomach. Winnie wasn't hurt. She couldn't be hurt. He would save her. He *had* to save her, or he could never go on. He could never face a world that would take his daughter away from him the same week that she'd come into his life.

Christina slipped her hand into his, and he realized that he had been standing there in silence as everyone else had started to move again, except the deputy who'd found the sweatshirt, who was documenting the scene and taking pictures.

"Let's go," Christina said, her voice soft but resolute and strong. "She needs you. You can't stop now. We have to hurry."

He followed her into the pasture, and they started moving again. Ahead of them was a small embankment. They slowly picked their way up the hill. Some of the dry grass had been trampled down where cows had moved through the area to the stock pond on the other side of the hill. He scanned the area, but aside from the cows' tracks, there was nothing to tell them that any other humans had been in the area recently.

Yet he knew she had to be close. He could almost feel her. It was strange to think that this little girl could now have such a pull on his heart. As he thought about Winnie, Christina and his family, he realized how alone he had been when he'd been away from the ranch. Part of him had been missing—the love of his family, a love as big as the sky over Montana.

He moved ahead of Christina and to the top of the hill. Cattails and weeds surrounded the stock pond, and some of the weeds were at least a few feet tall. Animals coming in for a drink had pushed some of the vegetation down, and bits of the detritus floated in the water. The trail that led down from where he stood had once been mud, but it was now frozen solid by the harsh, cold winds of winter.

It was odd to think that Christmas was only just around the corner. Winnie had been talking about it almost incessantly every time they had been alone. According to her, she wanted nothing more than a puppy.

He smiled at the thought of his mother's reaction if he showed up at their door on Christmas Eve carrying a puppy, complete with a big red bow. His mother would undoubtedly be mad, furious even, that he had brought another animal to the ranch, but she could never resist an animal in need—especially an animal that wagged its tail and promised licks.

It broke his heart as he looked out at the pond and was met with the rattle of dry grass and the lonely whisper of a long winter. Winnie needed the Christmas of her dreams. She deserved to be loved and cared for.

To get everything she ever wanted. If only they could find her. They had to find her. She had to be safe.

"Waylon," Christina said, her voice choked. "Look." She motioned toward the far side of the pond, where a patch of weeds leaned over the water. She took off running in that direction. He took a few steps after her before he saw the blue fabric bobbing in the water near the bank.

From the distance, he couldn't tell exactly what the fabric was, or what it was covering.

He sprinted after Christina.

It couldn't be Winnie. It couldn't be. No.

She hadn't been gone that long. Only about an hour. No one would want to kill the girl.

He didn't want to believe anyone would be crazy enough to hurt a child, but he knew all too well what people were capable of. He could only hope his gut was wrong—and his daughter was just fine and probably hiding in the weeds somewhere on the ranch, somewhere far away from the horror in front of him.

He rushed past Christina. She couldn't get there first. He had to shield her from whatever they were about to find.

"Go call the rest of the team," he ordered, but she paid him no mind. In fact, she didn't even slow down as she chased after him on the uneven path that led to the far side of the pond.

"Winnie!" she called, terror in her voice.

It wasn't his daughter bobbing there in the water like one of the weeds. It couldn't be. It just couldn't be.

He rushed down the steep bank and ran straight into the water. It was cold and ice had collected on the edges of the bank, but he barely noticed the bite. He reached into the water. In one solid motion he flipped over the body. It was Winnie.

Her little eyes were closed, and her lips were blue. Her skin wasn't mottled, and as he pressed his fingers against her neck, he could almost make out a sluggish pulse.

He pulled her from the water and carried her up onto the bank as he let his training take over. He started chest compressions.

"Come on, Winnie. Come on, baby." He pressed down. One. Two. Three. Four. "Come on, baby. Daddy's here. Breathe for me."

He pressed five more times. The little girl didn't move.

It was impossible to know how long she had been floating in the water, but if there was any higher power, they wouldn't let her die. She was just a child. She didn't deserve to pay the price for his mistakes. She had to live. She had to.

Christina fell to her knees beside the girl and held the fingers that stuck out from the end of the girl's bandage. "Come on, Winnie girl. Come on. Breathe for us."

He did another set of compressions on Winnie's chest, hoping like he'd never hoped before that the action would be enough to pull her back to the land of the living—to a world where they could be together. All three of them.

"Please, baby, please. I need you," he begged. "I love you. Please. Stay with Daddy."

Winnie's eyelashes fluttered, and water poured from her mouth. She coughed and gagged as she forced the fluid from her lungs. She moved to sit up, but her tiny body was so weak that she fell back to the ground.

He picked her up and pulled her into the safety of his arms. "I'm so sorry, Winnie. I'm so sorry, baby. Don't worry. Daddy's got you," he cooed as she coughed and sputtered on his shoulder.

He stood up as he looked over at Christina. "She's going to make it. We got her. We got her, honey."

Tears streamed down Christina's cheeks. "Now we just have to find the person responsible. They have to pay."

Chapter Seventeen

Christina couldn't stop watching Waylon and the way he hovered over Winnie as the emergency room nurse wrapped her in a warm blanket.

"Mr. Fitzgerald, you need to back up. I need to check her vitals," the nurse ordered.

Waylon stared at the nurse, and *shooting daggers* didn't even seem strong enough to describe the way he looked at the woman.

"Okay," the nurse said, not waiting for him to speak. "It's okay if you stay with the girl, but—"

"She's not just any girl. This is my daughter," he argued. "And I'm not going anywhere. I'm not leaving her again. Not until I know she's safe."

"She's safe in this hospital, sir," the nurse said, clearly not getting the message.

Christina moved closer to Waylon and took his hand as she glanced toward the nurse. "No one except hospital staff is allowed anywhere near the girl, do you understand?"

The nurse raised an eyebrow, almost as if she were surprised to be taken on by both Christina and Waylon, but instead of arguing, this time she answered with a nod. "I will have security come over and stand guard beside the door. No one will be allowed to come or go. I promise. But for right now, I need you both out of this room. You've done a great job in getting this girl to this point, but now she needs the help only this hospital and I can provide."

"Thank you, Nurse. Thank you." Christina pulled Waylon along by the arm. "Come on, honey. Come on. She'll be okay."

"I can't… I can't leave her," he said. "She needs us." He motioned toward Winnie.

His daughter's chest was rising and falling with the sleep of the exhausted.

"Don't worry, honey. She's going to be okay. They have her. Security is on their way. Don't forget, whoever is responsible for this—they're still out there. We need to find them. We have to stop them before they have the chance to do anything this horrible again."

Outside Winnie's room, they were surrounded by a sea of brown and black uniforms. There were at least ten police officers, both highway patrol and sheriff's deputies, milling around the unit. Near the entrance were Gwen and Wyatt, who rushed over as they noticed Waylon and Christina coming out of Winnie's room.

"Is she going to be okay?" Gwen asked. Her eyes were red and her skin blotchy from what must have been hours of crying.

Christina nodded. "She's alive. They are trying to get her warmed up and rested."

"Did she say anything about who was behind this? About what she saw?" Wyatt asked, looking toward Waylon.

Waylon stared out into space and slowly shook his

head. "She's just lucky to be alive. We're lucky we found her in time."

"Our guys are still going over the scene," Wyatt said. He reached into his pocket, pulled out his cell phone and opened a picture. He handed the phone to Christina. "But they managed to find the missing paperwork stuffed under a rock just inside the water's edge."

"What? Why would anyone do that?" she asked, staring at the picture of the papers under the water.

"I have no idea, but you think if they were after money, they would have simply sold the papers. Something like a passport can go for a lot of money on the black market," Wyatt said. "Sometimes they even use things like that for transporting kids across the border illegally."

Chills ran down her spine. Why were so many people determined to exploit kids? She must have lived in another world, because things like that didn't even cross her mind—not in the middle of Montana.

Several nurses and a doctor rushed into Winnie's room, and the people standing in the ER grew quiet. Another of the ER doctors, who had been standing at the nurses' station, looked over at them and slowly made his way over.

"Are you the parents of Winnie Bell?" he asked, motioning to Waylon and Christina.

She didn't really know how to respond. She wasn't the girl's mother, and now that Waylon had claimed his daughter, she wasn't really even the guardian.

"We are," Waylon said, squeezing her hand. "What can we do for you?"

The doctor gave them a weak but reassuring smile. "I heard about what happened. Don't worry. Every year we get a child who falls through the ice. We're practiced dealing with situations like this. The great thing about kids is that they are so resilient. From what I saw, you got to her just in time. If she's a fighter, she'll make it through this."

"She's a fighter," Waylon said.

"I'm glad to hear it," the doctor said with a thankful nod. "Now, about you both. How are you doing?"

"We're fine. We aren't the ones who were floating in the water," Waylon said, glancing over at the room where his daughter lay.

The doctor lifted Waylon's arm and pushed up the sleeve of his shirt. For the first time, Christina noticed red welts on his skin, covered in what looked like little pustules.

Waylon pulled his arm from the doctor's grip. "Don't worry, I'm fine." He pushed down his sleeve.

"Where did you guys say you found the little girl?" the doctor asked.

Wyatt stepped forward. "Does it matter?"

"Oh, no, don't get me wrong," the doctor said with a slight wave. "It's just that a rash like that is uncommon this time of year. Though—"

"I've been stressed. It's probably just hives or something," Waylon interrupted.

"No. A rash like this…" he said, taking Waylon's arm. The doctor touched the skin around the red welts. "These are from some kind of allergic reaction." He leaned in closer to take a better look. "It looks like poison ivy."

"We don't have poison ivy here. We're too far north."

"No, I know. It's probably something in the same family, maybe stinging nettles." The doctor leaned back and frowned for a moment. "Actually, I had a case just like this a few days ago. A woman came in presenting the same symptoms."

She had seen something like this before, on a ranch hand's Labrador retriever. The dog had been playing near the stock pond and had gotten into some kind of stinging underbrush.

"Who was the woman who came in with the rash?" Christina asked, more than aware that HIPAA laws, the restrictions that required medical confidentiality, would prohibit the man from answering. Yet she had to try.

"You know I can't answer that. I can't give you names."

A nurse walked out from Winnie's room and made her way over toward them. "Dr. Nay?" she asked, motioning toward the doctor standing with them. "Dr. Rogers needs your help."

The doctor looked back to Christina. "I'm sorry I can't be of more help."

"Don't worry," Wyatt said. "We'll be back, warrant in hand. If there's even a chance the woman you treated is the same woman responsible for Winnie's attack, the judge will give me anything I want."

"I look forward to helping," the doctor said, turning away to go to the room. "For now, you'll have to be satisfied that we are going to make sure Winnie's well taken care of. And," he said, motioning toward Waylon's arm, "you might want to take some Benadryl and lather that up with calamine lotion. If you take care of it, your rash should be gone within a few days."

"Thanks, Doc," Waylon said. His shoulders fell and there was an air of resignation in his voice. Christina felt the same way, for once again it was as if, when they finally started to make progress, everything in the world stood in their way.

She understood the need for privacy and HIPAA

regulations. She did. However, it didn't make it any easier when it impeded their progress in the investigation. They needed to find the woman with the rash.

No one went out to that stock pond at this time of year. No one—unless they were trying to hide something. Maybe Alli had been there, scoping out a place where she could kill Winnie. Or maybe she had been spending her nights at the place. It was well out of view from the staff at the ranch house and the vacationers who came and went from the guest houses and close enough that she could come and go unnoticed while she was waiting for her opportunity to take Winnie.

Christina could almost feel the pieces clicking together.

She couldn't wait to see her sister again. To confront her about what she had done and what she had put the family through. Perhaps she could even get some much-needed answers from her.

The nurse cleared her throat as she motioned to Waylon's arm. "That's a doozy of a rash," the nurse said. "The doctor's right, you definitely want to take care of it. My cousin had a rash like that a few days ago."

Her cousin?

Waylon's eyes lit up. "Oh, yeah?" he asked. "What's your cousin's name?"

"Lisa. Lisa Chase. Why?" the nurse asked, oblivious to what the doctor had been talking about—and the HIPAA laws that had stood in their way.

"Did she come in here to be treated?" Wyatt pressed her.

The nurse frowned. "Yeah. Dr. Nay told her exactly what he just told you. Benadryl and calamine. At this stage, with just the pustules and no oozing lesions, it's the only thing you want to do. The next step is anti-biotics if you've been scratching at them and they become infected."

Waylon nodded, but as he looked over at Christina, she could tell he wasn't really listening to anything the nurse had to say; instead, he was shifting his weight from one foot to the other just like a runner getting ready for a sprint.

"Thanks," Waylon said, "I'll get right on that."

"If you need, I bet I can get the doctor to pre-scribe—"

"No. I'm fine." He took Christina's hand and gave it a squeeze. They had answers. They finally had some kind of an answer.

"Wyatt?" he asked, turning away from the nurse.

His brother had a gleam in his eye. "I'll have my men stay here with Winnie. She'll be protected by at least three officers at all times in addition to the hospital's security."

It was really no wonder that both the brothers had gone into law enforcement—they knew how to keep a person at ease even when the world was falling apart.

Chapter Eighteen

Hate wasn't a new emotion in her world. No, it was a feeling Christina had become well versed in when she had watched her parents fight, when they had torn at one another, and the day her sister had repeated their cycle—and left her holding the strings to a life that she had never intended on leading. Yet she had never hated anyone or anything more than she hated Lisa Chase in that moment.

The woman had tried to kill one of the few people she truly loved.

She stared out the window as they pulled into William Poe's driveway.

Why did everything always come back to this vile man? He was like a poison. First Bianca, then Monica and Alli, and now they could even tie him to Lisa. He had always proclaimed his innocence—so far, he'd even been cleared of any wrongdoing in each of the cases, but he could only run for so long before the authorities would catch him playing in the shadows. Or at least, Christina hoped.

Then again, maybe he wasn't anything more than just a man who had the power to make women go crazy. She followed Wyatt and Waylon up to the front door of the evil man's house. Knowing her luck, he probably wasn't even home. He had a knack of being out of town when it came to the crimes that were rocking the community of Mystery.

Wyatt banged on the door. The sound was hollow and eerie.

A slight wheeze escaped her throat.

"What?" Waylon asked, taking her hand.

"Nothing," she said, and as the word ghosted from her lips, the front door opened.

Standing there was William Poe. He looked a bit haggard and tired, but his suit jacket was crisp from being freshly laundered and pressed. "What is it now?" he grumbled.

"Is your friend Lisa Chase here?" Wyatt asked.

"Why would you need to see her? She's done nothing." William's face contorted with rage. "I don't know what kind of thing you have against me or why, but this has to stop. You can't keep harassing me. This is ridiculous."

"We're harassing you?" Christina said, nearly hissing the words in her fury. "Ever since you entered our lives, everything has been going wrong. People have been killing each other, going missing, and stealing and hurting children."

"You think any of this has to do with me?" William laughed, the sound low and menacing. "You are just as crazy as your sister if you think I want to have anything to do with any of that or with any of you. Have you ever stopped to think that where everything truly stops and ends is at your family's goddamned ranch?"

"Shut your mouth," Waylon seethed.

"No. You all need to be put out of business—you

and your family have only brought trouble to this community. And once you're gone, that cursed guest ranch will be sold to the highest bidder. I'd be doing a public service if I got to be the one to take you all down."

"Is that a threat?" Wyatt asked, his voice even more dangerous than Poe's.

"Ha ha ha." William laughed, the sound as cheap and ridiculous as his suit. "I don't make threats. When I say I'm going to do something, I won't stop until it's done."

"How dare you think you can come at my family? My home?" Christina lunged toward the man, but Waylon grabbed her by the arms and pulled her back.

"Not here. Not now. Wyatt's going to handle this," he whispered, the sound harsh in her ear. "If you touch a hair on that man's head, we will lose any ground we have in going after him."

"We're not here to pick a fight with you, Poe. We're only here to speak to Lisa. Now, is she here or not?" Wyatt continued.

"Why in the hell would I tell you?" Poe sneered.

"If you don't help us, I have no problem getting more police and media involved. One little call and you and your personal life will be out in the open. I'd hate it if some pictures of you and one of your many female acquaintances would make it into the hands of a reporter or two."

"Now who's threatening?" William growled. "How dare you come here and treat me like I'm some kind of criminal. I haven't done a goddamned thing."

"If it walks like a duck." Wyatt shrugged.

Waylon leaned in close to Christina so only she

could hear him speak. "What photos is Wyatt talking about?" he whispered.

She turned to him and cupped his ear. "They found a set of incriminating photos when they were investigating Bianca's murder. There was one with Alli in a lace teddy."

Waylon sent her a look of surprise but then turned back to his brother and Poe. "I am sure the press would love to get their hands on the information that links you to Alli. Especially after everything that's happened."

"If those pictures are leaked, I will come after you. I will sue you and the sheriff's department for every penny—"

"Oh, don't misunderstand me, Poe. I have no intention of misconduct. However, I'm sure there are more copies of those photos we found," Wyatt continued.

It was a wonderful thing to watch the brothers work.

"That's ridiculous. Alli and I were done a long time ago."

Christina glanced over at Wyatt, but he didn't give anything away.

"Do you know where Alli is?" Christina asked, unable to hold herself back any longer. "I need to find my sister."

William turned to look at her. "Why do you think I'd give two shakes about what has come of your sister?"

The way he said the words made her unsettled. It was almost as if there was something he knew that she didn't—something sinister.

"What *has* come of my sister, Poe?" she seethed.

He laughed again, the sound filled with mirth. "I told you. Your sister is of no concern to me. She's been nothing but a thorn in my side ever since—"

"You threw her to the curb?" she interrupted. "You know, I have had a hard time understanding why my sister has done the things she has in the last few months, but now—talking to you for just a few minutes—I can almost understand why she was driven to the edges of her sanity."

Poe stepped closer, pressing his face close to hers. "Maybe you should look to yourself before you start pointing fingers at me, little girl."

Waylon's hands tightened on her arms.

"Before someone—namely you—gets hurt here, Poe, where's Lisa?" Wyatt said, motioning inside the man's house. "For once, take a moment and make a choice that will serve you the best in the end."

Poe took a few steps back and looked back over his shoulder, like he was looking for the woman in question.

"You know you don't love her. You don't love anyone but yourself. So, before you are pulled any deeper into our investigation, get out. Get her to come and talk to us," Wyatt pressed.

Poe said something Christina couldn't quite hear, but from the look on his face as he glanced back at them, she was glad she couldn't. "Lisa!" William called. "Get your ass out here, woman! The little deputy and his goon squad want to ask you some questions."

A small, dark-haired woman, the one she had seen the other day, stepped into the doorway.

"Don't speak to them. In the meantime, I'm calling my lawyer."

"For me?" the small woman squeaked.

William laughed, and the sound echoed off the

walls of the house. "Hardly. Whatever mess you are in, you are in it by yourself. I can't be associated with any more trouble." He stopped and pointed toward the brothers. "And I'm sure that no pictures will go public. I've played your stupid game. Do we all have an understanding?"

Waylon glared at the man. "One thing we will never have, Poe, is an understanding. I don't want you to think for one minute that we see you as anything more than the societal louse that you are."

Wyatt laughed as Poe stormed off down the hall. "Louse? That's the best you got for that guy?"

Waylon shrugged. "I would have called him an ass—"

"Stop," Lisa squeaked. "William may not be a perfect man, but he doesn't deserve to be talked about like that. Especially not by a civil servant," she said, pointing at the badge on Wyatt's uniform. "Your job is to protect the innocent."

Wyatt laughed. "Poe is far from innocent."

"Of course he is." Lisa looked around the driveway like a trapped animal as she scratched at the welts that ran up and down her arms.

"What makes you think he's innocent?" Wyatt asked.

"I'm the one who killed them. He never wanted me to hurt a hair on their heads. But I had to do what needed to be done. One must sacrifice for the greater good."

"Who did you kill?" Wyatt asked, his voice as cold as the snow on the ground around them.

"Alli was first." Lisa looked at Wyatt, but her expression was vacant—indifferent.

Christina's ears rang with the woman's words.

"You *killed* Alli?" Christina whispered, the words like weights that made her sink to her knees as they left her body.

"She had it coming. She was no innocent. The little girl, on the other hand, that was unfortunate. I didn't want to kill her. She just wouldn't come quietly. She kept trying to scream. Especially when I told her how I was going to sell her."

"You were going to sell my daughter?" Waylon seethed.

Lisa nodded, like the trafficking of children was among the most normal things in the world. "I would have been set up for life." She glanced over her shoulder and in the direction where Poe had disappeared. "I don't want to have to depend on anyone too much. Dependence leads to disaster." She turned back and leered at Christina. "Just ask your sister."

"Where is she? Where's Alli? What did you do with her?"

Lisa looked over at her. "How could you find one without the other? I went out of my way to make sure that mother and daughter could at least be together in the afterlife."

"How could you?" Christina started to lunge toward Lisa, but Waylon stopped her.

"How could I what? Kill your sister?" Lisa looked utterly confused, the face of a monster. "Don't worry. It was one quick bullet to the head. It was just like shooting out my tire. It was easy." She reached behind her and pulled out a gun. "In fact, it was just like this," she said, raising it and pointing the barrel toward Christina.

Before she had time to react, Waylon was on the

woman, pushing her to the floor and pulling the weapon from her hands.

Blood streamed from Lisa's nose as she looked up at Christina. She laughed. The sound was high and crazed. "I may not have gotten you, but your day is coming. All of your days are coming. I may not be the one pulling the trigger, but you're all going to die."

Waylon rolled Lisa over, pressing his knee into the center of the woman's back as he pulled her arms behind her. "That won't happen. I will stop at nothing to protect the ones I love."

Chapter Nineteen

She wasn't merely broken. No, Christina was destroyed, and all Waylon could do was hold her. He held her as they'd watched Wyatt cuff Lisa and stuff her into his car. He'd held her when they heard about her sister's body being pulled from the pond. And he held her as they lay in his bed and stared up at the ceiling.

If he had his way, he'd hold her forever.

She'd barely spoken all night, and he hadn't even mentioned eating.

Christina shifted in his arms, and her loose hair slipped over his chest. He ran his fingers through her locks in a feeble attempt to comfort her in the only way he knew how. There was no going back and undoing what had been done, or taking back the tragedy that seemed to have become a constant in not just their lives but those of all who lived and worked at Dunrovin.

She moved slightly and looked up at him. "What are you going to do?"

"What do you mean?"

"When are you leaving?" She sat up a bit more and lifted herself onto her elbow so they were eye to eye.

He cupped her face, running his thumb over the

soft skin of her cheek. "I will stay here as long as you need me."

She snorted. "We both know that can't happen. You've given your life to the army. They are going to want you back sometime."

He smiled, but the ache that had filled his heart—the one that had started the moment he'd realized his feelings toward her were more than mere friendship—expanded and threatened to make his chest explode.

"I have a couple more days here, but when I leave, you and Winnie...you can come back to Fort Bragg with me."

Christina looked out the window, where the bits of falling snow were shining like glitter in the moon's silver light. "I don't think it's a good idea to take Winnie away from this ranch. This is the only home she's known. She's already been through so much change." She looked back at him, a tear in her eye. "But ultimately the choice is yours. She's your daughter."

"Alli chose you to watch over her, to take care of her. She didn't choose me."

The tear slipped down her cheek. "What Alli wanted, or thought...it doesn't matter now."

"Yes, it does. She chose you because she knew what a good mom you would be. She chose you because you are a good person. She loved you. Just like I love you."

Christina's mouth opened with surprise, and she made a muffled, strangled sound, as though she wasn't sure what to say.

"Don't say anything at all," he said, filling the emotional gap between them. "You don't have to love me. I don't want you to feel like you need to say anything. Whether or not you love me, I love you. I love everything about you—your strength, the way you put Winnie and the needs of others before yourself. You're so selfless. So giving. You are one of the kindest people I've met in my entire life. I would be a fool not to love you."

"No," she said. "I'd be a fool not to love you." She leaned in and kissed him.

His body awoke, just as it always did when she was near. As their lips parted, he stared into her eyes, and a piece of his heart broke.

She loved him.

He loved her.

Yet there was too much between them to make anything work. Sometimes love just wasn't enough to bring two people together.

She'd never leave this place.

"I'm scared," she said, laying her head back down on his chest.

The words, though barely above a whisper, reverberated through him as though she had screamed them.

"Why? What are you scared of?" he asked, wrapping his arms around her.

"I'm scared of what the future will bring. And I'm scared of losing you." She reached up and took his hand, her ring flashing in the silver light streaming in from the window.

"I have to go back to work, it's true." He sighed. "But like I said, you and Winnie can come with me. Take a break for a week and get out of this place. You can check out the base. Then we can come back for Christmas."

"Then what?" she asked. "Whether or not we like the base isn't the issue."

He knew what she was saying was right, and he knew the answer—an answer that would change his life forever. When he'd come to the ranch, his career had been everything to him, but now, in a matter of days, Christina and Winnie had become the center of his life and the only things that filled his heart.

"I only have a few months left. I don't have to re-enlist. When I get out, I can come back here. We can set up a house. We can get married."

"Get married?" She wiped the remnants of the tears from her cheek as she smiled up at him.

He took her right hand and pulled her grandmother's ring from her finger. "If you don't want this ring, we can get another one, but…" He sat up slightly, but she wouldn't let him go. "Don't you want me to get down on one knee?"

She laughed, and the light from the moon filled her eyes. "The ring is perfect. And you are crazy if you think that, even for one minute, I'm going to let you go."

His laughter blanketed hers, and he kissed the top of her head. "So does that mean you will marry me?"

She sat up and moved on top of him, straddling him between her thighs. "Say it again. Something that good I want to hear twice," she said with an excited giggle.

He lifted her left hand and poised the ring to slip it on her finger. "Ms. Christina Bell, though this may be fast, I know with all my heart that I want to spend every waking moment with you. I never want to spend another day apart. And though life may get in the way and draw us in separate directions, I want to always come home to you. No matter where home is."

"Do you promise to not always be Mr. Serious?" She smiled. "And to love me unconditionally?"

"Always."

"Then, yes. Yes, Waylon Fitzgerald, I will be yours. Forever."

Regardless of everything that was going on in their lives or at the ranch, for one moment he was completely and blissfully happy. All the fears that had filled him, all of his apprehension and scars from the past were just that—in the past. Moving forward, they could have their fairy tale.

* * * * *

Don't miss the first book in the
MYSTERY CHRISTMAS *series:*

MS. CALCULATION

Available now from Mills & Boon!

"Love is always a weapon, Bennet."

"It doesn't have to be," he replied steadfastly, his blue eyes an odd shade in the light of the laptop screen.

Alyssa's chest felt tight, and her heart felt too much like it was being squeezed. She'd wanted to feel something, but not this. Not anything to do with love.

Before Alyssa realized what he was doing, Bennet had his hand fisted in her shirt and tugged her down. Then his mouth was on hers. Gentle, and something that kind of made her want to cry because there'd been so little of it in her life. His lips caressed hers, his tongue slowly tracing the outline of her bottom lip, and all she could do was soak it up. . .

STONE COLD
CHRISTMAS
RANGER

BY
NICOLE HELM

First Published in Great Britain 2017
By Mills & Boon, an imprint of HarperCollins*Publishers*
1 London Bridge Street, London, SE1 9GF

© 2017 Nicole Helm

ISBN: 978-0-263-92924-9

46-1017

Our policy is to use papers that are natural, renewable and recyclable products and made from wood grown in sustainable forests. The logging and manufacturing processes conform to the legal environmental regulations of the country of origin.

Printed and bound in Spain
by CPI, Barcelona

Nicole Helm grew up with her nose in a book and the dream of one day becoming a writer. Luckily, after a few failed career choices, she gets to follow that dream— writing down-to-earth contemporary romance and romantic suspense. From farmers to cowboys, Midwest to *the* West, Nicole writes stories about people finding themselves and finding love in the process. She lives in Missouri with her husband and two sons and dreams of someday owning a barn.

To late-night train whistles when everyone else is asleep
and the Janette Oke books that introduced me to
romance.

Chapter One

Bennet Stevens had learned how to smile politely and charmingly at people he couldn't stand before he'd learned to walk. Growing up in a family chock-full of lawyers and politicians, and many of the Texas rich and powerful, he'd been bred to be a charming, cunning tool.

His decision to go into police work had surprised, and perhaps not excited, his parents, but they weren't the type of people to stand in someone's way.

Everything was far more circumspect than that, and after five years as a Texas Ranger, easily moving up the ranks beyond his counterparts, Bennet was starting to wonder if *that's* how his parents were attempting to smoke him out.

Make everything too damn easy.

He was as tired of easy here at the Texas Rangers headquarters in Austin as he was of political parties at his parents' home where he was supposed to flirt with debutantes and impress stuffed suits with tales of his bravery and valor.

Which was why he was beyond determined to break one of the coldest cases his Texas Ranger unit had. The timing couldn't be more perfect, with his partner in the

Unsolved Crimes Investigation Unit taking some extended time off giving Bennet the opportunity to solve a case on his own.

He glanced over at said partner, Ranger Vaughn Cooper, who was leaning against the corner of their shared office, talking on his cell in low tones.

No amount of low tones could hide the fact taciturn Ranger Cooper was talking to his very pregnant wife. Bennet could only shake his head at how the mighty had fallen, and hard.

Vaughn said his goodbyes and shoved his phone into his pocket before he turned his attention to Bennet, assessing gaze and hard expression back in place. "Captain won't go for it," Vaughn said, nodding at the file on Bennet's desk.

"He might if you back me up."

Vaughn crossed his arms over his chest, and if Bennet hadn't worked with Vaughn for almost four years, he might have been intimidated or worried. But that steely-eyed glare meant Vaughn was considering it.

"I know you want more…"

"But?" Bennet supplied, forcing himself to grin as if this didn't mean everything. When people knew what it meant, they crushed it if they could. Another Stevens lesson imparted early and often.

"I'm not sure this case is the way to go. It's been sitting here for years."

"I believe that's the point of our department. Besides that, I've already found a new lead," Bennet said, never letting the easy smile leave his face.

Vaughn's eyebrows rose in surprise. "You have?"

"There was a murder around the same time as this case that the FBI linked to the Jimenez drug cartel. That victim's wounds were the same as the victim's wounds in our Jane Doe case. If Captain lets me take on this case, I want to find a connection."

Vaughn blew out a breath and nodded. "You have the FBI file?"

Bennet turned his laptop screen so Vaughn could read. Vaughn's expression changed, just a fraction, and for only a second, but Bennet caught it. And jumped. "What? What did you see?"

Vaughn sighed heavily. "I didn't *see* anything. It's just... Jimenez."

"What about it?"

"Alyssa Jimenez."

"I know that name." Bennet racked his brain for how, because it hadn't been in any of the files he'd been poring over lately. "The Stallion. Oh, she was with Gabby." Vaughn's sister-in-law had been the kidnapping victim of a madman who called himself The Stallion. Vaughn had worked the case to free Gabby and the handful of other girls she'd been in captivity with.

Including Alyssa Jimenez. "Wait. Are you telling me *she* has something to do with the Jimenez drug family?"

"I don't know that she does. But based on what I do know, I wouldn't be surprised."

"But you haven't followed up?" Bennet asked incredulously.

"Natalie and Gabby took her in after Gabby's release. They've adopted her like a sister, and I have yet to see anything that points to her being involved with any of the many members of the Jimenez drug cartel family."

"But you think she is," Bennet pressed, because Vaughn wouldn't have brought it up if he didn't.

"Alyssa is...different. It wouldn't surprise me if she

had connections to this family. She's built something of an underground bounty hunter business, and the contacts she has?" Vaughn shook his head. "I promised Gabby and Nat I wouldn't interfere unless it was directly part of my job."

"You? You, Mr. By-the-Book, promised not to investigate something?"

"She hasn't done anything wrong, and believe me, I've watched. *If* she's connected to that family, it's only biological. Not criminal. She's been through a lot."

"Wait. Wait. Isn't she the one who fought the FBI when they raided The Stallion's compound to release the women?"

Vaughn stood to his full height, disapproval written all over his face, but Bennet wouldn't let it stop him. Vaughn's family leave started tomorrow, and he couldn't stand in Bennet's way for weeks.

"She didn't fight them off. She just didn't exactly drop her weapon when they demanded her to do so. There is a difference. Now, Bennet, I need you to understand something."

Bennet held himself very still, especially since Vaughn rarely called him by his first name. They were partners, but Vaughn was older, more experienced, and Bennet had always looked up to him like something of a mentor.

"Do not let your need to do something big compromise your job, which is to do something *right*."

The lecture grated even though Bennet knew it was a good one, a fair one. But he didn't particularly want to be good or fair right now. He wanted to *do* something. He wanted a challenge. He wanted to feel less like this fake facade.

He would do all that by doing that something right, damn it. "I want her contact information."

"I didn't say I'd back you up. I didn't say—"

"I want her contact information," Bennet repeated, and this time he didn't smile or hide the edge in his voice. "I have found a lead that no one else has found, and I will rightfully and lawfully follow up on it once Captain Dean gives me the go-ahead. Now, you can either give it to me and smooth the way and let this be easy—for me *and* for her—or you can stand in my way and force me to drag her in here."

Vaughn's expression was icy, but Bennet couldn't worry about that. Not for this. So, he continued.

"You're out for a month to spend with your wife and your upcoming new addition. Take it. Enjoy it. And while you're gone, let me do my job the way I see fit."

Bennet couldn't read Vaughn's silence, but he supposed it didn't matter. Bennet had said his piece, and he'd made it very clear. He would not be dissuaded.

"If you get Captain Dean's go-ahead, I'll give you Gabby's contact information. It'll be the best way to get ahold of Alyssa."

When Bennet frowned, Vaughn's mouth curved into the closest it ever got to a smile on duty.

"Best of luck getting anything out of Gabby Torres."

Bennet forced himself to smile. "I can handle your sister-in-law." And he could handle this case, and the potential to crack it wide open. Starting with Alyssa Jimenez.

ALYSSA NEVER KNEW what to do when Gabby went into full protective mode. While Alyssa had grown up with five intimidating older brothers, they had protected her by throwing her in a room and locking the door, by teaching her to use any weapon she could get her hands on. They had protected her by hiding her.

Not ranting and raving about some half-cocked Texas Ranger wanting to talk to her.

Not that Alyssa needed Gabby's protection, but it was still interesting to watch.

"The *nerve* of that guy, thinking he can question you about something that doesn't even have anything to do with you!"

Alyssa sat with her elbows resting on her knees in a folding chair in the corner of her very odd little office. It was a foreclosed gas station in a crappy part of Austin, and Alyssa hadn't made any bones about making it look different from what it was. Shelves still stood in aisles, coolers stood empty and not running along the back wall. The only thing she'd done was add some seating—mostly stuff she'd found in the alley—and a desk that had a crack down the middle.

Her clientele didn't mind, and they knew where to find her without her having to advertise and attract potential…legal issues.

The only time the office space bothered Alyssa was when Gabby insisted on showing up. Even though Alyssa knew Gabby could take care of herself—she'd recently graduated from the police academy, and she'd survived eight years as a prisoner of The Stallion to Alyssa's two—Alyssa hated bringing people she cared about into this underworld.

"Alyssa. Are you listening?"

Alyssa shrugged. "Not really. You seem to be doing an excellent job of yelling all by yourself."

Gabby scowled at her, and it was moments like these

Alyssa didn't know what to do with. Where it felt like she had a sister, a family. People who cared about her. It made her want to cry, and it made her want to…

She didn't know. So, she ignored it. "I can talk to some Texas Ranger. I talk to all sorts of people all the time." Criminals. Law enforcement. Men who worked for her brothers, men who worked for the FBI, including Gabby's fiancé. Alyssa knew how to talk to anyone.

Maybe, just maybe, it made her a little nervous someone so close to Natalie and Gabby had possibly discovered her connection to one of the biggest cartels operating in the state of Texas, but she could handle it.

"Crap," Gabby muttered, looking at her phone. "Nat went into labor."

"Well, hurry up and get to the hospital."

"Come with me."

"No."

"Alyssa, you're ours now. Really."

"I know," Alyssa replied, even though it had been almost two years since escaping The Stallion and she still wasn't used to being considered part of the family. "But all that pushing and yelling and weird baby crap? I'm going to have to pass. I'll come visit when it's all over, so keep me posted. Besides, I have some work to catch up on. My trip to Amarillo took longer than I expected."

She'd brought a rapist to justice. Though she'd brought him in for a far more minor charge, the woman who'd come to her for help could rest assured her attacker was in jail.

It wasn't legal to act as bounty hunter without a license, but growing up in the shadow of a drug cartel family, Alyssa didn't exactly care about legal. She cared about righting some wrongs.

Some of that pride and certainty must have showed in her expression because Gabby sighed. "All right, I won't fight you on it. Get your work done and then, regardless of baby appearance, at least stop by the hospital tonight?"

"Fine."

Gabby pulled her into a quick hug, another gesture Alyssa had spent two years not knowing what to do with. But the Torres sisters had pulled her in and insisted she was part of their family.

It mattered, and Alyssa would do whatever she could to make sure she made them proud. She couldn't be a police officer like Gabby, or a trained hypnotist assisting the Texas Rangers like Natalie, but she could do this.

"See you tonight," Gabby said, heading for the door.

"Yes, ma'am."

Gabby left, and Alyssa sighed. Maybe she should have gone. Natalie had had a difficult pregnancy, enough so that her husband was taking almost an entire month off work to be home with her and the baby the first few weeks. And, no matter how uncomfortable Alyssa still was with the whole childbirth thing, they were her family.

Her good, upstanding chosen family. *Who don't know who you really are.*

Alyssa turned to her work. There was some paperwork to forge to collect her fee for the last guy she'd brought in, and then she had to check her makeshift mailbox to see if any more tips had been left for her. She worked by word of mouth, mostly for people who couldn't pay, hence the forging paperwork so she could pretend to be a licensed bounty hunter and collect enough of a fee to live off of.

Her front door screeched open, as the hinges weren't aligned or well oiled. She glanced over expecting to find a woman from the neighborhood, as those were usually her only word-of-mouth visitors.

Instead, a man stepped through the door, and for a few seconds Alyssa couldn't act, she could only stare. He was tall and broad, dressed in pressed khakis and a perfectly tailored button-down shirt, a Texas Ranger badge hooked to his belt. He wore a cowboy hat and a gun like he'd been born with them.

Alyssa's heart beat twice its normal rhythm, something unrecognizable fluttering in her chest. His dark hair was thick and wavy, and not buzzed short like most Texas Rangers she'd come into contact with. His eyes were a startling blue, and his mouth—

Wait. Why was she staring at his mouth?

The man's brows drew together as he looked around the room. He cleared his throat. "I'm sorry, are you… You are Alyssa Jimenez, aren't you?"

"And you must be the Texas Ranger Gabby's trying to hide me from," Alyssa offered drily. "How *did* you find me?"

"I followed Gabby."

She laughed, couldn't help it. She'd expected him to lie or have some high-tech way for having found her not-publicly-listed office. But he'd told her the truth. "Awfully sneaky and underhanded for a Ranger."

His mouth curved, and the fluttering was back tenfold. He had a movie-star smile, all charm and white teeth, and while Alyssa had seen men like that in her life, she'd never, ever had that kind of smile directed at *her*.

"You must know Ranger Cooper, antithesis of all that is sneaky and underhanded. We aren't all like that."

Something about all that fluttering turned into a spiral, one that arrowed down her chest and into her belly. She felt oddly shaky, and Alyssa had long ago learned how to ward off shaky. She'd grown up in isolation as part of a criminal family. Then she'd been kidnapped for two years, locked away in little more than a bunker.

She was not a weakling. She was never scared. The scariest parts of her life were over, but something about this man sent her as off-kilter as she'd ever been.

It wasn't fear for her life or the need to fight off an attacker, but she didn't know *what* it was, and that was the scariest thing of all.

"Why are you here?" she asked, edging behind her cracked desk. She had a knife strapped to her ankle, but she'd prefer the Glock she'd shoved in the drawer when Gabby had stormed in an hour earlier.

She wouldn't use either on him, but she didn't want him to think she was going to do whatever he wanted either. He might be a Texas Ranger, but he couldn't waltz in here and get whatever he wanted. Especially if what he wanted was information about Jimenez.

"I have some questions for you, Ms. Jimenez, that's all."

"Then why is everyone trying so hard to keep you from meeting me?" Alyssa returned, sliding her hand into the drawer.

The Ranger's eyes flicked to the movement, and she didn't miss the way his hand slowly rose to the holster of *his* weapon. She paused her movement completely, but she didn't retract her hand.

"Maybe they're afraid of what I'll find out."

She raised her gaze from his gun to those shocking blue eyes. His expression was flat and grim, so very *police*. Worst of all, it sent a shiver of fear through her.

There were so very many things he could find out.

Chapter Two

Bennet didn't know what to make out of Alyssa's closed-down gas station of an office. Could anyone call this an office? It looked like nothing more than an abandoned building, except maybe she'd swept the floors a little. But the windows were grimy, the lights dim, and most of the debris of a convenience store were still scattered about.

Then there was this pretty force of a woman standing in the midst of all of it as though it were a sleek, modern office building in downtown Austin.

She wore jeans and a leather jacket over a T-shirt. The boots on her feet looked like they might weigh as much as her. Her dark hair was pulled back, and her dark eyes flashed with suspicion.

Something about her poked at him, deep in his gut. He tried to convince himself he must have dealt with her before, criminally, but he was too practical to convince himself of a lie. Whatever that poke was, it wasn't work related.

But he was here to work. To finally do something worthwhile. With no help from any outside forces.

She didn't take her hand off what he assumed to be a weapon in the drawer of her desk—though it was hidden from his view—so he kept his hand on his. Alyssa might be a friend of people he knew, but that didn't mean he trusted her.

"I guess what you find out depends on what you're looking for, Ranger…" She looked expectantly at him.

Though she was clearly suspicious, defensive even, she didn't appear nervous or scared, so he went ahead and took his hand off the butt of his weapon. He held out his hand between them. "Bennet Stevens. And I don't know why your friends are being so protective of you. All I'm after is a little information about a case I'm working on. If you have no connection to it, I'll happily walk away and not bother you again."

Nothing in her expression changed. She watched him and his outstretched hand warily. She was doing some sort of mental calculation, and Bennet figured he could wait that out and keep his hand outstretched for as long as it took.

"What kind of case?"

"A murder."

She laughed, and something in his gut tightened, a completely unwelcome sensation. She had a sexy laugh, and it was the last thing he had any business noticing.

"I can assure you I have nothing to do with any murders," Alyssa said, still ignoring his outstretched hand.

"Then what do you have to do with?" he asked, giving up on the handshake.

She cocked her head at him. "I'm pretty sure you said that if I didn't have anything to do with your case, you'd leave me alone. Well, you know where the door is."

He glanced at the door even though there was no way he was retreating anytime soon. His initial plan had been to come in here and be friendly and subtle, ease into things.

It was clear Alyssa wasn't going to respond to subtle or friendly. Which meant he had to go with the straight-forward tactic, even if it ended up offending his friends.

He held up his hands, palms toward her, a clear sign he wouldn't be reaching for his weapon as he slowly withdrew two papers from his shirt's front pocket.

He unfolded the papers and handed the top one to her. "Is that you?"

It was a picture of a young girl, surrounded by five dangerous-looking men. Men who were confirmed to be part of the Jimenez drug cartel.

Bennet had no doubt the girl in the picture was Alyssa. Though she did look different as an adult, there were too many similarities. Chief among them the stony expression on her face.

She looked at the picture for an abnormally long time in utter silence.

"Ms. Jimenez?"

She looked up at him, and there wasn't just stony stoicism or cynicism in her expression anymore, there was something a lot closer to hatred. She dropped the picture on her ramshackle desk.

"I really doubt I need to answer that question since you're here. You've decided it's me whether I confirm it or not. You clearly know who those men are, decided I'm connected to them. I doubt you'll believe me, but let me head you off at the pass. I have not contacted any-one with the last name Jimenez since I was *kidnapped* at the age of twenty."

He wouldn't let that soften him. "Then I guess it's fit-ting that the case I'm looking into is sixteen years old."

Confusion drew her eyebrows together. "You want to question me about a crime that happened when I was eight?"

"Yes."

She made a scoffing noise disguised as a laugh. "All right, Ranger Hotshot. Hit me."

"Sixteen years ago, a Jane Doe was found murdered. She's never been identified, but I found some similarities between her case and a case connected to the Jimenez family. *Your* family. I'd like to bring some closure to this cold case, and I think you can help."

"I was eight. Whatever my brothers were doing, I had no part in."

"Brothers?"

She didn't move, didn't say anything, but Bennet nearly smiled. She'd slipped up and given him more information than he'd had. He'd known Alyssa was connected, but he hadn't known how close.

Yeah, she was going to be exactly what he needed. "I'd like you to look at the picture of the Jane Doe and let me know if you remember ever seeing her with your *brothers*. It's not an incredibly graphic picture, but it can be disconcerting for some people to view pictures of dead bodies."

Alyssa rolled her eyes and snatched up the picture. "I work as a bounty hunter. I think I can stand the sight of a…" But she trailed off and paled. She sank into the folding chair so hard it broke and she fell to the ground.

Bennet was at her side not quite in time to keep her ass from hitting the floor. "Are you okay?"

She was shaking, seemed not to have noticed she'd broken a chair and was sitting in its debris, the picture fisted in her hand.

"Alyssa?"

When she finally brought her gaze to his, those brown eyes were wide and wet and she was clearly in shock.

"Where'd you get this?" she demanded in a whisper, her hands shaking. Hell, her whole body was shaking. Her brown eyes bored into his. "This is a lie. This has to be a lie." Her voice cracked.

"You know her?" he asked, gently rubbing a hand up and down her forearm, trying to offer *something* to help her stop shaking so hard.

Alyssa looked back down at the picture that shook in her hands. "That's my mother."

THE TEARS WERE sharp and burning, but Alyssa did everything she could to keep them from falling. She forced herself to look away from the picture and shoved it back at the Texas Ranger, whatever his name was.

It wasn't true. It couldn't be true. Her mother had *left* her. She'd been seduced away by some rival of her father's. *That* was the story.

Not murder.

It didn't make sense. None of it made any sense. She tried to get ahold of her labored breathing, but no matter how much she told herself to breathe slowly in and out, she could only gasp and pant, that picture of her mother's lifeless face seared into her brain forever.

Murder.

She realized the Ranger had stopped rubbing her arm in that oddly comforting gesture and instead curled long, strong fingers around both her elbows.

"Come on," he said gently, pulling her to her feet.

Since the debris of the rickety chair that had broken

underneath her weight was starting to dig into her butt, she let him do it. Once she was standing somewhere close to steady on her feet, he didn't release her. No, that strong grip stayed right where it was on her elbows.

It was centering somehow, that firm, warm pressure. A reminder she existed in the here and now, not in one of the different prisons her life had been.

She blinked up at the Texas Ranger holding her steady. There was something like compassion in his blue eyes, maybe even regret. His full lips were down-turned, slight grooves bracketing his mouth.

He was something like pretty, and she'd rather have those cheekbones and that square jaw burned into her brain than the image of her dead mother.

"If I'd had any idea, Alyssa…" he said, his voice gravel and his tone overly familiar.

She pulled herself out of his grasp, pulled into herself, like she'd learned how to do time and time again as the inconsequential daughter of a criminal, as a useless kidnapping victim.

She'd spent the last two years trying to build a life for herself where she might matter, where she might do some *good*.

This moment forced her back into all the ways she'd never mattered. What other lies she'd accepted as truth might be waiting for her?

She closed her eyes against the onslaught of pain. And fear.

"My brothers didn't murder my mother, Ranger Stevens," Alyssa managed, though her voice was rusty. "I know they're not exactly heroes, but they never would have killed my mother."

"Okay." He was quiet for a few humming seconds. "Maybe you'd like to help me find out who did."

She didn't move, didn't emote. She'd worked with law enforcement before, but she was careful about it. They usually didn't know her name or her friends. They definitely didn't know her connection to the Jimenez family.

This man knew all of that and had to look like Superman in a cowboy hat on top of it. The last thing she should consider was working with him.

Except her mother was dead. Murdered. A Jane Doe for well over a decade, and as much as she couldn't believe her brothers had anything to do with her mother's murder—*murder*—she couldn't believe they didn't know. There was no way Miranda Jimenez had stayed a Jane Doe without her family purposefully making sure she did.

Alyssa swallowed. Making sure her mother had stayed a Jane Doe, all the while making sure Alyssa didn't know about it. Her brothers had always claimed they were protecting her by keeping things from her, and it was hard to doubt. They *had* meant well. If they hadn't, she'd have been dead or auctioned off to some faithful servant of her father's before she'd ever been kidnapped.

Ranger Stevens released her, and she felt cold without that warm, sturdy grip. Cold and alone. *Well, that's what you are. What you'll always have to be.*

"Take some time. Come to grips with this new information, and when you're ready to work with me, give me a call." He pulled his wallet out of his back pocket and handed her a card from it.

She took the card. That big star emblem of the Rangers seemed to stare at her. It looked so official, so *he-roic*, that symbol. Right next to it, his name, *Bennet E. Stevens. Ranger.*

She glanced back up at him, and was more than a little irritated she saw kindness in his expression. She didn't want kindness or compassion. She didn't know what to do with those things, and she already got them in spades from Gabby and Natalie and even to an extent from their law enforcement significant others.

Everyone felt sorry for Alyssa Jimenez, but no one knew who she really was. Except this man.

"Do you have a phone number I can reach you at?" he prompted when she didn't say anything.

She didn't want to give him her number. She didn't want to give him anything. She wanted to rewind the last half hour and go with Gabby to the hospital. She would have avoided this whole thing.

Not forever, though. She was too practical to think it would have lasted forever.

"Fine," she muttered, because, as much as she knew she'd end up working with this guy, the promise of solving her mother's murder was too great, too important, and she didn't want to give him too much leverage. She'd make him think she was reticent, doing *him* a favor when she finally agreed.

She grabbed a pen and scrap of paper from her desk and scrawled her number on it. He took it, sliding it into his pocket along with the pictures he'd retrieved. She'd wanted to keep them, but she had to keep it cool. She'd get them eventually.

"I'll be in touch, Alyssa," he said with a tip of his hat. He paused for a second, hesitating. "I am sorry for your loss," he said gravely, before turning and exiting her office.

She let out a shaky sigh. The worst thing was believing that kind of crap. Why would he be sorry? He didn't know her or her mother. It was a lame, placating statement.

It soothed somehow, idiot that she was. She shook her head and collected her belongings. She'd stop by the hospital to check on Natalie and Gabby, and then she'd go home and try to sleep. She'd give it a day, maybe two, then she'd call Ranger Too-Hot-For-Her-Own-Good.

She locked up and exited out the back, pulling her helmet on before starting her motorcycle. It was her most expensive possession, and she treated it like a baby. Nothing in the world gave her the freedom that motorcycle did.

She rode out of the alley and onto the street that would lead her to the highway and the hospital. Within two minutes, she knew she was being followed.

Her first inclination was that it was Ranger Stevens keeping tabs on her, but the jacked-up piece-of-crap car following her was no Texas Ranger vehicle.

She scowled and narrowed her eyes. Of course, anyone could be following her, but after the Ranger's visit and information, Alyssa had the sneaking suspicion it was all related.

Maybe her brothers had ignored her existence since she'd been kidnapped and then released, but that didn't mean they couldn't find her if they wanted to.

If they were after her now, they wouldn't give up until they got her. But that didn't mean she had to go down easy. Certainly not after they'd abandoned her.

She took a sharp turn onto a side street, then weaved

in and out of traffic the way the car couldn't. She took a few more sharp turns, earning honks and angry middle fingers from other drivers, but eventually she found herself in a dark, small alley. She killed her engine and stood there straddling her bike, breathing heavily.

Did her brothers know Ranger Stevens was investigating their mother's death? Did they have something to hide?

She squeezed her eyes shut, finding her even breathing. They couldn't have killed their mother. They couldn't have. Alyssa couldn't bring herself to believe it.

Her phone rang and she swore, expecting it to be news about Natalie's baby. Instead, it was a number she didn't recognize. Her brothers?

She hit Accept cautiously, and adopted her best take-no-crap tone. "What?"

"You're being tailed."

She scowled at Ranger Steven's voice. "I'm well aware. I lost them."

"Yeah, well, I'm tailing them now."

"Idiot," she muttered. How had this man stepped into her life for fifteen minutes and scrambled everything up?

"What?" Ranger Stevens spluttered.

Alyssa had to think fast. To move. Oh, damn the man for getting in the way of things. "Listen, I'm coming back out. I want you to let them follow me. And when they take me, I need you to not get in the way." Her brothers had never come for her, and she'd stopped expecting them, but if they were coming for her now... she was ready.

As long as she could get rid of the Texas Ranger trying to protect her.

Chapter Three

Bennet wanted to argue, but he had to keep too much of his attention on following the men who'd been following Alyssa to try to outtalk this girl.

Let them take her? "Are you crazy?"

"We both know it's someone from my family, or sent by them anyway. If I let them take me, I get information."

"And end up like your mother." Which was probably too blunt when she'd only just found out about her mother, but he couldn't keep compassion in place when she was talking about getting herself abducted.

He heard a motorcycle engine roar past him, and swore when Alyssa waved at him.

He tossed his phone into the passenger seat and followed. It was reckless and possibly stupid not to call for backup. But while Captain Dean had given him the go-ahead to take on this case, Bennet wasn't ready to bring in other people yet. He needed more information. He needed to know what he was dealing with.

The fact of the matter was he had no idea what he was dealing with when it came to Alyssa Jimenez.

She cut in front of the car that had originally been following her. He watched the streetlights streak across her quickly moving form, and she waved at those guys too.

She *was* crazy.

While Bennet had been worried in the beginning that the tail's goal had been to hurt Alyssa, it was clear they were after something else. If they wanted to hurt her, they could run her off the road and drive away. No one would know the difference except him, and Bennet didn't think they knew *they* had a tail.

It was clear they wanted Alyssa. Whole. She had wanted him to let them take her, so it seemed she knew she wasn't in imminent danger from these people, as well.

Was she working with them? Was he the fool here?

Except when she finally quit driving, he could only stare from his place farther down the street. She'd led them to the public parking of the Texas Rangers headquarters.

What on earth was this woman up to?

She parked in the middle of the mostly empty parking lot—employees parked in the back and public visitors rarely arrived at night. The car that had been following her stopped at the parking lot entrance. Clearly her followers didn't know what to do with this.

Bennet made a turn, keeping the parking lot in view from his rearview window. When the car didn't follow, the occupants instead kept their attention on Alyssa, he knew they hadn't seen him following them.

He made a quick sharp turn into the back lot and then drove along the building, parking as close as he could to where Alyssa was without being seen. He got out of his car and unholstered his weapon. He crept along the building, keeping himself in the shadows, watching as the car still idled in the entrance while Alyssa sat defiantly on her motorcycle in the middle of the parking lot, parking lights haloing her.

That uncomfortable thing from before tightened in his gut at the way the light glinted off her dark hair when she pulled off her helmet. Something a little lower than his gut reacted far too much at the "screw you" in the curve of her mouth. She looked like some fierce warrior, some underground-gang queen. He should not be attracted to that even for a second.

Apparently some parts of his anatomy weren't as interested in law and order as his brain was.

"What are you guys? Chicken?" Alyssa called out.

Bennet nearly groaned. She would have to be the kind of woman who'd provoke them.

"How about this—you send a message to my brothers. You tell them if they want me, they can come get me themselves. No cut-rate, brainless thug is going to take me anywhere I don't want to go."

The engine revved, and Bennet moved closer. He wasn't going to let these men take his only lead on this case. Even if she was trying to get herself killed.

But in the end, the car merely backed out and screeched away.

Leaving him and Alyssa in a mostly empty parking lot.

She turned to face him as if she'd known he was there all along. "I bet that got their attention, huh?" she said. She didn't walk toward him, so he walked to her.

"Yes. How smart. Piss off your criminal brothers you claim to have nothing to do with so they come after you."

"Yes, exactly."

"I thought you wanted me to let them take you." Which he never would have done.

"I was going to, but then I saw what cut-rate weaklings they sent after me. Afraid of a little Texas Ranger parking lot." She made a scoffing sound. "The only way to really get some answers is to get inside again, but guys like that? Dopes with guns? Yeah, I'm not risking my life with them. My brothers can come get me themselves if it's that important to them."

"You're not going back inside that family."

She raised an eyebrow at him. "Since when did you become my keeper?"

"Since I'm the reason you think you need to go back there. We'll investigate this from the outside. You don't need to be on the inside." He'd sacrifice a lot to actually accomplish something, but not someone else's life.

"Shows what you know. Not a damn thing. I've been gone a long time, but I still know how the Jimenez family works. I can get the answers we need."

"*We* need?"

She looked at her motorcycle, helmet still dangling from her fingertips. He'd watched her shake and tremble apart after seeing her mother's picture, but she was nothing but strength and certainty now.

Again, Bennet couldn't help but wonder if he was the sucker here, if he was being pulled into something that would end up making a fool out of him. But he'd come too far to back out. Gotten the okay on this case, gotten to Alyssa. He had to keep moving forward.

"My brothers didn't murder our mom," she said, raising her gaze to his. Strong and sure. "I know they didn't. I'm going to prove it. To you. And when you find out who really did it, you can bring them to justice."

Her voice shook at the end, though her shoulders-back, chin-up stance didn't change.

He couldn't trust her. She was related to one of the biggest drug cartels in the state. And while Gabby and Natalie had befriended her, and Vaughn thought she hadn't had contact with her brothers in years, this felt awfully coincidental.

She must have seen the direction of his thoughts. "You don't have to trust me, Ranger Stevens. You just have to stay out of my way."

"I'm afraid I can't do that." No matter what it took, he had knocked over whatever domino was creating these events. He was part of it, and whether he trusted her or not, he had some responsibility for bringing her into this.

"They must have my office bugged," Alyssa said, scowling. "The timing is too coincidental, too weird. It's been two years since the kidnapping rescue, and they've left me alone. They had to have heard you questioning me. So, they know. You have to stay out of my way so we can know what's *really* going on."

"How can you think they had nothing to do with it if they're stepping in now when they supposedly know what I'm after?"

"They didn't kill our mother, but cartel business is tricky. Complicated. Their never identifying her when she was Jane Doe, it could be purposeful or they feel like they can't now or... I don't know, but I have to find out. I'm going in. You can't stop me, and God knows you can't stop them."

He didn't agree with that. He could put a security detail on her, keep her safe and away from her brothers for the foreseeable future. Even if the Rangers pulled support, he had enough of his own money to make it so.

But it'd be awfully hard to make it so when she was so determined, and it'd make it harder to get the information he needed. It would make it almost impossible to solve this case.

He studied her, looking at him so defiantly, as if she was the one in charge here. As if she could stand up to him, toe-to-toe, over and over again. Some odd thing shuddered through him, a gut feeling he didn't want to pay attention to.

He'd made his decision, so there was only one way to settle this. "If you're going in, then I'm going in with you."

AND THIS TEXAS Ranger thought *she* was crazy.

"You think you're going to come with me. You think in *any* world my brothers would allow a Texas Ranger into their home or office or whatever without, oh, say killing you and making sure no one ever found out about it?"

"Except you."

Unfortunately, he had a point. Also unfortunately, her last name might keep her safe for the most part when it came to the Jimenez family, but she knew without a shadow of a doubt, if she outright betrayed her family, she'd be killed.

Like your mother.

She couldn't get over it, so she just kept pushing the reality out of her mind as much as she could. Still, it lingered in whispers. *Murdered. Murdered. Murdered.* How on earth could Mom have been murdered? It didn't make any sense.

Except she left. Betrayed your father. Maybe it makes all the sense in the world.

She couldn't. She just couldn't. She couldn't focus on possibility. She had to focus on truth.

"I can handle this," Ranger Stevens said resolutely.

"No. You can handle being a Texas Ranger. You can handle being a cop. You can't handle being inside a drug cartel. Even if they let you, you'd want to arrest everyone. And trust me, that wouldn't go well for you."

"They didn't hurt you. They ran away."

"Of course they didn't hurt me. Even if I'm not involved in the business, I'm the daughter of a cartel kingpin. I'm the sister of the people who run it. They hurt me, they're dead. It's a matter of honor, but that doesn't mean that protection extends to you." Or to her, if she betrayed Jimenez.

"So we'll have to find a way for them to think it's a matter of honor not to kill me."

"How on earth do you suggest we do that?"

"I have a few ideas, but I'm not discussing them here in this parking lot." He gestured toward the Texas Rangers building.

Alyssa laughed. "I'm not going in there. My brothers are going to think I'm working with you on a lot more than Mom's…" she cleared her throat of the lump "…murder."

"You know it isn't just me at stake here. Natalie and Gabby. Their families. They're a part of your life, and now—"

She took a threatening step toward him—or it might have been threatening, if he wasn't about six inches taller than her and twice as wide. "You don't think I know that? You don't think I have made my life very separate so they would never get pulled into this if I had to be?"

"I don't know you at all, Alyssa. I don't know what your plans are."

"My plan is to live a normal life. That's all I want." She realized, too late, she'd yelled it, shaking all over again. Normal had seemed almost within reach lately, and then this Texas Ranger had walked into her office and everything had changed.

She was Alyssa Jimenez again. Not bounty hunter and friend, not even kidnapping victim, or the inconsequential relative of very consequential people. She was in danger and in trouble, and she couldn't do anything about it.

He reached out, and she hated that something like a simple touch on her arm could just *soothe*. She'd never understood it, but Gabby would hug her back in that bunker, and even out here in the open, and everything would feel okay. This guy, this stranger of a Texas Ranger, touched her, and it felt like she could handle whatever came if he was touching her.

It was insanity.

"If they bugged your office, it's likely they've bugged your house."

Alyssa thought of her little apartment above Gabby and Jaime's garage. Was it bugged? Was the whole house bugged? Had she brought all of her family's problems into the house they'd been kind enough to open up to her?

Guilt swamped her, pain. Tears threatened, but she wouldn't be that weak. She'd fix this. She had to fix this.

"Come home with me."

She jerked her head up to look at Ranger Stevens and

carefully pulled herself out of his grasp. Everything in her rebelled at the idea of going home with him. His house. His life. Him.

"I have a big house. Multiple rooms. You can have your own bathroom, your own space. We can get some sleep, and in the morning we can talk knowing that no one has bugged my place."

"They know who you are now. If they bugged my place, they know your name. They know what you're after."

He seemed to consider that with more weight than she thought he would. "All right. I have somewhere else we can go. It might require a little bending of the truth."

Alyssa frowned at him. "What kind of bending of the truth?"

"We'll just need to pretend this isn't related to my job. That you're not so much a professional acquaintance but a, ah, personal one."

"Where the hell are you taking me?" she demanded, touching her bike to remind herself she was free. He couldn't take her anywhere unless she agreed.

And if you go home, would you be putting Gabby and Jaime in jeopardy?

"My parents have a guesthouse. I use it on occasion when necessary. I can say I'm having my house painted or remodeled or something and they'll believe it, if they're even home. But if I'm bringing you with me, they're going to need to think…" He cleared his throat.

Alyssa's mouth went slack as it dawned on her what he was suggesting. "You want me to pretend to be involved with you like…sleeping-over involved?" Her voice squeaked and her entire face heated. Her whole body heated. She'd never been sleeping-over involved with anyone, and she was pretty sure that was a really lame way of putting it, but she didn't know how else to say it.

She didn't know how to wrap her head around what he was suggesting.

"My parents aren't invasive exactly. Actually, they're incredibly invasive, but like I said, it's unlikely they're there. They have some of the best security in Austin, so we'll be safe, or at least forewarned. Should one of the staff mention I had a woman over, then they'll assume it's personal and we'll just go with it."

"Your parents have a guesthouse and staff?"

"Your father runs a drug cartel?" he returned in the same put-off tone.

She wanted to laugh even though it wasn't funny in the least little bit. "No one's going to believe I'm involved with...*you*."

Something in his expression changed, a softening followed by an all-too-charming smile that had her heart beating hard against her chest.

"Am I that hideous?" he asked, clearly knowing full well he was *not*.

"You know what I mean. I look like a street urchin," she said, waving a hand down her front. "You look like..." She waved her hand ineffectually at him.

He cocked his head. "I look like what?" he asked, and there was something a little darker in his tone. Dangerous. But cops weren't dangerous. Not like that.

"I don't know," she muttered, knowing she had to be blushing so profusely even the bad lighting couldn't hide it. "A guy who has servants and guesthouses and crap."

"They'll believe it because there's no reason not to.

Street-urchin chic or no, my parents wouldn't doubt me. They might assume I'm trying to give them an aneurism, but they won't suspect anything."

Alyssa looked at her bike. She could hop on, flip him off and zoom away. Zoom away from everything she'd built in the past two years, zoom away from everything that had held her prisoner for the first twenty-two.

But she hadn't left Austin on her release from her kidnapper, and she had people to protect now. She couldn't leave Gabby and Natalie in the middle of this, even if they were both married to men or living with men who would try to protect them.

She studied Ranger Stevens and knew she had to make a choice. Fight, and trust this man. Or run, and ruin them all.

It wasn't a hard choice in the slightest. "All right. I'll go."

Chapter Four

Bennet drove from the Texas Ranger offices to his parents' sprawling estate outside Austin. It wasn't the first time he'd been self-conscious about his parents' wealth. Most of the cops and Rangers he knew were not the sons and daughters of the Texas elite.

Nevertheless, this was the life he'd been born into, and Alyssa hadn't been born into a much different one. Just on opposite sides of the law, but if her father was the Jimenez kingpin, then she'd had her share of wealth.

She followed him, the roar of her motorcycle cutting through the quiet of the wealthy neighborhood enough to make him wince. There would be phone calls. There would be a lot of things. But the most important thing was they were going somewhere that couldn't have been infiltrated.

He drove up the sprawling drive after entering the code for the gate and hoped against hope his father was in DC and his mother was at a function or, well, anywhere but here. Because while they might ignore his presence, maybe, they would never ignore the presence of the motorcycle.

Parking at the top of the drive, he got out of his running car and punched the code into the garage door so it opened.

"*This* is a guesthouse?" Alyssa called out over the sound of her motorcycle.

Bennet nodded as the garage door went up. He walked back to his car and motioned for her to park inside the garage. Maybe if the evidence was hidden, and it was late enough, it was possible no one would notice the disturbance. A man could dream.

Alyssa walked her motorcycle into the garage and killed the engine. She pulled off her helmet. It seemed no matter how often her hair tumbled out like that, his idiotic body had a reaction. He really needed to get a handle on that.

"Follow me," he said, probably too tersely. But he felt terse and uncomfortable. He felt a lot of things he didn't want to think about.

He slid the key he always kept on his ring into the lock of the door from the garage to the mudroom. He didn't look back to see how she reacted to the rather ostentatious guesthouse as they walked through it. It wasn't his.

He led her into the living room. "Feel free to use anything in the house. The fridge probably won't be stocked, but the pantry is. The staff keeps everything clean and fresh for visitors, so—"

"You keep saying 'staff,' but I have a feeling what you mean is servants."

He gave her a doleful look. "I'll show you to a bedroom and bathroom you can use. I suggest we get some sleep and reevaluate in the morning."

"Reevaluate what?"

"How we're going to handle getting me into see your brothers with you."

"There's no way. There's *no* way. They'll kill you on sight knowing you're a Texas Ranger. They have all this time while we're 'reevaluating' to plan to kill you and make it look like an accident, make you just disappear." She snapped her fingers. "It will be suicide. I don't think you get that."

"I told you I had some ideas."

"Like what?"

"Like what we're doing right here."

She threw her arms up in the air, clearly frustrated with him. "What are we doing right here?

"If your brothers think that we…" He cleared his throat, uncomfortable with his own idea, with telling it to her, with *enacting* it. But it made sense. It was the only thing that made sense. No matter how much he didn't want to do it. "If your brothers think we are romantically involved, there's a chance they wouldn't touch me. If I were important to you."

Alyssa blinked at him for a full minute. "First of all," she said eventually, "even if that was remotely true, if they have my office bugged, they know we just met. It was part of that conversation."

"We'll say it was a lure."

"You can't be this stupid. You can't be."

That offhanded insult poked at a million things he'd never admit to. "I assure you, Ms. Jimenez, I know what I'm doing," he said, crossing his arms over his chest and giving her a look that had intimidated drug dealers and rapists and even murderers.

Alyssa rolled her eyes. "Spare me the 'Ms. Jimenez' crap. It makes far more sense for me to go there on my own and handle things my own way. You can trust me when I say I want to get to the bottom of my mother's murder more than you do. I have no reason not to bring you whatever information I find so my mother's murderer can be brought to justice."

"I think you're bright enough to realize all of this is so much more than a murder case. The things your brothers are involved in aren't that easy. It's not something I can trust a civilian to go into and bring me back the information I need to prosecute. I need to go in there with you. I need to investigate this myself."

She shook her head in disgust, but she didn't argue further. Which was a plus.

"How far are you willing to go?" she demanded.

"As far as I need to. This case is my number one priority. I won't rest until it's solved."

She sighed while looking around the living room. "I can't sit anywhere in here. I'll stain all this white just by looking at it."

He rolled his eyes and took her by the elbow, leading her to a chair. It *was* white, and it was very possible she'd get motorcycle grease or something on it, but it would be taken care of. Stains in the Stevens world were always taken care of.

He pushed her into the chair. She sat with an audible thump. "What about this? You tell them I'm a double agent. That I want to be a dirty cop."

"They wouldn't believe that."

"Why not?"

"Because you are the antithesis of a dirty cop. You look like Superman had a baby with Captain America and every other do-gooder superhero to ever exist. No one would believe you want to be a dirty cop."

"Have you ever had any contact with a dirty cop?"

"Well, no."

He took a seat on the couch, leaning forward and resting his elbows on his knees. He never took his eyes off her—this was too important. "It has nothing to do with what you look like and everything to do with how desperate you are. How powerful you want to feel. Cops go dirty because… Well, there are a lot of reasons, but it's not about how you look or where you're from. It's about ego, among other things."

"Okay, it's about ego, which I'll give you you've got, but that doesn't mean they're going to believe any of it."

"It doesn't mean they won't."

"You're not going to give up on this, are you?"

"We can do it the easy way or the hard way. The easy way is where you work with me. The hard way is where you work against me. Either way, I'm doing it."

She sighed gustily, but he could see in the set of her shoulders she was relenting. Giving in. One way or another, she was going to give in.

"Fine. But we're not doing it your way. If we're doing it together, when it comes to my brothers, we do it *my* way. I tell them I'm using you to get information. I don't know if they'll buy it hook, line and sinker, but it's better than all your ideas."

"Gee, thank you."

"I'm afraid you're going to have to leave your ego at the door, Mr. Texas Ranger."

"I'll see what I can do."

Alyssa rubbed her temples. She had to be exhausted and stressed and emotionally wrung out from the things she'd found out today.

"Let's go to bed. We'll work out the details in the morning."

She sighed and pushed herself out of the chair. "Fine. Lead me to my castle."

"You're awfully melodramatic for a street urchin."

"I'm not the one living in this place."

"I don't live in this place," he muttered, standing, as well.

"You also don't live in an apartment above a garage."

"Is that where you live?" Which was neither here nor there, knowing where she lived or anything about her current life. All that mattered was her connection to the Jimenez family.

"Yes. I live in an apartment above the garage of my friends' house. My friends who are now in danger because of me, because of this." She let out a long sigh and faced him, her expression grave, her eyes reflecting some of the fear she'd kept impressively hidden thus far. "I need them safe, Ranger Stevens."

"I may not know Gabby very well, but I've worked with Jaime on occasion, and Vaughn has been my partner for a long time. I care about your friends. They're *my* friends, too. Nothing's going to happen to them."

"My, you are a confident one."

But no matter how sarcastically she'd said it, he could see a slight relaxation in her. His confidence gave her comfort. "Confidence is everything."

"Except when you have nothing."

Bennet didn't know what to say to that, so he led her down a hallway to the bedrooms. The farthest one from his. It would be the best room for her, not just for keeping her far away from him. He wasn't that weak to need a barrier, or so he'd tell himself.

"That door back there leads to a private bathroom. Feel free to use it and anything in it. I'll see you in the morning."

"Hey, have you heard anything from Vaughn about Nat?"

Bennet looked down at his phone. "I don't have any messages."

"I don't know what to tell them. They'll expect me to visit, and…" She shook her head, looking young and vulnerable for the first time since she'd seen the picture of her mother.

He wanted to help. He wanted to soothe. Which was just his *nature*. He was a guy who wanted to help. It had nothing to do with soft brown eyes and a pretty mouth.

"You're a bounty hunter, right? Well, an unauthorized and illegal one, anyway."

She frowned at him. "Yes. I have my reasons."

"Criminals always do." But he grinned, hoping the joke, the teasing, would lighten her up, take that vulnerable cast of her mouth away. "Tell them you had an important case, and you'll be back as soon as possible. You're not going back to your place, so it's not like they'll have any reason to believe you're in town."

"I don't like lying to them."

"It's not my favorite either, but—"

"I know. It'll keep them safe, and that is the most important thing to me."

"It's important to me, too. Never doubt that."

She nodded, hugging herself and looking around the room. "You know this kind of insane show of wealth is usually the sign of a small dick, right?"

He choked on his own spit. That had not been at all

what he'd expected her to say, but from her grin he could tell that's exactly why she'd said it.

"I suppose that's something you'd have to take up with my father, since this is neither my show of wealth, nor is that a complaint I've ever received."

Two twin blotches of pink showed up on her cheeks, and Bennet knew it was time to close the door and walk away before there were any more jokes about…that.

"Are you sure your parents won't get wind of this?"

"Unless it furthers their political agenda, my parents won't be sticking their nose anywhere near it. They'll stay out of it and safe."

"Political agenda?"

"Oh, didn't you put it together?" he asked casually, because he knew much like her small-dick comment had caught *him* off guard, this little tidbit would catch *her* off guard.

"Put what together?"

"My father is Gary L. Stevens, US senator and former presidential candidate. My mother is Lynette Stevens, pioneer lawyer and Texas state senator. You may have heard of them."

She stared slack-jawed at him, and he couldn't ignore the pleasure he got out of leaving her in shock. So he flashed a grin, his politicians' son grin.

"Good night, Alyssa."

And Bennet left her room, closing the door behind him.

ALYSSA TOSSED AND TURNED. Between trying to come to full grips with the fact that Bennet Stevens was the son of two wealthy and influential politicians, and Gabby being mad about her taking a job before coming to see the baby, she couldn't get her mind to stop running in circles.

She hated when someone was mad at her and had every right to be. She hated disappointing Gabby and Nat. But this was keeping them safe, and she had to remember that.

And more than all of that, the thing she kept trying to pretend wasn't true.

Her mother had been murdered. She knew Ranger Stevens suspected her brothers. No matter what horrible things they were capable of, though—and they were enormously capable—Alyssa rejected the idea they could be behind the murder of her mother. *Their* mother.

Maybe she could see it if her father was still in his right mind, but he had succumbed to some kind of dementia before she'd even been kidnapped. He was nothing but a titular figure now, one her brothers kept as a weapon of their own.

Once it was finally a reasonable hour to get up, Alyssa crawled out of the too-comfortable bed and looked at herself in the gigantic mirror. She looked like a bedraggled sewer animal in the midst of all this pristine white.

It was such a glaring contrast. Though she'd grown up surrounded by a certain amount of wealth, it had all been the dark-and-dirty kind. She'd lived in a sketchy guarded-to-the-hilt home for most of her life, and then been kidnapped into a glorified bunker.

But what did contrasts matter when she was simply out for the truth? She tiptoed down the hallway, wondering where Ranger Stevens had secreted himself off to last night. What would he look like sleep-rumpled in one of those big white beds?

She was seriously losing it. Clearly she needed something to eat to clear her head. She headed for the kitchen, but stopped short at the entrance when she saw Ranger Stevens was already sitting there in a little breakfast nook surrounded by windows.

"Good morning," he offered, as if it wasn't five in the morning and as if this wasn't weird as all get out.

"Morning," she replied.

On the glossy black table in front of him, he had a laptop open. He was wearing sweatpants and a T-shirt, and while the button-down shirt he'd been wearing last night hadn't exactly hidden the fact this man was no pencil pusher, this was a whole other experience.

He had muscles. Actual biceps. Whether it was on purpose or not, the sleeves of his T-shirt hugged them perfectly and made her realize, again, how unbearably hot this man was. And how unbearably unfair that was.

"There's coffee already brewed. Mugs are in the cabinet above it. As for breakfast, feel free to poke around and find what you'd like."

"Not much of a breakfast eater," she lied. She didn't know why she lied. She just felt off-kilter and weird and didn't want to be here.

"I'd try to eat something. Got a lot of work to do today."

"Don't you have to go to, like, actual work?"

"My actual work is investigating this case."

"If my brothers get ahold of you and you don't report for work, what's going to happen then?"

He looked at her over his laptop with that hard, implacable Texas Ranger look she thought maybe he practiced in the mirror. Because it was effective, both in shutting her up and making those weird lower-belly flutters intensify.

"I'll handle my work responsibilities," he said, his voice deep and certain.

Alyssa rolled her eyes in an effort to appear wholly unaffected. She walked over to the coffeepot. She didn't drink coffee, but she figured she might as well start. That's what adults did after all. They drank coffee and handled their work responsibilities.

"Sugar is right next to the pot. No cream, but milk is in the fridge."

"I drink it black," she lied. She tried to take a sophisticated sip, but ended up burning her tongue and grimacing at the horrible, horrible taste.

"You take it black, huh?" And there was that dangerous curve to his mouth, humor and something like intent all curled into it. She wanted to trace it with her fingers.

So, she scowled instead. "Let's worry less about how I take my coffee and more about what we're going to do."

"First things first, we're going to go back to your office and check for a bug. We need to know exactly what your brothers know about me and what I'm looking for."

She wasn't in love with him deciding what they were going to do without at least a conversation, but unfortunately he was right. They needed to know for sure what was going on.

"Once we've figured that out, we'll move on to trying to lure your brothers out."

"I'm guessing my leading their cronies to Texas Rangers headquarters and yelling probably did it."

"Probably, but we need to make sure. We also need to make sure it seems like we don't want to be caught."

She studied him then because there was something not quite right about all this.

"This is official Ranger business, right?"

He focused on the computer. "What do you mean 'official'?"

"This isn't on the up-and-up, is it?"

His mouth firmed and his jaw went hard and uncompromising. He was so damn hot, and she kind of wanted to lick him. She didn't know what to do with that. She'd never wanted to lick anyone before.

"I've been okayed to investigate this case," he ground out. "It's possible we'll have to do some things that aren't entirely by the book. I might not tell my superiors every single thing I'm doing, but this is one of those cases where you have to bend the rules a little bit."

"Doesn't bending the rules invalidate the investigation?"

"Depends on the situation. Do you want to find the answers to your mother's murder or not?"

Which she supposed was all that really mattered. She wanted to find the answers to her mother's murder. Everything else was secondary. "Okay. Well, let's go, then."

His mouth quirked, his hard, uncompromising expression softening. "Aren't you going to finish your coffee?"

She glanced at the mug, and she knew he was testing her. Teasing her maybe. She fluttered her eyelashes at him. "You make shitty coffee."

He barked out a laugh, and she was all too pleased he

was laughing at something she'd said. All too pleased he would tease her. Pay attention to her in any way.

It was stupid to be into him. So she'd ignore that part of herself right now. Ignore the flutters and the being pleased.

A door opened somewhere, and Bennet visibly cringed when a voice rang out.

"Bennet? Are you here?"

It was a woman's voice. Did he have a girlfriend? Something ugly bloomed in her chest, but Bennet offered some sort of half grimace, half smile. "Well, Alyssa, let's see what kind of actress you are."

He pushed away from the table, and an older woman entered the room. He held out his arms.

"Mother. How are you?"

"Surprised to find you here." She brushed her lips across the air next to Bennet's cheek.

Alyssa pushed herself into the little corner of the countertop, but Bennet wasn't going to let her be ignored. He turned his mother to face her.

"Allow me to introduce you to someone," he said easily, charmingly, clearly a very good actor. The woman's blue gaze landed on Alyssa.

"This is Alyssa… Clark," Bennet offered. "Alyssa, this is my mother, Lynette Stevens."

"Alyssa Clark," Mrs. Stevens repeated blandly.

Alyssa didn't have to be a mind reader to know Mrs. Stevens did not approve. She might have squirmed if it didn't piss her off a little. Sure, she looked like a drowned sewer rat and was the daughter of a drug kingpin rather than Texas royalty, but she wasn't a bad person. Exactly.

Alyssa smiled as sweetly as she could manage. "It's

so good to meet you, Ms. Stevens. I've heard *so* much about you," she said, adopting her most cultured, overly upper-class Texas drawl.

Mrs. Bennet's expression didn't change, but Alyssa was adept at reading the cold fury of people. And Mrs. Stevens had some cold fury going on in there.

"I didn't realize you were seeing anyone at the moment, Bennet," Mrs. Stevens murmured, the fury of her gaze never leaving Alyssa.

"I don't tell you everything, as you well know."

"Yes, well. I just came by to see what all the noise complaints were about. If I'd known you were busy, I wouldn't have bothered you."

"It was no bother, but I do have to get ready for work."

"And what's Ms. Clark going to do while you work?"

"Oh, I have my own work to do," Alyssa said. She smiled as blandly and coldly as Bennet's mother.

"Yes, well. I'll leave you both alone then. Try to avoid any more noise disturbances if you please, and if you're around this evening, bring your young lady to dinner at the main house."

"I'll see if our schedules can accommodate it and let Kinsey know," Bennet replied, and Alyssa had not seen this side of him. Cool and blank, a false mask of charm over everything. This was not Ranger Stevens, and she didn't think it was Bennet either.

"Wonderful. I hope to see you then." She gave Alyssa one last glance and then swept out of the kitchen as quickly as she'd appeared.

Alyssa looked curiously at Bennet. "That's how you talk to your mother?"

"I'm afraid so."

"Why did she hate me so much?"

"You're not on her approved list of women I'm allowed to see."

"She doesn't have a list."

Bennet raised an eyebrow. "It's laminated."

Alyssa laughed, even though she had a terrible feeling he wasn't joking. "So, she wants you to get married and have lots of little perfect Superman babies?"

"It's a political game for her."

"What is?"

"Life."

Which seemed suddenly not funny at all but just kind of sad. For her. For Bennet. Which was foolish. She'd grown up in a drug cartel. What could be sad about Bennet's picture-perfect political family?

"Why'd you give her a fake name when you introduced me?"

"Because her private investigators will be on you in five seconds. If you've ever stripped, inhaled, handed out fliers for minimum-wage increases, I will know it within the hour. But a fake name will slow her down."

"She checks out all your girlfriends?"

"All the ones I let her know about. Which is why I don't usually let her know. Which I imagine is why she's here at five in the morning and overly suspicious. But you don't have to worry."

"Because you didn't give her my real name?"

"Because I think you can eat my mother for lunch."

Alyssa glanced at the way the woman had gone. She didn't think so. She might be a rough-and-tumble bounty hunter, but Mrs. Stevens had a cold fury underneath that spoke to being a lot tougher than she looked.

Still, Alyssa didn't mind Bennet thinking she could take his mother on.

"Let's head over to your office."

Alyssa nodded and followed along, but Bennet's mother haunted her for the rest of the day.

Chapter Five

"I can't find a damn thing," Bennet muttered. They'd spent over two hours searching Alyssa's office from top to bottom. Meticulously. They'd taken her desk apart, pulled at loose flooring, poked at soft drywall.

It was possible they'd overlooked something, but Bennet didn't have a clue as to what. Surely, surely the office had been bugged. How else would anyone have known to follow Alyssa last night?

He tried to push the frustration away, since it wouldn't get him any further in this case—and he'd already come further than he'd expected to in twenty-four hours—but something about knowing who the Jane Doe was, and who cared about her, made it seem all the more imperative to unravel this mystery.

Alyssa tossed some debris into a corner. "This is pointless. It could be anywhere. In anything."

"We've been through everywhere and everything. Maybe there was no bug."

"Then why would they have followed me last night?" She looked out her smudgy windows, frowning. Her profile reminded him of last night, when she'd stood in the middle of that parking lot and all but dared two thugs to harm her.

He shifted, trying to ignore the uncomfortable way his body reacted to that memory. "Maybe it's something else. Something seemingly unrelated. Had you ever seen those guys before?"

"No... Wait. Wait." She rushed over to her desk, pulling a crate off the floor.

"We already went through that."

She waved a hand. "Did you get the license plate off that car last night?"

"License plate. Make. Model. Picture on my phone."

"Pull it up."

He pulled out his phone and pulled up the information and placed it on the most level side of the desk. She pulled a little notebook from a seemingly endless supply of them and began rifling through it.

She found a page, read it, then glanced at his phone screen and swore. She shoved the notebook toward him, poking her finger at a few lines of chicken scratch. "I have seen those guys—well, their car. It was following me when I was on my last skip in Amarillo. Kept getting in my way. I thought it was friends of the skip trying to stop me, but..." She shook her head, forehead furrowed in confusion. "It is the same car. Same plate."

"So, your brothers have sent someone after you before, which means your office might not be bugged."

"But why? Why now?" She shoved her fingers into her hair, pulling some of the strands out of the band they were in. "Two years. I..." She trailed off, shaking her head, grappling with something bigger than this case.

She hardened her jaw, tossing the notebook back into her crate of notebooks. She stalked around the desk, shoving his phone back at him, something like fury in her gaze. A fury that definitely did not come from this alone.

"Okay, what's next?"

Bennet stilled. Next? Hell if he knew. He'd expected to find a bug and then go from there. He hadn't expected this twist.

"You're the Ranger. You have a plan. Don't you?"

"Why don't we take a deep breath and—"

"You *don't* have a plan."

"Alyssa—"

"You're probably not even really a Texas Ranger. Your mommy and daddy gave you a badge and everyone plays along. Pretends you aren't some idiotic—"

"Have a seat," he barked, gratified when she jumped a little.

"You don't order me around," she replied, lifting that chin, leveling him with that furious glare. It was only the fact there was some panicky undercurrent to it that he didn't bark out another order.

But he did advance, no matter how defiantly she kept his gaze. He stared her right down, getting up in her personal space until they were practically touching. "I said, have a seat," he growled.

Her screw-you expression didn't change, but she did blink and, after a few tense seconds, where he was thinking far too much about the shape of her mouth and not nearly enough about the threat he was trying to enact, she glanced behind her and pulled one of the folding chairs toward her.

She sat carefully, scowling at him all the way.

"I understand this is emotionally taxing for you, Alyssa." She scoffed, but he kept talking. "You will not lash out at me if you'd like me to allow you to—"

"Allow me, my a—"

She tried to stand up, but he took her by the shoulders and firmly pressed her back into the seat. "You're an asset, but don't forget you are working with me because I consider you one. Should you stop being one, I will no longer require your assistance."

"Perhaps," she said, speaking in the same way she had this morning when his mother had been around, mimicking a smooth, soft drawl, "I no longer require your assistance, Ranger Stevens." She shoved his hands off her shoulders with a flourish.

Which irritated him about as much as her words and her fake drawl and everything else about today that wasn't adding up.

So, he took her by the face, which was a mistake, his big palms against her soft cheeks. He felt her little inhale of breath, could see all too easily the way her pupils dilated as he bent over her.

He could feel the way her cheeks heated, the little puffs of breath coming out of her mouth, and there was an insane, blinding moment where he forgot what he was doing, why he was here. All he could think was that if he pressed his mouth to hers he'd know if she tasted as sharp as she always sounded.

He released her face and stepped back, shoving his hands into his pockets. "Getting pissed off at each other solves nothing. We need to arrange a meeting with your brothers somehow. Ferret out what they know." He paced, trying to focus on the information he had rather than the way the strands of her hair had felt trailing against the back of his hand. "Did your skip have something to do with them?"

"No," Alyssa said quietly. "At least, I don't think so."

"But he could have?"

She frowned in concentration. "I think I would have found a connection somewhere, something that rang familiar, but…"

"But what?" he demanded, no patience for her inward thinking that she wasn't sharing.

"I didn't know much about cartel business. I was kept very separated and very isolated from their world. My brothers always acted like I was in imminent danger. They told me if I ever went somewhere alone, there'd be a target on my chest. They were protecting me, they always said."

She seemed to doubt it now, in retrospect, and he couldn't help but wonder if they'd been so protective, so diligent in keeping her separate, then how had she been kidnapped? He hesitated to point that out, then berated himself for it.

He had an investigation to figure out. He could not be ignoring pertinent questions to spare her feelings. "How were you kidnapped?" he asked, gently. Softly. Certainly not in a tone befitting a Texas Ranger.

She hugged herself in that way she seemed to do only when she was really rattled, gaze sliding away from his. "I don't know," she whispered.

Something about that whisper, the vulnerable note, made the desperation wind inside him like a sharp, heavy rock, and he knew then and there he'd find out. He'd find out just how she'd come to be kidnapped, regardless of his case.

And if that was stupid and foolish, well, so be it.

ALYSSA DIDN'T WANT to talk about the kidnapping. She didn't want Bennet to talk to her in that gentle way that had to be a lie. Gentleness spoke to care, and all she was to him was a means to an end.

"What do you mean, you don't know?" he asked, and all of that fury and those hard edges from before when she'd insulted him and he'd ordered her to sit down were gone, softened into this…*concern.*

Which was too tempting, too alluring. She wanted to tell him everything, when she'd never told or wanted to tell anyone anything. Even Gabby knew only bits and pieces, because Alyssa didn't like to bring that pinched, pained look to her friend's face. Gabby had been a prisoner for eight years. Nearly all of her twenties. It wasn't right. It wasn't fair.

But life never had been, Alyssa supposed. Which meant she had to tell Bennet the facts. She wouldn't let emotion get wrapped up in it. She'd just tell him what had happened, and if this had something to do with that…

She closed her eyes, trying to breathe, trying to work this all out in a way that made her want to act instead of cry.

"Take your time," Bennet said softly, giving her arm a quick squeeze, nothing like the way he'd grabbed her face and had those blue eyes boring into her, dropping to look at her mouth as though…

She snapped at him to keep her thoughts from traveling too far in that way-wrong direction. "Don't tell me what to do."

His mouth firmed, some of that softness going away, thank God.

"All I know about the kidnapping is one minute I was asleep in my bed, the next moment I woke up in the back of a van with a hood on my head. I was taken inside some giant warehouse, and there wasn't one person I recognized. A guy examined me, The Stallion, and I got taken to one of his little lairs."

"You would've had to have been drugged," Bennet said, focusing on the details of the kidnapping rather than the emotional scars as if he could read her mind and what she wanted.

"It's the only explanation," Alyssa replied. "I just don't know…how. My brothers kept me locked away. *They* brought me my food. *They* protected me all those years. Before my mother disappeared. Before…" Well, she didn't feel right about letting Bennet in on their biggest family secret—that Dad wasn't in his right mind, or even in his right body. He was a shell in a locked-up room, just like she'd been.

"There's no way *they* could have arranged it?" Bennet asked, with something like regret on his face.

Or maybe that was projection, since she regretted this conversation, regretted and hated the doubts plaguing her. "Why would they protect me for twenty years, keep me safe and from harm, then with no warning hand me over to some crazy guy?" *Who only ever kept me as locked up as my brothers did.*

"I don't know," Bennet said carefully. "But if they protected you so well for twenty years, I don't understand why all the sudden you were kidnapped."

She swallowed at the lump in her throat and did everything she could to appear unaffected. "Well, neither do I."

"Come to think of it, the other night, they followed you. Not me. Alyssa, maybe this doesn't have anything to do with me and what I talked to you about, and everything to do with you."

She forced herself to breathe even though panic threatened to freeze her lungs. Why would it have to do with her? Why had they left her alone for *two* years? Why would they come *now*?

"I could be wrong," Bennet said, and he studied her with those soft eyes that made her want to punch him.

That's not really what you want to do with him.

She shook her head trying to focus, trying to *think*. "We need a next step," she said more to herself than him. "We need to get this over with so that I can enjoy Christmas with my…" She almost said "family." She'd let Gabby and Natalie become her family because her brothers hadn't come for her.

They'd left her. Abandoned her. And now they were back, lurking around the corners of her life.

Bennet reached out to touch her again, but before he could say anything, her door violently screeched open.

Two men in ski masks stepped inside, one with a very large gun, and when Bennet reached for his gun, they fired off a warning shot all too close to Bennet for Alyssa's comfort.

"On the ground," one of the men growled. Bennet didn't move, his face impassive, his hand on the butt of his weapon, though he didn't move another inch.

Alyssa knew she should move off her chair, should follow instructions, but Bennet's stoicism kept her calm, as did the way the man without the gun tapped long fingers against his thigh.

"I said get on the ground," the gunman said in that fake raspy voice.

Alyssa slowly stood, staring at the shape of the man's mouth, the breadth of his shoulders. The way he held that gun.

"Jose," Alyssa said, making sure it was clear she *knew* it was him, not just suspected. She glanced at the man without the gun, the brother closest in age to her. "Oscar. It's been a while."

Both men froze. Jose glanced at Oscar, still training the gun on Bennet. "How did she know it was us?" Jose demanded in a sad attempt at a whisper.

"I told CJ she wasn't stupid," Oscar muttered in disgust.

Alyssa swallowed at the odd lump in her throat, blinked at the stinging in her eyes. Four years. Four years ago her entire life had been torn from her, and now here was half of her entire life, the brothers who'd kept the closest tabs on her, in ski masks and with a gun.

Men she'd trusted her entire childhood to keep her safe. At least she'd always thought that's what they'd been doing. Had she been so wrong? So naive and stupid?

Two years she'd been imprisoned with that madman, The Stallion, and had slowly gone crazy realizing she'd *always* been imprisoned, for her entire life, but she'd waited. Waited to be rescued. To be found by the men she'd loved and trusted.

But she hadn't been rescued by them. She'd been rescued by the FBI. And for two years her brothers hadn't done a damn thing to contact her. They'd left her for dead.

Now, *now* they'd crashed back into her life and were just *standing* there discussing whether CJ was right about her intelligence level.

Furious, and more than a little emotional, Alyssa stomped over to them and their sad little whispered argument. Jose's eyes widened, but he kept the gun

trained on Bennet, who was standing calmly and plac-
idly near where she'd been sitting.

She ignored Jose for the time being, and instead
stood toe-to-toe with Oscar, her closest brother, her
sweet and kind and caring closest brother, and slapped
him across the face as hard as she could.

"What did you do that for?" Oscar howled, cradling
his smacked cheek.

She tried to yell all the reasons why she'd hit him, but
what she really wanted to do was cry, so she couldn't
manage a yell, or anything more than a squeak.

She moved to slap Jose, too, for good measure, for
mixing her up and making her want to cry, but before
she could do anything, three more men stormed into
the office.

Two with masks and guns just like Jose's went
straight for Bennet. They jerked his arms behind his
back and had him pressed to a wall, face-first, in seconds flat.

The other man stared straight at her, maskless, dark
eyes cold and furious.

"I knew I couldn't trust you two," he muttered, glancing disgustedly at Jose and Oscar. "It's broad daylight.
What the hell are you taking your time for? Eric, Benji,
get the Ranger in the van. *Now.*"

"What about Alyssa?" Oscar asked, still cradling
his cheek.

CJ, her eldest bother, the leader of the cartel, looked
her over as if she was some kind of cargo. "Alyssa
comes with me."

If she had any sense in her head, she'd let CJ take
her. Her oldest brother had always been cold, remote
and mostly ruthless, and it didn't make sense to cross

him when she and Bennet had been planning on being taken anyway.

But slapping Oscar had only unleashed more fury rather than soothed any of it. She wanted to hit all of them. She wanted to beat them until they bled. She wanted answers, and hell if she was going to be calm or patient in the getting of them.

"Let him go," Alyssa said calmly and evenly, coolly even, matching CJ's cold stare with one of her own.

CJ leaned down, so close their noses almost touched. "Are you warming that Texas Ranger's bed, Alyssa? I didn't think we raised you to be a whore."

Those words, that tone, lit a fire to something inside her that had been simmering for all of these four years. She'd never acknowledged it, this blistering hurt and rage.

They'd abandoned her, to be kidnapped, to be let go. They'd given up any claim to her in four years of silence.

Now they had Bennet pressed to a wall with a gun to his head, and she wasn't stupid enough to think her brothers were *that* much stronger and smarter than him. No, Bennet was standing there *letting* them press him up against the wall.

For her.

No. No, for the *case.*

But it didn't matter, because she wasn't giving her brothers this kind of power. They'd run her life for years, but those years were over.

In a move she'd practiced for as long as she'd known how to walk, she pulled the gun out of her coat so swiftly, she had it shoved to CJ's gut before he'd even blinked an eye.

His mouth hardened, but he made no other reaction. "Am I supposed to believe you'd shoot me, my sweet Lyssie girl?"

She could almost believe he cared when he used that voice, that old nickname, but four years of separation had given her too many questions, too many doubts. "If you don't think I have the guts to shoot you right here, right now, then you don't know the woman you raised."

"You'd shoot your own brother? Whatever happened to loyalty?"

"Loyalty? You dare speak the word *loyalty* to me?" Alyssa shoved the gun against him harder, and he winced. "Family was supposed to be the only thing that mattered to you. Family was the rallying cry in *protecting* me. But I wasn't protected. I got kidnapped. I've been free from that for two years, and where have you been?"

"It's complicated," CJ growled.

"It's not. You weren't there, and now I don't need you." She looked down at the gun in her hand, surprised to find herself steady. When she looked back up at CJ, she smiled. "But I may spare your life."

CJ scoffed. "Jose, give me that gun."

"I'll shoot him if you move, Jose. And what would the world do without CJ Jimenez in it to pull its strings?"

"What do you want?" CJ asked, feigning boredom, but Alyssa could see a faint line of concern on his forehead.

She fiddled with the safety of her gun, just to show him she wasn't messing around. "Our mother was murdered, and I want to know why."

CJ's mouth curved and his gaze moved to Bennet, who somehow looked calm and model-like pressed to her grimy office wall. "I think your Ranger has a few more answers about these things than he lets on."

Alyssa didn't jerk, didn't react, though inwardly her stomach tightened into a painful cramp. Had Bennet been lying to her? Someone was. It could be him. But CJ was her impending doom right now, and she had to take care of him first.

"Drop the guns, let the Ranger go, or I shoot CJ. I'll count to ten."

She watched as her brothers all stood wide-eyed and frozen as she counted down. Finally, CJ inclined his head. "Let the Ranger go," he grumbled.

"And drop the guns. Now."

The two brothers holding Bennet let go, slowly putting their guns on the ground along with Jose. Bennet didn't scurry away, didn't scowl, didn't outwardly react in any way. He simply picked the guns up and used the straps to sling them onto his shoulder.

"I want you all lined up in front of the door," Alyssa said, pushing CJ back toward the door with the gun.

They scrambled to do her bidding, and Alyssa couldn't ignore the thrill it gave her. She was in charge. *She* had outwitted them. *She* was going to get what *she* wanted for once. For damn once.

And there they were. All five of them. The men she'd loved and trusted for her entire life.

She'd spent the past two years fearing they didn't love her. Being so afraid she didn't matter or that they thought she was tainted in some way. But none of that fear or sadness was inside her right now. All she felt was rage. Rage that they'd abandoned her. After giving her very few skills with which to survive—only violence and suspicion.

Bennet came to stand behind her, and she expected him to tell her what to do. She didn't know what, but she expected *something*. He hadn't uttered a word this entire altercation.

He still didn't. He just stood there. Behind her. A calming, supportive force. Because it was her turn. *Her* turn to be in charge of her life.

"I want all the information you have on my kidnapping and our mother's murder. And if I think you're lying, I'll pick you off one by one."

"And I'll help," Bennet added cheerfully, holding one of the guns in his hands, sights set on CJ.

Chapter Six

For a few moments Bennet could only stand behind Alyssa and stare. He hadn't known she had a gun on her. How could he have missed that, and what kind of Ranger did it make him that he had?

But that moderate shame was no match for the other feeling that assailed him. Awe. She'd fended off an attack from all five of her brothers. Who did that? They were the leaders of a *cartel*, three of them had guns, and yet she'd gotten them to drop their weapons, all without his having to lift a finger.

He'd been content to let her brothers think they had the upper hand, eager for them to pull him into their world so he could find his answers.

But Alyssa had a gun on them and point-blank asked for those answers, and so he'd stood behind her and backed her up. It was the only thing to do.

"Why don't you ask your Ranger, Lyss?" the clear leader of the group said, dark eyes zeroed in on him.

Alyssa didn't flick so much as a glance back at him, but he saw the way her shoulders tensed, the way CJ insinuating Bennet knew something he wasn't telling her bothered her.

"If I knew anything about either, I wouldn't be here," Bennet replied coolly.

CJ cocked his head, and even if Bennet didn't know about her brothers and their documented work in cartel dealings, he'd know this man was dangerous. Powerful.

But this man had cowered to Alyssa, and that was something to use.

"When are you going to run for office like Mommy and Daddy, Ranger boy?" CJ asked.

Something prickled at the back of Bennet's neck, that telltale gut feeling something was seriously wrong, but he didn't have enough to bluff his way through this one. So, he had to go with the truth. "I'm not a politician."

"Hmm." CJ considered Bennet as if two guns weren't pointed at him. "And I suppose the name Sal Cochrane means nothing to you."

Bennet racked his brain, every memory, every case, every person he'd ever met, but he came up blank.

"Salvador Dominguez, then?"

Bennet was very careful to keep the recognition off his face. The Dominguez cartel was newer and less powerful than the Jimenez one, but it had been gaining in power of late. But who the hell was Sal Cochrane?

CJ kept studying him, but Bennet didn't know what the man was looking for. What the man thought Bennet knew.

"Politics is dirty business, Ranger Stevens," CJ said, putting extra emphasis on his last name, and there was that scalp prickle again. Foreboding.

"I suppose it is, but like I said, I'm not a politician. That's my parents."

"I guess we'll see," CJ murmured.

"Who the hell are you here for, CJ?" Alyssa demanded. "Me or him?"

CJ's mouth curved in what Bennet assumed was supposed to be a smile. "If I wanted either of you, I'd have you."

Which sent a cold chill down Bennet's spine, because he was beginning to realize this was all a little too easy. For five men involved in a drug cartel with an insane amount of weaponry, one woman—sister or not, remarkable or not—they hadn't actually been bested.

This was all an act. Bennet kept his gun aimed at CJ, but he started looking around. There was a back entrance, but he'd not just locked it when they'd entered through it, he'd barred the door. They at least couldn't be ambushed without warning that way.

Alyssa shoved the gun in CJ's gut again, with enough force that CJ coughed out a breath. "Why was I kidnapped?" she demanded. "You're not leaving here without telling me. How the hell did someone drug me and get me out of the house?"

CJ's mouth firmed, and the one who'd come inside without a gun stared at his feet. Whatever the reason, these men all knew it, which meant they were probably part of it.

Which, unfortunately, Bennet knew would hurt Alyssa immeasurably. She'd seen them as her protectors all this time, and not coming after her had been a betrayal—even if Bennet thought she was better off without them—but this?

"You never came for me," Alyssa replied, and on the surface her voice was calm, collected, but there was something vibrating underneath, something Bennet figured she was trying to hide. Emotion. Hurt. "And now you're here spouting threats at *him*. What is this?"

"Still dying to be the center of attention after all these years, Lyssie?"

Bennet opened his mouth to say something, anything to put the man in his place, but that's when he saw a flicker of light outside the grimy windows, and when the glass exploded seconds later, he couldn't be sure what was coming through, but he knew it wasn't good.

And far too close to Alyssa. He lunged for her, knocking her onto the ground and underneath him. He couldn't make out whatever words of protest she was making, because something exploded.

He could feel heat, bits of debris painfully pelting his back and Alyssa breathing underneath him.

She was swearing, pushing at him, but breathing. In and out. Bennet was almost afraid to see what had caused the explosion, afraid to see what casualties there might be, but he could still feel the heat on his back, which meant the place was on fire.

He pushed off her and onto his feet, offering his hand to help her up, but she scrambled past him unaided.

"Where'd they go?" She stared at the door and the flames licking around it. None of her brothers or her brothers' bodies were anywhere to be seen. There was only a line of flame slowly spreading down the length of the front wall.

She whirled on him. "Where'd they go?"

"Alyssa…"

"You let them get away. You…" She slapped her palms to his chest and pushed. Hard, and while in normal circumstances it wouldn't have hurt him in the least, a searing pain shot through his shoulder and back at his body's movement.

He hissed out a breath, and some of her desperate fury was replaced by confusion, and maybe concern. She tried to move past him, but he moved with her, keeping his back hidden.

"We need to get out of here," he said, sucking in a smoky breath before reaching his arm out to take hers. To usher her out the back way. The fire wasn't huge, but they needed to get out before the smoke got worse, and they really needed to leave before anyone saw them.

He nudged her in front of him, pushing her down the hall no matter how often she scowled over her shoulder at him. He pulled the heavy rack he'd pushed in front of the back door earlier away, no matter how his back screamed, then pushed her out the door and into the alley where they'd parked his car.

He wasn't sure how he was going to drive like this, but they had to get out of here before they were seen. If he had to explain this to the Rangers, other law enforcement would be brought in, and he wasn't ready for that yet. Not when he knew so little.

Not when CJ Jimenez had dropped hints about his parents.

No, he had to figure out what this whole thing was about before anyone else got involved. If his parents were connected to something… He could hardly stomach the thought, but he wouldn't protect them. He couldn't. Not at the cost of everything he'd sworn himself to.

But he had to be sure first.

"Oh my God. You're bleeding," Alyssa gasped when he passed her to head for the driver's side.

Bennet paused and glanced down his back as best he could. "It's just some glass," he muttered.

"We have to get you to a hospital."

"No," he said, leveling her with his most serious glare. "We have to get the hell out of here."

"Bennet, there are *shards* of glass sticking out of your back. How do you suggest we get the hell out of here?"

He looked down at the keys in his hand and then shrugged, wincing in pain. He tossed her his keys, trying not to show how the move hurt him. "You're driving."

ALYSSA DROVE BENNET'S fancy car through the streets of Austin, back to his parents' guesthouse, glancing occasionally in the rearview mirror to the back seat, where Bennet was pretzeled into a position where his back wouldn't hit anything.

It looked awful, and Alyssa was half-tempted to drive him to the hospital against his will.

But none of this made sense. Not her brothers' appearance, not their disappearance and not Bennet's refusal to stick around and deal with it as an official law enforcement agent. He'd called 911 and given the pertinent information, but not his name.

Luckily she didn't really care if her office burned to the ground. She still had her gun and her motorcycle, which were the most important possessions she owned. The paperwork she kept in the office was helpful, but not necessary. The few important documents she had, she kept in a safe-deposit box at the bank. Losing the office meant nothing.

Losing out on answers meant everything.

She glanced at Bennet again as she drove the long, winding drive to his parents' guesthouse after he'd ground out the code to the gate and she'd punched it in.

She supposed that man meant a little bit. He'd certainly jumped between her and harm. She could be the one with shards of glass sticking out of her if he hadn't acted so quickly.

As much as she might want to blame Bennet for letting her brothers get away, she wasn't stupid. Everything that had happened—from her knowing Jose and Oscar on sight even with masks, to the firebomb that allowed the Jimenez brothers to escape—had all been part of a plan.

CJ hadn't given her any information he hadn't wanted to, and while he'd given her nothing, he'd planted all sorts of new doubts about Bennet in her head.

She parked the car at the garage door and pulled the keys from the ignition. "Let me guess, you have a magic doctor on staff who's going to stitch all that up?"

"No, I'm afraid that's going to have to fall to you. Hope you're not squeamish." On a grunt, he shoved the door open. Wincing and breathing a little too heavily, he maneuvered himself out of the car without any help.

Alyssa scrambled to do just that—help. No matter what insinuations CJ had made, this man had stepped between her and an explosion. His first instinct had been to protect her, which was not an instinct apparently any of her brothers shared. And even before all that, Bennet had given her something no man in her entire life had ever given her: power.

He'd let her hold a gun on her brothers and question them without stepping in, without riding roughshod. He'd given her space, and he'd protected her.

Maybe he knew more than he'd let on, but she wasn't about to let CJ manipulate her into doing what *he* wanted. No, she was going to make up her own mind. Slowly. Carefully. Once she had all the evidence laid out before her.

She followed Bennet inside, through the vast white rooms and plush hallways and into a bathroom that was about the size of her entire above-the-garage apartment.

He bent over, hissing out a breath as he pulled a white box out from under the sink. He dropped it on the beautiful countertop. "First aid kit. I doubt there will be anything to pull the glass out with, though."

Alyssa unzipped her jacket and turned slightly away from Bennet. Once her front was shielded from his view, she pulled her Swiss Army knife out of her bra before turning around and holding it up. "I've got tweezers."

His mouth curved, and his little exhale of breath was something close to a laugh. "Of course you do." He reached behind him and tugged at his collar, but winced and dropped it. "Help me get this off," he ground out, turning his back to her again.

The shirt was ruined—torn, bloody—and if she focused on that she would maybe not focus on the fact he'd just asked her to help him take his shirt off.

"I, uh, should maybe get some of the glass out first." Which was the truth, not some excuse to keep from having to touch his naked back.

"Go for it."

"Right." She blew out a breath and ignored how her hand shook as she pulled the tweezer tool out of her Swiss Army knife.

She had to splay her hand across the least torn-up

shoulder blade to try to find her balance and leverage. Some of the tenseness in his shoulder relaxed at her touch, and she didn't know what to make of that. That or the too-hard beating of her heart.

She took a deep breath and focused on the largest piece of glass sticking out of Bennet's back. She bit her lip and used the tweezers to pull it out. Bennet didn't move, didn't make a sound. She placed the stomach-curdling piece of bloody glass on the sink, wincing a little at the thought of the blood staining the countertop.

"Well, I think it might look worse than it actually is," Alyssa offered hopefully, shuffling awkwardly closer to get the next piece of glass.

"Great," Bennet muttered.

"This would be easier with you lying on a bed."

He glanced at her over his shoulder, something about the wide-eyed look and slight curve of his mouth causing her face to heat.

"J-just for…leverage."

His mouth curved even more. "Leverage," he repeated, far too amused.

She scowled at him. "You want this glass out of you or not?"

"The bed it is. You want to take my shirt off first?"

She pretended to study his back if only so she didn't have to meet his gaze. "All right," she said, refusing to let any of her uncertainty come out in her voice.

She flexed her fingers, willing away the slight tremor in them before touching the hem of his T-shirt. She could do this. Take some glass out of his back, take off a shirt. It was all just…business.

Sort of.

She swallowed and pulled the shirt away from Bennet's back, then lifted the fabric. "You're, uh, going to have to bend over or pull it or something."

He reached back with only a minimal sucked-in breath and pulled the shirt off, leaving his back completely bare. And broad. And strong. And bloody.

"Oh." His injuries weren't anywhere near serious, but it looked so ugly. Glass and blood and scratches. She touched her finger to an unmarred spot, feeling oddly protective, hurt by this silly little attack on him.

"Not looking so great now?"

She pulled her hand away, something like guilt washing over her. "You'll live."

He made a considering noise then gestured toward a second door. "To the bed, then?" And somehow this man with bits of glass shards in his back was grinning at her. Charmingly.

She'd faced down her brothers, a madman of a kidnapper and all his goons, a parcel of FBI agents in an attempt to garner some power, admittedly foolish in retrospect. She'd faced all those people down without a qualm, but it was always the quiet moments she didn't know what to do with.

Gabby and Natalie's kindness. A charming smile from an all-too-handsome Texas Ranger. It made her feel young and stupid.

She grabbed the first aid kit and lifted her chin at him. "I'll follow you."

He walked out the door and into a huge bedroom, all white and black just like every other room in his bizarre place. Where was the color? The charm? The—

Bennet got on the bed, lying stomach down on the pristine white blankets. He crossed his hands under his head and rested his temple on the back of one hand, studying her.

She looked away and placed the kit on the nightstand and focused on getting out and opening bandages and not staring at a Texas Ranger all sprawled out half-naked on his bed after saving her from…well, minor injury.

"I do have an investigation to start if we could hurry this damn thing up."

"Right." Except he was lying there, and she wasn't sure why she thought this would give her more leverage. Oh, she could reach all places on his back easier, but she'd have to lean over him. Brush against him. Hell, it'd be easiest if she could just straddle his legs and go at it that way.

She was *not* going to go at it that way. But she did have to do it. So, enough of being a silly little girl. Maybe she was a sheltered virgin in the oddest sense of the word, but she had a job to do. Bennet had helped her out, and now it was her turn to help him.

So, she focused on the glass shards and pulling out all she could see. She focused on using the antibiotic ointment on the cuts and bandaging them up. And if she noticed that his skin was soft, or that his muscles rippled appealingly any time he moved, well… So what? Adult women did that sort of thing, didn't they? Noticed attractive men.

"There might still be debris in there," Alyssa said, bandaging up the last of the cuts. "I only got out what I could see."

"It'll be good enough," he replied, pushing himself into a sitting position on the bed.

"You should go to the hospital. Some of those bigger cuts might need stitches."

He shook his head.

"Why aren't you reporting this?" There was a reason, and she was a little afraid she knew what it was.

His jaw firmed, but he didn't look away. That blue gaze pinned her in place. "First off, they'd put me on medical leave for a day or two and give someone else the case. Second of all…"

"Your parents?"

"That was your brother's insinuation."

"And you believe him?"

Bennet looked away for a moment. "I don't know. It could be a trick. It could be true. It could be a lot of things, but I want to be the one to figure it out."

"I should go."

He looked back at her, brow furrowing. "Go where?"

"Home. No one was bugging my place, and my brothers didn't hurt me or take me, which means they aren't going to. There's no reason for me to stay here."

He scooted to the edge of the bed and took her hands with his before she could think to step away. "Alyssa, that doesn't mean you're not in danger," he said seriously.

"I've been in danger before. I can handle myself."

He studied her, and she couldn't read his expression or guess what he was looking for, but when she tried to tug her hands away, he only held on tighter.

"I know your brothers insinuated that I know something about your mother, about anything, but I don't. You have to believe that."

"I do." Maybe she shouldn't, but why would he have

come to her with her mother's picture as a Jane Doe if he knew anything?

"If either of my parents is involved in some kind of crime, I will not hesitate to turn them in, Alyssa. I took an oath. For what it's worth, my parents took an oath, and if they are not representing their constituents in a lawful fashion, then it's out of my hands."

She blinked at the vehemence in his tone. "O-okay."

"So you don't need to worry."

"What do you think I'm worried about?"

"You're trying to leave. You must be worried about something."

"I'm… You don't need me, Bennet. You got your Jane Doe name, and there's no point trying to get drawn into my brothers' world now. They know too much." She was useless to him. *Just like you're useless to everyone else.*

Again she tugged her hands, but Bennet held her in his grasp.

"Until we know how this all connects, until we can be certain you're safe, you're under my protection."

Tears pricked her eyes unexpectedly. Protection. She was so tired of being under someone else's protection. And yet, today Bennet had let her fight her own battle within that protection. He hadn't abandoned her or allowed her to be hurt like everyone else had.

"And you're right, we can't go into your brothers' world now, but we have a much bigger challenge ahead of us," he said gravely.

We. *We.* As if they were a team, working together, protecting each other. "We do?" she managed to ask past the lump in her throat.

"I have to bring you into mine."

Chapter Seven

Bennet didn't bother to find a new shirt, and he didn't bother to try to figure out what Alyssa's silence meant. They had work to do.

"Did you recognize either of the names your brother mentioned?"

Alyssa blew out a breath. "Sal Cochrane not so much."

"And Salvador Dominguez?"

Her expression shuttered, and he supposed it was answer enough, though it didn't sit well with him that she knew.

"I've been a bounty hunter—"

"Illegal bounty hunter," he interrupted, because he liked the way she scowled at him when he did. "You don't only know Dominguez from the past two years. Don't insult me with a lie at this point."

She had the decency to look a little shamed. "I don't know Salvador Dominguez, but I have heard of him."

"From your brothers?"

She shook her head almost imperceptibly.

"Then from who?" he demanded, as irritated with her hesitation as he was with the burning sensation in his back.

"My father, but…" Alyssa rubbed her hands together, clearly working out something in her head without letting him in on pertinent information.

"But what?"

"He wasn't… He isn't… When he told me about Dominguez, none of it made any sense. And when I told CJ, he…"

"He what?"

Her gaze flew to his. "Oh my God. He made me think Dad was crazy. He convinced me Dad had lost his mind but… But Dad said Salvador Dominguez had our mother. That she hadn't left, that someone had double-crossed him and *I* would be next and… Bennet, they convinced me Dad was crazy, but maybe he wasn't."

"Why tell us? And what does it have to do with Sal Cochrane?"

She shook her head, eyebrows drawn together, hands clasped. "I don't know. I don't know." She paced, fury taking over her features. "I hate that we have to find out when that's just what he wants us to do."

"Maybe it's some kind of warning. Some kind of way to help you, and if we find out—"

She laughed. Bitterly. "I might be able to convince myself of that if it had been any of my other brothers, but CJ has been in charge too long to have any decency left in him. Whatever reason he has for showing up, for letting me go, for dropping those little breadcrumbs, it is for the cartel's well-being and that alone."

She wrapped her arms around herself, and he curled his hands into fists so he didn't reach out. They could probably stand a little less touching, a little less close quarters, and a lot less his being an idiot and trying to make her blush.

How this unbelievably strong fighter of a woman could *blush* at the remotest sexual thing was beyond him, and he liked it far too much.

But *sexual* was not something he could afford to be thinking about. No matter how gently she'd tended his wounds, or how brave she was, or how much he wanted to protect her.

"Does The Stallion have anything to do with the cartels?" she asked, still hugging her arms around herself.

"The Stallion has been in prison for two years," he reminded her as gently as he could.

"Before that, I mean. It all has to connect, don't you think? Not just now, either. This is sixteen years in the making, if it connects to my mother."

Bennet sighed. He didn't know. It seemed there were a million connections and he didn't have a clue about any of them. It was more than possible a rival cartel could have killed Alyssa's mother, but that didn't explain why she'd been left a Jane Doe.

There were too many unanswered questions, and what clues he had came from criminals with their own agendas. If he thought he'd been frustrated at the prospect of a Jane Doe, it had nothing on *this* frustration.

But this was what he wanted. A challenge. To do something good for once. All on his own.

"Bennet," a voice boomed from the entryway.

Bennet swore. The last thing he wanted to do right now was go toe-to-toe with his father.

"I assume that's not the staff," Alyssa offered drily.

"It's my father."

"Do your parents know how to knock?"

"Not if it doesn't suit them." Bennet glanced at the door. It was no use to hide Alyssa when Mother would have already told Father about her, but he didn't want to waste time trading fake niceties or old-hat arguments with his father.

He took a step toward Alyssa. There was one possible way to get his father out of here quickly. And he was already shirtless.

"I need you to go along with something, all right?"

"With what? Being Alyssa Clark? I did this morning. I don't see why…"

She trailed off when he slid his arms around her, her eyes widening as she looked up at him.

"W-what are you doing?"

"We need time, and if my father comes in here he won't be sweeping out anytime soon. Not like my mother. He'll want to stay and chat and charm and who knows what all. We don't have time for that, so we're going to pretend we are otherwise engaged."

"Bennet?" the voice boomed again, closer.

"Otherwise. Engaged," Alyssa repeated breathlessly, and though she leaned away from him she didn't jerk away or try to escape.

So, he pulled her close and lowered his mouth close to hers. "It's only pretend. Like…undercover work."

Her eyelashes fluttered and her breath came in short bursts, and he had no business wondering if the attraction he felt wasn't one-sided. If she might feel some of that in return. If she might…

"Bennet?" This time followed by a knock on the bedroom door as the knob turned.

Bennet pressed his mouth to Alyssa's, but all she did was stand there. Frozen and wide-eyed and not at all pretending. She didn't slap him either, but she didn't relax or even feign a kiss back.

"You have to kiss me back," he whispered across her mouth.

"B-but I don't know how."

Hell.

BENNET WAS KISSING HER. His mouth was on her mouth, and no matter that he held her sturdily against him, that he'd called it pretend, she didn't know what the hell to do with her mouth or her arms or with anything.

His father was stepping inside the room and—Bennet's fingers tangled in her hair, angling her whole head so that his mouth slid more easily across hers. Sweetly. Gently. It was warm and…nice. Nice enough to relax into, to soften. She very nearly sighed.

So, this was kissing. Well, she supposed having her body pressed up against the large, hard body of a man while his soft, firm mouth angled over hers had its appeal. It made her whole body feel warm and heavy, it made every place her body touched his seem to sparkle to life, and to taste another person—

A throat cleared, and Alyssa jerked. She didn't know how she'd lost so much track of where she was or what…

She could only blink up at Bennet, but his expression was blank, his jaw hard and his gaze not on her.

"Sorry to interrupt," an unfamiliar voice drawled, sounding very much not sorry.

Alyssa finally gathered enough sense to step away from Bennet and look at their intruder. Which made Alyssa blink all over again.

"*Are* you sorry to interrupt, Father?" Bennet asked, his voice cool and unaffected. "Because a gentleman would perhaps just step back out."

Mr. Stevens smiled widely and looked so much like his son Alyssa could only stare.

"Gary L. Stevens," he said in that charming drawl, holding out a hand to her. And Alyssa would have to give him credit. He might have worse timing than Bennet's mother, but he was certainly kinder.

"I would really prefer it if you weren't introducing yourself to women in my bedroom when we are in the middle of something."

"So traditional," Mr. Stevens said with a wink to Alyssa.

"What are you doing here? I am busy," Bennet said through gritted teeth.

"Your mother sent me on a fact-finding mission, and you know how she gets. I wasn't about to return empty-handed. You must be Alyssa. Clark, was it?"

Alyssa nodded mutely. Where Mrs. Stevens had put her back up with her cold disapproval, she didn't know what to do with Mr. Stevens's easy friendliness. Much like she didn't know what to do with Bennet's fake kisses that apparently affected him not at all.

"I know it's incredibly rude of me, Ms. Clark, but I need just a few moments in private with my son or I'll never get any peace at home."

Bennet opened his mouth, presumably to argue, but Alyssa didn't think that would do anyone any good. She adopted her smooth, fake drawl and smiled sweetly at Mr. Stevens. "Of course." She glanced at Bennet, reminded herself she was playing a part. And the part was that of possible floozy girlfriend.

She patted his bare chest and attempted to look pouty and alluring even though she had no idea how to look that. "You might want to put a shirt on, honey."

Especially if he was going to keep the injuries hidden from his father.

Alyssa walked out the door, pulling it almost closed behind her, but she left a crack. When no one finished closing it, she took a few steps down the hall, then stood exactly where she was, gratified when she could hear everything being said.

"Her last name isn't Clark," Mr. Stevens offered with no preamble.

"You think I don't know that?"

Mr. Stevens sighed heavily. "Your mother is having a conniption."

"Then everything's normal, I assume."

"She wants a name."

"She won't get it from me."

"If the girl has nothing to hide, let your mother run her little background checks. And if she does have something to hide, well, you know your mother won't go exposing her. It would only look poorly on us."

"Regardless of what's in her background, I don't want you two poking around in it or coming after her. She is none of your business. If Mother can't get that through her head after all this time, I don't know what to tell you."

"And yet you're here, under our roof."

Alyssa edged closer to the door, trying to see through the crack in the door. She could see a sliver of Bennet—who'd pulled on a sweatshirt at some point—but she couldn't see his father. She couldn't help but be curious about what Mr. Stevens's reaction might be to that cold fury in Bennet's expression. And, more, she couldn't understand Bennet's relationship with his parents.

She knew her family was warped beyond belief, and

she knew that her brothers fought, sometimes furiously, over cartel business, but she'd assumed that was the life of criminals. Not the life of someone like Bennet and his parents.

"What do you know about Sal Cochrane?" Bennet asked with no finesse, no easing into it. Alyssa frowned. Couldn't he be smoother than all that?

"Is that a friendly question, son, or an official one?" Mr. Stevens returned easily.

"Is that a political evasion or you just being difficult?"

After another long sigh, Mr. Stevens answered. "He's one of your mother's silent donors, I believe. Never met the man myself, so that's about all I know. You're not going to bring your mother into trouble."

Which was not a question. Even Alyssa knew that from her eavesdropping spot in the hall.

"If she isn't already in any."

"Bennet, we've never stood in your way when it came to police work or joining the Rangers. We've never—"

"I'm not going after Mother," Bennet interrupted, clearly irritated by his father's line of conversation. He stepped out of her slim view through the crack in the door. "Sal Cochrane is who I'm after, and it's only for information, so if you have any information, I'd appreciate it. Officially."

"I'll see what I can do." Mr. Stevens stepped into view. "In return for that young woman's last name."

Bennet made a scoffing noise, and Mr. Stevens turned his head, in a seemingly casual move. But as Alyssa didn't have time to move out of the way, she doubted there was anything casual about it.

He'd either known she was there or suspected it, and

she wasn't stupid enough to believe Mr. Stevens hadn't caught her spying. Crap.

Still, better to give the illusion she didn't know she'd been caught. She hurried as silently as possible down the hall and to the bedroom she'd slept in last night. She desperately wanted to listen to the rest of that conversation, to see if Bennet would trade her name for the information he wanted, but as she stepped into the blindingly white room, she realized she had bigger fish to fry.

"What are you doing here? How did you get in?"

Oscar smiled sheepishly. "Hi, sis."

"You...you can't be here." It would be bad enough if Bennet saw him, but if Mr. Stevens saw him, too? Alyssa didn't have a clue as to what might happen, but she knew it wouldn't be good. At the very least her brother would be arrested, and while he might be deserving of that...

Oscar had snuck her checkers and Baby-Sitters Club books. He'd given her sweets and taken her on walks when none of her other brothers would. He'd treated her like a girl, a sister, not just a possession. A statue to protect.

She couldn't let anything happen to Oscar. Not like this. She grabbed him by the arm and tried to pull him toward the door, but he jerked out of her grasp.

"I don't have time, but I had to warn you. Don't try to figure this out. Don't get involved. Stay low, get your Ranger to stay low, and you'll be fine. But if you let CJ drag you into this, you will get hurt."

"Drag me into what?"

"I'm risking my life here, Alyssa. That's all I can say."

"Os—"

But before she could even get the words out of her mouth, he was climbing out the window Alyssa hadn't realized was open. She might have followed him, she might have grabbed him again, but she could hear footsteps in the hall and she couldn't risk being discovered.

"Alyssa!" Oscar hissed from outside.

She pushed the curtains back and looked at her brother standing in the perfectly manicured yard of the Stevenses' guesthouse, a figure all in black, the faint scar across his cheek he'd never told her how he'd gotten.

"Don't tell your Ranger I was here. Please." And then he was gone, running silently around the corner of the house.

"Well, I hope you know how to clean up," Bennet said, and Alyssa whirled away from the window. Probably the only thing saving her from being caught was the fact Bennet's attention was on a card in his hand.

"Clean up?" she echoed stupidly, her heart hammering a hundred times in overdrive.

He looked up at her, that charming smile so easily camouflaging his true emotions.

"We're going to a ball, Cinderella."

Chapter Eight

Bennet sat at the kitchen table, casually eating his dinner, while Alyssa continued to rant. And rant. And rant, rant, rant. It was almost amusing, really, considering he'd watched this woman fly down a highway on a motorcycle waving at very bad men, watched this woman hold a gun on her brothers, and yet those weren't the things that caused her to come unglued.

No, she was losing it at the prospect of going to one of his parents' idiotic Christmas balls or galas or whatever they were calling this one.

"I'm not going."

"Yes, you are."

"I don't work for you, Bennet."

"No, but you're working with me."

"Are you always this infuriatingly unruffled?"

He shrugged, grinning at her. "When it suits." He hadn't been unruffled this afternoon. Not with his father, and certainly not with Alyssa and the kiss.

The *fake* kiss. That had made him far more irritable with his father than he should have been. Too direct. Too…everything.

"Maybe we shouldn't," Alyssa said, and when he looked up at her, she had her back to him while she pretended to make herself a sandwich. Pretended because she'd been doing so for the last twenty minutes without finishing.

"Maybe we shouldn't what?"

He watched her shoulders lift and fall as though she was inhaling deeply, steeling herself for something. She turned, and though she looked at him, he got the distinct impression she was staring at his nose instead of meeting his actual gaze.

"Maybe we shouldn't work together. Work…period. If my mother's death was cartel business, what does it matter?"

Bennet stood slowly. "It's an unsolved murder case, that's what it matters." He narrowed his eyes at her. Suddenly she was fidgety, and backing off, and that was very much not the Alyssa Jimenez he'd come to know in a short few days.

So maybe you don't know her at all.

"You said yourself that CJ *wants* us to find this all out, and I'm worried about playing into that trap." She hugged her arms around her even as she kept looking at him defiantly. But something had rattled her, and Bennet wasn't about to let her get away with it.

"Why?"

"What do you mean *why*? Did it escape your notice my brother is a dangerous man?"

"Who didn't hurt you when he had the chance."

"That doesn't mean he won't ever hurt me or…"

"Or what?"

"Or you, idiot," she snapped. "He wants us to go looking for this information, but what will happen if we find it? Why can't he find it himself? It's stupid to go after it. It's like helping him."

Bennet took a few steps toward her, and no matter that what she said held some truth, this was all a sudden change from how she'd been earlier. A woman didn't change her mind like this without provocation. "Alyssa. What happened?"

"Noth—"

He curled his fingers around her shoulders and cut her off. "Do not lie to me again. What happened?"

She swallowed, but she didn't lose that defiant tilt to her chin. "It isn't safe to go after this, and I don't want to go to your dumb ball."

"Is that all this is, Princess? Don't want to wear a dress?"

"It isn't funny."

"Then what is it?"

"Dangerous! And not just to us, or to my family, but to your parents. CJ wants to bring them into this. All of us. Why are we falling for it?"

"And why are you suddenly skittish?" Something inside him went past irritation to worry, but that only served to irritate him. He had no business worrying about her state of mind. He had a case to solve.

She gave him a push, stalking past him, though she didn't leave the kitchen, just started pacing across it.

"Alyssa, we'll get nowhere if you lie to me."

Her breathing hitched, and a little sob escaped, and no matter how clearly she tried to fight back the tears, they slipped down her cheeks.

"I don't know who to trust. Who to believe," she said in a squeaky voice, tears tracking down her jaw.

Bennet knew he should keep his hands to himself, but he'd known a lot of things in his life that feeling had taken over, and this was no different. He stepped toward her and brushed the tears off her cheeks. "I know what that's like, and I know I can't make you believe or trust me, but I haven't let you down yet, have I?"

She shook her head.

"I grew up in a world of lies and deception, where it mattered more what people thought than what people did. 'Oh, Mr. So-and-So beats his wife, but the checks he writes for the campaign are quite large, so we'll look the other way.' I hated it, always, so I sought out the exact opposite of that world. Not truth, not honesty, but—"

"Justice," she finished for him in a whisper.

He blinked at her, but he shouldn't have been shocked she understood. She'd grown up in a cartel, and since her kidnapping release had built a bounty hunter business. It might not be legal, but it was a search for justice.

Just like him.

He should stop touching her face, and he would. In a minute or two. "Yeah, I guess you know something about that, don't you?"

"Oscar was here," she said in a whisper.

His hands dropped from her wet face. "What?"

"While you were talking to your father. He...he was in my room. He told me not to listen to CJ. That it was dangerous."

Bennet wanted to yell at her, demand to know why she'd kept it from him for *hours*. Demand everything, but he'd seen that look on her face in so many victims he'd come across in his work.

Fear, and—worse, so much worse—a kind of grim acceptance that pain and suffering were just around the corner.

So, he swallowed down his anger, flexed his fingers

from the fists they wanted to curl into. He breathed evenly, doing his best to unclench his jaw. "And you believe him?"

"Oscar was always the nicest of all of them. The one with a heart, if you can believe it. There'd be no nefarious reason to warn me off. No self serving ones. He was trying to warn me so CJ didn't hurt me. Didn't hurt both of us. He told me not to tell you, Bennet. He's afraid, too. If CJ found out…" She closed her eyes as if she couldn't bear to think about it.

"I know they're your brothers, but I need you on my team, Alyssa. I need your eyes, and I need your brain and memories. I need you to be in this with me so we can find out what happened to your mother, and to you. Justice. For both of you. But you have to trust me, and if Oscar contacts you again, I have to know you'll tell me. I have to be able to trust you. It is necessary."

She used the back of her hand to wipe off her cheek.

"Is there anything else you're keeping from me?"

She looked up at the ceiling as if she was shuffling through all her memories of what she might have kept from him. She eventually shook her head. "No. You've been with me every moment except that one."

"And last night."

"I was sleeping last night," she said, her tear-stained cheeks turning an appealing shade of pink.

There was something seriously warped with him. He should still be angry. He should be nervous and worried and thinking about Sal Cochrane.

But all he could think about was that kiss. *Fake kiss. Fake.*

"Why'd you say you don't know how to kiss?"

Her cheeks darkened into a shade closer to red, but

she met his gaze, attempting and failing at looking regal. "Because I *don't*. My brothers didn't exactly let me out of the compound to *date*, and then I was, you know, kidnapped by a psycho who wouldn't touch me because my belly button wasn't symmetrical."

"Your belly button wasn't… What?"

But she was bulldozing on. "So, I haven't exactly been kissed or anything else, thank you very much."

"You've been free two years." Which he shouldn't have pointed out, nor should he continue this line of conversation, or step even closer.

But he did. Stepped closer and continued.

Her eyes were wide and dark and on him like she couldn't quite force herself to look away. "I… I… I've been building a business," she said, her voice something like a squeak. "And a f-family of sorts, and I… Guys aren't really impressed when you can kick their ass."

His mouth curved. "I don't think you could kick my ass, but you can try if you'd like."

"Bennet," she said so seriously he held his breath, afraid to speak and ruin the moment when her eyes held his and she looked like she was going to confess the world.

Or move in for a real kiss.

"I can't go to a ball," she said in that same serious, grave tone. "Look at me."

His breath whooshed out and he cursed himself for an idiot. She was not going to kiss him, and he should hardly want her to. She was innocent on every level and involved with the most important case of his life.

He needed to get himself together. Focus. Channel a little all-business Vaughn Cooper. "Admittedly your current look is a little bedraggled, but I can fix that."

"*You* can fix that?"

"Well, my staff can make you blend right in."

She folded her arms over her chest and scowled at him skeptically, but he noticed she stopped arguing.

"The ball will be attended by a variety of my mother's political supporters and donors, which means the possibility of Sal Cochrane being there is high. I need you there, on the off chance you recognize him or something about him. I'll need an extra set of eyes who knows at least enough about the Jimenez and Dominguez cartels to notice something that might connect. You're integral, Alyssa."

She seemed to consider that very hard and then finally rolled her eyes. "Fine."

Bennet grinned. "Who knows, you might even enjoy it."

WHEN ALYSSA WOKE the next morning, it was with her cheek stuck to a variety of printouts Bennet had given her last night to pore over. She yawned, peeling the paper off her face. She'd dozed off before finishing the read-through.

But lists of people she'd never heard of and the kind of money they handed over to Bennet's parents for political crap was not exactly tantalizing reading. She'd much prefer criminal records or something with a little pizazz.

She stretched out on the big bed and sighed. Oh, a girl could get used to this kind of luxury. She'd had nice things growing up, even if she had been kept mostly locked up and away, but between two years with The Stallion and two years on her own, luxury had been sorely missing from her life.

But this was a luxury borne of the investigation into her mother's murder. Which caused her to think about last night. A few too many things about last night, but mostly Bennet saying she deserved justice, too.

She was afraid of how much that disarmed her. How much all those little touches that seemed to come so easy to him—an elbow touch, wiping tears off her cheeks— kept throwing her off balance, changing something.

Alyssa blew out a breath. She had to find some kind of power against him. Something to shield herself from all that charm and random acts of sweetness or saying things that felt like soul-deep truths.

Justice. For both of you.

Her life had been unfair, and she knew dwelling on that would send her spiraling into the same awful mental space she'd been in when she'd been kidnapped by The Stallion, but justice had been a foreign concept. The fact it no longer was, the fact someone wanted to fight for her own justice was… Overwhelming. Scary.

Irresistible. And she'd never had to resist anything before. There'd been nothing to resist. She'd only ever wanted freedom, and she'd been given it at twenty-two and somehow created her own little box to exist in.

But all her boxes were colliding, and she didn't know what to do with that. Unfortunately, staying in his comfortable bed was not an option. Something had to be done, and…

She stared hard at the ceiling above her. Bennet had said he needed her. Her help. Her brain. No one had ever needed her before. Gabby had been the first person in her whole life to ask her for help, but Gabby had always been the clear leader in the kidnapping house. Alyssa had followed, had helped, but Gabby hadn't needed her. Not really.

Bennet used the word *need*. Repeatedly. It filled her with hope and fear and a million other things she didn't know what to do with, but the possible only positive of living in basic captivity was that she'd learned to deal with just about anything.

All you could do was keep going.

She slid out of bed and went to pull on her jeans, but noticed that just inside the door was a stool with a pile of neatly folded clothes. She frowned, uncomfortable that she'd slept through someone putting something in her room.

She peered at the stack and noticed a note on top.

Amazing what staff can do. Should fit well enough.

She scowled at the note and then the stack of clothes. Arrogant man. Still, it *would* be nice to put on some clean clothes. Of course, it reminded her she still hadn't visited Natalie in the hospital. They were probably going home today.

Alyssa shook her head as she got dressed. She had to do what she had to do, and with Oscar clearly knowing where she was and how to get inside without tipping any security off, Alyssa had to be careful. She couldn't bring Natalie and Gabby into this.

So, she grabbed her phone and texted her most sincere apologies to both women. She'd make it up to them, explain everything, she just had to make sure she was out of danger first.

And if you're never out of danger?

A question for another day. She headed for the kitchen, where she had no doubt she'd find Bennet hunched over his computer.

"You're terribly predictable, Ranger Stevens," she offered in greeting, heading for the coffee. She was going to get used to the stuff if it killed her. "How's your back?"

"Sal Cochrane does not exist," Bennet said, ignoring her question.

"What?"

"I have been through every lawful search I can make on that name, every spelling, everything. There is no Sal Cochrane in Austin, Texas. And expanding the search doesn't give me any leads either."

"Maybe he doesn't live in Texas."

"Maybe, but why would someone who doesn't live in Texas donate anything to my mother's campaign? She's a state senator."

"Well, that's if we're working under the assumption Sal Cochrane is on the up-and-up." She felt bad bringing it up, because it implicated his icy mother, but still. It was true. "I could ask Jaime for help. He might have access to some different searches than you guys do, or maybe the name has been involved in an FBI investigation or two."

His face blanked. "We're not bringing in the FBI."

"Not even just for information?"

"It's never just information with the FBI, Alyssa."

Which was maybe true, but it didn't help them any. She wanted to argue with him, but she'd figured enough out about Bennet that arguing only made him dig his heels in deeper. She could always contact Jaime herself, ask for any information he could give without the FBI getting involved, but she didn't think lying to Bennet would go over well. Especially after she'd kept the Oscar thing from him, no matter how briefly.

"I emailed my father's assistant for a list of Mom's campaign donors, along with the guest list of the ball. Maybe that'll give us something to go on."

"Why did you email your father's assistant for information about your mother's campaign donors?"

Bennet smiled wryly. "Because if my mother got wind of my asking her assistant for anything, the barrage of questions I would be piled under would make a criminal interrogation look like a walk in the park. Dad already knows I'm nosing around, so it made sense to go through his people."

"And he won't tell your mother?"

"I believe he'd also like to avoid the interrogation." Something on his computer pinged. "There it is." He gestured for her to come next to him where she could see the screen, too.

He opened one of the email attachments, and they both started scanning it.

"There," Alyssa said, pointing at the name. "S. Cochrane."

"S. Cochrane. SCD Enterprises LLC," Bennet muttered. "That sounds like a front company if I ever heard one."

"A front for what?"

"Anything. Money laundering. Drugs."

"A cartel?"

He sucked in a breath, let it out. "It could be."

Which meant his mother might be connected to cartel business. "Bennet—"

"I don't suppose those names mean anything to you or what you know about your family's business."

"I wouldn't know anything about actual business. I

sometimes overheard names or connections, but nothing official like this."

"All right, well, I'll start doing some searching on this LLC and we'll see what I find, but first…" He pulled up the other document, the guest list for the Stevens Christmas Gala.

"He's on the guest list." Bennet nodded firmly. "That's good. That's very good."

Alyssa studied him. He was all tense muscles and clenched jaw and steely gaze today. No charming smiles, no little insinuations over how close they were standing. He wanted to pretend this was all business, but it wasn't. It was family, too.

"If you did turn this over to the FBI, you wouldn't have to be the one who—"

His cutting blue gaze stopped her dead.

"If my mother is knowingly involved in something illegal," he began firmly and forcefully, "then it is my duty and my right to bring her to justice."

"It isn't always that easy."

He stood abruptly from the table. "For me, it is." He stalked over to the coffeepot and Alyssa glanced at the guest list. For a second, it felt as though her heart had stopped.

"Bennet?"

"Please don't try to argue—"

"My father is on the guest list."

Chapter Nine

Bennet stared at the name he hadn't paid any attention to. Carlos Jimenez.

"My parents did not invite a known drug cartel king-pin to our Christmas gala. The press would crucify them both. This is insanity." In no world would his parents invite *Carlos Jimenez* to their Christmas gala. Good lord.

"Bennet…"

"It's a mistake of some kind. A different Carlos Jimenez. Some horrible prank by a political opponent."

"Bennet."

He glanced at her then instead of the completely insane name on his computer screen. She was pale, hugging herself, wide-eyed.

"What is it? You're not going to have to see him. It can't be true."

"I know it isn't true. Bennet, my father… He isn't well. Mentally or physically. CJ runs everything now. He couldn't possibly come even if he wanted to."

Bennet tried to process that, *understand* it. The FBI, the Rangers and probably half of the Austin police department were trying to find Carlos Jimenez, and he wasn't *well*.

"This is bad. This is wrong and bad and…" She

looked up at him, looking as scared as he'd ever seen her. Which, per usual when it came to Alyssa, didn't make any damn sense.

"It's got to be some other Carlos Jimenez. That's a common enough name. It's just a coincidence."

"It's not a coincidence. It's a warning. It's… Something is very, very wrong here. There aren't coincidences right now."

"We'll go to the gala and find out ourselves. Whatever's wrong, whatever's weird, we have the upper hand."

"How?"

"We're on the right side."

She laughed bitterly. "Oh, you are Superman, without the invincibility. Right is not an upper hand. Nothing is an upper hand with all this. CJ is screwing with us, and maybe not just CJ. We don't know who all is involved, and this… Something is very, very wrong, Bennet."

"Yes, we have some question marks, but that's the point. We have to find out, and if we do it right, we will. We'll find out and we'll bring them down."

"Or they kill us, Bennet. Because they can."

She was exhausting. Every time he thought he'd gotten through to her she backed away. Got scared.

"How do you ever track down a skip with this kind of attitude?"

"I'm not tracking down a skip. I'm trying to keep myself and the people I care about *safe*. I'd been safe for two whole years until you showed up."

"So, you're blaming me?"

She raked her hands through her hair. "No!"

"Do you want to stop?" he demanded.

"I…"

"Because we can stop. We can name the Jane Doe, call the case cold, leave it all alone. The end. There are plenty of other cold cases I can work on. Your brother and whoever else was involved in your mother's murder and *your* kidnapping can go along doing whatever they're doing. Justice can just die here, if that's what you really want."

"Oh, screw you," she muttered, and stalked out of the kitchen.

Which he'd take as a no, that's not what she wanted. She wanted justice just as much as he did. More, maybe. She was scared, clearly, though it surprised him. She'd described an awful childhood, a terrible ordeal being kidnapped for *years*, was an illegal bounty hunter for Pete's sake, and yet she was running scared. Constantly.

Something didn't add up, and he didn't like that. She'd promised him she'd told him everything, and he needed to be able to trust her. How could he do that—

An odd noise broke through the silence. Bennet frowned and listened. Silence. Well, maybe Alyssa had just stomped or punched a wall or something. She *was* quite pissed.

Something else, a squeak or a groan or... The back of his neck prickled with foreboding, and maybe he was overreacting, but in the current state of things it didn't hurt to check out a little overreaction.

He moved down the hall silently, listening for any more sounds. Silence, silence, then something that sounded like a bump. Alyssa was probably just stomping around her room, but...

Bennet curled his fingers around the butt of his gun in the holster on his hip as he approached Alyssa's room.

She'd probably laugh at him, but maybe she'd stop being so scared if she laughed at him.

He eased the door open, and Alyssa was standing by the window.

"Oh, good. I thought I—"

The distinct sound of a safety clicking off and the cold press of metal to his temple pissed him off. Not nearly as much as the drop of blood trailing down Alyssa's cheek from her temple.

"Keep your head forward and drop any weapons and kick them behind you," the man with the gun whispered. "You try anything, I kill you both."

"Oh, come on now. You're not going to hurt your sister."

"You think I'm Jimenez? Insulting."

The gun dug harder into Bennet's temple, and he'd admit there was a little fear now. Was this really not one of her brothers? That couldn't be good, but it *did* mean they were moving in the right direction.

"Drop the weapons."

Bennet forced himself to remain calm, to carefully pull his weapon from its holster. Jumping out of the way or swinging the gun at this man was too dangerous. He would fire off a shot one way or another, and it could hit Alyssa.

So, Bennet had to worry about disarming him before he worried about weapons. He set the gun on the ground, gently nudged it behind him as he held up one finger at his side where the man couldn't see him, then held up two, adding his best questioning eyebrow, hoping Alyssa understood his code.

She lifted her bound hands to the wound this man must have inflicted on her, and would pay for. Bloodily. But as she dropped her hand, she held up one single finger.

One he could take.

"On your knees," the man demanded, jabbing the gun harder against his head again.

"Just don't shoot," Bennet said, trying to inflict his voice with some fear, even though the last thing he was was afraid. He was furious.

"No use fighting, idiot. I'm taking her, and if you try to stop me, you will die. Maybe not today, but soon, and painfully, and in a way no one will ever find your body. Do we understand each other?"

"Perfectly," Bennet replied, and before he'd even gotten the word out he struck, landing a tight-fisted blow to the man's throat.

The gun went off at almost the exact time Alyssa launched herself across the room and against her assailant. The man fell and Bennet flung himself on top of the assailant, who'd fallen to the ground at Alyssa's attack, ignoring the pinpricks of pain in his back from yesterday's wounds. The attacker fought viciously, kicking and nearly landing an unmanning blow before Bennet had him pinned to the ground. But pinning him meant he didn't have any limbs left to inflict a blow.

He glanced up at Alyssa. "Break his nose."

"Gladly." And with perfect form, even with her hands bound together, Alyssa jabbed her elbow into the man's nose with a sickening crack and a satisfying spurt of blood.

The man screamed in pain, and Bennet used the distraction to shift enough so he could roll the man onto his stomach, using his knee to hold him down while he jerked the man's arms behind his back roughly.

"I think he has more zip ties in his pocket," Alyssa said, nodding behind her back.

This man had broken into his home, restrained and hurt Alyssa, and he had *more* zip ties in his pocket. Bennet dug his knee harder into the man's back. "Kneel on his hands."

"Oh… I… Okay." Alyssa shuffled one way and then the other before lowering into a kneeling position on the back of their assailant.

"Really dig your knees into his wrists so he can't move, and I'll grab the zip ties."

The man groaned in agony, and Bennet flashed a grin. "Good girl." With absolutely no finesse, he roughly searched the man's pockets until he found the zip ties. He gave Alyssa a boost back to her feet then as roughly and tightly as he could, he connected the ties around the man's wrists and ankles.

Bennet stood and watched as the man writhed and groaned. Bennet was tempted to kick him for good measure, but Alyssa still had her hands bound and he wanted to get her freed as soon as possible.

"Where's your knife?"

She cleared her throat. "Well, it's where it always is."

"Which pocket?"

"Um… Well…"

"Where, Alyssa?"

She met his gaze, something indecipherable on her face. "My bra." She bent her elbows, clearly trying to maneuver her fingers into her shirt, but she couldn't bend her elbows or twist her fingers enough to fish it out.

Bennet forced himself to look away from her attempts. "I'll just go get the, uh, kitchen scissors."

Alyssa rolled her eyes. "And leave him here? Just pull it out of my bra, for heaven's sake."

Bennet laughed, couldn't help himself. "And here I thought this job couldn't surprise me any more."

ALYSSA'S TEMPLE THROBBED from where it had hit the bed after the strange man had pushed her down after she'd stepped inside her room. She had no idea where he'd come from, since she'd kept the window locked ever since Oscar had snuck in that way.

She was furious, just righteously livid, that this man had caught her so off guard he'd managed to knock her down and tie her hands. When he'd heard Bennet's approach, he'd jerked her to her feet and told her to stand by the window without saying a word.

She would have told him to take a flying leap, but she hadn't wanted to risk Bennet's life, and she'd trusted that Bennet could get them out of this, and he had. Not just gotten them out of it, but let her break her attacker's nose.

It felt good. It felt like teamwork.

Now Bennet Stevens, Texas Ranger, one hundred tons too charming for his own good, was retrieving the knife from her bra like he was afraid of a pair of breasts. *Her* breasts in particular.

"Don't act like you've never gotten to know your way around a woman's underwear before," she muttered, irritated that no matter how nonchalant she tried to act, her skin felt prickly and tight and all too desperate to know what Bennet's fingertips might feel like across her skin.

He let out a sigh, and then his hand was moving inside her shirt. He paused briefly and cleared his throat. "Um…right or left?"

It was her turn to laugh because, dear Lord this was the most ridiculous situation she'd ever found herself in. "Right."

His fingers brushed the outline of her bra, tracing the seam, touching her skin with the rough, blunt tips of his finger. Oh, God. She was dizzy. Which was possibly the head injury, or the fact he was touching the wrong breast.

"I—I meant *my* r-right," she managed to squeak out. "Not your right."

"That would have been helpful to know before feeling up the other one."

Cheeks on fire, Alyssa did her best to scowl. "You'll live." She knew without a shadow of a doubt she should keep her gaze on the floor, or look up at the ceiling, or even at the bad guy writhing around on the floor, but her gaze drifted to Bennet's.

Who was smiling, all lazy, Texas charm. "Yes, I do believe I will live," he murmured, pulling the Swiss Army knife out of her bra and shirt. "Now, hold out your wrists so I can cut those off."

"What are we going to do with him?"

Bennet stared icily at their attacker. "We're going to leave him here for the time being."

"Here?"

Bennet carefully pulled the knife against the plastic of the zip ties until they snapped, freeing her hands. Then he bent over and retrieved the man's gun and handed it to her. "Keep this on him. He so much as moves a muscle, you have my permission to shoot. I'll be right back."

"Bennet—"

But he was already gone, striding out of the room and picking up his gun he'd been forced to put down on the way out.

"You'll be a dead woman by week's end," the man hissed.

Alyssa kicked his shin. Hard. Then waited for him to finish howling before she spoke. "But I'm not one yet." He would have had her if not for Bennet, and that was humiliating, but Bennet had been there, and Alyssa was no longer running scared.

No, from here on out every clue that led them closer would only firm her resolve. Someone wanted to murder her like they'd murdered her mother? Well, it would take a damn army. No amount of brothers or her father's name could change that.

Bennet returned with a pair of handcuffs and a roll of duct tape. Whistling something that sounded an awful lot like "We Wish You a Merry Christmas," he handcuffed one of the man's bound hands to the foot of the bed. Then, still whistling, he ripped off a length of duct tape and fastened it over the man's mouth.

Without another word, he stood and took Alyssa's arm and led her out of the room. Once in the hallway, any smiles or humor or whistling stopped. Bennet's face went hard and, if Alyssa wasn't totally bad at reading him, furious.

"Wh-what are we going to do?" she asked, because no matter how she tried to free her arm from his grasp, it was like iron. Leading her through the house and to the door to the garage.

"We're going to get you over to my parents' house. They have much heavier security over there."

"What about him?"

"Once I get you settled, I'm going to call the police and report an attempted burglary, of course."

"You're going to lie to the police?"

He stopped her before they walked out the door, taking her by both elbows and pulling her close. "He was one minute away from kidnapping you, and possibly killing you. This isn't just your brothers anymore, and your safety is paramount. I will do whatever it takes to keep you safe while we solve the case, including lying to the local police. Now, can I count on you to do the same?"

"But—"

"But what if my parents are in on it?" he finished for her, clearly irritated by her line of thought.

Still, she nodded.

"Mother will be at her lunch meeting. Dad is at some charity thing until three. Once I get this situated, you are not leaving my sight until we figure this out, and we won't be going anywhere unarmed."

"I'm always armed."

"More than a Swiss Army knife in your bra."

"So, you're going to follow me to the bathroom? Sleep with me?" Which was possibly not the right wording of her question.

"If I have to," he replied unperturbed, beginning to pull her again. Through the garage and out into the open, one hand on her elbow and the other on his holstered gun. He moved quickly and efficiently, scanning every inch of the landscape as they moved from guesthouse to main house.

"He had to have gotten here somehow. Do you think someone else is out there?"

"Maybe," Bennet said in that cold, detached Texas Ranger tone. "If someone else is, they can't be too close with a vehicle. They'd never get past the gates. But we need to hurry on the chance someone is out there, and make sure they don't come looking for our friend."

Bennet keyed a code into the main house's garage door. Practically silently, it glided open and Bennet moved them inside, closing the garage door behind them.

They stepped into what was some sort of finished basement cellar-type thing—stainless steel deep freezer, matching fridge, a pantry full of canned goods and alcohol and all kinds of nonperishables.

Bennet led her up a staircase, and they stepped out in a kitchen where two people were sitting at a table sipping tea.

Bennet nodded at them. "Mrs. Downy. Kinsey. Can you make sure no staff enter my room for the next few hours?"

The older-looking woman nodded. "Of course."

Then Alyssa was being led out of the kitchen, down another hall, through another room she couldn't ascertain the use for. Then they were clearly in the main entryway because a giant chandelier glittered above them.

It was like a movie. There was a grand staircase in the middle, all gleaming polished woods decorated with garland and red bows. On the other side of the staircase she could catch a glimpse of what had to be a gigantic tree decorated completely in gold.

But Bennet didn't give her any time to soak it in. He was pulling her up the stairs and down a long hall and into another giant room. This one wasn't white, though.

It was a kind of forest green and some kind of tan color. Very woodsy and masculine.

"This is *your* room."

"Well, it was when I lived here. Now you're going to sit tight," he instructed, going through and checking all the windows even though they were on the second story. "Don't leave. Don't move, and on the off chance someone comes in this room, you shoot," he ordered, pointing at the gun he'd handed her earlier.

Alyssa frowned at the weapon she held. "What if it's someone from your parents' staff?"

"You heard me leave instructions for no one to enter. So, if someone does, you can almost be certain it's nefarious."

And clearly she wasn't as smart as she'd always fancied herself to be because she finally understood what was happening. "So, I'm just supposed to sit here in this room? Locked up."

Bennet didn't even pause, already striding for the door. "It's for your own protection, Alyssa."

"That's what they said, too."

He stopped and turned, frowning at her in that way she might have been intimidated by if she wasn't so irrationally hurt by all this.

"It isn't fair to compare me to your brothers."

"Isn't it?" she returned, shrugging as if she didn't have a care in the world.

"I don't have time for this," he muttered, raking a hand through his hair, but he didn't walk out. "I can't have you call the police because then you have to explain why you're in my parents' guesthouse. It's too complicated. You can't go milling around the house because I don't know who in this house we can trust.

I actually don't know who we can trust, period, and neither do you. This is temporary while I deal with the police, and I need you on board."

"You need me to sit down and shut up."

"Hey, I let you break that guy's nose. Never accuse me of not using your unique talents." He smiled, but she couldn't bring herself to smile back. This was all too familiar, all too…much. She couldn't stand the idea that she'd felt like Bennet's partner there for a little bit, and now he was going to lock her away, too.

"Alyssa, I can't imagine what this might feel like from your perspective, but try to think about it from mine, okay? I'll be back." And then he was gone and the door was locked. End of discussion.

Alyssa sat down on the bed, fury and hurt pumping through her. But the worst part was knowing he was right and that she had to, once again, sit in a locked room and twiddle her thumbs.

Chapter Ten

Bennet dealt with the police, half his mind elsewhere. He wanted the squad car gone before either of his parents returned home, and he wanted to get back to Alyssa ASAP.

Everything had gotten completely out of hand, and he was half-tempted to send the whole of the Texas Rangers after CJ Jimenez.

But it wouldn't solve his case, and it wouldn't help Alyssa.

Luckily, being a Ranger himself helped speed up the Austin police investigation, and by the time Bennet was allowed to go, they even had a suspected partner in crime and vehicle for the getaway car.

He didn't know who'd sent the men, though, and that was a problem. All of this was an increasingly complicated problem. Bennet grabbed his laptop, his extra sidearm, all the clothes he'd gotten for Alyssa and shoved everything into a bag.

He didn't like the idea of staying at the main house whether his parents were involved in this mess or not, but he couldn't think of a safer place for them right now. Security was tight, and if one of his parents turned out to be his enemy, he'd keep them close and smoke them out.

That was something he couldn't allow himself to think too deeply on. Whatever happened, whatever *justice* was, he'd deal with the emotional fallout when it was over.

He entered through the garage again. When he got to the kitchen, Kinsey was still there, though she was no longer sipping tea with Mrs. Downy, who was in charge of the kitchen. Kinsey was sitting at the table, alone, a computer in front of her.

She'd run this house like a military institution since Bennet could remember, so when she gestured for him to approach, Bennet could only obey.

"Shall I tell your mother you and a guest will be staying with us?"

"You haven't yet?"

Kinsey's mouth curved just a fraction, but Bennet had known the severe woman most of his life. Which meant he knew that smile was a feat indeed, just like when he was a teenager and she'd finally allowed him to call her Kinsey instead of Ms. Kinsey.

"The girl was bleeding. Police cars. I don't want to be the one to break all that to your mother."

"Then don't."

"Someone will."

"*I* will." At least that way he could control the information, gauge his mother's reaction. Did she know? Was she part of this? He hated having doubts about his own parents. No matter how little he got along with them, they were still his family. He loved them.

And it was looking more and more likely one of them had cartel ties.

Kinsey pushed a small box toward him. "Clean her up first."

Damn. He'd been so worked up about getting the attacker and police taken care of, he'd forgotten all about Alyssa's head wound.

"She's pretty," Kinsey commented as Bennet took the box.

"She's work," he replied firmly.

Kinsey made a noncommittal sound that Bennet didn't have time to argue with. He strode through the house and to his room. He knocked, offering his name.

The door unlocked and opened a crack, the barrel of the gun the only thing appearing in the crack.

"Alyssa."

"Just making sure." The door opened the rest of the way, and she was smirking, gun still in her hand. It should not arouse him in the least.

"Uh-huh."

Alyssa set the gun down on the nightstand once he'd entered and closed and locked the door behind him.

"So, what happened?"

"They arrested the guy for breaking and entering and attempted burglary. They think they have a lead on the car that was waiting for him outside the gates. Did you recognize our guy?"

She shook her head. "I tried to pay attention to anything that might have been familiar or connect to anything, but he was nobody I've ever met."

"What about this man?" Bennet asked, pulling out his phone and bringing up the pictures he'd had the Austin officer send him. "He's our suspect for being the driver of the getaway car."

Alyssa frowned, leaning closer to the screen. "He looks familiar. He... He used to work for my father."

"Used to?"

"Yeah. Eli... I don't know last names, or even if that's his real name, but his name was Eli and he worked my father, but he defected." She looked up at him. "I'm sure of it."

"What exactly does *defected* mean?"

"I'm not sure of the exact cartel meaning. I used to think it was going to the cops, but it's what my brothers said about my mom. She defected. To a cartel rival. And if we put it together with what my father told me about Dominguez having my mother... Maybe that's the connection."

"Except we don't know what Dominguez has to do with any of this."

Alyssa swallowed, and though she was trying to look tough, to act tough, he could see the worry in her eyes. "He wants me, though. For whatever reason, he's after me."

"Why now? You've been free for two years. If he wanted you as revenge, he's had years to do it."

"There has to be an inciting incident we don't know about."

"That started recently, but before I came to your office, if your brothers' men were following you on your last job."

"But... I don't know what it would be."

"We'll start looking into cartel cases and see if we can't find some recent dustup we might make a connection to."

"And if we can't?"

Bennet didn't know what to say to that. He was

tempted to make a joke about crossing bridges once they were burning behind them, but she didn't look like she'd laugh. Or smile. Or do anything except maybe break.

He couldn't bear the thought of breaking her.

"I don't want to be a prisoner anymore, Bennet. Not one of my family, or a madman, or whatever the hell is going on here. I don't want to be locked up and shoved away. I won't live like that, even if it puts me in danger. I'd rather be dead."

"You're not going to end up dead. Not on my watch."

"What do you care? I shouldn't be anyone to you."

It was such a vulnerable statement, clearly speaking to all those hurts she'd somehow survived. Trust broken over and over again.

He didn't know what it was like to be a prisoner, not in any sense of the word. Even in the world his parents had created he'd broken mostly free. Maybe they'd greased some palms for him that he'd wished they hadn't, but it was hardly kidnapping or betrayal.

But somehow, despite his complete lack of experience in the matter, he could feel that pain of hers, and he wanted to soothe it. He wanted to be as honest as she was being when he should be cagey or stone-faced or whatever would best benefit this case.

But as gung-ho as he'd been just days ago about solving *this* case, the oldest cold case on file at the Texas Rangers, it had irrevocably become about something else. About her.

"What do I care?" He shook his head. "You hold your own. You make me laugh at the wrongest of times. You're smart, and we understand each other. Justice. We understand that. Not everyone does. Maybe you shouldn't be anyone to me, but you are."

He stepped forward and more than anything else he'd ever wanted in his whole life, he wanted to press his mouth to hers. Not in some ploy to convince his father to leave, or just because he wondered what it might be like. No, he wanted to kiss her because she was her and he thought somehow their mouths fitting together would make everything all right.

But it wouldn't. So, he held up the first aid box Kinsey had given him. "Now, it's my turn to bandage you up."

ALYSSA HATED PORING over paperwork. It was boring. As much as she often had to do some investigating when she was hunting down a skip, she at least got to do stuff. Call people. Go places. Plan.

This was all looking for some magical clue, one that could be absolutely anything. She glanced at Bennet, who was sitting on the window seat, legs stretched out in front of him and crossed at the ankles, focus lasered on the computer screen in front of him. He didn't lean against the wall, likely because of his cuts, but he still looked…powerful and smart and a million other things she should ignore.

Anytime he found something he thought might be important or relevant, he printed it out and made her read it.

She wanted to be useful, but she also wanted to make a move. She'd already learned that being kidnapped with someone wasn't all that much different from being kidnapped alone. In The Stallion's house, there'd been three other girls with her, but it hadn't changed the fact she'd been alone and shut in.

"You can go to bed if you're tired," Bennet offered, never taking his gaze off the screen.

"I'm not tired," Alyssa muttered, poking at the tray of food an older woman had brought up a few hours ago. "I'm bored."

"You'd make a terrible policeman."

"Why do you think I'm a bounty hunter?"

He glanced over at her, mouth curved at one side. "Illegal bounty hunter."

She flashed him a grin. "Even better. Don't have to worry about following any pesky laws."

"How's your head?"

"How's your back?"

"Fine. How's your head?" he repeated, clearly unamused by her unwillingness to answer the question.

"You should see the other guy."

"I believe I did. Impressive indeed. Seriously, though?"

"It's fine." If fine was painful throbbing. "Didn't even lose consciousness."

"Look, we'll have to sleep in shifts, so you might as well try to grab a few hours."

"Why do we have to sleep in shifts?"

"Well, for starters I'm not going to sleep on the floor."

She cocked her head. She'd sort of assumed she'd sleep on that cushy window seat he was on. He was too tall to fit, but she'd be able to stretch out just fine. It was a little interesting he hadn't thought of that, though. He'd gone straight to the only option being him sleeping on the floor.

Apparently with her was not an option. *You know it's not.* And it shouldn't be something she was imagining. She needed to focus on reality. "You don't think we're safe."

"I don't *know* if we're safe. For the time being, one of us is always on guard. We sleep in shifts. And, while one is sleeping, the other one is working. Until we get to the bottom of it."

Alyssa flopped back on the bed, frowning. "And how am I supposed to sleep with all the lights blazing?"

Without Bennet even moving from the window seat, the lights flicked off.

"Your computer—"

He made a move with his arm without even looking and suddenly he was pulling a curtain from behind him to enclose the little window seat alcove. The room was completely dark.

"Good night, Alyssa," he said from behind the curtain.

Since it was dark and he was behind a curtain, she indulged in the childish impulse to stick her tongue out at him.

"It's too quiet in here," she grumbled.

"No, it isn't, because you keep whining."

She scowled and shifted deeper into the unbelievably soft sheets. She wasn't tired in the least, but she also wasn't *whining*. She was going insane. The walls were closing in, and at least complaining kept them at bay for a while.

How could she sleep when she was locked up again? Oh, this was by far the nicest room she'd been locked in, but amenities didn't matter when you were essentially a prisoner. Hands tied from *doing* anything because they didn't know what the hell was going on.

She scowled over at the curtain Bennet was behind.

The irritating thing was she understood why they had to do all this. She just hated it. Hated feeling locked up and ineffective. She wanted to do something. Even if it meant smashing her elbow into some assailant's nose.

At least that had been action. At least that had *felt* good. She wanted something that felt good instead of dark and oppressive. Instead of like her life would only ever be some terrible, lonely prison.

But she wasn't exactly alone right now, curtain or no curtain. Her mind drifted to her kiss with Bennet. *Fake kiss.* Except no matter how the pretense had been fake, the kiss hadn't been. His mouth had been on hers, and more than once his hands had been on her.

Sometimes he looked at her and she was almost certain that whatever she'd felt in the midst of that fake kiss—attraction and need and the desperate curiosity of what more he could do with that all-too-charming mouth of his—he felt it, too.

She didn't know *why* he'd be attracted to someone like her, and she realized she probably wasn't the world's leading expert in men and attraction, but she also wasn't stupid. He'd gently bandaged her head, but on occasion his gaze had drifted to her mouth.

That meant something. She'd spent the past two years in the orbit of Gabby and Jaime, who couldn't seem to keep their hands off each other no matter how committed they got. So, she may not have experience with attraction or lust or anything, but she did know what it looked like.

She'd really like to know what it *felt* like. She'd spent the past two years building something of a free life, but she hadn't dated or flirted or even put herself out there in any way, shape or form because she'd been waiting for something to come to her.

Like all her life she'd waited for freedom. What a waste all that waiting was.

"Bennet?" she asked into the quiet of the room.

"What?"

"How many women have you kissed?"

He made a sound, something like a cough or rough inhale. "I... How is that relevant to anything?"

"I didn't say I was going to ask you a *relevant* question. I'm just asking you *a* question."

He cleared his throat. "I... I don't know. I don't have a running tally."

"Oh? That many." And on some level she wanted to know everything about them. Why he'd kissed them. How far it had gone. What he'd felt.

And on some level she wanted to elbow every woman in the nose just as she'd done to the man who'd attacked her.

"It isn't about how many, it's just... I'd have to do the math and... Why are you asking me this?"

"Well, you know, I've only kissed you."

There was a moment of heavy silence. "That wasn't a kiss," he said, his voice something closer to a growl.

"Oh? What was it then?"

"A...charade."

"A *charade*," she repeated, because even though it had been an act, a fake, *charade* seemed such an oddly proper word.

"That's what I said."

"But I was just thinking if I'm going to die—"

He jerked the curtain open, the harsh computer light

glinting off the angry expression on his face. "You're not going to die."

"You can't *promise* I'm not going to die, and God knows someday I will. So. You know. I should probably know what it's like."

"What what's like?"

"Sex."

He didn't move, didn't speak, and she was almost certain he didn't even breathe. Which was kind of funny, all in all. That it just took the mention of sex to catch Ranger Stevens off guard.

And since he was off guard, she slid out of bed and walked over to him. He watched her approach warily, but he didn't ward her off, and he didn't tell her to stop. She walked all the way until her knees were all but touching the window seat. She looked down at him.

He held her gaze, but he still didn't say anything. Everything she knew about Bennet suggested he'd be the kind of man who'd make the first move, and yet he just *sat* there. Not making *any* move.

"It would be something of a no-no, wouldn't it?" she asked, her voice a little breathless with something like nerves but not quite that. Adrenaline, maybe. *Anticipation*. "Because I'm involved in this case."

"First of all, please never say the phrase 'no-no' again. Second of all, yes. It would be incredibly wrong. On every level."

"Come on. Not *every* level."

"Okay, nine out of ten levels," he returned, and she could tell he was trying very hard not to be amused.

"So, maybe we explore that one-out-of-ten level," Alyssa offered hopefully, covertly moving to take the computer off his lap. Except as she glanced at the screen she noticed something oddly familiar. Something she hadn't seen in years.

"What is this a picture of?" she asked breathlessly, this time not nerves or anticipation or anything other than the excitement they might find a lead.

"What… What?" Bennet asked, clearly not making the leap to work quite as quickly as she had.

"The picture you have on the screen," she said, pointing at it as she leaned in closer. "What's it of?"

"Uh… I… The FBI believes the man on the right is Salvador Dominguez. It's the only known picture of him law enforcement has as far as I know."

"And the man next to him?"

"No one's identified him. It's too shadowy, he's looking away from the camera and there're no markings to give any clues."

"But there is an earring."

Bennet squinted at the screen. "I suppose."

"It's one of my brothers."

His head jerked toward hers. "How do you know that?"

"The earring. It's a *J* with dragon horns. It was my father's. Now, that definitely isn't my father. This guy is too tall, too broad. But it's one of my brothers, I can almost guarantee it. My father wouldn't have given that earring to anyone else. When was this photo taken?"

"Last month."

"So, one of my brothers is photographed talking with the head of a rival cartel a month ago."

Bennet blew out a breath. "Well, it looks like we might have our inciting incident, doesn't it?"

"I don't know what *I* have to do with it, though."

"Your brothers love you. To bad men trying to hurt each other, love is a weapon. A weakness."

She glanced at Bennet, feeling unaccountably sad for some reason. "That isn't just to bad men trying to hurt each other, Bennet. Love is always a weapon."

"It doesn't have to be," he replied steadfastly, his blue eyes an odd shade in the light of the laptop screen.

Her chest felt tight, and her heart felt too much like it was being squeezed. She'd wanted to feel something, but not this. Not anything to do with love, especially when it came to her brothers. *If* they loved her, that love had only ever been used as a weapon, no matter what Bennet thought.

"Well, I guess we've got something to go on now," she said, straightening and wrapping her arms around herself. She felt sad and alone and suddenly she wouldn't mind just going to bed and being locked away. "I'll take my sleeping shift, then."

Before she realized what he was doing, Bennet had his hand fisted in her shirt and jerked her down so that she had to grab his shoulders or risk just falling into his lap.

Then his mouth was on hers. Gentle, and something that kind of made her want to cry because there'd been so little of it in her life. Softness. His lips caressed hers, his tongue slowly tracing the outline of her bottom lip, and all she could do was soak it up.

She felt like melted wax and a firework ready to burst all at the same time, and underneath her hands his shoulders were just these steady rocks to lean on.

He pulled away, though his hand was still fisted in her shirt, and his breath wafted across her still-wet lips.

"*That* was a kiss," he murmured. He released her and grabbed the curtain. "Now go to sleep," he ordered, and snapped the curtain closed between them.

Chapter Eleven

Bennet woke with a start and then a groan of pain. He'd dozed off on the stupid window seat and now his neck and shoulders were paying the price, the cuts on his back throbbing. He rubbed his eyes, realizing through the gauzy fabric of the curtains that covered the window, daylight shone far brighter than he'd have liked.

He should have been up hours ago. He should have never fallen asleep. Sleep was wasting precious time they didn't have to unravel all of these confusing clues.

He fumbled for the curtain that separated the window seat from the room and managed to shove it open.

Alyssa was sitting in the bed, cross-legged with his laptop perched on her thighs. There was a tray of fresh fruit and bagels and a coffeepot on the bed next to her.

"How'd you get that?"

"Ms. Kinsey brought up the food and coffee—much better than yours, FYI. The laptop? I took it while you snored away. Very unattractive, I might add."

Bennet grunted irritably, remembering exactly why he'd allowed himself to doze off on the window seat.

The thought of waking up Alyssa, asleep in his bed, warm and soft and more alluring than she had any right to be, had been a little too much to bear at two in the morning. He'd been afraid that if he'd even simply nudged her shoulder he'd want to touch all of her.

And that was most wholeheartedly a *no-no*. Which made kissing her last night inexcusable and irrational and something he had no business considering in the light of the morning.

"Coffee?" she asked sweetly.

"Are you always this obnoxious in the morning?"

"Morning is the absolute best time of day."

He grabbed the coffeepot and one of the mugs and poured. "You're evil."

She laughed, and no matter how much he hated mornings or the awful, digging pain in his neck and the fact his back felt like it was on fire, he liked hearing her laugh. He liked a few too many things about Alyssa Jimenez, drug kingpin's daughter.

Yeah, that was never going to fly in any of his lives— Texas Ranger, politicians' son. The conclusion of this case would be the conclusion of their time together.

You can't promise I'm not going to die, and God knows someday I will. So. You know. I should probably know what it's like.

Those words kept bouncing around in his brain, completely unwelcome. Someday she *would* know what it was like, but it wouldn't be with him. For all the reasons he'd gone through a million times over.

"Find anything?" he asked, easing onto the other side of the bed, enough space and a tray of food between them, to keep his head on the case.

Maybe.

"Well, I found that no matter how hard or zoomed in I look at the picture, I can't tell which of my brothers is in that picture. I have committed Salvador Dominguez's face to memory, though, and I can't help but thinking he's behind yesterday."

"Agreed."

"How did you connect my mother to me when she was a Jane Doe?"

"Happenstance. I was searching old case files and happened to notice a similarity in a murder that was committed by a known member of the Jimenez cartel. The victim in that murder had the exact same wounds and was buried in the exact same way not too far from where…"

She'd looked away, but he understood that thinking of her mother's wounds and where her body was found was too much even for Alyssa.

"What I didn't know when I came to see you was that my Jane Doe *was* a Jimenez."

"Who was the man convicted of the other murder?"

"Dom Coch… Holy hell. Dom Cochrane. Spelled differently, but that's too much of a coincidence to the name your brother gave us."

"I don't remember anyone named Dom, but I wouldn't have known everyone, I guess."

Bennet gestured for her to hand over the laptop. She did so, and he logged into the Ranger system while he sipped his coffee. "I'm going to do some searches for Dom Cochrane and see what pops up."

Alyssa took one of the bagels off the tray between them and spread cream cheese across the top. She frowned at it while Bennet typed the name into the database.

Something was bothering her, and she wasn't saying what. He didn't like knowing she was keeping some-thing from him, even if it was feelings rather than information. He wanted to know everything. About the case. About her.

Which was the absolute last thing he needed right now. He tried to focus on the results of his search, but Alyssa licked a smudge of cream cheese off her thumb. Which he shouldn't watch. Or think about.

Either she felt his gaze or just happened to look over, but somehow their gazes met as her thumb disappeared into her mouth. Everything inside him tightened and ached, and would it really be *that* bad to indulge in something this potent? He'd still solve the case, and maybe it was morally ambiguous to get involved with someone connected to one of his cases, but hell, Vaughn had done it, and he was the most morally upstanding person Bennet had ever met.

A sharp knock sounded at the door, and they both nearly jumped a foot, the tray tipping over and spilling the remaining bagels onto the bed.

"Who is it?" Bennet growled.

"Kinsey."

He shoved the computer off his lap and strode over to the door, doing everything he could to take his mind off the completely untimely erection.

He opened the door a crack. "Yes?"

Kinsey looked vaguely amused, but her message was brief.

"Ms. Delaney is here with the dresses. Shall I send her up here?"

"That would be perfect. Thank you."

Kinsey nodded and Bennet shut the door. He had half a mind to bang his head against it. Instead, he turned back to the bed to find Alyssa staring at him, her eyebrows drawn together.

"You really grew up like this?"

"Like what?"

"Servants? Everything at your beck and call. Dresses… Wait." She sat up straighter on the bed. "What did she say about *dresses*?"

Bennet tried not to smile, but half his mouth curved of its own accord. "You'll need something for the ball."

"But…"

"We can't exactly go to the *mall* after you've been attacked, so I asked Kinsey what we could do. She suggested calling one of my mother's personal shoppers with your size and have them make a house call."

"B-but… I can't afford…"

"Alyssa, honestly."

"I don't want you paying for stuff," she said stubbornly.

"Except I'm the one *forcing* you to go to this gala, and you'll need to fit in if we have hope of getting any information. Which means jeans and a T-shirt aren't going to cut it, and neither is…well, no offense, darling, but anything you'd pick out on your own."

She scowled at him, which was good. Better her to be angry with him than anything else.

"And, just so you can settle into the idea before Friday night, I'll also be hiring a hair and makeup person to do all that stuff women do."

"What stuff?"

"Hell if I know, but the person I hire will, and that's all that matters. Now, you can pick whatever dress you'd like. Cost is no option."

"Oh, well, then why don't you shower me with jewels, too," she returned sarcastically.

"Don't tempt me."

She opened her mouth, likely to say something scathing, but another knock sounded at the door.

Bennet opened it, smiling at Tawny Delaney, whom he'd met on occasion at events such as the Christmas gala. Her father was in oil and a dedicated donor to his father's many political endeavors.

Tawny also *might* have been on the list of women he'd kissed, and he couldn't help but be glad Alyssa didn't have any such list.

"Ben. It's so good to see you again," Tawny said, smiling up at him.

"Thank you for coming," he returned, ushering her in. A man with a rolling rack of what Bennet could only assume were dresses began to push the rack inside, but Bennet slapped a palm to the rack.

"I'll take it from here, sir. You can wait down in the foyer, if you'd be so kind."

"Ben?"

"Sorry. Can't be too careful right now."

"Oh. Well. That's fine," Tawny replied, though she looked a little nervous. "Where's our client?"

Bennet gestured to the bed, where Alyssa was sprawled out, defiantly so, scowling. Bennet wanted to laugh even though it was ridiculous.

"Oh, well." Tawny cleared her throat, her smile looking so forced Bennet winced. "Won't this be fun?"

"Yes, it will. Won't it, Alyssa?" he said, giving her a meaningful look he hoped she realized meant *get your butt off the bed.*

"Sure it will, *Ben*," Alyssa said, emphasis on the shortened name, still lounging on the rumpled covers.

It was more than likely he was going to end up paying very dearly for this.

ALYSSA WATCHED AS Tawny the tall, put-together blonde started taking the covers off the dresses on the rack. She chattered on about jewel tones and coloring, and all Alyssa could think was she would never in a million years look like this woman.

There would always be a little drowned sewer rat in her. A girl who'd grown up locked in a room with only men for companions. Even when her mother had been alive and around she hadn't spent much time *around*. The kids were supposed to play with each other while the adults did the serious business of running a cartel.

"Where should we do the trying on?" Tawny asked brightly.

"There's a bathroom through that door there," Bennet offered.

"Perfect." Tawny turned her attention to Alyssa, all bright smiles and comforting drawl. "We'll start with three. More than three and it gets overwhelming." She plucked three dresses off the rack and rested them across her arm before marching for the bathroom. "These are my top choices based on your coloring and build."

She stepped inside the bathroom and waited for Alyssa to hesitantly enter before she closed the door shut and hung the dresses on the shower curtain.

"My, the Stevenses do know how to build a house, don't they?" Tawny said conversationally. She handed Alyssa a blindingly gold dress. "Let's start with this one."

Alyssa recoiled. Visibly. "No."

Tawny blinked, and for a fraction of a second Alyssa felt kind of crappy for her antagonistic behavior. It wasn't this woman's fault she was everything Alyssa wasn't and never could be.

"It's a beautiful dress," Alyssa offered, shoving her hands into her pockets. "It's too loud for this. I need to blend in."

Tawny smiled indulgently. "Isn't it every woman's fantasy to stand out?"

The question landed a little hard, right in the heart. Stand out? All standing out had ever gotten her was locked up, and somehow she still wanted that moment. A moment when the attention was on her for something *good* for once.

But, this wasn't that moment. "This is more a business venture than a personal, womanly venture."

"Okay, well, let's try the black, then." She held out a black dress with a fluffy thing of green hanging off it.

Alyssa wanted to refuse this one, too, but it was no use. She did have to fit in, and fitting in meant some fancy dress the likes of which she'd never even dreamed about wearing it was so foreign to all the lives she'd lived.

She took it and waited for Miss Texas Perfect to leave, but Tawny just waited expectantly.

"Oh, well, I'm supposed to stay with the dresses," Tawny explained. "Part of the job. I do it all the time." Sensing Alyssa's continued hesitation, Tawny nodded. "How about I turn my back?"

"Sure," Alyssa muttered. Maybe it was stupid, but the last thing she wanted was Tawny seeing her subpar underwear. Tawny probably had a matching set. All silk or lace or something beautiful and expensive.

And what would you ever do with something like that?

Hoping to get it over with as quickly as possible,

Alyssa shucked her clothes and roughly pulled on the dress. It was black, somehow fit like a glove, and though she'd probably *never* feel comfortable in a dress, it wasn't scratchy or uncomfortable or anything.

"So, how do you know Ben?" the woman asked conversationally, trailing her perfectly manicured pink nails across the decorative towels hanging off a rack next to the sink.

"Uh. Work," Alyssa muttered, tugging the zipper in the back up as far as she could.

"Oh. Are you a Ranger?" Tawny asked, as if it was somehow possible her scrawny self could be a Ranger.

Alyssa couldn't help but smile. "No. Just…helping out."

"It must be dangerous if you're working with the Rangers. Aren't you scared?"

"Sometimes, but I know how to protect myself."

Tawny sighed. "No wonder Ben likes you. He's one of the few men I've ever met who wasn't impressed or enthralled by weakness."

Alyssa didn't know *what* to say to that, so she smoothed her hands down the dress. "Uh, I'm done."

Tawny turned and clapped her hands together. "Oh, isn't that perfect!"

Alyssa had her doubts about perfect, but Tawny was immediately fussing, pulling the zipper up the rest of the way, tying the green ribbon around her waist into a beautiful bow Alyssa would never be able to replicate.

Tawny nudged her over to the full-length mirror, forcing Alyssa to look at her reflection.

"You'll want to sweep your hair back, and have someone do your makeup, obviously," Tawny said, pulling Alyssa's hair back herself, artfully brushing some hair to hide the bandage on her forehead. "Maybe a tasteful necklace. Diamonds or rubies. Nothing ostentatious. You'll fit right in without standing too far out."

Even with no makeup and someone else holding her hair back, Alyssa didn't recognize herself. It was like someone had put a fancy filter over the girl she'd always been.

"Do you want Ben's opinion?"

Even though she'd warmed to the woman a little bit, Alyssa still *hated* her calling Bennet Ben. "No. I think I'd like it to be a surprise."

The woman smiled somewhat wistfully. "He isn't an easy man to surprise, but this might do the trick."

"Do you know him well?"

Tawny's smile didn't change. "Sometimes I wonder if anyone knows him well. And for the record, I call him Ben because it irritates him and that's about the only time he'll pay me any mind."

"Oh."

"But you don't seem to have that trouble."

Alyssa turned away from the mirror. This woman was confusing, and Alyssa didn't have any idea how to talk to her. She seemed…well, perfect for Bennet's world of icy mothers and charming fathers and smooth, Southern drawls.

And somehow this tall blonde with class and elegance for miles seemed to be under the impression Bennet liked Alyssa. And that wasn't weird, just something to sigh over.

Alyssa moved back to her regular clothes, and Tawny dutifully turned her back again. "W-why do you think he likes me?" Alyssa couldn't help but ask, pulling the zipper down. "This is all work."

"You're in his bedroom, sweetheart. He might be calling it work, but men are apt to say lots of things to get a woman into their bedroom."

It all sounded so worldly and adult, and Alyssa felt like a child again. A child playing at being an adult.

Except she was twenty-four. And she'd survived what might kill most people. She was not some little girl. She was just a little inexperienced.

But Bennet had kissed her last night. Of his own accord, with no pretending it had been meant to throw anyone off. It had been a *real* kiss. He'd said so himself.

So, it was time. Time to get rid of the inexperience, and if she ended up doing that before they unraveled their myriad of mysteries, well, so be it.

She had a life to live, after all, and she was tired of it being thwarted.

Chapter Twelve

Once Tawny left with the dresses, Bennet made himself scarce. He knew Alyssa wasn't happy with him for running some mysterious errands, but he also knew she was losing her mind locked up in that room. So, he set about a safe way to give her a little excursion.

It wasn't necessary, and it would take time away from the case he was trying to solve, but...

Hell. He hated that wild look in her eyes like she was reliving all the ways she'd been a prisoner in her life. He hated the way she paced that room like it was some kind of cage. And, worst of all, he liked way too much the way she'd sometimes stare at him, considering, assessing. The same look she'd had in her eyes last night when she'd approached him before seeing the picture on his computer and recognized one of her brothers.

One of her brothers. Possibly fraternizing with a rival cartel. A lead, something to go on. What he should be focused on instead of Alyssa's state of mind.

But no matter how he chastised himself for his lack of focus, he still secured his parents' screening room, checking every nook and cranny, locking it down in a way that eased his worries. It was still just another locked room, but it wasn't the room he currently had her locked in.

He had no idea if she'd appreciate it, but it was worth a shot. And she could pick a movie and some snacks and he could still focus on finding a connection between Sal/Dom Cochrane, Salvador Dominguez and one of Alyssa's brothers.

So, he was hardly ignoring his duties or his case. And if he'd told Captain Dean he was taking a vacation until after Christmas even though he was working on this case 24/7, it was only to keep Alyssa safe. It wasn't lying to his superior. It was protecting a vulnerable piece of the case.

He'd work on believing that. He left the movie room, locked sufficiently, and went to collect Alyssa for their little…night in. Not theirs. Hers. It was like a gift.

Certainly not like a date.

He forced that thought out of his head and walked up the stairs, hand on the butt of his weapon, scanning every corner for anything suspicious.

It was strange to walk through his parents' house feeling like danger could be lurking anywhere. He'd grown up in this house and there had been a lot of feelings it had prompted. Suffocating, cold, frustration, disgust. But never fear.

It made him sick to his stomach to think too hard about his mother being involved in this, but if Sal Cochrane was connected to Dom Cochrane, and they were both connected to Salvador Dominguez…

Ambition had made worse monsters out of people. He just hated to believe it of his mother even with as strained a relationship as they had.

But he would find the truth regardless. Justice. One way or another.

He walked down the hall to his room, something uncomfortable jittering in his gut, and it wasn't the fear of danger or worry over his mother's involvement.

It was anticipation and nerves. No one had ever affected him quite like Alyssa did, and he wasn't altogether certain he liked it, but he seemed incapable of resisting it.

He knocked, three hard raps. "It's Bennet."

The door edged open, just a crack. She didn't open it farther, so he pushed in himself.

He made a noise, one he couldn't have described to save his life. Everything just kind of whooshed out of him.

She was standing there in one of his button-down dress shirts. And that was all. Her long legs bare from midthigh on down to her toes. She'd left the top of the shirt unbuttoned far enough he could see the enticing tops of her breasts.

"This is your shirt, right?" she asked, her expression unreadable.

"Uh, yup. That's…my shirt." He glanced around the room and found her jeans and pointed at them. "You should put some pants on."

She cocked her head, toying with the top buttoned button of his shirt. If she undid it…

"Why?"

He'd completely lost his train of thought. "Why what?"

"Why should I put pants on?"

"Oh, right." He cleared his throat, trying to speak past the dryness there. "I have a surprise for you."

She took a few steps toward him, still toying with that button, and no matter how strictly he ordered himself to look away, he simply couldn't. She looked impossibly soft, even knowing how tough and strong she could be.

She reached out, pressing her palm against his chest, looking up at him from underneath her lashes. "Let's do my surprise first."

He should not ask for details on that. He should not be deterred. He should... Hell.

He managed to clear his throat and put his hand over hers, gently pulling it off his chest. "I have a feeling your surprise isn't very...appropriate."

"No, it's very, very inappropriate." She grinned up at him, and he shouldn't smile back, but he couldn't help it.

"Alyssa..."

"Don't say no to the virgin throwing herself at you. That'd scar her for life."

He reached out and touched the edge of the bandage on her head. She hadn't complained about it once. "Nothing I could do would scar you for life."

She stepped closer. This time instead of pressing her palm to his chest, she stood on her toes and wound her arms around his neck. She was all soft curves against him, the fragrance of his own damn soap on her skin and in her hair.

"I want you, Bennet. And you want me, too... I think."

"I do."

"Okay, well, you may have gotten most of the things you've wanted in life, but I've gotten very few. So, it's my turn to get something, have something, I want."

"I thought you wanted to get out of here."

"This'll do." Then her mouth was on his, and what could he do but pull her closer, sink into that kiss. He slid his hands down the sexy curve of her back, exploring her mouth with his tongue. When his hands slid over her ass, he realized she was not, in fact, wearing any underwear.

"Hell."

She laughed against his mouth, pressing her body more firmly against his. "I figured if the shirt didn't work, full-on naked would do the trick."

"You do the trick all on your own," he murmured, lifting her up.

She clung tighter, smiling against his mouth as he maneuvered her onto the bed. He should resist. He knew he should resist, but she smiled up at him from beneath his body, and who had that kind of willpower? He'd wanted her since she'd reached for the gun in her desk all those days ago, and it had only intensified each second of getting to know her.

She was beautiful and seemed so sure, but he knew she'd been sheltered. She was untouched.

Except she wanted him, and she might be innocent, there might even be hidden fragile pieces of her, but Alyssa Jimenez knew what she wanted, and who was he to keep it from her?

"After all this is done, I can't promise—"

"I didn't ask you to promise anything, Ben."

He scowled. "Don't call me that."

Her mouth curved. "Why do you hate it so much?"

"It isn't my name."

"Hmm," she murmured, tracing his hairline with her index fingers. "It's half of your name. Why don't you like it?"

Bennet sighed. He had *no* idea why they were talking about this when they could be doing far more interesting things that she'd initiated, but he also knew she wouldn't just let it go. "It was my grandfather's name. Well, Bennet was, but he went by Ben. Everyone loved him."

"It doesn't sound like you did."

"He used to hit me."

Everything on Alyssa's face morphed into shocked outrage. "What do you mean hit you?"

"It's the Stevens way. Beat you into proper behavior."

"And your parents *agreed* with that?"

"They didn't practice it themselves, but they didn't stop it either. You can hardly be shocked by that. You grew up in a cartel. You must have seen far worse things."

"I was sheltered from the good and the bad, I suppose." She studied his face then wiggled beneath him. "Let's focus on the good right now, huh?"

"Yes, I like the sound of that. Why don't you unbutton the rest of that shirt?"

She smiled up at him as she brought her fingers to the buttons that were still buttoned. She pushed one button free, and then the next, and next until they were all free and he could pull the fabric apart and reveal her body completely.

She was petite, all bronze skin and slight curves. Everything inside him tensed and hardened.

"You're beautiful." And his, somehow. She was his.

ALYSSA DIDN'T QUITE know how to handle Bennet's words. Whether it was that sad little story about his grandfather, or telling her she was beautiful with such awe she almost believed it.

So, she pulled his head down and kissed him, because she knew what to do with her mouth then. Absorb the warmth of him, trace his lips with her tongue until he groaned and invaded her mouth with his.

She pressed her naked body to the rough fabric of his jeans and then pulled at the hem of his shirt, wanting to feel *him* against her. Skin and skin and hearts beating erratically against each other.

He pulled the shirt up and off his body, discarding it on the floor before his mouth returned to hers. But only briefly. Then it was moving down her jaw, her neck, feather-light brushes, the occasional brush of his tongue.

His palm slid up her stomach and rib cage until he was cupping her breast, kissing down her chest until his tongue touched her nipple. Her body would have jerked off the bed if Bennet hadn't been above her, a solid, warm wall of muscle.

She felt as though she was pulsing with something. Need probably, because the more his tongue played with her nipple the more restless she became—needing to move, needing to press against him, needing more. More, so much more.

But he seemed content to kiss and lick her everywhere but where she needed him most.

Nothing in the whole world had ever felt like this. Not the sight of the sun after two years of confinement. Not the closure on someone's face when she put a dangerous skip away. Nothing. Nothing had this kind of physical and emotional charge to it.

"Let me go get a condom," he said in a raspy voice that sizzled over her skin.

"You have condoms?" she asked dazedly.

"Sure. Rangers are like Boy Scouts. Always prepared."

"I hope Boy Scouts aren't prepared in *that* way," she called after him when he disappeared into the bathroom. When he reappeared, she grinned at him. "Wait. Please tell me you were a Boy Scout."

"Of course I was. Made it all the way up to Eagle Scout. You have no idea the things I can do with my hands." He grinned.

She spread out on his bed. "Show me."

He tossed the condom on the bed then undid his belt, eyes never leaving hers. Goose bumps rose on her skin at that steady, brazen gaze. He thought she was beautiful. He wanted her as much as she wanted him.

And still that need coiled deeper, no matter that she didn't think it could. She could barely sit still as he pushed his jeans and boxers off in one quick push, and then he was standing there naked.

He was just always so impressive. Tall and strong and broad. Long and hard and something close to intimidating. But no matter how nerves hammered in her chest, she didn't even think of backing out or changing her mind.

Not because she only wanted something good or to cross some adult rite of passage off the list, but because she wanted him. Only him.

He slid onto the bed, over her again, spreading her legs apart with his knees. His fingers trailed up her calves, over her knees, her thighs.

She should do something, too, but all she could seem to do was lie there and breathe, watching his blue eyes intent on the most intimate part of her. He stroked her there and she whimpered, much to her own chagrin.

But his fingers *were* like magic. Sparking, spiraling the pleasure of magic as they entered and stroked, found places inside her that had her panting, writhing, pleading. She'd never felt this out of control, this desperate for something, except freedom.

But she didn't want freedom now. Not from Bennet. She wanted more of him. More of him inside her, on top of her.

"Please," she whispered, so close to some unknown cliff she didn't understand but knew she wanted to fall over. Over and over again.

He paused for a second, grabbing the condom and pulling it out of its package. She watched as he rolled the condom on his thick erection, and Alyssa couldn't quite fight the little kernel of panic that settled in her chest. "Bennet."

His blue eyes met hers, sure and steady as he positioned himself at her entrance. "Shh. It's all right. I'll take care of you."

She relaxed. "I know." It'd probably be easier if she could stop believing in people, but everyone who'd come into her life since she'd left that bunker had proved to her that her brothers' betrayal was their shortcoming. Not hers.

She could feel the tip of him slowly take the place of where his fingers had been. She was still pulsing with that lost orgasm, and as he slowly pushed inside she tried to chase that almost pleasure as much as she tried to ignore the uncomfortable tightness.

Everything was too big and too much, and yet ev-

erything she'd wanted was right there. Bennet inside
her, Bennet on top of her, Bennet. Hers.

He moved, and there was a dull pain mixed in with
that pleasure, but it was diluted enough she could enjoy
that pleasure. Chase that joy that needed release. He
moved slowly, his body hard against hers, and it made
her feel safe. Protected.

All without being locked in or hidden away. He was
bringing her to life even as he made sure nothing bad
happened to her.

"Alyssa," he said, sounding pained, and that's when
she realized a few tears had escaped her cheeks.

"It's not bad crying," she managed, because it wasn't.
It was a release like any other. Too many emotions and
feelings built up and leaking out.

"Good." He kissed a tear, his hand curling around
her hip, angling himself differently, and this time when
he slid deep, she gasped.

So, he did it again. And she forgot about that odd
fullness and focused instead on the way he pulsed
through her, uncoiled that heavy tight knot deep in her
belly. This time she moved with him, and something
seemed to explode inside her, waving through her, an
intense, pulsing pleasure she wanted to bask in forever.

And still he moved inside her, making it all last longer, spiral harder, brighter. Until he was pushing deep,
groaning and holding her tight to him.

She was so crushed to him she couldn't even wrap
her arms around him like she wanted to. She wanted to
hold on and never let go.

Someday you'll have to let go.

She closed her eyes against that thought, listening to
the heavy beating of his heart. This was just like any

other captivity. You only had the time you had. She'd enjoy it while she had it.

"Don't sleep on the window seat tonight," she said into his chest.

His mouth brushed across her temple. "I won't."

Chapter Thirteen

Bennet knew they were falling into too much of a routine, and yet he couldn't seem to help himself. What man in his right mind could?

They explored each other at night, researched all angles of the case during the day and sometimes distracted themselves with more sex then, too.

They hadn't gotten anywhere, and it should irk him more than it did. But it was hard to be irked about anything with Alyssa in his bed.

Even now, when they were both dressed, focused on reading through different things to do with Dom Cochrane's case. It felt…right. Right to be working in the company of someone he could quickly talk into getting naked.

Which seemed like a hell of an idea right now, since they'd have to start getting ready for the gala soon. He slid the laptop off his lap and rolled onto his side.

Alyssa was engrossed in the papers she'd been rifling through, her eyebrows drawn together, her bottom lip pulled between her teeth.

The feeling in his chest scared him more than a little. He'd told her he couldn't make her any promises a few days ago, but every time he looked at her he wanted to make a million. He wanted to make sure she was always with him.

There was something warped in that probably, but no matter how often he told himself he was being an idiot, he wanted her beyond measure. In bed and out. Now and later. She just seemed to belong here, at his side.

So, he tugged one of the papers out of her hand, but she slapped his hand away. "Wait."

"My charm can't be wearing off *this* quickly."

"No, I think I've got something. Bennet, what if…" She arranged some papers he'd printed off for her. The picture of Salvador Dominguez and one of her brothers. The paperwork on Dom Cochrane's murder case.

She spread them all out, pointing at the pictures of Dom and Salvador. "What if Sal Cochrane, Dom Cochrane and Salvador Dominguez are all the same person, just different aliases? They've got the same nose. Same mouth. Salvador is older, obviously, but it has been sixteen years."

"Salvador has a clear scar on his chin."

"He could have gotten it in the time between pictures."

Bennet rubbed a hand against his jaw. "And if that's true, a man who worked for your father got out of jail, started a new identity and built a cartel to rival your father's. And is now a donor to my mother's campaign."

Alyssa blew out a breath. "What reason would she have?"

"I don't know. Getting donations has never been a problem for the Stevenses, but perhaps things have gone south and I don't know about it."

"Maybe they're not the same person."

"He was convicted. Dom was convicted of murder,

a murder that was probably ordered or sanctioned by your father. Yeah?"

Alyssa nodded, studying the pictures, so he did, too. Dom Cochrane and Salvador Dominguez certainly did look alike if you looked hard enough.

"Typically a cartel doesn't let that happen. They don't want one of their own talking to lawyers. They don't want to risk connections."

"I guess that's true, but he was the one stupid enough to get caught."

When he raised an eyebrow at her, she shrugged. "That's how they'd think about it. He got caught, and we never have. I love my brothers, Bennet, because... Well, a lot of complicated reasons, but I'm under no illusion they're good men or have never killed anyone. It's the life."

"Why were you sheltered from it?"

"I'm a girl." She shrugged again. "It's the only reason I ever got. Even before my mother left or whatever it is that happened, the way they'd talk about her... They thought she was weak, and maybe she was. She never spent much time with me."

"So, what was she doing if she wasn't spending time with her daughter and was too weak to be part of things?"

"I don't know."

Bennet studied the pictures again. "Let's work off the theory they're all the same man. Dom Cochrane had orders from your father to kill someone as part of cartel business. Dom gets caught, tried, sent to prison. Who would Dom be most angry with?"

"My father, but like I said, my father hasn't been well for years. Years upon years. CJ runs the show."

"So, maybe he transfers the revenge. It's personal enough, and the cartel family is actual family. It all works together."

"Except one of my brothers meeting with him."

"You still don't know which one?"

"It would make the most sense if it was CJ. He's the head of things, and it would make sense if Dad passed that earring on to him, but… It doesn't look like CJ to me. Something about the hand."

"What about it?"

"CJ is always angry. Fists clenched or on a weapon. My other brothers are always armed, except Oscar." She paused, her finger touching the hand of the man in the picture. "It can't be Oscar," she whispered, shaking her head. "But everything points to Oscar."

"Are you certain?"

"No. But he taps his fingers on his legs when he's nervous. Did you see him do it at my office? He's always done it. This man's fingers are on his leg, as if he's tapping them out of sight of Dominguez."

She looked up at him, her expression sad and a little lost. "Oscar was the sweet one, sweet to me. I can't believe he'd double-cross the family. It's not in him. Not like the others."

"So, maybe it's not him."

Alyssa swallowed and nodded, looking back at the picture of Dominguez. "How did we turn out okay? I mean, assuming your parents are part of this. How did we…"

"You know, I learned something from dear old Grandpa Ben."

She frowned and reached out and touched his cheek. "I don't like your making light of that."

"You can't beat who someone is out of them or beat who you are into them. I'm not saying it doesn't shape them or leave a mark, but it never does exactly what the bad wants it to do." He took her hand and kissed her palm. "We are who we are because that's what we are."

"So, we'll still be what we are after this is all over?"

Which wasn't as simple a question as he'd like. She was the daughter of a drug cartel kingpin, and whether his mother was involved in all this or not, he was the son of a US senator and, more, he was a Texas Ranger. It would be complicated. It would be…

She withdrew her hand from his, and he wished he had the words to make it right. To say they could be.

"Your hair lady is going to be here soon."

"My nothing. *Your* hair lady. *Your* dress. *Your* party."

"I'll pass on wearing a dress tonight, but we need to go over the plan one more time," he said, ignoring her irritation, really ignoring her hurt. They didn't have time for that. Not right this second. Afterward when he could work it all out, he'd figure them out, too, but they had to do this first.

Alyssa rolled her eyes. "Never leave each other's side. Be on the lookout for Dominguez and anyone he talks to. File as much away as we can, and if we have the opportunity to follow him we do, as long as we're together. That about cover it?"

"Trust no one."

"Except you."

"We'll trust each other."

A knock sounded at the door, and Alyssa sighed heavily.

"Who is it?" Bennet called.

"Ms. Delaney is here," Kinsey returned.

Bennet got off the bed and headed for the door to let Tawny in.

"Wait. Tawny's doing my hair and makeup?"

"When I asked her for referrals for someone, she suggested herself. I figured that'd work out, keep fewer new people from traipsing in and out."

"If I look ridiculous after this, I'm blaming you," Alyssa muttered.

"Be very hard on me. I probably deserve it," he replied, grinning at her as he opened the door.

ALYSSA FELT LIKE HYPERVENTILATING. Tawny had done her hair and makeup, chattering on and on about statement colors, and had put diamonds around her neck, and all Alyssa could think was this was all wrong.

Tawny should be going to this party, talking to debutantes and rich politicians and whatever. Alyssa should be in a little apartment above her friends' garage in her jeans and T-shirt, considering her next bounty-hunting case.

But Alyssa was in some expensive gown, her hair swept back in ways she never would have dreamed it could be curled and coiffed. She was wearing lipstick of all things, and anytime she caught a glimpse of herself in the mirror, she wanted to rip off the weird little gold hairpiece Tawny had pinned into her hair and run screaming in the opposite direction.

But Bennet was counting on her, and no matter how he'd hesitated when she'd mentioned *after* earlier, she couldn't let him down. He'd given her too much, even if they were coming to the end of that particular line.

"Now, I know you don't want to draw too much attention, but I brought two possible pairs of shoes. One is the sensible choice, and one is the little flash-of-fun choice." Tawny pulled out two pairs of heels from her bag.

Heels. Tall, tall, impossible-looking heels.

"I've never walked in heels before."

"Never walked in… Honey, where *did* you come from?"

Now that was a question.

"They aren't any different from regular shoes. Mostly," Tawny offered brightly.

"I don't believe that for a second."

Tawny laughed. "Okay, it requires some balance and some…well, beauty is pain and whatnot." She handed Alyssa the less flashy pair. "Here, these are shorter."

Alyssa slid her feet into the heels and tried not to wince as she stood.

"Just balance on your heels and it'll be all good. Besides, Ben will catch you if you fall."

"Did he ever tell you why he doesn't like that?" Alyssa asked, failing at the breezy, conversational tone Tawny always used.

"Like what?"

"Shortening his name to Ben."

Tawny cocked her head. "No. Why?"

Alyssa knew she shouldn't say anything. It was none of her business. But, well, Bennet was always protecting *her*. Maybe it was time for her to do the same for him. "Maybe you just shouldn't."

Tawny stood there and didn't say anything for the longest time. Eventually, she nodded. "All right. Well, you're all finished. I'll leave you to make a grand entrance." Tawny collected all her things and opened the door with a wink.

"Hey, um, I know you're getting paid for this and all, but thanks. I appreciate it."

Tawny smiled that big, pretty smile Alyssa knew even with years of practice she wouldn't be able to duplicate. "You're very welcome, Alyssa. Good luck to you." She slid outside, and Alyssa knew she had to follow. No matter how desperately she wanted to avoid *any* gala, but especially *this* gala, it was a job. One she had to do well.

Which meant she had to ditch the heels. She kicked them off and grabbed her tennis shoes. The dress was long enough it would cover the faux pas, she hoped. And if not, well, hell, she'd at least have the ability to run if she needed to, and the dress was already enough of a detriment.

A knock sounded on the bathroom door. "Are you coming?" Bennet demanded. "Tawny said you were done."

Alyssa took a deep breath and took a few halting steps toward the door. All the nerves were just worry over what they might find out tonight and what danger they might be in. It had nothing to do with Bennet seeing her in this getup.

"Don't say anything stupid," she called through the door.

"Well, thank you for that wonderful vote of confidence. Now, would you get the hell out here so we can—" He stopped abruptly as she stepped into the bedroom.

Then he didn't say anything at all. He didn't even move. He just stared at her. Expressionless.

Alyssa fidgeted. "I know I said don't say anything stupid, but you could say *something*."

"You…" He reached out and touched the cascade of golden circle things Tawny had fastened into her up-swept hair. "You look like some kind of goddess."

"That counts as stupid."

"That counts as a compliment," he returned, leaning in.

She shoved him back. "You cannot ruin my makeup. I don't know how to fix it. Besides, you said we needed to get going."

"I think I changed my mind." His hands landed on her hips, and no matter how she pushed him away, his mouth brushed her neck.

And, okay, maybe she didn't push all that hard. It was entirely possible she just sighed and leaned into him while his mouth did unfathomable things to her neck.

She didn't want to go out there. She didn't want to face strangers or even try to solve a mystery or catch any bad guys. She wanted to stay right here, because once they did all that solving and catching, she wasn't so sure right here would exist anymore.

Since that caused an annoying lump in her throat, she gave him a little nudge. "We have to go."

He sighed heavily against her neck, but he pulled away. He looked her in the eye, Mr. Texas Ranger all over his face.

"We're going to go over this one more time—"

"Bennet."

"We don't separate unless absolutely necessary. You have your cell phone, your knife and your gun on you at all times." He swept his gaze over her. "Where the hell did you put the gun?"

She grinned, lifting the long skirt up to her hip,

where a thigh holster held her Glock. "I mean, God help me if I need it quickly, but at least it's there."

"And the knife is in your bra?"

"Always."

He grinned. "A very, very unique goddess." He cocked his head as his gaze followed her dress hem back down to the floor. "Are you wearing tennis shoes?"

"Don't you dare tell Tawny. She'll kill me."

Bennet chuckled as they moved toward the door, but any humor left them both. What lay ahead of them was risky, and potentially dangerous, most especially for her since her attacker a few days ago had said she'd be dead within the week.

But that only made her more determined. She'd been through one horrible thing in her life already with the kidnapping, and no pissant minion who botched the simplest kidnapping attempt was going to make her cower in fear.

Dead within the week? Not without a fight.

Bennet stopped abruptly with his hand on the knob. He turned to face her, staring at her intently, and Alyssa didn't know what he was looking for, what there was to say in this moment.

"No unnecessary risks," he said eventually.

"What if it leads to the answer?"

He released the knob and curled his fingers around her upper arm. Hard. "No unnecessary risks. Promise me." No jokes, no charming smiles. This wasn't even that Texas Ranger stoicism thing he had down so well. It was dark and dangerous.

But she wasn't about to promise things he wouldn't. "You first."

His mouth flattened into a grim line, and the tight grip he had on her arm didn't loosen.

"No unnecessary risks is a two-way street, Bennet. Either we both take them, or neither of us do."

It took him another few seconds of whatever inner arguing he was doing to speak. "Fine. Neither."

Which was not the answer she had expected in the least. "But… We have to figure this out. It's your important case. It's my mother's murder. You can't honestly think we should play it safe."

"Yes, that's what I honestly think," he replied grimly.

"Why? When we've worked so—"

He took her other arm, giving her a little shake. "You mean more to me than whatever this is," he said, so darkly, so seriously, Alyssa could hardly catch her breath.

He blinked, his grip loosening, as if he was a little surprised at his own vehemence. "So, we play it safe. Got it?"

She could only stare at him. Mean more to him? When had she ever meant more to someone? When had her safety ever been paramount to an end result? Oh, her brothers had kept her safe for twenty years, but for the cartel. She'd been a burden and a duty, not something someone cared about. She'd maybe never thought of it that way, but she understood it now.

Understood it because she'd never felt like a burden to Bennet. She felt…important. Central.

"Alyssa."

She nodded stupidly. "I got it." She swallowed down all the tremulous emotion in her throat. "No risks."

He released her from his grip, holding out his elbow

with one arm and opening the door with his other hand. "Then, let's go."

She slipped her arm through his, still looking up at the hard planes of his face. Clean-shaven and so dashing-looking in his suit. And she meant something to him. Something enough that he'd rather her be safe than solve this case that had been so important to him just days ago.

It was a big deal, no matter what she tried to tell herself. It was a big deal he'd think that, say that, prioritize keeping her safe over solving this case.

He led her to the staircase, and she had to focus on the steps instead of his handsome face. Even though everyone in the house would be attending the party, it was still decorated to the hilt. Christmas lights and evergreen garlands sparkled over the curving banister of the grand staircase.

The floor gleamed, clean and expensive. Even the wood trim seemed to glow in the twinkle of the Christmas lights. The Christmas tree shone bright white from the living room, and it was like walking through a magazine or a castle or anything but anywhere she belonged.

She'd never fit into this sparkling world of wealth and appearances. No matter how many dresses Bennet bought for her or how often Tawny did her makeup. She was a Jimenez. Criminal by association no matter whom she might help bring down.

Bennet could never accept that. She might mean something to him, but once this case was over, the only way they could go was in opposite directions.

So, there was no use getting her hopes up and, more, no use keeping her promise.

Chapter Fourteen

Bennet scanned the crowd for a flash of anyone who might resemble the photograph he had of Salvador Dominguez. He scanned the crowd for any of Alyssa's brothers. He scanned the crowd over and over again.

But all he ever saw were legions of his parents' friends and donors and Texas elite. From the looks of it, Alyssa was just as frustrated about it as he was.

"Let's dance."

Alyssa grimaced. "You think I know how to dance?"

"It's just swaying to a beat." He used the arm that had been situated around her waist the whole evening to lead her to the small cluster of people dancing to slow, jazzy Christmas music. Once on a corner of the dance floor under sparkling lights and all the sparkling jewels on bodies all around them, he drew her close.

She put one hand on his arm and the other she clearly had no idea what to do with. He took it in his, placing it on his shoulder. He eased her into a simple side-to-side step.

"Why do you know how to dance?" she grumbled. "They teach that at Texas Ranger school?"

"Cotillion."

She wrinkled her nose. "What the hell is that?"

He laughed, drawing her even closer. "If I explained it, it would only horrify you."

"That I believe." Her gaze did another scan of the room before returning to his. "Is he not coming? Is he hiding?" she whispered.

"I don't know."

"This is crazy-making, all these questions. All this waiting. Why doesn't he grow a pair and make a move?"

Bennet wanted to laugh, but the thought of any one of the numerous potential "bad guys" out there making a move filled him with dread. They'd already been too close to Alyssa being hurt.

But all he could do was sway to the music, holding her close and watching the room diligently. Maybe whoever it was—Sal or Dom Cochrane, Salvador Dominguez or one of Alyssa's brothers—wouldn't dare try anything as long as he was by her side.

Well, if that were the case, he wouldn't leave it. And no matter how much she'd chafe at the idea, it didn't bother him in the least.

A moody version of "I'll Be Home for Christmas" started playing, and Alyssa rested her cheek against his chest, and he could all but feel the sadness waving off her.

He wanted to promise he'd get her back to her old life by Christmas next week, but how could he possibly promise that? No matter how many little clues they managed to put together, they were still as in the dark about the end game as they'd ever been.

"It'll be all right," he murmured, rubbing a hand down her back and up again.

She sniffled a little. "What if they don't forgive me?"

"Who?"

"Gabby and Natalie. I haven't visited the baby. I've been ignoring their calls. If I miss Christmas... What if they don't forgive me? It's not like we're related by blood or anything. They don't owe me anything, and then I'd be alone. Again."

"You won't be alone." No matter how many qualms he had about what might happen *after*, he couldn't imagine his life anymore without Alyssa in it. Didn't want to.

She'd stiffened in his arms, and she didn't raise her head. He could all but feel the questions in her, but she didn't voice any of them.

"Besides, they'll forgive you. Even if you're not blood related, they're family, and you'll be able to explain this all to them afterward. They'll understand. They know how these kinds of things work. Not only are they both involved with law enforcement, but they've both been in danger before. They know what it's like."

She finally pulled her head back and looked up at him. "Did you really mean—"

There was a tap on Bennet's shoulder and a loud, booming voice. "May I cut in?"

Bennet glanced back at his father, who had his best politician's smile plastered on his face. Bennet tried to fight the scowl that wanted to take over his mouth.

"You've been hiding your date all night, Bennet," Dad said jovially, clapping him on the back a little hard. "Let one of us old hats have a turn."

"It looks like your mother's free," Alyssa said, nodding toward Mom walking away from the cluster she'd been talking with earlier. "Why don't you go dance with her?"

He should. He should do some digging about Sal Cochrane here where things would be so busy and booze-filled Mom was likely to forget his questioning in the morning. And Alyssa wasn't just a grown woman, but a capable, *armed* grown woman who could handle his father for a quick dance. Even if Dad said something asinine.

He wanted to finish their conversation. He wanted to assure her he meant *everything*. And he downright hated the thought of leaving her, stupid as it was.

But what could happen to her if she was dancing with Dad? It wasn't like whoever they were waiting for was going to pop out and snatch her away when she was dancing with a US senator, for God's sake.

"All right," Bennet said, smiling tightly and probably not at all convincingly. "Just return her to me after the song, huh?"

Dad rolled his eyes, taking Alyssa's hand off Bennet's shoulder and clutching it in his own.

"Such a caveman I raised, Alyssa. I hope this boy has a few more manners than that." Dad slid his arm around Alyssa's waist and started leading her away.

Bennet stood at the corner of the dance floor like a fool. Dad was either trying to piss him off or... Well, no, probably just trying to irritate him. Bennet shouldn't let him win.

He forced himself to walk over to his mother, tried to make the scowl on his face soften into something bordering on pleasant.

"Are you having fun?" Mom asked.

"The time of my life," Bennet replied drily, causing his mother to chuckle.

"You look quite cozy with that girl."

Bennet merely grunted. Once the case was figured

out he'd fight Mom on this battle, but not before. For now, he'd be as discreet and noncommittal as possible.

"You know, there were a few names on the guest list I didn't recognize," he offered, failing hard at casual.

"Worried about security, dear?"

"Something like that. I don't remember you ever mentioning Sal Cochrane before."

Mother's eyebrows drew together. "Cochrane. That name doesn't ring any bells."

"He's a donor of yours."

Mom chuckled. "No. Honey, trust me. I know all my donors. I make sure of it."

Bennet frowned. Mom could be lying, he supposed, but he knew his mother fairly well. He knew her politician charm and the way lies could fall out of her mouth with the utmost authenticity, but she was rarely flippant about lying.

He pulled out his phone and brought up the email from Dad's assistant with the donor list and handed it to her. "It says Sal Cochrane right here."

Mom took the phone and squinted at the screen before scrolling. "Mariah must have made some kind of mistake. This isn't my donor list."

"You're certain?"

Mom nodded, scrolling more "Julie Dyer is on it. Trust me, she wouldn't give me a cent if her life depended on it. That's your father's donor list." She handed the phone back to him, and Bennet nearly dropped it.

If this was Dad's list, then Dad was the connection.

And he was dancing with Alyssa.

THE WHOLE NOT-KNOWING-HOW-TO-DANCE thing was a little less concerning when she was dancing with Bennet. Dancing with his father, no matter that there was far more distance between their bodies, made her inordinately tense.

"This is a nice…party. Gala. Thing." Alyssa wanted the floor to swallow her whole. She sounded like an idiot.

"My wife just loves her…party gala things," Mr. Stevens replied with a wink.

Alyssa took a deep breath and tried to relax. Mr. Stevens was nice. A little slick, but nice nonetheless. None of Mrs. Stevens's ice.

"Are you all right, dear? You're looking a little peaked. Why don't we step out onto the balcony? Get a little fresh air."

"No, I'm all right."

But Mr. Stevens was tugging her through the swaying throng of dance-floor people and across the room.

Alyssa wasn't quite sure what was going on, but something didn't sit right. She glanced over at where Bennet had been. His head was bent over his phone as he talked to his mother.

Mr. Stevens all but pulled her onto the balcony, and she was about to scream, jerk her hand away, anything, but there were people on the balcony, even a waiter carrying around trays of champagne with little red fruit floating in the top, sprigs of what looked like holly decorating the bottom of the glass.

It could hardly be that sinister if there were plenty of people around. It could hardly be that sinister considering Mr. Stevens looked downright jolly.

Mr. Stevens took two champagne flutes as a waiter passed, handing her one. She took it even though she had no plans to drink it.

"Now, you've made quite an impression on my son, and that is a hard thing to do. God knows he'll keep you away from my wife and me as long as that's the case, so I wanted to corner you a bit. I hope you don't mind."

"Well, um, no. I guess not," she managed. It was stupid to want to impress him, please him, but no matter how strained Bennet's relationship might be with his parents, he did love them. And no matter how she told herself there was no future for her and Bennet… She couldn't quite bring herself to blow up that tiniest inkling of a chance.

"Tell me about yourself, Alyssa." He took a sip of his champagne, looking like some ritzy watch or cologne ad.

"Oh, well, there's not a whole lot to tell."

"Where'd you grow up? What do you do? How'd you meet my son?"

Alyssa opened her mouth, hoping some kind of lie would just fall out, but it didn't. Nothing did. Not even a squeak.

"Are they really that difficult of questions, Ms. Jimenez?"

Alyssa froze. He knew her name, and something about that slick smile that had never quite settled right with her now suddenly seemed sinister.

But he was as relaxed as ever, watching her as he sipped champagne and waited for her to answer.

"Cat got your tongue? Have a few drinks. Might loosen things up for you."

Alyssa swallowed, trying to think straight and not panic. "What exactly is it that you want from me?"

"I'm just concerned about my son, Alyssa. Surely you understand what kind of good, upstanding man

Bennet is. He has such a clear sense of right and wrong. I'd hate for him to get wrapped up in the wrong kind of people and get himself hurt."

"Your son can take care of himself," she returned, trying to figure out an exit strategy that wouldn't draw attention. But the people on the balcony were dwindling, and the waiter had disappeared.

Pretty soon she'd be out here alone with Mr. Stevens, and she didn't think that would be very good at all.

"Are you so sure about that?" He said it so casually, so offhandedly, it shouldn't mean anything. It couldn't mean anything, but Alyssa couldn't help but read it as a threat.

This was all wrong. All wrong.

"I should get back," she muttered, taking a retreating step backward.

Mr. Stevens's hand shot out and clamped onto her wrist in less than the blink of an eye. "Now, now, Ms. Jimenez. Surely you don't need to rush off just yet."

"Let go of me," Alyssa said between gritted teeth. She tugged at her arm, but he held fast, something in his expression hardening.

Alyssa wanted to panic, but she fought it off. She just had to break his grasp and run inside and to Bennet. She could always grab one of her weapons with her free hand, but she didn't think waving a knife or gun at a US senator for some veiled threats was going to go over very well.

She heard the click of a door and jumped, jerking her gaze to the doors that led to the balcony. The now-empty balcony, one door shut and, if that clicking sound was any indication, locked.

But there was still one open. She just had to break his grasp and get through it.

She pulled hard, but Mr. Stevens only jerked her toward him.

"What is this?" she demanded.

"This, Ms. Jimenez, is business. Now, I suggest you stop trying to put up a fight. I'd hate to bruise that pretty face of yours, and I'd hate to have to get my son involved. Bennet's an excellent policeman, but we both know he'd put himself in harm's way before he let you be put in it."

"You would hurt your own son?" she asked incredulously.

"Oh, Ms. Jimenez, I'll do whatever I have to."

Before he finished the sentence, Alyssa pivoted and elbowed Mr. Stevens as hard as she could in the chest. He stumbled back, releasing her grasp, and she ran for the open door.

But a man stepped through, closing it behind him. Alyssa stopped short at the sight of her youngest brother blocking her exit.

"Oscar, what are you doing?" She took a few more steps toward him, reaching out to him. Even if Oscar was working with Mr. Stevens, he wouldn't hurt her. "Oscar, you have to help me," she whispered, looking at him imploringly. "Let me through. Please."

"Sorry, Lyss," Oscar said, sounding truly regretful.

Before she could beg, or push him out of the way, pain exploded in her head. And then there was nothing but darkness.

Chapter Fifteen

"You're sure he came this way?" Bennet demanded of the shaking waiter who was leading him down a back hallway out of the hotel.

"Y-yes, sir."

"Then where the hell is he?" Dad and Alyssa hadn't been anywhere in the ballroom. No hallways, no bathrooms. Bennet had tactlessly started asking questions, all the glitzy attendees of the ball looking like he was crazy, but the waiter had spoken up and said he'd seen Dad.

But there was no sign of him or Alyssa. There was nothing but an empty stretch of hallway. Bennet felt sick to his stomach. He didn't want to believe this of his father, but they'd been there one second, and gone the next.

Gone. Just gone. In the few minutes he'd discussed donors with his mother, they were suddenly nowhere to be found.

He scrubbed his hands over his face and focused on the waiter. "And you didn't see the woman either?"

"No. No woman. Nobody really. I mean. Except Mr. Stevens. Who went this way." The waiter swallowed with a loud gulp.

Something about the way the kid looked away and took in an unsteady breath poked at Bennet. He took a threatening step toward the shaking, sweating waiter. "Are you lying to me?" he demanded, getting in the guy's face.

"N-no, sir. Mr. Stevens… He told me… I mean…"

Bennet grasped the man's shirt in his fist and gave him a hard shake. "You are talking to a Texas Ranger in the middle of a life-or-death investigation, so if you want to keep your nose intact and your ass out of jail, you better start telling the truth."

The waiter started crying.

"Look, I don't know what he threatened you with, if anything, but if someone dies because you kept it to yourself, you're an accessory, and I will do everything in my power to punish you to the fullest extent of the law."

The waiter started crying even harder. "I don't know, man. I was just following orders. All he told me was to tell you he went this way, but I don't know where he went."

Bennet swore. A distraction. "What else do you know?" he demanded, giving the guy another hard shake.

"I don't know. I don't know," the man sobbed. "There was someone with him. A guy named Oscar. But that's all I know."

Bennet released the man and swore, barely acknowledging the waiter crumpling to the floor. He had to calm down and think. *Think.* What the hell could his father possibly be doing?

Oscar. Alyssa was so sure her youngest brother was the nice one, but Bennet couldn't let that console him right now. There were too many variables, and since he knew Alyssa would under no circumstances disappear of her own volition, they were all really shitty variables.

He didn't even know where to start. He had no idea what he was dealing with. All he knew was she was gone, and she wouldn't have done that to him.

Which meant he had to focus. He had to be the Texas Ranger he'd been trained to be. He had to find Mom. Based on the conversation he'd had with her earlier, he didn't think she was involved, but she would know all the places Dad could go.

He left the waiter sobbing on the floor and strode back toward the ballroom, but before he made it down the length of the back hallway, Mom pushed through some doors.

"Bennet. There you are. You've made something of a scene. What's going on?"

"I'll tell you what's going on. Your husband has kidnapped my…" What the hell was she? He didn't know. "I need a list of all the property you and Dad own jointly or separately. Emailed to my work address ASAP." He pushed past her. He'd start at the main house. It was a long shot, but maybe there'd be some clue in Dad's office or…

"Bennet, you don't honestly think—"

"You're right. I don't think, I know. I know what he did, what he's done." He turned to face her. "Mom, if you really have nothing to do with any of this, I'd suggest getting your lawyers together."

"What on earth are you even talking about? Bennet? Bennet! I don't have any earthly clue—"

"My, my. What is all this commotion?"

Bennet turned incredulously to find his father pushing through the doors, then standing there, brushing at his sleeve as if there was some minuscule piece of lint. Pristine and politician perfect in his suit as if everything was fine. Normal.

Bennet lunged, missing only because two of Dad's plainclothes security guards stepped in and grabbed him, holding him back. "Where is she?" he demanded, shoving against the guards.

Dad had the gall to look incredulous and quizzical. "Where is who?"

"You were the last one with her. Now I want to know what you've done with her."

"You mean Alyssa? Oh, she said something about going to the bathroom and—"

"Bullshit," Bennet spat. "You don't think I've put it all together? You and Dominguez and Jimenez. I've got more evidence than you can possibly imagine, and if you think kidnapping her—"

"You aren't making any sense, son. Should I perhaps put in a call to Captain Dean? I have to say I have been worried about your mental state as of late."

Bennet laughed. As if the threat of his job would get through this haze of fury and fear. "Come after me, Dad. Throw it all at me. I will destroy you," Bennet said and then, with a well-placed elbow, escaped the security guard's pathetic hold and pushed past his father and back into the ballroom.

It was teeming with people, many who gave him odd looks, and there was just too much of a world out there. He couldn't do this on his own.

He hadn't wanted to bring in anyone else this whole time because it was his case to solve, but Alyssa's safety trumped all of it. He would find her, and if anyone had hurt her he'd kill them himself.

He pulled his phone out of his pocket, jogging through the ballroom to the exit to the parking lot. He searched his email for an old correspondence with Jaime Alessandro over The Stallion case, found the phone number he needed and called.

"Hello?" Alessandro answered, clearly skeptical at the unknown number.

"Agent Alessandro, this is Bennet Stevens with the Texas Rangers."

"Ah, yes, I've been hearing your name quite a bit around these parts. Not exactly kindly."

Which might have been funny in any other situation. "I need your help. Alyssa needs your help."

There wasn't a second of hesitation. "I'm all ears."

WHEN ALYSSA CAME TO, head throbbing painfully, stomach roiling, she was in a basement of some kind. She took a deep breath in and out to fight the nausea and the panic at the realization she was tied to a chair, her hands behind her back, her ankles each to a leg of the chair, and then another cord around her thighs and the seat of the chair.

But she could see, and she could breathe. Important things to focus on. If she panicked, nothing good could happen. If she panicked, she *would* end up dead.

Of course, how she was still alive was a mystery. Surely a US senator wasn't going to leave loose ends lying around. *If* she escaped his life would be over.

And what will Bennet think of that?

She had to close her eyes against the painful thought of Bennet. He would not be taking any of this well. But he would save her. He would. He knew the last person she'd been with was his father.

And he's going to choose saving you over bringing his father down?

She couldn't think like that. Besides, Mr. Stevens had said it himself. Bennet had a clear sense of right and wrong. Even if he wanted to protect his father, his conscience wouldn't allow him to do it at her expense.

She hoped.

She was still in her dress, but she could tell the gun she'd had strapped to her thigh was gone. She could feel the outline of her knife against her breast, and that was good. If she could get untied, she had a chance.

Something sounded behind her, a squeak and groan. A door opening maybe. She tried to turn her head, but the way her arms were tied behind her back limited how much she could look back.

Footsteps approached, and Alyssa did everything in her power to breathe normally. To stay focused and calm no matter who appeared.

"You're awake. Good," Oscar offered cheerfully.

Alyssa could only stare at her brother as he stepped in front of her. He'd knocked her out, and by all accounts was the one who'd tied her up here, and he was acting as if it was all normal.

"You hit me."

"You didn't listen," he returned as if they were arguing semantics, not whether or not he'd knocked her out in the middle of a party.

"What is going on?" she said, her breathing coming too fast, the panic rising too hard. "Oscar, please, explain this to me." She might have tried to hold back the tears, but she had to hope they would get through to her brother. Her sweet brother. How could he be doing this to her?

"You should have listened to me, Lyss." Oscar paced the concrete room, tapping his fingers on his leg. "I'm running out of options here. Why'd you have to keep pushing? I could have kept you out of this if you'd only listened."

"Kept me out of *what*?"

"He wants you."

"Who? Stevens?"

Oscar laughed. "Please. Gary Stevens is nothing more than a pawn. A distraction to get you here. Dominguez is who you should be afraid of. He wants revenge, and it has to be you. Stevens only helped because Dominguez owns him."

"And Dominguez owns you?"

Again Oscar laughed. "No one owns me, Lyss. Dominguez and I are like partners."

"Why are you working for Dominguez?"

Oscar scoffed. "You have to ask that question? CJ wouldn't even let me carry a gun, or run a raid by myself. He thought I was stupid and weak. Well, he'll see who's stupid and weak now."

"Oscar. He's our brother. I'm your sister. Whatever is going on—"

"He killed our mother, you know. CJ. Our own brother. He killed her. And then he gave you over to The Stallion, all so The Stallion wouldn't encroach on cartel business."

Even though it confirmed too many suspicions, Alyssa could only shake her head, the tears falling faster now. "No."

"He did, Alyssa. On Dad's order he killed our

mother. And when The Stallion threatened us and all we built, he offered you."

She couldn't get a full breath. She couldn't...

"Dominguez might not be blood, but he's honorable. He'd never ask me to kill you."

"But he had you kidnap me."

Oscar shrugged, as if that was neither here nor there.

"I'll die anyway. His men who tried to kidnap me last week said he wants me dead."

"But I won't be the one to do it. He'd never ask that of me."

Alyssa had no rebuttal for that. None at all. He didn't care if she died, as long as he didn't have to do it.

"He might not kill you, Lyss. If you can prove some worth, he might just keep you."

"Prove some... Have you lost your mind? Have you lost your heart? What happened to you?" Alyssa demanded, trying so very hard not to sob.

Oscar refused to meet her gaze, and the sound from before echoed in the concrete room. A door opening. Oscar straightened as footsteps approached.

"Good work, Oscar. I knew I could count on you," a booming voice said.

Oscar beamed and Alyssa thought she was going to throw up as a new man stepped into view. Definitely the man from the picture they had of Salvador Dominguez. Tall and lanky, his graying black hair pulled back in a ponytail, the faint scar on his chin. His dark eyes glittered with something that looked eerily close to joy.

"And here she is." He shook his head as if she was some long-lost friend he was so happy to see. "You look just like your mother." He reached out to touch her cheek and Alyssa flinched, trying to back away from the touch but held too still by the ropes.

"Well, where are my manners? Introductions are necessary, of course. Salvador Dominguez, at your service." He made a strange little bow. "I know we haven't met yet, but I know so many of your family. Oscar here, of course. And I used to work for your father before he became something of an imbecile."

He smiled widely, and Alyssa tried to keep herself still, to not react at all.

Salvador cocked his head. "You don't seem surprised by that information. My, my, maybe you and your Ranger were more thorough than I gave you credit for. Good thing we moved when we did, Oscar." Salvador clapped Oscar on the back as he continued to smile at Alyssa. "Your brother is quite the prodigy. I've been very impressed."

Alyssa wished she could wipe the tears off her cheeks and put on some unemotional, screw-you manner. As it was, she couldn't imagine how foolish she looked tearstained, makeup streaked, hair falling out of all Tawny's ruthless pinning.

"A quiet one. How unlike the Jimenez clan. Even your mother was quite the chatterbox. Of course, I loved to listen to her chatter. You see, I loved her. What a beauty she was, and so…passionate." He reached out and touched her face again, the skim of his index finger down her cheek causing her to shudder as her stomach roiled more viciously.

Salvador leaned in close, so close she could feel his heavy breath on her neck. "I bet your Texas Ranger would say the same about you."

Alyssa wished she could throw up on him, but no

matter how nauseated she felt, all she could do was sit there and try not to cry no matter how disgusting his breath felt across her bare skin.

"Don't worry, little girl, I would never test out that theory…in front of your brother," he whispered.

Alyssa worked on her best withering glare. "I don't know what you want, but—"

"Oh, that's simple," he said downright jovially, stepping back and straightening to his full height. "Your family let me rot in jail for years, and while I did, they killed the woman I loved." He waved his arms dramatically as he spoke. "So now, I'm going to kill you."

Alyssa didn't gasp. She didn't allow herself to. She simply stared at her brother imploringly, no matter how he avoided her gaze, until Salvador stepped between them.

"Eyes up here, beautiful."

"You won't kill me," she said, even if she wasn't certain she believed it. She wasn't going down without a fight. Without some backbone.

"Well, maybe not *now*. We might need to have a few *conversations* first, but then you will definitely die. On camera. For all of the Jimenezes to see."

Chapter Sixteen

Bennet and Jaime had split up the list of properties Mom had emailed him and were checking them out one by one. Austin PD was currently questioning his father and had put out an APB for Alyssa. To Bennet's surprise, Mom had snapped into her own kind of action, scouring Dad's financial records for any transactions that might give them a hint.

But still nothing was *happening*, and even as Bennet searched another of his father's Austin properties, he knew it was damn pointless. He was fighting a losing battle, and he didn't know what else to do.

His phone chimed, and he brought it to his ear. "Stevens."

"Gabby found something," Jaime said with no preamble.

"Gabby?"

"I figure if you can do a few things off the record, so can I. She's a better analyst than half my men anyway," Jaime muttered. "I had her look through the files on a raid the FBI did on a house a few months ago. We'd gathered information Salvador Dominguez was doing business there, but the raid found absolutely nothing."

"Well, that doesn't exactly sound promising," Bennet

replied, heading back to his car after another property was completely empty.

"It doesn't. Until we tracked down the owner of the house. Originally we hit nothing but dead ends and fake LLCs, but Gabby discovered a tie to your father."

"Address," Bennet barked, starting his car.

"Austin, luckily. I'll text it to you and meet you there."

Bennet hit End and backed out of the parking lot and added the texted address into his GPS. It was all the way on the other side of the city, but the link to both Dominguez and his father was too much to ignore.

He flew through town, then slowed down as he approached the address, looking for an inconspicuous place to park his vehicle.

It was a nondescript-looking house in the middle of a very middle-class neighborhood. Dark had descended, but most of the houses in the neighborhood had lights of some kind on. Except this one. Dark shrouded it so much Bennet could barely make out anything, especially with a privacy fence extending around the front yard as well as the back. Bennet parked his car three houses down and got out of the car, trying to canvas the best way to approach.

If Alyssa was here, there had to be some kind of security in place. Not just alarms, but cameras surely, and if there'd been an FBI raid here a few months ago that had found nothing, surely they were not dealing with amateurs.

He wouldn't let that make him feel sick, because the most important thing wasn't anything except getting Alyssa out, and he'd do whatever it took. Whatever it took, enough that he had to pray she was here, and safe.

He glanced down the road as another car approached.

It stopped five doors down and on the opposite side of the street. The headlights stayed on as Jaime got out casually, scanning the neighborhood in the exact way Bennet had. He nodded to Bennet and turned off the lights of his car, shrouding him back in darkness.

What had Bennet's hand resting on the butt of his weapon was another car three houses up from the current house parking as conspicuously. Of course, the minute the driver stepped out of the car and into the light of the streetlamp, Bennet could only stare.

"Is that Vaughn?" Jaime asked as he came up to Bennet's side.

"It is," Bennet replied, watching as his partner approached. "What are you doing here?"

Vaughn studied the privacy fence in front of them. "Gabby told Natalie all the details, and I was instructed to help or be excommunicated or something, and I'm not keen on arguing with a woman and a newborn. Three law enforcement officers are better than one. At least when they're the three of us."

"Then I don't have to brief you?"

"Alyssa is missing. We're likely dealing with the Dominguez and Jimenez cartels in some capacity. We have no idea who or what is in that house. That about cover it?"

"About," Bennet muttered, eyeing the privacy fence again. "The fence is weird, and I assume if this really is some kind of cartel headquarters or meeting place or whatever, it's got cameras everywhere."

"Likely," Jaime replied. "Gabby found me possible floor plans, though," he said, holding out his phone. "This was on the developer's website, and it looks about right. Now, we don't know what kind of modifications the owners might have made over the years, but it gives us an idea."

They each took a turn looking at the floor plan and committing what they could to memory.

"We don't know what kind of arsenal they have," Bennet said. He didn't mind risking himself, but he couldn't put these two men at risk like this. He needed their help, he knew that, but he couldn't risk their lives like this. "I want you two to stay back."

Vaughn scoffed and Jaime shook his head.

"Look, they could be watching for us. They could be armed. You really want to get your head blown off? You're supposed to get married soon," he said, pointing at Jaime. "And you just had a kid."

"We've both done raids, Bennet," Vaughn said. "We know the risks, and the best practices. I've got a vest on. You?"

Jaime and Bennet nodded.

"So, we do what we'd do in any other situation. We're careful, but this is still our job. If something goes bad, it's the risk we took when we took those badges. And I think Natalie and Gabby would understand since they consider Alyssa their sister."

"Fine. We do this together, but I take the risks, you understand? I screwed this up, and I let her out of my sight. This is on me." Bennet knew Vaughn wanted to argue, but they didn't have time. "We'll split up to check the perimeter and see if there are any vulnerabilities in the fence. Vaughn, you stay here and watch for any comings and goings. Stay in the dark so no neighbors get worried and call the cops. Jaime, you take the east side. If they have a monitoring system, they won't know you as any different from a neighbor walking down the street. I'll start on this side, and we'll meet in the back. Understood?"

Vaughn had stiffened, and Bennet knew his partner well enough to know Vaughn didn't particularly care to take orders from him. But, Vaughn didn't argue. He and Jaime both nodded.

Which was all Bennet needed to take off. He walked down the fence that hid the side of the house, running his hands up and down the surface, trying to find a weakness. He'd brought a few tools when he'd started out in case he'd have to do some not-quite-lawful breaking and entering. If he could find a decent crack or opening, he could possibly pry a section open and sneak in undetected.

He had to believe they had the element of surprise on their side. They wouldn't expect him to figure out their hiding spot, at least not this quickly, but that didn't mean they weren't being diligent.

Bennet made it down the entire side of the house, and when he turned the corner, the shadow of Jaime was turning the one across from him.

Bennet was half-tempted to just blow a hole in the damn fence, but that'd probably draw unwanted attention, and he might as well go through the front if he was going to go down that route.

But there was something of a joint at the corner of the fence here. Where the side had been one long sheet of whatever material the fence was made out of, where they connected at the corner had something of a space. Oh, the materials butted up against each other and were clearly screwed together tightly, but Bennet had to believe with enough force he could pry it open.

Jaime crossed to him. "You're going to need a crowbar or something like it."

"Luckily, I came prepared to do a little breaking and entering." He'd had no trouble jamming the crowbar into his pocket. It had torn the fabric of the pocket, but the curved part of the tool had hooked onto his waistband well enough to keep it secured.

"Good thinking," Jaime said, looking around the back. The house behind them had inside lights on, but none in the back to cast a light on them. Jaime positioned himself in front of Bennet so that if anyone did look out, they hopefully wouldn't notice a man crowbarring open a fence.

Of course, they might notice the tall, broad man just standing there, but Bennet couldn't worry about that. He shoved the sharp edge of the crowbar into the small space between joint and fence and worked to pull it apart.

It took longer than he wanted, but eventually the fence began to give, and once he'd separated the parts, he used his body weight to bend the joint enough he could step through and into the pitch-black of the backyard.

"I'm going in. Get Vaughn."

"And if they pick you off?"

"You know not to come this way, and you call in every law enforcement agency to handle the situation."

"We could do that right now, you know."

Bennet looked at the dark shadow of the house. "I can't risk her safety like that. If she's in there, if we let SWAT or some other high-handed assholes handle this, you know as well as I do she has less of a chance."

"Normally I'd argue with you."

"But you won't, will you?"

"No. I care about Alyssa, and apparently so do you. So, we'll do this our way first."

Bennet was already stepping through the space he'd

made in the fence. He stayed close to the side fence, using it as a guide to bring him closer to the house.

There were no lights on, and with the moonlight hitting the upper half of the house, he could make out that there were no windows. Not one.

Interesting. He couldn't make out the bottom half of the house, but he could feel his way. He started at one edge and moved his body across the siding of the house until he felt the indentation of a door.

He paused, listening to the quiet of night. Nothing moved, no shots rang out, and if there *were* cameras on this side of the house, he didn't know how they'd be able to see anything.

He had a chance. He crouched next to the doorknob he'd felt out. He pulled out the tiny penlight from his pocket, followed by the lock-picking kit he'd shoved into his jacket pocket.

He heard Vaughn and Jaime quietly approach and went to work. If his picking the lock drew attention, ideally Jaime and Vaughn would have a chance to surprise anyone who came out.

He didn't care about his own safety right now. He'd gladly die if it meant they got Alyssa out of here in one piece.

Still, he pulled the gun out of his holster and placed it next to his feet while he worked. He'd die for Alyssa in a heartbeat, but he wouldn't die without a fight.

SALVADOR HAD LEFT her and Oscar alone while he "readied his supplies," and Alyssa racked her brain for anything she could say to get through to her brother.

"They'll only kill you, too."

Oscar looked at her as though she were a fool. "I'm

Dominguez's right-hand man. Not only will he protect me, but hundreds of men who work for us will, as well. CJ can't touch me. I'm nearly as powerful as him, and with Stevens in our pocket, it's only a matter of time before we use every law enforcement agency in Texas to take down the Jimenez cartel."

"Dad would be so disappointed in you."

"Dad doesn't know what century it is, Alyssa. He's completely gone."

"So, you're going to let this man rape and murder me?"

Oscar's throat worked for a few seconds before he turned away from her. He pressed his forehead to the concrete wall of the basement. "You don't understand, Lyss. I have to do this. I don't have a choice. Can't you understand the position CJ put me in?"

Alyssa opened her mouth to yell at him that she didn't care about CJ or Jimenez or anything, she just wanted to live, damn it, but the doorknob on the door across from her seemed to...make a noise.

Considering Oscar and Dominguez had appeared from behind her, she could only assume this door led somewhere else. Maybe even outside?

Then the doorknob downright jiggled. She jerked her head to look at Oscar, but he didn't seem to notice, either in alarm or to go open it for anyone. Not with his head pressed to the wall.

Alyssa's heart leaped in hope. Maybe it was foolish to hope, but Bennet wouldn't give up. He'd do whatever it took. She knew he would, and if it was a chance...

"Can't you do one favor for me, Oscar?" she breathed, trying to sound sad and terrified instead of elated. "One last favor before you let me die?"

"It's not up to me, Alyssa," he said, sounding sad and resigned as he thunked his head against the concrete of the basement wall. Over and over. "I don't have a choice. You forgive me, don't you? You will. I think you will. Once you understand."

"Can't you bring me milk and cookies? One last time?" Even though it was a fake request, it caused a lump to rise in her throat, but she had to speak loudly enough that the increased shaking of the knob didn't get his attention. "Please, Oscar, I'll forgive you if you show me this one kindness."

Oscar turned slowly, and Alyssa forced herself to hold his gaze instead of looking at the jiggling knob. She had to keep his attention on her, or on the wall, but nowhere near that door.

"You will? Really?"

"I promise. I'll do whatever you want of me, if you just… Bring me milk and cookies like you used to."

Oscar swallowed and nodded slowly, then more quickly. "Okay. Okay, I mean, I doubt we've got milk and cookies, but I'll find a snack. A good one. He'll have to let me do that. A show of respect. It's a show of respect," he said, and leaned down to kiss her cheek.

She tried not to flinch, tried to smile tremulously as she squeezed her eyes shut, hoping a tear would fall over.

"A delicious snack coming right up," Oscar whispered, heading behind her where she couldn't see. She could only hope he'd have to leave the room they were in. She could only hope whoever was on the other side of that door was someone who could save her. Who would.

She heard the door open and close behind her and

then prayed, fervently, for the shaking knob to do more than just shake.

"Please, please for the love of God," she whispered, watching the door and wishing with everything she had it would open and Bennet would be on the other side.

When that happened almost exactly as she imagined it, she nearly couldn't believe it. But the door opened with a click, slowly inching open, before Bennet appeared.

She nearly cried out with joy, swallowing it down at the last minute. Tears erupted, but she swallowed down the sobs. For a brief second Bennet kneeled there looking around the edge of the door as if shocked to see her, but then he was all action and movement before she could even register it.

He was at her feet, pulling the knife out of her bra before she could manage a word.

"Tell me everything you know," he whispered, the command calm and clear and helping to keep her focused.

"There're two men that I know of," she whispered as he began to cut all her ties quickly and efficiently. "Dominguez and Oscar. But I woke up right here so I don't know what's up there. Oscar's getting me a snack. Dominguez is getting what he needs to kill—"

The telltale sound of the door behind her squeaking open had her stopping, icy fear gripping her. They'd kill Bennet and then her and—

But the last of the ties fell off and Bennet shoved the knife into her hand as he pulled his gun. A shot fired and Alyssa cried out because she knew Bennet couldn't have fired yet. His gun clattered to the ground, and he stumbled back.

Alyssa clutched the knife in her hand, turning to see Salvador standing there, gun in each hand pointed at both of them. She tried to step in front of Bennet, but he was already on his feet, pushing her back behind *him*.

"Are all Rangers this stupid?" Salvador demanded, pointing both guns at Bennet. Bennet stood there, shirt ripped and blood dripping from where the bullet must have grazed. He was standing, though, looking defiant and pissed as ever, so Alyssa had to believe he was okay. She had to.

"Are all common criminals this stupid?" Bennet returned conversationally.

Salvador's laugh was low and horrible. Alyssa shuddered, trying to think. A knife didn't trump a gun, but maybe she could throw it? Maybe she could lure him close enough to...

"Oscar. Tie up the Ranger. He's going to be our audience, I think. Yes, I think he'll enjoy what I have planned for our little lady."

Bennet whistled, high and quick. Salvador frowned, and then a shot was fired from somewhere behind her and Bennet.

One of Salvador's guns clattered to the ground on a howl of outrage, red blooming near his elbow. "Oscar," he screamed. "Shoot them!"

"I... I left my gun in the kitchen," Oscar whispered, wide-eyed and terrified.

"You have three seconds to drop the weapon, Dominguez," a man from behind them ordered. Alyssa looked back, and her knees nearly gave out. Vaughn and Jaime were standing at the door, weapons trained on Salvador and Oscar.

Jaime began to count off. "Three, two—"

But Salvador grinned. Everything else after that awful, soul-freezing grin went too fast. The next thing Alyssa fully understood was Bennet on top of her and the sounds of at least two gunshots being fired.

"Bennet?" she managed, barely able to breathe between his crushing weight and the hard, cold concrete ground.

He groaned, and panic clutched her throat. She tried to get out his name again, but her throat felt paralyzed. *She* felt paralyzed.

"Vest," he finally wheezed, pushing off her.

"Vest?" she returned dumbly, but he was getting off her. He was standing up. He had to be okay. She rolled onto her back as he straightened to full height, looking a little too pale for her comfort. But he held out his hand as if she was supposed to take it.

She could only stare. Surely, he'd been shot, but he was standing there trying to help her up.

"You're one lucky bastard," Vaughn muttered, standing behind Bennet and studying his back. "That bullet isn't even an inch away from the edge."

Bennet merely grunted, now not waiting for her to find the wherewithal to grab his hand. He bent over and took her hand and tugged her onto her feet.

"Are you hurt?" he asked, his fingers curling around her shoulders as he studied her intently.

"You've been shot. Twice," she returned, staring at his gorgeous face, a little afraid this was all a dream.

"Yeah, and I'm still standing. Now, are you hurt?" he repeated, more forcefully this time.

"No. I mean, Oscar knocked me out, but—"

Bennet whirled around, but whatever he'd been about to do, Vaughn stepped in front of him.

"Let's let the law handle the rest of this."

That's when Alyssa finally felt like things were real. This had all happened. She looked over at Jaime, who stood above the two men who'd kidnapped her. Jaime was talking on his cell, Salvador laid out in a pile of blood, but his hands were cuffed behind his back as he lay there facedown, so it was possible he was still alive.

Oscar was in a sitting position, rocking back and forth, his hands also cuffed behind his back. Everything seemed to fade away at that moment except her brother.

Her brother who had knocked her out. Who had been a part of a plan to rape and kill her. Who had considered that *fine* because he wouldn't be the one doing it. All for revenge. All because CJ wouldn't respect him.

Alyssa pushed past Bennet. Whatever Vaughn and Bennet said to her, she didn't hear any of it. She stormed over to Oscar, who was looking up at her with tears in his eyes.

"I'm so sorry, Lyss. So sorry. Can't you forg—"

Alyssa didn't want to listen to another syllable, so she bent over and elbowed him in the nose as hard as she'd elbowed the man who'd tried to abduct her last week.

Oscar cried out, blood spurting from his nose.

"I *hate* you," she spat at him, a few tears spilling over her own cheeks. "And I'll never forgive you, you weak, soulless bastard." She turned away from him then, and Bennet was right there. Bleeding and beautiful.

"You saved me." It was all she could think to say, standing in this basement, surrounded by injured men and lawmen and this man. This wonderful man who had saved her from the worst thing she'd ever faced, and that was saying something.

His throat worked for a few seconds before he spoke. "I never should have let you out of my sight."

"But—"

Suddenly men were pouring through the door. Police and FBI, all talking and ordering things, radios squawking, paramedics jogging.

And somehow she was being led out of the basement, away from Bennet, too many questions being asked of her, too many hands prodding at her when all she wanted to do was cry in the comforting circle of Bennet's arms.

But he was still in that basement, not looking at her, and Alyssa realized she might have been saved, but nothing much had changed. He was still a Ranger, and she was still a Jimenez.

Nothing could change that.

Chapter Seventeen

Bennet was doing everything in his power not to shove the paramedic working on his arm. He didn't particularly feel like having his wounds tended to right now.

Nor did he feel like answering anyone's endless questions, not when Alyssa had been taken out of the basement that was now crawling with all manner of law enforcement.

"We're going to have to transport you, Ranger Stevens. Even a minor bullet wound is a bullet wound."

Bennet tried to make his face do anything other than scowl, but it was a lost cause. He didn't want to go to a damn hospital. He wanted to sit down and go through everything that had happened. Not with FBI or other Rangers or anyone. Just Alyssa.

Who had been led away and hadn't reappeared.

"I'll go see if the second ambulance is here, if you'll wait."

Bennet nodded, staring at the chair Alyssa had been tied to when he'd gotten inside. Tied up. *This* close to dying. Because of him and all the mistakes he'd made along the way.

Jaime reappeared from wherever he'd been outside. Bennet glanced up at the man who'd helped him. Bennet didn't know much what to say. What could be said when you'd made this kind of a mess of things?

"Paramedics checked Alyssa out, and she was cleared to go home. Vaughn is taking her back to his house. Gabby's there, and she'll take good care of her."

Bennet nodded. "They're going to make me go to the hospital."

"Bullet wounds will do that to you. I'll let Alyssa know once she's had some rest. Don't want her rushing off to the hospital."

Bennet laughed bitterly. "I'm the reason she was put in this position. I wouldn't worry about it."

"Come on, Bennet. We've both been doing this too long to talk like that."

"I let my guard down. I trusted the wrong people. She could have been killed."

"But she wasn't. You know those seconds matter. The end result matters. Justice matters in the end."

"It's different," Bennet said flatly, because some man he barely knew, no matter what help he'd offered, couldn't absolve this black cloud of guilt.

"Why? Because you're involved with her?"

When Bennet didn't respond in any way, because yes he *had* been involved with her but he wasn't so certain he would be from here on out, Jaime continued.

"Been there, done that, buddy. It's really not different. Not when you've both survived relatively unscathed and have a chance to build a very nice future."

"She was knocked out, tied to a chair and seconds away from being killed. We must have different definitions of *unscathed*."

"We don't get out of life unscathed. Not a one of us.

Alyssa's tough. She's had to be. If you think she's going to wither away—"

"I don't think that. I know she's tough. She's tougher than she should have to be, because she's had shit thrown at her her whole life."

"Then how about this? Don't be more of the shit. I didn't get to save Gabby when she was in trouble. She mostly saved herself. I didn't like it, but you know what I did like? Getting someone I loved and wanted to marry and have a family with out of the deal. So. Stop being a dumbass."

"Thanks for the pep talk," Bennet muttered as the paramedic reappeared.

"Go to the hospital. I'll let Alyssa know you'll be by when you're released. Don't disappoint her, or you'll have a whole slew of intimidating women to answer to."

Bennet nodded absently as Jaime went over to talk to another FBI agent and the paramedic started leading him out of the house.

He *was* being a dumbass, feeling sorry for himself, blaming himself, and as much as it felt right to wallow in that, Jaime had a point. This was over now, and Alyssa *was* safe.

There'd be fallout to deal with. His father was a part of this, and Bennet... He didn't know how to absorb that, or how she would. How anyone would.

But Alyssa was safe. Alive and safe and able to go home, and maybe she hated him a little bit now. He could deal with that. He could deal with any range of emotions she had toward him, but that didn't mean he had to sulk and give up and stay away.

Not when he'd fallen in love with her, and damn it if she wasn't tough enough to take it.

ALYSSA HAD SHOWERED as much of the day off her as she could. She'd been fussed over by Gabby, had a newborn baby shoved into her arms and been plied with tea.

She hated tea, but she hadn't found her voice. Not since Vaughn had ushered her away from the house she'd been tied up in and driven her to his house.

Natalie and Gabby had done *all* the talking since then. It was nice, all in all, since Alyssa didn't know what to say or what to feel. Her entire body felt cold and numb.

A knock sounded at the door, and Vaughn disappeared to answer it. When he returned, Jaime was with him.

Alyssa had approximately eight thousand questions she wanted to ask him, but in the end she just looked down at the baby sleeping in her awkwardly positioned arms. The little girl was so tiny, her face all scrunched up in sleep.

Alyssa's chest felt too tight, her eyes too scratchy. Everything ached and hurt and didn't make any damn sense.

She swallowed at the lump in her throat, still watching the baby in her arms. "How is everything?" she managed to ask, her voice squeaky.

"Everyone has been transported to the hospital. In Bennet's and Oscar's cases that's more of a precaution than a necessity. I arranged to have your bike brought here, and it's out in the driveway." He placed her keys on the table next to the couch.

"Wait. You didn't give her a chance to talk to Bennet before you brought her home?" Natalie demanded, turning toward Vaughn.

"Bennet was a little busy. Would you sit down? You shouldn't be up around pacing."

"I'm not pacing, I was getting Alyssa more tea, and I will not sit down. Is your memory faulty?"

"Alyssa hasn't drunk the tea she's got and my memory is fine," Vaughn replied, pressing Natalie into the chair.

Natalie whipped her accusatory gaze to Jaime. "You, too?"

"He needed to be transported to the hospital. The entire place was crawling with law enforcement. That's not exactly the time to talk."

"Even though you both know talking after these kinds of ordeals is important?" Natalie returned.

But Alyssa had been glad. She didn't want to talk to Bennet just yet. Not when all she felt was this horrible numbness interrupted only intermittently by the need to cry. She wouldn't cry in front of him in the aftermath. She needed to be strong the next time she spoke to Bennet.

Strong enough to pretend she didn't care that they didn't have a future together.

"Bennet will be by once he's released," Jaime said. "They'll be able to talk in a calm, comforting environment instead of in the middle of a crime scene."

"Unless that's not what you want?" Gabby said, sliding onto the couch next to Alyssa. It was the first time in this conversation anyone had talked to Alyssa directly.

Which Alyssa wanted to shy away from. She wanted to live in this numb bubble for right now. She didn't want to think about Bennet or the impossibility of their future. She didn't want to think about Oscar or what he'd been willing to do. She didn't want to think of CJ killing her mother or any of it.

She just wanted to stare at a sweet little sleeping baby who would always know her parents loved her.

"We can tell him not to come, sweetie. Until you're ready." Gabby squeezed her arm, and Alyssa barely felt it. She wasn't sure she'd ever feel ready. What had she ever been ready for in her life? She'd only ever had things happen to her and learned to deal, or learned to fight, or learned to be the victim. Time and time again.

Something poked through all the numbness. Anger. She was so damn tired of being a *victim*. So tired of things happening to her and her having to learn how to fight, how to survive.

When was it going to be her turn to live? To make choices without worrying if she was going to inconvenience someone or get them connected to something they shouldn't be connected to. When did she get to have a *life*? With ups and downs and successes and failures and...

"Can you take her?" Alyssa asked abruptly, nodding toward the baby she was still afraid to jostle.

Gabby obliged and Alyssa stood as soon as she was free of the baby. "I have to go," she announced to no one in particular.

"You're not going anywhere, Alyssa."

Alyssa ignored Gabby. "What's happening with Gary Stevens?" she demanded of Jaime.

"He's been arrested. He has a team of lawyers working to get him released, but there's a lot of damning evidence to him being an accessory. Including Oscar's throwing him under the bus."

"And Dominguez?"

Jaime shoved his hands into his pockets, rocking back on his heels. "Died en route to the hospital."

"Good. And my brother?"

"Oscar is being checked out, and once he's fit for confinement, he'll be transported to jail. We're also applying for warrants on your brother CJ in the murder of your mother."

"Oh." Alyssa cleared her throat. "Good. Good, I'm glad." They should all pay for what they'd done. Every last one of them. "I need to go then."

Jaime glanced at Gabby as if asking permission. Alyssa scowled. "I don't want to wait for him to get here. I have some things to say to him. I'm not waiting. I'm done with waiting."

Jaime inclined his head. "I can't argue with that. Can you?" he asked pointedly at Gabby.

Alyssa looked back at her friend, her *sister*—more her family than any of the horrible men related to her— and Gabby sighed heavily.

"Just drive her to the hospital."

"I can handle myself," Alyssa retorted.

"We all can, but it doesn't hurt to let the people who care about us take care of us either. Got it?"

That numbness receded further. Care and taking care. *That* was what she wanted out of her life. She crossed back to Gabby and gave her a hug. "Thank you," she whispered, then did the same to Natalie. "Thank you for being my family," she said firmly. Damn if she'd ever be afraid or hesitant to say that again.

"And I appreciate the taking care," she continued. "But this is something personal and I want to drive myself. Okay?"

Gabby gave a nod. "Just keep us informed on where you are so we don't worry, okay?"

"I will." Because that's what family did, and she was most definitely part of a real family now.

Chapter Eighteen

Bennet signed the paperwork to get him the hell out of the hospital. It shouldn't take that long to stitch up a little bullet wound, Bennet thought.

Captain Dean had debriefed him on the status of Alyssa's mother's murder case, including a warrant for CJ Jimenez. Bennet couldn't begin to guess what Alyssa would think of that when she'd been so certain her brothers hadn't done it.

But no matter how she took it, he wanted to be the one standing by her as she did. Now, he just had to hope she'd let him.

The nurse ushered him out of the room he'd been in, and when Bennet stepped into the waiting room, he stopped short. "Mother."

Mom stood from the chair she'd been sitting in. She'd changed out of her gala finery, and in fact looked pale and as mussed and bedraggled as he'd ever seen her in his entire life.

"Have you been released?" she asked as if she was asking him how the weather was.

"Yes."

Mom swallowed, clutching her purse in front of her. "The police are crawling all over my home and guesthouse. I'd relish the opportunity to stay away and drive my son back to his house." She swallowed, and Bennet realized no matter how calmly she spoke, she was as affected as her appearance might suggest.

Bennet sighed. "They arrested Dad?"

Mom nodded tersely. "Obviously his lawyers are working overtime to find some loophole."

Bennet didn't know what to say to that. Didn't know what to do with this. What he wanted was to see Alyssa, to talk to her, to sort things out, but maybe this was as important to sort out.

"I had no idea," Mom said, her voice more a whisper than that cool politician's tone she'd been employing. "Apparently his assistant was the only one who did. I don't know why he'd risk it, Bennet. Working with a cartel, no matter what the money, is political suicide."

"Unless no one finds out and you can use it to aid your cause."

Mom shook her head. "It's unconscionable. Maybe you don't believe me, maybe he could have convinced me otherwise, but I swear to you, if I had known... I would have had to have turned him in. My career is everything to me, Bennet. It always has been for better or worse, but I never could have condoned this kind of..." She shook her head, a tear slipping over her cheek.

It was impossible not to believe his mother at this point. She wasn't an emotional woman. She hadn't even cried at her own mother's funeral. For her to be this distraught, she had to be caught completely unaware, and he supposed as separate as his parents had been conducting their lives, it was more than possible.

"I'm sorry you got caught up in it."

Mom nodded jerkily. "You, as well. I hope Alyssa wasn't hurt."

"Not physically."

"Good. I… Well, I suppose I wasn't overly polite when I met her."

"Are you going to apologize how you treated a woman in my life, Mother?" Bennet asked incredulously.

Mom sniffed. "Well, it perhaps took my life being ruined before my eyes to get me to that point, but yes. And, though I'm sure you'll think it makes me cold and callous, your father's ruined our name completely now. It doesn't really matter what women you consort with at this point."

Perhaps it shouldn't be funny, but after this long-ass day, Bennet could only laugh. He laughed and did something he hadn't done for years, maybe over a decade.

He hugged his mother.

"Oh, well, it turns out you might be busy," Mom said after giving him a quick squeeze back. When he pulled away, his mother pointed to the doors of the waiting room.

Alyssa stood there, arms crossed over her chest, looking beautiful and pissed off. And for the first time since she'd shown him the gun strapped to her thigh just *hours* ago, he finally relaxed again.

She was here. They were both all right. If they could both survive a kidnapping plot orchestrated by members of each of their families, they could probably figure just about anything out.

"Go to my house. Stay there until the police clear out of yours. I have…business to take care of," Bennet told his mother absently.

"Bennet, I'm going to tell you something I'm likely never to admit aloud again."

"Yeah?"

"I quite like her."

He managed to tear his gaze away from Alyssa and stared at his mother, who shrugged and began walking for the exit. She paused as she approached Alyssa, said something, and then she was gone.

Then it was just the two of them. And a handful of people in the waiting room, but he barely noticed. He walked toward her, and she didn't move. Just stood there staring at him as though they were about to fight.

"They stitch you up?" she asked.

"Yes."

"And you're okay?"

"Aside from a bruise the size of Jupiter on my back and some stitches on my arm."

"Well, you got something to say to me?" She lifted her chin, all brave defiance, and he grinned.

"Yeah." But he didn't say any of it. He kissed her instead, tangling his fingers in her hair, drowning in the taste of her he'd never be able to live without no matter how he might fail her in the future.

ALYSSA HAD NOT come to the hospital to make out in the waiting room in front of a handful of people, but now that Bennet's arms were around her, his mouth on hers, it was hard to remember what she had planned to do.

She wanted to stay here, in this moment, for good. They were safe. They were together. He was *kissing* her regardless of her last name or his.

"Bennet," she murmured against his mouth. She'd come here with things to say. Things to demand, and he was dismantling it all because this was all that mattered. All she wanted. Him, him, him.

His hands moved to cup her cheeks, his mouth brushing across her mouth in between his words. "If you're going to yell at me, can it wait?"

"For what?"

He pressed his forehead to hers, his eyes still closed. "My wounds to heal, the case to be over, fifty years—take your pick."

"No, I didn't mean wait for what, I mean what would I yell at you for?"

His eyes opened, blue and vibrant. "You didn't come here to yell at me?"

"No, I came here to tell you that I'm tired of waiting and being pushed aside and we will talk about everything on *my* time, and when *I* want to."

"Okay," he returned all too reasonably.

"And I don't want to do it in this damn waiting room with all these people listening to me."

"Okay."

"And stop saying okay!"

He grinned at her again, and she didn't know whether to laugh or cry, tell him she loved him or kiss him a million times over no matter who they were in front of.

"All right," he said, feigning seriousness. "This is where I point out I don't have a car or any way of getting us out of here."

"I guess you'll have to ride on the back of my bike. If you think you're up to it."

"I guess it's fitting punishment all in all."

She frowned at him. "Why do you think I'm going to yell at you or you need to be punished? You recall saving my life earlier, right?"

"I'm the reason you were in that position. I let my father convince me to do something I knew I shouldn't. I didn't want to leave you with him. It went against every gut feeling I had, but I let it go because..."

"Because he's your father. You think I don't understand the way loyalty and family love can screw with you? I trusted Oscar. I trusted CJ. They... Bennet, you want to love your family, and it's an awful thing when they don't deserve it. But it's not our fault."

His thumb brushed her cheek, back and forth, and all she wanted was to be in a bed somewhere with him and shut the world and their families and this awful day away for good. But his next words made her breath catch.

"I love you," he said in the middle of a hospital waiting room, earnestly and looking her right in the eye as if there was no greater truth in the world.

Alyssa tried to make sense of those three simple words. Except, she hadn't expected them, and they were anything but simple. "Wh-what?"

"'What' as in you didn't hear me or you don't believe me or you don't want me to?"

"I..."

"Because I'm not sure how to talk you into loving me back without knowing which objection I'm fighting."

"You don't have to talk me into it," she managed to say through her tight, scratchy throat.

"I don't?"

"I may not have had very good luck with the kind of love a person is born with, but I've been pretty good about finding it myself these past few years." With shaky fingers, she traced the impressive cut of his jaw. "I love you, Bennet."

"Just took a week, a few kidnapping attempts and successes, a dramatic shootout."

"Don't forget the involvement of family members."

"No, who could forget that?" He inhaled deeply, then let it out. He looked at her so intently Alyssa wasn't sure she'd ever get used to it, but she'd gladly spend a very long time trying.

"We managed to turn today around, I think," he murmured, still touching her face, still looking at her in that heart-melting way.

Alyssa glanced at the clock. "It's after midnight. It's tomorrow."

"Even better."

Then he was kissing her in the middle of this waiting room again, and she didn't care anymore at all.

Epilogue

One Year Later

"The timing is so funny," Tawny said, attaching a golden hairpiece to Alyssa's impossibly perfect updo. "I swear we were just doing this a year ago."

"We were," Alyssa returned. "Except I was wearing black."

"And now you look positively radiant in white." Tawny stepped back and studied her handiwork. "Please wear the heels. Please. I beg of you."

"Sorry. Tennis shoes are tradition."

"So is kidnapping. I'm hoping we avoid that this time around."

"You and me both."

Tawny pouted at Alyssa's feet. "Well, at least they're white. But everyone is going to see them when you walk down the aisle."

"They'll survive the shock."

"Ready for the great unveiling?" Tawny asked.

Alyssa took stock of herself in the mirror. It was no different from how she'd felt a year ago getting ready for a Christmas gala, and yet it was completely different. As uncomfortable as she felt all dressed up, she was going to her wedding this time.

And that made all the difference in the world.

Tawny opened the bathroom door and ushered her out into the bedroom where the photographer and her bridesmaids waited. Natalie and Gabby were both dressed in beautiful forest green, Nat holding pretty little Sarah dressed in red toddler finery on her hip, Gabby lying miserably on the bed.

But both looked at Alyssa as she entered the room, brown eyes shiny.

"Oh, you look like a princess," Natalie said with a little sniffle. "It's perfect."

"You look great, Lyss," Gabby added. "I've got a bet with Jaime that Bennet cries, so do your best for me, okay?"

Alyssa managed a laugh, feeling a little teary herself. "You going to make it down the aisle?"

"Do you want me to go get you some ginger ale?" Tawny asked.

"No, I'd prefer a time machine so I can fast-forward out of morning sickness land," Gabby replied.

"You're getting there," Nat offered.

Gabby simply groaned, but Alyssa had to grin. She'd spent much of her life alone and isolated, and now she was getting married surrounded by her surrogate family. Her sisters, her friends. And soon enough she'd be walking down the aisle to the man she loved.

She swallowed at the lump in her throat, because she did not want to go through the arduous process of redoing her makeup.

A knock sounded at the door, and when Tawny opened it she screeched and slammed it right back shut.

"You are not supposed to see the bride, Bennet Stevens," she scolded through the door.

"I'm not superstitious," Bennet returned from behind the closed door.

"Well, I am," Alyssa said, crossing to the door. "So get the hell out of here."

"Open the door."

"No."

"Just a crack. We don't have to see each other. I just want to give you something."

"If it's jewelry, I don't want it."

"It's not jewelry. Open the door and hold out your damn hand, woman."

She looked at the door, unable to stop grinning. How she'd gotten here, she'd never know, but she was so happy. So, so happy, and what's more, she knew she darn well deserved it.

She cracked the door open and stuck her hand out the crack. Bennet placed something in her palm, and she curled her fingers around the slim piece of metal and pulled it to her.

When she uncurled her fingers, she was staring at a Swiss Army knife. A *monogrammed* Swiss Army knife, with her soon-to-be initials on it.

"If I'm not fishing that out of your dress later, you're going to be in very big trouble," Bennet said from behind the door.

Tawny peered into Alyssa's palm and wrinkled her nose. "What kind of gift is a *knife*?"

Alyssa slid the knife into the top of her dress, making sure it was secure before she flashed a grin at Tawny. "The perfect gift." She cleared her throat and peeked out the crack in the door.

Bennet was standing there looking all too pleased with himself, polished and perfect in his tux.

She kept her body hidden behind the door, but stuck her head out the crack.

"Hi," he offered.

"Hi," she returned. She stuck her finger out the crack and crooked it at him so he'd step closer.

"If I come closer, I'm going to kiss you," he warned.

"On the cheek," she said, offering her cheek, but as he moved closer, he only cupped her face with his hands and bent his face close enough their noses were touching.

"Not the cheek," he whispered, touching his lips to hers. It would ruin her lipstick, but she was a little too happy to care. She kissed him right back.

There were protests from inside, but Alyssa didn't care. Today she was marrying the man she loved, and no luck—good or bad—could stand in her way.

"I love you, Ranger Stevens," she murmured against his mouth.

"And I love you." He pulled away, that charming grin firmly in place. "See you soon, wife," he offered, heading back down the hall toward the grand staircase. They would be getting married at the bottom of it, then having their reception in the huge living room decorated with the giant gold tree she'd admired last year.

Bennet hadn't loved the idea of getting married at the Stevenses' house, what with his father being in jail, but Alyssa thought it was fitting. It was where they'd had their first real kiss, where they'd made love for the first time, where they'd spent all that time together that had led them to this wonderful moment.

Yes, it was perfect, even in all its glitz and glamour, and when they went home tonight to Bennet's less flashy house that he'd insisted she help decorate over the past few months, they'd have their low-key, very naked wedding night, and celebrate the start of a very wonderful, *loving* life together.

And if everything in her life had led her to this wonderful point, she wouldn't trade any of it and risk missing out on that. Because the life she'd built in her newfound freedom wasn't perfect, but it was full of love, and love, it turned out, wasn't a weapon.

It was freedom.

* * * * *

MILLS & BOON®

INTRIGUE
Romantic Suspense

A SEDUCTIVE COMBINATION OF DANGER AND DESIRE

MILLS & BOON®

Why shop at millsandboon.co.uk?

Each year, thousands of romance readers
find their perfect read at millsandboon.co.uk.
That's because we're passionate about
bringing you the very best romantic fiction.
Here are some of the advantages of
shopping at www.millsandboon.co.uk:

* **Get new books first**—you'll be able to buy
  your favourite books one month before they
  hit the shops

* **Get exclusive discounts**—you'll also be
  able to buy our specially created monthly
  collections, with up to 50% off the RRP

* **Find your favourite authors**—latest news,
  interviews and new releases for all your
  favourite authors and series on our website,
  plus ideas for what to try next

* **Join in**—once you've bought your favourite
  books, don't forget to register with us to rate,
  review and join in the discussions

Visit **www.millsandboon.co.uk**
for all this and more today!